"ALL I WANT IS A KISS"

"A simple, harmless, kiss," Colin murmured with dangerous softness, and Ariadne felt her flirtatious grin freezing to her mouth. Wide-eyed and unable to move, she watched his head lowering to hers, felt one arm going behind her neck and lifting her face up to his, the other hand pulling at the closure of her shirt, with an intent that was all too obvious.

Ariadne began to panic.

"I'm sorry, Colin, I was just t-teasing—"

"I've had it with your teasing, Ariadne. One of these days you're going to push somebody too far. It's about time you learned that kissing can be about as harmless as setting a spark to gunpowder!"

And then, before she could protest, cry out, or even raise her hand to slap him, his mouth came down hard upon hers . . .

Taken By Storm

Danelle Harmon

AVON BOOKS ◆ NEW YORK

TAKEN BY STORM is an original publication of Avon Books. This work has never before appeared in book form. This work is a novel. Any similarity to actual persons or events is purely coincidental.

AVON BOOKS
A division of
The Hearst Corporation
1350 Avenue of the Americas
New York, New York 10019

Copyright © 1995 by Danelle F. Colson
Inside cover author photograph by the Keegan Photography Studio
Published by arrangement with the author
Library of Congress Catalog Card Number: 94-96864
ISBN: 0-380-78003-8

First Avon Books Printing: August 1995

AVON TRADEMARK REG. U.S. PAT. OFF. AND IN OTHER COUNTRIES, MARCA REGISTRADA, HECHO EN U.S.A.

Printed in the U.S.A.

RA 10 9 8 7 6 5 4 3 2 1

This book is dedicated
to my dear friend, Andrea Coursey

I am indebted to the following individuals at Tufts University School of Veterinary Medicine in Grafton, Massachusetts, who gave so generously of their time and knowledge in order to give my 19th century veterinarian a decent education: Franklin M. Loew, DVM, PhD, Dean; Sylvia J. Bedford-Guaus, BVM, MS; W. Robert Cook, FRCVS, PhD; Angela E. Frimberger, DVM; Kris M. Koss, DVM; Mary Rose Paradis, DVM, MS, and Nicholas Trout, MA, VetMB., MRCVS.

Your knowledge, advice and help are gratefully appreciated; any mistakes, however, are mine.

I also wish to thank Doug Coursey for his help in handling Shareb-er-rehh; Pac Man, Magic, Windy, Chuckie, and Tommy for rejuvenating my interest in horses, along with 1930 Triple Crown winner Gallant Fox, who was the inspiration for Shareb-er-rehh; my editor, Christine Zika and agent, Nancy Yost for direction, enthusiasm, and (pardon the pun) free rein; Andrea Coursey, Trena Haroutunian, and Karen Hayes for care and feeding of the manuscript; Barbara Brown; and, of course and always, my family for their continuing encouragement and support.

And, with special love, my beloved English husband, Dr. Chris Gatcombe, for restoring my belief in happily-ever-afters and proving that real-life romance heroes really *do* exist.

May God bless you all.

Danelle Harmon
Oxfordshire, England

Taken By Storm

Prologue

Weybourne House,
London, England
1810

The fire started as a spark set to hay, a twisting viper of black smoke before a draft from the stable's open door blew it into life.

With a savage, whooshing roar, the hay burst into flame.

Satisfied, the man tossed the lantern into the loose straw and stepped back as the fire's hot breath hit him. He stood watching the hay blacken, crackle, and disintegrate, mesmerized by the flames, feeling their heat pressing against his face and sucking the moisture out of his pores, drying out his eyes, searing the inside of his nose, and crawling into his lungs with deadly malice.

Take this, you bastard. Teach you to go breaking agreements. If I can't have the Weybourne fortune—and the horses—no one can.

Acrid smoke blackened the air and banked down from the rafters. Coughing, he whipped out his handkerchief, covered his mouth, and stepped back, toward the safety of the door and the cool-

1

ness of the night beyond. Already, the fire was out
of control, a frenzied demon swallowing up stacks
of hay, leaping up the partitions that separated the
empty stalls, and charging toward that one, single
box at the end that was not empty at all.

A shrill whistle pierced the night, and then,
hooves knocking desperately against wood.

The panicked stallion was the most valuable
horse in England, if not the world, but the man
made no effort to save it. He heard its whistle become a terrified scream, felt the fire growing hotter,
louder, angrier, pressing hot clothing against his
skin, beginning to scorch, blister, and suffocate
him. Smoke caked his tongue, and he tasted burning wood and hay, turpentine, leather, and dirt.
Eyes watering, his lungs constricting in the searing
heat, he retreated from the stable while the fire
raged at his back.

From behind him came the stallion's frightened
scream, piercing the hellish clamor of fire and heat.
It was a horrible, ghastly sound of pure terror, and
he pictured the flames reaching for the proud animal, engulfing it, burning it.

Such a waste.

It could've been otherwise, Weybourne. You old fool.

Outside, the night air engulfed him like a cool
blanket, and he sucked huge gulps of it into his
lungs to rid them of smoke and heat. At his back
the inferno roared, and he heard the great timbers
of the stable caving in upon themselves, a last distant battering of shod hooves meeting wood. . . .

And then, a crescendo of thunder rising behind
him.

He whirled and saw the stallion.

Wild-eyed with fury and terror, its tail streaming
smoke and fire, the horse came charging out of the
flames like a winged specter of death. It made
straight for him; he saw the fire reflected in its sav-

age black eyes, against its burnished coat, in its wide, flaring nostrils that burned an unholy red—

He jumped out of the way just in time.

The great beast galloped madly off into the night, its mighty hooves making the earth tremble beneath him.

Shaken, his trousers smudged with dirt, the man pulled himself to his feet. Sweat poured down his hot face and sheets of fire snapped and popped and reached for him. Flames danced within the collapsed building like legions of angry devils. And now, faintly, he heard hoarse cries, and turned to see old Weybourne himself running from the house, trailed by servants who were trying in vain to catch up to him.

"Shareb!" the old man cried. "Shareb-er-rehh!"

Silhouetted in the conflagration's bright light, the fire starter moved backward, behind a stately elm whose leaves were already curling in agony against the intense heat. Smiling, he watched as the earl came rushing toward the stable, arms waving, legs pumping, his nightcap trailing from his head.

"Shareb!" the old man cried, and then his voice rose in a desperate scream of bleak agony: *"Shareb-er-rehh!"*

"Stop him!" shouted one of the servants, running as fast as he could. "My lord, no!"

Another section of the stable roof imploded, spouting a fountain of sparks and churning black smoke toward the stars above.

"Shareb!"

"No, milord! Don't go in there, *it's no use!*"

"Shareb-er-rehhhhhhh—"

The old earl ran blindly through the sheets of flame and into the burning stable; the servants charged toward the back of the building in the hope of gaining a safer entrance; then, there was only Weybourne's horrible screams as the fire caught him. His clothing ablaze, he came staggering out, gaining fifteen, maybe twenty feet, before he fell, clutching his chest.

The arsonist moved out from behind the elm and stood staring coldly down at the dying man.

"You..." the old earl gasped, the flames casting a glow against his face as he dragged open his eyes and saw who stood over him. "Knew it was you...did it for revenge, didn't you... should have trusted my instincts about you...."

The fire crackled and sighed. Pungent billows of black smoke enclosed them, cut them off from the shouts and screams and calls that pierced the darkness.

The arsonist knelt down to the old man's level. "Pity, pity, Weybourne. I suppose young Tristan told you all about me, did he not? Is that why you wanted to break the agreement?" He arched a brow, a faint smile touching his mouth as the earl stretched a wizened hand toward him, fingers clawing the glowing earth in a spasm of agony. "Well, *I'm* in debt, too...and I'll be damned if I let you break your promise to me. Good-night, Weybourne. May you rot in hell."

He stood, still looking at that pitiful old hand reaching toward his boot. Above the fire's roar, he heard Weybourne's wheezing gasps, watched the feeble hand jerk and stiffen, saw, in the unholy glow from the burning stable, the skin going ashy and gray.

And heard, off in the distance, the thunder of hoofbeats.

Hard, fast, and furious.

The stallion was returning.

This time, the man slithered off into the night, while behind him the stable burned....

And burned.

Chapter 1

WANTED: *Any information leading to the where-abouts of Lady Ariadne St. Aubyn, daughter of the late Earl of Weybourne, who disappeared on Sunday last following the stable fire at Weybourne House in which Lord Weybourne perished. Her Ladyship, who is nineteen years of age, is described as having a very small frame, a most remarkable shade of red hair, and has in her possession a bay stallion. A REWARD of one thou-sand five hundred pounds has been offered by her brother, the new Lord Weybourne, for the return of said horse, of which he is the new and rightful owner. En-quiries may be made to Weybourne House, Brompton Road, London.*

"That ought to do it."

Seated at the carved mahogany desk that was now his, the new Lord Weybourne scanned his words a final time, put his seal on the document, and briskly handed it into the care of his waiting butler. "Make sure a copy of this gets posted at every inn and public house from here to Kings Lynn, and get it into the *Times* as soon as possible." He picked up his gloves, took his hat from his valet, and slapped it atop his dark russet hair. "For

5

all the good it will bloody well do. My sister is probably halfway to Norfolk with that horse by now."

The door opened and a groom stood there. "Your mare is saddled and ready, my lord."

"Yes, well pray God it's a fast one," Tristan said darkly, and slammed the door as he walked out.

Outside, the servants were already lined up on the lawn to see their young lord off. As he strode swiftly down the steps of Weybourne House, they quailed at the look in his eye, the grim set to his mouth.

"May God be with our dear Lady Ariadne, wherever she is," a maid whispered to the footman who stood rigidly beside her. She wrung her hands. "Oh, William, I only hope she reaches Norfolk before *he* does!"

"She has a good head start," the footman said, out of the corner of his mouth. He kept his face fixed and attentive. "*And* Shareb-er-rehh. He'll not catch her."

Tight-lipped and silent, the servants watched as their new master checked his horse's girth, scowling at the hapless animal as though damning it for not being one of the fast Norfolk Thoroughbreds. Tension crackled in the air, and tense sideways glances passed up and down their waiting ranks. Lady Ariadne had lost so much in the last two months alone. First the strange epidemic at the country house in Burnham Thorpe that had killed all but one of the Norfolk Thoroughbreds; then the London stable fire that had claimed her father, and nearly Shareb-er-rehh as well—and, finally, the opening and reading of his will. It had been the final blow. Surely, old Lord Weybourne had meant well . . . but it was unbelievable that he had been blind enough to bequeath Shareb-er-rehh, the last remaining stallion, to his derelict rakehell of a son.

Who could blame Lady Ariadne for stealing the horse and fleeing London?

It was a good thing young Tristan was ignorant of their thoughts—and where their sympathies lay. His handsome face exhibited no sign of grief as he passed the gutted stable on its black and ugly patch of charred ground; his eyes revealed no emotion as the damp London wind skated over the rubble and brought with it the acrid stench of ashes and dead dreams. There was nothing in his countenance but fury—and grim resolve.

Sensing it, the mare fearfully rolled her eyes as he pulled on his gloves, took the reins, and snapped out final instructions to his grave-faced butler. "If anyone comes looking for the reward money, put them off until my return. God knows I don't have the funds—*yet*—to pay it out. But I will, as soon as I catch up to my sister and get my hands on that stallion. *So help me God I will.*"

Then the young master of Weybourne swung himself up in the saddle, wheeled his horse, and in a clatter of hoofbeats, was gone.

"There sir! In the street!"

Colin Nicholas Lord took one look at the dog and knew it was dying.

Gripping his bag, he sprinted toward the animal even as a woman broke from the confused group that milled around it. She hurried to meet him, her skirts flying, her face flushed and anxious. "Oh sir, they said you're an animal doctor! Please, do something for our precious Homer—you've got to save him, sir, oh, *please* you've got to save him, he's my son Tommy's only companion and if he dies—"

The crowd parted, ushering him through. The big black mastiff was lying on its side, lips pulled back in a grimace of agony, body stiff, eyes glassy and staring into nothingness. A little boy, six or seven years old by the look of him, was huddled on the street next to the dog, his skinny arms wrapped around its massive neck, his bright blond head buried in its fur. He looked up, his eyes huge and blue, his grimy cheeks streaked with tears.

"H-Homer. . . ." he choked out. "My doggie—"

"Let me get in here and take a look at him," Colin said gently. "All right?"

The boy's lower lip quivered, and a huge tear rolled from his eye. Wordlessly, he turned and fled into his mother's arms.

Colin knelt down on the cobblestones beside the dog. "Easy there, big fellow," he murmured, setting his bag down and running a calming hand over the animal. Beneath the heavy warmth of its hind leg, he found the femoral pulse beating too rapidly, too faintly; he lifted the slack lip, saw that the mucous membranes were nearly as white as the teeth they enclosed. But it was the dog's abdomen, huge, hard, and swollen tight as a drum, that gave him his diagnosis.

"When was the last time he ate, madam?"

"A few hours ago," she said tightly, holding Tommy against her skirts and clutching his hand. "Oh, sir, is he going to—"

"Any vomiting?"

"Well, yes, he tried—I made him a big plate of meat and potatoes for supper, then he drank his whole bowl of water, went outside to run and play with Tommy—he does that every night and he's such a gentle old dog and all the little ones in the neighborhood love him so much—oh, sir, is he going to live? Please, tell us he's going to live—"

Tommy broke from her side, fell to his knees beside the dog, and wrapped his arms around its big neck. "Oh, Homer. . . . Oh, Homer, please, don't die! Please, please, *please* don't die. . . ." Sobbing, the boy looked imploringly into Colin's grave face.

"Please, mister, don't let him die. *Please.* ... You won't let him, will you?"

Colin opened his bag and took out his spectacles. "I'll do what I can, Tommy. Now, you do *me* a favor and go stand with your mama, all right?"

The little boy's throat worked, but he obeyed the order.

Colin put on his spectacles and once more returned his attention to his patient.

Commotion surrounded him. Traffic stopping in the street, carriage wheels grinding against worn cobblestone, running footsteps, someone shouting, the hollow clatter of a horse's hooves. Colin never raised his head, intent on the dog, and the dog only. He passed his hand over its abdomen as the crowd pressed close, some unwashed and rank with sweat, others heavily perfumed, all of them blocking out sunlight, air, thinking space—

"Give the fellow some room, folks!" a man shouted, from somewhere above. "Clear away, get back. *Back.* ..."

The dog stared glassily into space through half-closed eyes, whimpering through its nose in pain.

"Do you know what ails him, sir?" the woman asked, tightly.

"Gastric dilatation. Bloat, if you will."

"Bloat?"

Colin was already eyeing the hugely swollen abdomen, praying silently that the stomach was not twisted up inside; if it was, the animal was as good as dead. But the woman didn't have to know that. Not yet, anyhow.

As gently as he could, he answered, "There's a large amount of gas trapped in your dog's stomach, madam—if it is not released, he'll die." His hands still resting on the mastiff's side, Colin twisted around, looking up at the anxious faces until he found the man who'd summoned him. "Sir?

If you'll please restrain Homer for me while I attempt treatment.... Yes, like that. Just put your hands on his neck and shoulders. Good."

Little Tommy hid his face in his mother's skirts, crying bitterly. Colin's chest constricted. He glanced at the woman, and she stared beseechingly into his eyes with that frozen plea he was all too familiar with, that blind faith and hope and trust that the animal lover bestows upon the one person in the world who might be capable of saving a beloved pet.

"Please do your best, sir," she said quietly. "For my son."

There was no time to waste. Reaching for his bag, Colin hurriedly searched its depths for the small bottle of rum, a cloth, and the trocar, a short needle that was Homer's only hope of survival. He lifted the instrument out, keeping his face perfectly blank and his features composed for the sake of the mastiff's distraught owner. He'd used the fine needle on sheep—but never on a dog.

There was no other choice.

Palming the mastiff's distended belly, Colin found its highest point. The dog tried to roll into an upright position, but Colin gently pushed him back down. As the crowd went hush-silent around him, he poured rum onto the cloth and cleaned the area. Then he leaned over the dog so the little boy might not see what he was about to do—and drove the needle straight down into the hard, swollen stomach.

Behind him, the woman gasped.

The needle pierced the stomach wall. Fluid, sunset-colored and fetid, shot from the top of the trocar, spattering his cheeks, his brow, his spectacles. He blocked out the sudden, overpowering stench and the alarmed murmur of the crowd, aware of only the malodorous fluid bubbling out of the trocar and the pent-up gas escaping the dog's stomach in a frenzied hiss.

At his side, the man was staring at him in shocked horror.

Please, God, let the stomach wall be healthy, Colin thought desperately—for if it were not, the organ would burst inside the abdomen and the resulting peritonitis would surely kill poor Homer.

The moments crept by.

The crowd was silent, not even breathing.

He laid his fingers against the inside of the dog's hind leg, checking its pulse once again. Counting. Feeling his helper's gaze upon him and searching his face for some sign of encouragement, hope, promise.

Come on, big fellow, he thought, holding the needle in one hand and stroking the dog's heavily muscled neck with the other. *Don't bow out on me now. Come on, Homer . . . make little Tommy happy. . . .*

The gas hissed out, taking forever. He was aware of Tommy's mother hovering over him, her hand resting against his shoulder and her fingers biting into his flesh as she stared down at the needle in horrified awe. There was no sound but that of the dog's faint respiration, a horse trotting past on the street, and the steady, persistent whisper of the escaping gas. The crowd had gone deathly still. Watching.

Come on, big fellow, he urged again, silently.

At the perimeter of his vision, just beyond the crescent of pavestone at the dog's back, Colin saw a hundred shod, slippered, and booted feet . . . an ant crawling through the tiny valley between two pale cobblestones . . . loose pebbles, grains of sand, a flattened twig of yellow straw. He shut his eyes, oblivious to the bits of gravel driving into his knees, the sunlight toasting the back of his neck, feeling only the dog's ribs moving steadily beneath his palm, up and down, up and down. Five minutes went by. Ten. The hiss of the escaping gas dropped in pitch, then faded out, and gently he withdrew the needle, his heart pounding, his brow flushed and damp.

He risked a glance up and saw some fifty anxious faces, all staring down at him, all expecting nothing short of a miracle, and he was suddenly terrified of failing them all.

He looked away—and it was then that he saw her. A woman, refined and elegant, sitting astride a deep-chested bay stallion and staring directly into his eyes. Her hair was pulled up beneath a wool cap, breeches molded her shapely thighs, and only the fine arch of her red brows, the clarity of her skin, and the hint of a bosom beneath her coat betrayed the fact she was not the lad she might appear to be at first sight. Her head was high and her dark eyes glittered with triumph, as though she secretly shared his success; she gave the faintest of nods, and in her gaze he saw more than just blind faith in his abilities—he saw complete, unflagging confidence that he would succeed in saving the dog.

Suddenly flustered, Colin's gaze shot back to his patient.

And then, beneath his hand, he felt it. The slowing and strengthening of pulse and the return of spirit, the defiant rush of blood, of promise, of life, through veins and arteries and heart—

He forgot the woman on the horse.

"Yes!" he said through clenched teeth, bending anxiously over the dog as the crowd closed in and their shadows fell over both of them. "Come on— what's your name, big fellow?—Homer. Come on, Homer," he urged, stroking the dog's thick neck

and gazing intently into its half-shuttered eyes.
"Come awake for me, Homer. . . ."

The dog whimpered and stirred. Its foreleg
jerked, the huge paw scraping the cobblestones, its
whimper becoming a harsh cry deep in its throat
as full consciousness began to return, and with it,
pain. The crowd murmured excitedly, their voices
rising in a sudden, thunderous din; the little boy's
sobs caught, held—and then the mastiff's eyes
opened, and it lifted its huge, noble head to regard
the man who had just saved its life, its dark eyes
looking deeply, gratefully, into the gentle, lavender
ones of the veterinarian.

Colin smiled.

The dog's tail thumped once, twice, on the cobblestones.

And the crowd went wild.

"*Home-e-e-e-e-e-e-r!*" Tommy shrieked, tearing
himself from his mother and plunging to his knees
at the mastiff's side.

His head ringing with that elated screech, his
ears filled with the cheers of the crowd, Colin stood
up and passed a shaky wrist across his brow. People were clapping him on the back, congratulating
him, jabbering excitedly amongst themselves. He
took off his spattered spectacles and turned to
speak to Tommy's mother, but her fond gaze was
on her son, who was bent over the dog, sobbing
into its fur, embracing it and hugging the big body
ecstatically.

"Oh, Homer!" Tommy cried, sobbing happily.
"Oh, Homer, Homer, *Homer!*"

Colin dropped the spectacles into his pocket,
wiped his face with a handkerchief, and gazed
down at the happy pair as the boy's mother moved
to stand beside him. "I think," he said with a helpless grin, "that Homer here will live to eat many

more atrociously huge meals—though I would advise against them."

She touched his arm. "Oh, sir, how can we *ever* thank you for what you have done?"

He smiled modestly and looked away. Involuntarily, his gaze swept the crowd in search of the tiny woman on the bay stallion—but the spot where the horse had been was empty.

His guardian angel was gone.

"I want that man."

Daniel and Simon, walking on either side of Shareb-er-rehh's hooded head as they hurried away from the cheering crowd, simultaneously came to such an abrupt stop that the action might have been choreographed. They stared up at her.

"What do you mean, you *want* him?"

Lady Ariadne St. Aubyn tugged her cap down over her brow and, pressing her heels to Shareb's side, urged the stallion on. Again, she relived that silent drama: the veterinarian down on his knees in the street, his dark blond head bent over a mastiff, the dog's tongue hanging out to rest lifelessly upon the cobblestones. Again, she saw the concentration in that intent, handsome face, the hair falling unheeded over his brow, the blood spraying his spectacles, and he never once flinched, faltered, never lost that expression of purpose and will. She remembered the steady hands, the muscles beneath his rolled up sleeves, the horror and nausea she'd felt at seeing that needle plunging into the dog's swollen abdomen—

"My lady?"

And the dog. Coming back to life as though raised from the dead. Lifting its massive head to look up at its savior, and the humble gratitude in its dark eyes before the happy shrieks of the little boy, the roar of the crowd, had drowned everything out.

She would never forget it, not as long as she lived.

"I said, *I want him*," she announced blithely, keeping her eyes straight ahead and her gaze directed on a point just beyond Shareb's fine ears as the stallion pranced beneath her.

"What do you mean, my lady, you *want* him?"

Ariadne lifted her chin and gazed imperiously down her nose at the two grooms. "What I *mean*," she said, patting the stallion's neck, "is that I need an escort who is capable of ensuring Shareb-er-rehh's health en route to Norfolk. And what I *want*"—she smiled then, her eyes mischievous and reminiscent of her old self—"is for you to follow him back to his practice and wait there until after it grows dark."

"Why?"

"Because I want you to abduct him."

They stared at her as though she'd lost her senses. "But my lady, *we* can escort you to Norfolk, keep you from harm, make sure your brother doesn't recognize or find you along the way—"

"Yes, but you cannot cure a sick or injured horse. *That* man, obviously, can. I want him. *Period*."

She directed her gaze straight ahead, her nose high, her spine stiff, her manner already shutting the book on the subject. "Daniel, you will go back and learn his name. Simon, you will go across the street and secure me a dozen of those black currant tarts that I can see in that shop window, and several bottles of ale. Then I shall expect to see the both of you in Hyde Park one hour after sunset—*with* the veterinarian."

Shareb-er-rehh stood safely hidden behind the trees where Lady Ariadne had left him. The night was cool, but he never felt it; a mosquito buzzed about his ears and he shook his head to ward it off. Two horses—mares, by the scent of them—were coming down the drive that ran through the park, and he could hear the low voice of a man, the answering giggle of a woman. Concealed by the darkness, the trees, and his own color, he pricked his ears forward as the horses approached, his roving eye passing over each of them with a bored, assessing air.

He was long in the limb and unusually deep through the chest, not remarkably tall but lean, strong, elegant. His head was noble, with a broad brow and wide, intelligent dark eyes, the right one ringed with white and giving him a perpetual look of curiosity and coltish wonder. His blood was impeccably blue, his existence the result of four decades of careful planning on the part of the late earl of Weybourne, his worth—as the last and only heir to his heritage—beyond value. But right now, none of that mattered. Only the mares mattered, and now, they had caught his scent and were prancing and preening for *him*, captivated—as all equine ladies were—by his fatal charm and good looks. With a soft whicker of invitation, Shareb-er-rehh stepped boldly from behind the trees—

And heard Her Ladyship's light footsteps racing over the grass.

He froze.

"Get *back*, Shareb!" With one hand cupped over his muzzle, and the other pushed against his chest, she drove him backward. "Do you want someone to see you?"

The stallion's dark eyes remained fixed on the mares; then their riders urged them past and they were gone, their scent lingering on the wind to fill his dilated nostrils long after their hoofbeats faded into the night.

He sucked the air into his lungs and let out a deep, defeated sigh, the expansion of his great sides making the girth and saddle creak loudly in the still darkness.

Stroking his sleek neck, Ariadne reached into her pocket for a last bit of pastry. The stallion ignored her. She uncorked the flagon of ale she had brought for him and offered it, instead. Petulantly, the stallion turned his head away, refusing to be placated. She sighed, staring at his sulky face in dismay before finally shoving the cork back into the flagon. Poor Shareb. First, her father had hustled him from Norfolk to London to save him from the strange sickness that had claimed the other horses; now, she was hustling him *back* to Norfolk to save him from her wastrel of a brother. And rushing away this afternoon, then waiting about because of her sudden, impulsive plan to abduct the veterinarian . . . poor Shareb, it was more turmoil than he deserved.

Rewrapping the untouched pastry and putting it back in her pocket, she leaned close to the stallion's velvety nose, feeling his soft breath blowing warm against her cheek.

"I know what you're thinking," she whispered. Lowering her voice, she adopted a suitably deep and husky tone, as might befit a noble stallion. "A veterinarian. What use do *I*, Drinker of the Wind, have for an animal doctor? Lud, but I'm not even sick!"

Ever so slightly, Shareb-er-rehh turned his head back toward her, and then raised his foreleg, as though entreating her to take off the thick bandages she'd used to conceal his long cannons from the knees down.

"That *is* what you're thinking, isn't it?"

The stallion slammed his head against her shoulder, trying to dislodge the black hood that covered most of his face. He rubbed up and down, the stiff cups of leather that framed his eyes scraping painfully against Ariadne's arm. She caught the cheekpiece of his bridle, and stared off into the night. In the darkness, every noise was amplified—the damp wind stirring the trees above her head, the crickets chirping in the grass, the distant sound of a horse and carriage traveling down Park Lane.

She swallowed nervously, suddenly feeling very alone and unprotected. Daniel and Simon, the grooms she'd hastily recruited from her father's London stable, should be along soon with the veterinarian. Again, she thought of that handsome, fair-haired man bending over the dog, the emotions—horror, amazement, and finally, awe, despite the fact the sight of the needle plunging into the dog's belly had nearly made her swoon— that had swelled her heart, and the hot current of shared triumph when he'd looked up and his gaze had collided with hers.

Somehow, the thought of the veterinarian made her feel safe.

And the sooner they got him and fled London, the better.

Her heart pounding, the little noblewoman led her charge farther into the trees to wait, and tried not to think about how many people out there in the darkness were searching for her.

Night had long since fallen outside the livery where Colin ran his practice. As was his habit, he strode the length of the barn, carrying a lantern and looking in on each horse before closing the place up for the night. A small office and two box stalls at the stable's far end were his to use in exchange for veterinary care for the owner's horses, and now, all three of those stalls were empty.

He looked at the last empty stall on the left for

a long moment, his fingers tightening around the wire handle of the lantern as a familiar pain tightened around his heart. Poor Old Ned, who'd served him so faithfully these past three years ... sickly, arthritic, and chronically lame ... he was one animal Colin had *not* been able to save.

"I miss you, old boy," he whispered, gazing sadly at the empty feed bin, the empty water bucket, the empty hay net. Around him, the other horses abruptly stopped munching their hay, listening. He reached out and ran his fingers over the stall door's worn top, where a few white hairs still clung. "Miss you like hell," he said softly. Then he turned away and continued on, the chronic ache in his right leg joining the one in his heart and warning him of impending rain.

Every horse in the stable turned its head to watch him as he passed, though he never noticed the love and adoration in their large, dark eyes. The livery's owner had long since gone home and the two stable hands were off for the night to drink themselves into a stupor at the Blue Rooster. As usual, they had invited Colin to join them; and as usual, he had politely declined. It wasn't that he didn't like people; he simply wasn't a gregarious man, a trait that he'd first become aware of back in his navy days when, alone in his cabin and cut off from the rest of the ship, he'd found a haven in isolation where others of his rank had often complained of finding it a self-imposed prison.

He reached out to stroke the nose of a stout gray gelding whose head hung over a stall door. Better not to think of those glorious years. Nor of the shame and disgrace that had ended them forever, toppling him from the pinnacles of public and military acclaim to spend his life in forgotten obscurity. He might as well have just disappeared off the face of the earth. And yet, the man he had been still remained, and the parallels between the two, vastly different careers were not lost on him. Once, he'd been a hero. And sometimes—like today, he thought with a little smile, as he remembered the mastiff coming alive under his hands, the boy's tearful shriek of glee—he still felt like one.

Giving the horse a last, fond pat, he continued on, his limp more pronounced than usual, remembering that beautiful, elegant woman sitting coolly astride the stallion.

Watching him.

What had *she* thought?

He'd probably never know. Just as he'd never know who she was, nor why she had concealed her gender, nor why she'd been staring at him so intently.

He hadn't been able to get her out of his mind all day. Surely, such obsessions were a direct result of spending too much time with animals instead of people. Perhaps he *should* have joined the two stable hands for a wet or two at the local tavern, just for a change of scenery. . . .

He completed his nightly tour, the soft mixture of straw, wood chips, and dirt sighing beneath his boots. For a moment he stood listening to the sounds of a happy, healthy stable: the horses munching their hay, the occasional swish of a tail across a back, the stamp of a foot, the rattling of an empty feed bucket. All was as it should be. Satisfied, he stepped into his small office, intending to retrieve his bag and his nightly dose of educational reading.

He stopped in surprise. A farmer stood there, shy and obviously ill at ease, a stained red hat clenched between his stubby fingers.

"Can I help you?" Colin asked, politely.

The man put out a thick, broad hand. "Name's John McCarthy. Just wanted to stop by and thank ye for savin' that dog today—he belongs t' me son, ye know."

Setting the lantern down, Colin returned the handshake. He heard himself making some inane comment about what a good patient Homer had been.

"I know ye don't remember me," the farmer went on, the lanternlight gleaming off his balding head as he gazed in wide-eyed wonder at the vials and jars of salves, pills, and powders on the wall shelves. "But I came to the talk ye gave last week at the lecture hall, the one on lameness in the horse. Enjoyed it a real lot, Mr. Lord. Thank ye for leavin' out all those eee-ses and oh-ses so that us plain folk could know what ye was talkin' about."

Colin nodded, smiling in amusement as the man screwed up his brow and peered at a bottle of pills whose cobalt color he seemed to find particularly attractive.

"I, uh . . . I'm sorry to be botherin' ye, 'specially at this hour when ye probably want to go home and eat yer supper, but . . . well, I was wonderin', Mr. Lord, if ye might suggest a remedy for me little mare. She's got a cold—you know, runny eyes 'n' nose an' the whole lot, and I've already had her bled once. It didn't do no good, sir, and I was just wonderin' what *you*, bein' one of these new *vet-rinarians*, think I ought t' do."

"Do you have her with you, Mr. McCarthy?"

"Well, er, no . . . figgered she was best left at home since she was feelin' so poorly."

Overhead, rain began to drum softly upon the roof, and Colin felt his leg throbbing right along with it. Leaning against the examination table to take the weight off his thigh, he bent his head, raking a hand through his hair and pushing it back off his brow.

"F'rgive me, Mr. Lord. Ye look tired—I can come back in the maw'nin—"

"No, no, I'm fine, really." Colin looked up and gave a reassuring smile, still thinking of the woman. The memory of that lovely face would put off any hopes of a peaceful night's sleep, as surely as the pain that was plaguing his leg. "About your little mare . . ."

"Do ye think I ought t' get her bled again, Mr. Lord?"

"Absolutely not."

"But the farrier said—"

"I *know* what the farriers say," Colin said, with more sharpness than he intended. "*And* the cow leeches, *and* the surgeons, *and* my own colleagues, even. Phlebotomy is the accepted treatment for everything from colic to pneumonia. But it is cruel and unnecessary, and I don't believe in it. Cover your little mare with a blanket instead, give her a hot bran mash, get her away from your other stock so she does not infect them, and rest her from her work for a day or so."

The farmer stared at him for a moment, mentally digesting the information. Then he nodded, slowly. "Blanket, bran mash, and rest," he said, counting off on his fingers. "No bleeding."

"No bleeding."

The man beamed and pumped Colin's hand in gratitude. "Thankee, sir. Much obliged. And what do I owe ye for yer good advice?"

"Not a thing. Just your promise that you won't have her bled. And please, if she doesn't improve, send for me and I'll come take a look at her, personally."

"I'll do that, Mr. Lord." Smiling, the farmer clapped his hat down atop his balding pate and pulled open the door. "Thanks again ... and I'm sorry for botherin' ye."

"You're not both—"

He was gone before Colin could finish his sentence, his cheerful whistle and heavy footsteps fading into the rainy night. For a moment, the veterinarian stood leaning against the examination table, listening to the gentle tap of rain against the roof. He could smell it as it came sweeping through the still-open door on a feathery wave of wind, and the fresh, earthy scent of springtime—damp dirt and grass, blossoming flowers, clean, newly washed air. He looked forward to a refreshing walk home this evening.

Another trait, left over from his many years at sea. He liked weather, in all of its many facets and moods.

Straightening up, Colin unlocked his bookcase, selected the second volume of Delabere Blaine's *The Outlines of the Veterinary Art* and Bracy Clark's recently published *A Series of Original Experiments on the Foot of the Living Horse*—the former for its discussion of laminitis, the latter for its theories regarding elasticity of the foot, complete with an anatomical and physiological dissertation long and complicated enough to keep him well distracted into the wee hours of the morning. Heavy reading, but certainly easier to rest on than the memory of that cool beauty. Tucking the books beneath his coat, Colin shut the door to the barn and picked up his bag.

He was just turning when, out of the corner of his eye, he saw a shadow slide past the window.

His head jerked up and he stared at that ominous pane of glass for a long moment. The rain suddenly seemed louder, the room darker, and, unconsciously, his hand went to his hip. But his sword was no longer there; that had been part of his former life, though the instinctual motion remained.

Frowning, he put the books down. Then, carrying the lantern, he moved toward the door, his gaze on that black window, the hair rising on the back of his neck.

He tore the door open and stared out into the rainy night.

Nothing.

Let it go, Colin. You are no longer an officer on watch, with the responsibility of a man-of-war and some eight hundred men resting on your shoulders. You're just a London veterinarian. Get used to it.

Feeling a bit foolish, he picked up his books, blew out the lantern, and set it on the floor. For a moment he stood listening, all alone in this room with only his thoughts, and two years worth of warm memories played out within its walls—of saving, healing, and helping those poor, gentle creatures who could never voice their complaints of just how much it hurt.

Pushing open the door, he stepped out into the cool spring night. Rain tapped against his face, moist wind kissed his cheeks. He locked the door and pocketed the key.

He was just turning when something crashed against the back of his skull. The books tumbled from his hand, and the grassy earth rushed up to meet him.

Stars winked before his eyes.

Colin Lord heard himself groan, and then knew no more.

Chapter 2

～◎〇◎～

Lady Ariadne waited restlessly in the darkness. Around her, Hyde Park lay black and silent beneath a silver pillow of mist. The grass was wet at her feet, her breeches were damp, and her leather boots were nearly soaked through. She peered through the trees toward the carriage drive running parallel to Park Lane, her stomach in knots. It was nearly ten o'clock. Surely, Simon and Daniel would be along with the veterinarian any time now.

She was terrified.

A part of her vast inheritance was sewn into the blanket that covered Shareb-er-rehh's back, but the thought of having it stolen from her by thieves was not the only cause of her fear.

It was the veterinarian.

What if he recognized her as the most wanted fugitive in London? What if he didn't wish to abandon his veterinary practice to escort her to Norfolk? What if he refused the money she was prepared to offer, and turned her in to the authorities instead?

As though sensing her distress, Shareb-er-rehh moved forward, shoving his head against her arm and rubbing hard. She threaded her fingers through his mane, trying to calm her racing heart. Moonlight was infusing the mist now and making it look ghostly and ethereal; shadows crept from the trees, stretching across the ground and reaching for her, and from somewhere off in the night, she heard two cats fighting, their angry, drawn out wails winding through the darkness before ending on a high screech of synchronized fury.

Shareb-er-rehh lifted his head, dismissed the sound with a heavy sigh, and dropped his muzzle to crop the wet grass around Ariadne's toe. The fresh-cut, musky scent rose, mingling with that of soggy earth, leather, and damp horse. The stallion was alert, his ears swiveling back and forth on his noble head as he grazed, and Ariadne lamented what she'd had to do to her beloved horse to keep him safe.

His once-lustrous, pitch-colored mane had been singed by the fire and was now trimmed sparse and short. His scorched tail had been chopped, racehorse style, to the level of his hock. The blinkered hood enclosed his expressive head, the blanket covered most of his back beneath the saddle, and weighted leg bandages threw his long, fluid gait off enough to disguise it. No one would know who—or what—he was. But Ariadne was still nervous. She couldn't risk Tristan or anyone else tracking them down by Shareb's description.

Or, she thought, looking down at her manly attire, her own.

Clenching her fists, she tilted her face up to the moon now sailing through the silver clouds, her silent vow so vehement that it squeezed tears from the corners of her eyes with its very intensity.

Oh, Papa ... I'll not let Tristan get his hands on Shareb-er-rehh. He is our horse, and I'll do whatever I have to do to keep him safe and healthy.

She opened her eyes and stared at the moon's pale, shimmery disc.

"Even if it means abducting a London veterinarian," she whispered, the tears trickling silently down her cheeks as she thought of her beloved papa.

Papa, whom she hadn't even had time to grieve for yet.

The stallion was suddenly there, snuffling loudly and lipping at her coat. Ariadne had barely managed to get the flagon of ale out and uncorked before Shareb had it between his teeth. He lifted his head high and, closing his eyes in bliss, guzzled deeply. Then he flung the bottle away with a toss of his head and nosed her coat once more.

She smiled through her tears. "What?" she asked, though she knew what he wanted.

His muzzle shoved against her pocket. Ariadne stepped back. The stallion moved with her.

His antics were enough to drive away the tears. Funny, how animals sensed your feelings, how they were always there to comfort you in your hour of need. . . .

Laughing now, she shoved him away.

"Would you wait a minute? Lud, you're the most impatient animal Papa ever bred!"

She reached into her pocket, unwrapped the last piece of pastry, and broke off a chunk of it. Hearing the crackling of the paper, Shareb-er-rehh grew frantic, eagerly nosing her hand and lipping at her fingers. She put the treat on her palm, felt his velvety lips brushing her skin. Only his quiet munching, and the sound of water dripping from the leaves above her head, broke the stillness of the night.

That—and now, something else.

Shareb-er-rehh heard it, too. Crumbs peppering his whiskers, he jerked his head up in mid-chew and stared off toward the carriage drive, every muscle in his big body tense, his eyes gleaming like jet in the moonlight.

Voices. *Male* voices, low and familiar. Ariadne closed her eyes on a shaky sigh of relief, thanking God above that Simon and Daniel had arrived at last.

She stepped forward—and her eyes went wide with horror.

"For heaven's sake!" she hissed, rushing from the concealment of the trees. "You didn't have to blindside him, you *fools!*"

The grooms exchanged worried looks and stared down at their senseless burden; one of the veterinarian's arms was hanging, the hand curled loosely and the knuckles just brushing the grass. Sheepishly, Daniel said, "Well, it wasn't as though we could just *ask* him to help you, my lady, you being a fugitive and all."

Anger burned through her. "Set him down."

"But—"

"Immediately!"

Ariadne was already taking off her coat and kneeling in the wet grass beside the veterinarian. Biting her lip, she slid her hand beneath his nape and gingerly lifted his lolling head. Shivers raced through her as her fingers made contact with his warm skin, and it was all she could do not to snatch her hand away and let his head thump heavily to the ground. After all, she didn't even know this man, was betrothed to another, and had no business laying her ungloved hand upon a stranger.

But she did not let go of him, and as she cupped the back of his head, steadying it while she made a pillow of her coat, her fingers threaded through his damp hair and found the swelling just behind his ear.

"A lot of use he's going to be to me *now*," she muttered angrily, and glared up at the two sheepish servants.

"Really, my lady, we didn't hit him that hard. . . ."

"You shouldn't have hit him at all," she snapped, and carefully lowered the veterinarian's head to the makeshift pillow. "It was totally unnecessary and *extreme*."

Anxious and worried, she gazed down at his still features as the grooms told her where his practice had been located, what his name was, and a host of other things she only half heard. His hair was fashionably cut, silky, and devoid of curl, his brow high and intelligent, his nose a bit long and a shade too prominent, but showing no weakness of soul. It upset her to see him, a gentle healer, laid low by her grooms' senseless violence, especially after viewing his heroic actions on behalf of the dog. Wishing to negate it, she reached out and gently smoothed the wet hair back from his forehead. Her hand trembled, and a spasm of nervousness made her shudder. Could he somehow know she was touching him? But no, his eyes were closed, the long lashes lying still against his cheeks; she remembered those eyes as being clear and intelligent, direct and almost piercing.

He had known who she was. Or surely, would've guessed. Maybe they'd had no choice but to abduct him so forcibly. . . .

The veterinarian moaned softly, and Ariadne snatched her hand away.

"Bring the lantern, Simon," she said impatiently. "He's waking up."

She sat back on her heels, watching him anxiously. *Please God, let him be all right*, she thought. His eyelids fluttered, and then he pressed his palms to his temples, rolled to his side, and pushed himself up onto the heel of one hand, head hanging, bits of wet grass clinging to his coat, his hair tumbling over his brow in a wave of silk. He remained swaying, supporting himself on one arm—then he fell, landing on his back and dragging open hazy, blinking eyes to peer dazedly up at her.

She waved the groom back. "Not that close, Simon, the candle is hurting his eyes!"

Colin Lord squinted and gazed up into the suddenly dark space above him. It took him a moment to focus on the present, and then he became slowly aware of several things at once: the damp, spongy ground beneath him, moisture creeping through his clothes; light, and the scent of burning wax; the cool night wind against his cheeks; the presence of several people—*scoundrelly thieves*, he thought angrily, *what on earth could they possibly want from me*?—all staring down at him, and someone trying to shove something soft and lumpy beneath his aching head. . . .

His eyes fell shut. He felt someone slapping his hand, frantically. "Mr. Lord! Wake up, I beg of you!"

The voice was sharp, scared, and *female*, and, with an effort, Colin dragged his eyes open once more. He stared blankly at the face that loomed above him—then, recognition.

"Dear God," he murmured, thickly, " 'tis you."

"Forgive me, Mr. Lord, I had no intention of harming you; it was an accident, should never have happened; I just wanted to talk to you—"

He felt sick, dizzy, awful. Wanted to move. Couldn't. Wanted to drift back into oblivion. Couldn't. Wanted to ask her to lay her soft, tiny hand against his pounding head. Didn't.

On the faintest of smiles, he whispered, "You deliver a devilish mean wallop, madam."

"Oh, it wasn't me, but my servants. They should

never have hurt you—you're all right, aren't you, Mr. Lord?—I shall not forgive them, or myself, if we have done you any lasting injury."

She was talking too fast, too nervously, for him to keep up with her. Colin pressed his palms against his throbbing skull and tried to focus his eyes on the three other lanternlit faces looming above him. Two were men, one with a good-humored cast to his mouth, an aquiline nose and bright eyes; the other, black-haired, watchful, rather effeminate; and the third was . . . the stallion. Beneath the edge of its blinkered hood Colin could just see the tapered muzzle and wide, shell- shaped nostrils meant for taking in vast amounts of air; the animal lowered its head, sniffed him, and, as though dubious and disdainful, craned its neck to look at . . .

Her.

"How gallant you were today, saving that little boy's dog as you did," she said, hurriedly, as though praise could make amends for the hurt she had caused him. "I commend your persistence, your skill, and your knowledge. I have never seen anything quite like it in my life. You were magnificent. Simply brilliant!"

He gazed hazily up at her lovely face; already, the cool night air was clearing his head, restoring his senses. But she didn't have to know that. Oh, no, it was far more amusing to let her gush on with her hurried apologies, her worried chatter, and come to think of it, it wasn't so bad that she thought him "magnificent," either. . . .

He smiled and shut his eyes against the feigned dizziness.

"Where did you learn such a thing, Mr. Lord? You must be appropriately educated."

"Veterinary College, London," he whispered, with a groan of pain for effect. "Graduated from there . . . did an apprenticeship with Delabere Blaine. . . ."

"Ah yes, the Veterinary College. My father, God rest his soul, had great faith in the future of the veterinary art and gave much money to support that institution. Always said it was a pity that France had a veterinary college before England did. . . . After today, I can certainly see why he harbored such belief in your profession. Your knowledge far surpasses that of the common farrier and I think you'll do quite nicely." She knelt close, her dark eyes worriedly searching his face, her fingers resting on his arm. "Can you get up, Mr. Lord?"

"I . . . really don't know."

"Here. Try. I shall help you."

She got down on her knees, slid her arm beneath his nape, and helped him into a sitting position. The world made a slow, sickening revolution and he felt himself falling, into space, into her arms. She caught him and he felt her stiffen, as though she didn't quite know what to do with him. Or perhaps, didn't want to touch him. Oh, this situation was growing more and more amusing by the moment. Bending his head to hide his grin, he shut his eyes and leaned heavily against her tiny frame, enjoying her obvious discomfort and embarrassment while he pretended to recover. He felt the damp scratchiness of her coat beneath his cheek, heard the erratic race of her heart beneath his ear, and happily drowned in her scent, a heady potion of lavender, leather, and fresh rain.

She moved beneath his weight, trying to wrestle him into a position that was less intimate, less invasive. The two youths stepped forward to help but she angrily waved them off, lashing out with a peppery admonition that their actions had done more harm than good. It was obvious she wasn't finding the situation as amusingly absurd as he did; in fact, he hadn't had this much excitement since his navy days—

It suddenly occurred to him what she'd just said. *Do quite nicely?*

"Ah, yes," he murmured, pushing away from her and supporting himself with a palm splayed firmly in the wet grass. He reached up to touch the swelling knot just aft of his ear. *Subperiosteal hematoma*, he thought, wryly. "You obviously want something from me."

"Yes, but I am willing to pay handsomely for it."

He pretended a weak smile. "Pray, madam, do not keep me in suspense. I don't know if I can stand it."

Satisfied that he was in no danger of fainting, she stood and pulled off her cap. In the lantern's soft glow her hair tumbled down, gleaming rich and red and lustrous, like a warship's new copper. She drove a hand through it, obliterating the flat imprint left by the cap and making the glossy tresses spring and bounce to life around her fine shoulders. For the first time, he saw her features in all their delightful glory—the impudent little nose, the roses in her cheeks, the saucy, spoiled tilt to her perfect mouth. Her skin was the color of his mother's finest china, her eyes alight with piquancy. She was more lovely than he'd imagined, and he suddenly found it too hard to breathe.

"What?" she asked, a bit flippantly, cocking her head. Her eyes sparkled, and he caught the challenging, almost teasing, note to her tone. "Have you never seen a *lady* before?"

"Not one garbed so charmingly."

It was a bold reply, and he saw her brows shoot up, the quick burst of color in her cheeks before she quickly turned her back on him and moved to stand beside the stallion, her hand stroking the horse's white muzzle with rapid, nervous movements.

"You have aptly demonstrated your knowledge of dogs, Mr. Lord," she said, her hand moving faster now. "Tell me . . . what do you know about horses? Say . . . racehorses?"

"Thoroughbreds?"

"*Racehorses.*"

Thoroughbreds, he thought. "Well, they have four legs, a mane and tail—"

"I am dead serious, Mr. Lord!" she protested, turning to face him with a little laugh.

He sighed. "Really, madam, I'm not feeling well enough to go into a lengthy discourse about the merits of the various breeds, nor the illnesses that each of them are predisposed to. What do you want me to tell you about thoroughbreds? That the lot of them are a sick and fragile collection, cruelly forced to run themselves to death merely for the pleasures of a few privileged rich folk who have no better means of amusing themselves?"

One copper brow lifted, ever so slightly. Her eyes gleamed, a hint of a smile touched her mouth, and she shot a triumphant glance at the two silent youths. Her hand encircled the stallion's muzzle, and, still watching him, she rested her cheek against the side of its face. "Sick and fragile, Mr. Lord? How so?"

"Are you testing me?"

"As a matter of fact, I am. Answer the question, please."

He shrugged. "I worked with racehorses at Newmarket for a bit—I saw broken-winded animals, many with bones too fragile to withstand the rigors those poor beasts were asked to endure—God and the devil, but my head hurts. . . ."

"Enough, Mr. Lord. You will do. Help him up, Daniel."

The youth moved forward, offering his hand; Colin grasped it, found his feet, and, still pretending to feel much worse than he actually did, stumbled to a nearby tree. He leaned his brow against its rough trunk and shut his eyes, keenly aware of her soft footsteps as she came up behind him and wondering if he had dreamed of her fine, tiny hand smoothing his hair back from his brow . . . or if she really had.

"Are you well, Mr. Lord?" Her voice was soft, concerned, and he felt her fingers hesitantly touch his shoulder.

"I will be, madam."

"Because if you're not, I can go find another veterinarian to give the one thousand pounds to."

Colin's eyes shot open. He twisted his head around to look at her, all pretense of nausea and dizziness suddenly forgotten. "One thousand *pounds?*"

"Yes. It is what I will pay you to accompany me to Burnham Thorpe in Norfolk. I wouldn't expect you to know where it is, of course, but—"

"On the contrary, madam," he murmured, bracing himself with a hand against the tree as he thought of all that he could do with such a staggering amount of money. "I . . . had a friend who hailed from there." A shadow crossed his face as he remembered that friend—Horatio, Lord Nelson—dead now for almost five years and sleeping forever in the crypt of St. Paul's, not far from where he now stood.

"Well!" She snatched her hand away from his shoulder. "Such a small world, is it not? Burnham is just a tiny village tucked up in the corner of Norfolk, near the sea; probably no one in England had ever even *heard* of it until Lord Nelson put it on the map—"

Something caught in his throat. "Yes, of course. . . ."

"So are you interested in earning one thousand pounds, Mr. Lord?"

His head was spinning. One thousand pounds was more than his practice made in an entire year. One thousand pounds would enable him to buy his own establishment, perhaps even one in the West End of the city. One thousand pounds would more than fund his research on equine laminitis. One thousand pounds . . .

"It would seem, madam—"

"My lady."

"—that before I agree to *anything*, I should know who you are. . . . Since you have put me at a decided disadvantage in that you seem to know more about *me* than I do *you*, I think it is only sporting that you introduce yourself—and explain to me precisely what services I shall have to perform in order to earn such a sizable sum of money."

Silence. She was looking uncertainly at the grooms, as though hesitant to reveal her identity; then, she raised her chin, her shoulders went back, and she faced him resolutely. He saw her chest rise and fall on a deep, steadying breath, almost as though she was bracing herself.

"I am Lady Ariadne St. Aubyn," she announced, "daughter of the late Earl of Weybourne."

He looked at her blankly, then glanced at the grooms. "Forgive me, but . . ."

Her eyes widened. "You don't know who I *am*?"

"No. Should I?"

She glanced at the two young men; all three exchanged fleeting, relieved smiles. Then her shoulders relaxed, and he heard her release her breath as she met his questioning gaze. "I'm a fugitive, Mr. Lord. The whole of London is after me, and probably East Anglia as well."

He looked at this lovely elfin creature of mystery and mystique, and grinned. "For what? Stealing male clothes and going about dressed as a lad?"

"No, for stealing my own horse and fleeing the clutches of my horrid brother."

"Oh. How nice. So you wish to involve me in a family dispute."

"For one thousand pounds, I should think it wouldn't matter *what* I ask you to involve yourself in."

He rested the side of his head against the tree, smiling. "Are you implying that I might want for money?"

"Well . . . you *are* just a commoner, and a lowly veterinarian besides. And your clothes do not suggest to me that you are a wealthy man."

"Yes, well, I wouldn't want to wear my everyday velvets and silks for crawling around in cow manure and performing rectal exams on colicky horses—"

Her face went white with shock before turning a brilliant crimson. "*Really*, Mr. Lord!"

"Forgive me, my lady," he murmured, still a bit peeved by her presumptuousness. "Perhaps we should get straight to the point, and you can tell me exactly what services you require of me in order to earn this one thousand pounds. I understand it has something to do with accompanying you to Norfolk and looking after a horse?"

"Yes. Not just *any* horse, but the fas—"

"*My lady!*" cried the two grooms in unison.

Her eyes flashed to them and she raked a hand through her coppery hair, looking flustered and blown off course. "Yes, er, a horse, Mr. Lord. He's not ill, but he has great . . . sentimental value, and I'm terrified that something will happen to him. Unfortunately, my wicked, horrible brother Tristan—he's the new Lord Weybourne, you know—wants Shareb-er-rehh as much as I do. He's even posted a reward for the return of this horse. *My* horse. A sister-brother dispute, right, Daniel?"

"Yes, my lady. A sister-brother dispute."

Colin looked at her suspiciously. There was more here than met the eye, but for one thousand pounds he was hesitant to dig too deeply.

"So, it is *this* horse you want me to look after, then?"

"Yes. Shareb-er-rehh, 'Drinker of the Wind.' "

"And just what is so valuable about this animal that you're willing to pay me one thousand pounds to protect him?" Colin asked, stretching out a hand toward the stallion. The animal flung its head up with violent force; its ears swept back, and thick white teeth gleamed savagely in the darkness.

"I wouldn't get too close," Her Ladyship warned. "He's very protective of me and quite jealous besides."

"Yes, well let's pray he never requires any medical attention," Colin said, dryly.

"No, I doubt that he shall. But to answer your question, Mr. Lord . . . my father, the sixth earl, had a lifelong interest in breeding horses. He—"

"*My lady!*" Daniel and Simon cried once more.

"Yes, you two, I *know*." Her eyes flashed, and she was looking mildly irritated now. "In any case, Mr. Lord, my father devoted his entire life to developing a . . . very special breed of horse. Superior in intelligence, and . . . other things. Shareb-er-rehh is the last surviving male to represent it."

"And just what is so special about this breed?"

She looked away. "It is, um . . . renowned for its . . . high-stepping gaits."

"I see."

"With the exception of one mare, who is in the possession of Lord Maxwell of Norfolk, the rest were all lost to a mysterious illness two months ago." Her eyes grew sad, and she looked down at her toes. "Four decades of careful breeding, Mr.

Lord. My father's legacy. Wiped out, just like that."

He began to stretch his hand toward her tiny shoulder in sympathy; thought better of it and pulled back.

"And you don't know what this 'mysterious illness' was?"

"No. All I can tell you is that the horses went out of their minds, and had strange convulsions and behavior just before they died . . . thank God my father got Shareb-er-rehh out of there and down to London before he could catch it as well." She turned to him, her eyes haunted and bleak. "What do you think it might have been, Mr. Lord?"

"I'd have to see the clinical signs and examine the animals," he said evasively.

"A guess, then?"

He shrugged. "Could be one of many things. Moldy corn disease, perhaps."

"Moldy corn dis—"

"Aye, sometimes the corn goes bad and upon ingestion, proves fatal to the horse."

"Oh."

She stood there, looking miserable. "Well," he said brightly, "all is not lost. You say there is one mare left?"

"Yes, Mr. Lord. My father gave her to Lord Maxwell—he also resides in Norfolk, you see—and her name is Gazella. She is the *real* reason that I must get Shareb-er-rehh to Norfolk—so that they can be bred, a foal can be got, and the horses that were my dear father's legacy, preserved." Her eyes grew angry and she turned away to stroke the stallion's sleek neck. "But my wicked brother Tristan cares naught for our father's forty years of dreaming and planning! All he cares about is catching up to me, claiming Shareb-er-rehh as his own, and then handing him over to his creditors in order to pay off his immense gambling debts!"

"Aaaah. So now I understand your desperation to get to Norfolk," Colin mused, rubbing his still-aching head.

"Can you help me, Mr. Lord? Will you travel with us to Norfolk, look after Shareb-er-rehh, protect us from Tristan and any other threat to my stallion's well-being?"

"Well, I—"

"I'm an heiress; I'll pay you well for your trouble, Mr. Lord!"

He nodded, thinking. "You say that this animal is superior for its high-stepping gaits. Yet his build—from what I can see of it—is extraordinarily lean and rangy."

"He's . . . been off his feed."

"Sick?"

"No, just . . . stressed."

"Forgive me, but your stallion does not *look* like a fancy gait horse," Colin said dubiously, wishing the animal would let him get close enough for a more careful examination.

She tossed her head. "*That's* because he's in disguise."

"In case your brother happens to see and recognize him?"

"Of course."

"Of course," Colin said, smiling.

"Just as *I* am in disguise, for the same reason."

"And just how much is your brother offering for the horse's return?"

"Fifteen hundred pounds," she said unthinkingly.

"Aaah. So, fifteen hundred pounds to return him to your brother"—he pushed the hair off his forehead and gazed sideways at her as though in deep thought—"and yet, only *one* thousand pounds to get him to Norfolk? I daresay, it would be a most unwise business decision on my part if I were to settle for a mere one thousand pounds when I can earn another five hundred by simply turning you over to your brother."

She stared at him, stunned and openmouthed with horror.

"Furthermore," he mused, "such a course of action would require far less work on my part, and I would merely have to travel across town as opposed to a hundred miles or so up to Norfolk—"

"Why, you rotten scoundrel! I wouldn't have thought you were a devious man!"

"I am not a devious man. Merely a logical one."

"Fine, I'll pay you fifteen hundred pounds!" she snapped.

"I want two thousand."

"Sixteen hundred!"

"Two thousand."

"Eighteen hundred!"

"*Two thousand.*"

"I am *not* giving you two thousand!"

"Very well then. I'll settle for the fifteen hundred offered by your brother instead. Come with me, my lady—"

"Daniel! Simon!" she cried. "Don't just *stand* there!"

The two youths exchanged nervous glances, unsure what to do. "But my lady, that stallion is worth far more than—"

"Never mind what he's worth!" she cried, stamping her foot and cutting them off before they could do more damage. "A fine lot of help *you* two are!"

"Sorry, my lady," they said in unison.

She glared at the veterinarian. He merely stood watching her, an infuriating, amused little smile playing about his lips, his keen eyes regarding her with confident challenge. Heat prickled her skin beneath that calmly assured gaze, exacerbating her anger. "Very well, Mr. Lord," she seethed, "I shall pay you the two thousand pounds, you deceiving blackguard! But let me tell you, I think you're *despicable*."

"Thank you. But actually, I would rather you tell me I'm a shrewd businessman. 'Twould be far more flattering, I think."

She clenched her fists at her sides.

"So, do we have an agreement then?" he asked, lifting a brow.

"Yes, we have an *agreement*!"

"Ah, splendid. I suppose we should get started right away, then. But first, I must return to my lodgings so I may pack some clothes, hang a sign proclaiming my absence, and collect my medicines and surgical instruments. Do you wish to accompany me?"

"Just lead the way," she said angrily, and, waving off the grooms' offers of help, swung herself agilely up onto the stallion's back. "But let me tell you, Mr. Lord, I am in great haste to get this horse to Norfolk and will not wait about for you!"

"Which leads me to one last question, my lady."

She spun around in the saddle, her eyes flashing. "What?"

"Just what sort of refuge do you expect to find once you reach Norfolk?"

"Oh, did I not tell you? The mare belongs to Lord Maxwell." She glared down at him. *My betrothed*."

Chapter 3

In the dark street just outside Mr. Lord's rooms in Chelsea—a most-deplorable and *un*fashionable part of London, she thought with a sniff!—Lady Ariadne St. Aubyn waited impatiently for the veterinarian.

Already, she regretted her rash decision that had put her in this current position. She did not quite know what to make of Colin Lord. He angered her with the way he had shrewdly outsmarted her. He confused her, with an attitude of command she would not have expected in such a gentle healer. And he unnerved, annoyed, and flustered her—with his patient ways, his smiles of private amusement, and the way he had looked at her. *Especially*, the way he had looked at her. Directly. Appreciatively. Too hard, and for far too long.

She suddenly felt hot all over.

Just who did he think he was?

His eyes had been no less keen upon studying Shareb-er-rehh, and she knew he would have liked nothing more than to strip off the blanket and hood and see the animal beneath. Thank heavens he had not discerned the truth about the stallion. *Gait horse?* Imagine! Well, it was safer to let him—and everyone else—believe such rubbish. It was only a matter of time before the veterinarian realized that Shareb-er-rehh was no gait horse at all. . . .

With a start, she realized Daniel and Simon were talking to her.

"My lady, we *insist* on coming with you to Norfolk," Daniel was saying, and she wondered that his throat wasn't raw from repeating the same words so many times in the last two hours. "You don't even know this—what d'you call him, Simon?"

"Veterinarian."

"*Veterinarian*. You don't even know him, my lady—he may take liberties with you, he may steal the stallion, he may do you dreadful bodily harm—"

"Or worse," Simon said, evasively.

She looked at them, puzzled. "Or worse?"

The two young men exchanged glances. "Never mind, my lady. Suffice it to say that you cannot travel alone with a *man*—"

"Oh. And so you wish me to travel alone with *three* of them."

"Yes, but we're—"

"I *know* what you are. And I appreciate your concern, but you will remain here in London, at Weybourne House in case Tristan comes looking for me. You must tell him I've gone to be with—who can I think of who lives in the *opposite* direction? . . . ah yes, with Lady Chadwick and her family at Greenvale Manor in Milford, Hampshire. Yes, tell him *that*."

Lud, what was taking that veterinarian so long?

"But my lady—"

"No 'buts,' Daniel. You and Simon will stay here in London, and I wish to hear no more on the matter. If you are truly so worried as all that, I shall send word to you when I reach Lord Maxwell's protection."

"Yes, and what is Lord Maxwell going to think, when you show up on his doorstep wearing a coat and breeches with another man in tow?"

Ariadne raised her chin and pretended to study the detail of a window ledge, fifty feet away. "He'll not say anything. My Maxwell is kind and generous, patient, understanding, and good. We're betrothed, for pity's sake, with the mare Gazella to seal the agreement. Besides, he loves me, and I love him, and nothing and no one can get in the way of *that*. Now, go. And Godspeed."

"But my lady, please—"

"Go!" she cried, keeping her gaze fastened on the window ledge so they wouldn't see the glimmer of tears in her eyes. Another part of her life, gone. The horses, her father, the servants who had shared her childhood . . . one by one, they were all being stolen from her.

She heard the two grooms sigh and then walk off into the darkness, their footsteps dejected.

Ariadne stared straight ahead, swallowing hard and rhythmically stroking Shareb's sleek neck as she fought to regain her composure.

Think of Maxwell. Handsome, dear Maxwell, who worships the ground you walk on. He will make everything all right. He will keep you safe, and Shareb-errehh, too. Tristan will never be able to get Shareb once you reach Maxwell's protection. . . .

Her father was gone, his horses were gone, her reputation, surely, was gone.

At least she still had Maxwell.

Her words came back to her. *Besides, he loves me, and I love him, and nothing and no one can get in the way of* that—

Colin Lord's door opened, and the veterinarian, with a small, curly-haired mongrel twirling about his heels, came out. He had changed into a loose-fitting morning coat of navy blue; a simple waist-coat, a clean white shirt, and a muslin cravat gave him a dash of panache and elegance, and buckskin breeches tucked into military style riding boots emphasized the long, muscled leanness of his legs. He seemed much recovered from the blow he had suffered earlier, and for that, she was thankful. Her conscience would not easily bear the guilt of having hurt another person; it was bad enough to find herself wondering why he seemed to favor one leg.

Probably kicked by a horse, she thought.

However, her vulgar admiration for his masculine splendor, and her curiosity over how that slight limp had come about, were quick to turn to annoyance—especially in light of how he'd neatly turned the tables and gotten another thousand pounds out of her. *The blackguard*. She watched impatiently as he locked his door, positioned a sign upon it that took him a full minute to arrange until it hung to his exact satisfaction, and stooped to pick up the large trunk he had set on the steps. As heavy as it looked, he never staggered under its weight, and, lifting it to one broad shoulder, he called for the dog and came toward her.

He set the chest down and picked up the dog, fondly ruffling its ears and holding its squirming body out toward Ariadne.

"Lady Ariadne, meet Bow. Bow, meet Lady Ariadne. Shall we be on our way?"

"*Bow?*"

"Aye, Bow." He grinned, still holding the salt-colored mongrel toward her and waiting for her to make a response. The animal's pink tongue slid out, and its button eyes fastened on Ariadne. "As in ship."

From her lofty perch atop Shareb-er-rehh's back, she stared in disbelief down at the veterinarian's fair head, wondering if Daniel's blow had knocked the sense out of it.

"Mr. Lord, what do you think you're doing?"

"The task you're paying me for, my lady," he said, tickling the dog's fat pink stomach and setting it down.

"And just where do you propose to put that trunk?"

"It's not a trunk." He stepped back, and she looked down to see that, indeed, it was not a trunk, but a heavy wooden chest emblazoned with, of all things, a beautifully engraved drawing of a ship, and letters picked out in gold that spelled HMS *Triton*.

"Dare I ask what it *is* then?" she asked, with mounting ire.

"A sea chest. It goes everywhere with me, and has many sentimental memories attached to it. But lest you think I'm toting useless frippery, I'll have you know that this chest contains medicinals and surgical instruments, as well as several changes of clothing."

"I hope you've considered just how you plan on bringing it along," Ariadne said sharply, "because I can't imagine that you intend to *carry* it!"

"You're absolutely right. I have no intention of carrying it." He looked up at her, studying her as though he thought *she* was the addle-pated one. "Come, follow me."

Hoisting the chest to his shoulder once more, he turned his back and strode off, the little dog yapping at his heels. Miffed at his superior attitude, Lady Ariadne angrily sent Shareb-er-rehh trotting after him.

"I'll have you know, Mr. Lord, that I quite object to your high-handed ways. And I'll thank you to remember your station in life, and how you address your betters. Furthermore, may I remind you that you are working for *me* and I'm the one giving orders here!"

Ignoring her, Colin suppressed a grin and dug his fingertips into the sea chest balanced atop his shoulder. *I know more about giving orders and ensuring that they're obeyed than you ever will*, he thought. But it was best to let her remarks go by the board. Let her assume what she wanted. She was young. She wouldn't understand. Whereas he . . . knew better.

Favoring his bad leg, he led the way around the back of the building to the little courtyard, her peppery words stinging the air behind him, the stallion following in his footsteps and mincing like a fop. She was lying about the beast, that was for damned sure. Even for a gait horse, it had a strange and singular way of moving, throwing its feet high and strutting like a damned peacock.

Well, she must have her own secrets, and for two thousand pounds, he wasn't going to thrust his jibboom where it didn't belong.

Reaching the tarpaulin-covered chaise he'd brought over from the livery with the intention of repainting it, he set the trunk down and looked up at Her Ladyship. She was staring at the shrouded lump, and frowning.

"And what, pray tell, is *that*?"

"A chaise."

"And what do you intend to do with it?"

"Why, harness your fine steed to it." He saw the color rushing into her face, and added, "Besides, it will enhance his disguise. No one will suspect a carriage horse as being a fancy riding hack, will they?"

"Now see here," she began, "Shareb-er-rehh is the bluest of bluebloods. He can*not* be made to pull a chaise—"

"My dear lady." Colin had more patience than

cold treacle, but it was beginning to wear quite thin. "We have between us, your belongings, my sea chest, Bow, and over a hundred miles between here and Burnham. In case you have not noticed, we also have only *one* horse, with no time to hire another. I personally don't care if he's a damned mule or the most valuable stallion in England, he is still a horse, and I'll be damned if I'm going to walk all the way from here to East Anglia!"

Ariadne's eyes shot open, and she drew back in surprise. The veterinarian's anger was the quiet type, restrained but effective, the kind that was all the more dangerous because one was unable to discern its depth. Beneath her, Shareb-er-rehh stiffened, as though he had understood the animal doctor's logic—and his words.

Her mouth tight with indignation, she glared out past the soot-stained buildings of this deplorable part of town that, even now, were starting to gain shape and color from the blossoming pink-and-gold dawn. "Fine," she announced, loftily. "But I'll have you know he has *never* had to stoop to such a base level as pulling a *chaise*."

"He can learn."

"He'll balk. He'll shy. He'll refuse to budge."

"Then I guess we won't get him to Norfolk, will we?"

She glared at him, rankled by his logic, his patronizing air, his quiet authority. He gazed calmly back, awaiting her answer.

"I can see right now that this is going to be one miserable journey."

"Only as miserable as you choose to make it."

"I'm beginning to wish I'd never hired you."

He shrugged and began stripping the tarpaulin cover from the chaise. "It is not too late to change your mind."

"What, and have you go running straight to

Weybourne House to tell Tristan that I'm still near at hand? Oh, no. You know too much as it is, and you're coming with me whether you like it or not, Mr. High-and-Mighty Animal Doctor!"

"And *you* are going to hitch that horse to this chaise whether *either* of you like it or not, My Spoiled and Sassy Ladyship."

"How dare you insult me so!" she hissed, staring angrily down at him.

He merely grinned, leaned insolently against the side of the chaise, and gazed calmly back at her.

And as the first fingers of daylight breathed color into the morning, she saw that his eyes were a clear, matchless shade of lavender shot through with gray.

Beautiful, arresting, keenly-perceptive eyes.

She wasn't supposed to notice things like that. Not when her heart, and her future, belonged to another. She jerked her gaze away, staring at the shoddy stone and brick buildings so she wouldn't have to look into those knowing depths.

"Very well, then," she snapped. "Finish uncovering the thing."

Out of the corner of her eye, she saw him touch his brow as though in salute, turn, and resume where he had left off. The temptation was too much, and despite herself, she slowly twisted her head to look at him, wearing an appropriately haughty expression on her face and ready to jerk her gaze away in case he straightened up and caught her watching.

For a lowly commoner, Colin Lord possessed no small degree of charm and dash, and he issued orders as though doing so came second nature to him. She didn't like the feelings he evoked in her, the flustered jolt to her senses, the febrile tension that flashed between them every time their eyes met. It was unnatural; he was far beneath her in station and status. And, of course, there was no comparing him to Maxwell. He wasn't nearly as handsome as her betrothed. Didn't dress fashionably, or as richly. Didn't possess a title, breeding, or bloodlines, nor even a dog that could boast of a pure pedigree.

There was no reason she should even look at him twice.

Yet—

She watched as the fat little mongrel sidled close to her master's legs, cocking her head at the sound the night's rain made as it rolled off the tarpaulin. Yapping, she dived at the droplets trickling to the ground, inciting a burst of laughter from the veterinarian before he playfully shooed her away.

Losing interest, the tiny creature came up to the stallion. Then she went down on her forepaws before him, barking happily and looking up at Shareb-er-rehh with sparkling, mischievous eyes. Her tail waved madly; Shareb pricked his ears and took a step forward, blowing softly through his nose. Then his head went down, the reins slipped through Ariadne's fingers, and the mighty stallion touched his nose to the little dog's.

Bow, the veterinarian had called it. Part of a boat. What kind of a name was *that*?

"Your chariot awaits, my lady."

Startled, she raised her head to look. The chaise, a white, two-wheeled contraption with a collapsible top and a red leather seat, was barely large enough for two people. Ariadne gauged the size of that seat and swallowed hard. She'd have to sit closer to this man than propriety, her liking, and her own betrothed status would have permitted.

Yes, beautiful, unusual eyes. And his features aren't so bad, either. Even if he is just a commoner.

He leaned over to pull a harness and bridle from just beneath the seat. She could see the muscles stretching taut across his shoulders and back, and the fabric of his coat was light enough for her to pick out the nuances of their depth and definition. Sudden warmth coursed through her. Did Maxwell have shoulders that looked like that? After all, she'd never really thought to study Maxwell's shoulders—

"Well?" he said, holding the tack and looking expectantly at Shareb-er-rehh.

"What *I* don't understand," she said loftily, "is that you have a chaise but no horse of your own to pull it."

"I *did* have a horse to pull it," he returned.

"Well, why don't we hitch *him* to the chaise, then?"

"Because he died three days ago."

"Lovely. You're a veterinarian and your horse *died*." She tossed her head and said flippantly, "Oh, I feel supremely confident now about hiring you to look after *my* animal, truly, I do."

He had been reaching into the chaise to wipe a bit of dampness from the seat when she saw his back go stiff; he turned around slowly, *too* slowly. "My horse," he said softly, "was twenty-nine years old."

His gaze met hers. Ariadne swallowed hard, felt the color coming up in her face and a strange constriction in her chest.

She gazed down at Shareb's mane and knotted her fingers in the silky black strands, her cheeks flaming. Twenty-nine years was a long time for a horse. He must have looked after the animal quite well indeed.

Unable to meet his eyes, she murmured, "I'm sorry, Mr. Lord. That was very mean of me."

"Horrifically so."

She bit her lip and glanced at him. He merely stood there, the harness and bridle slung over one arm and a little smile playing across his face to soften the awkwardness of the moment. She tried to smile back, and felt small and insignificant in the face of his patience.

"Friends?" he murmured, raising one pale brown brow.

She raised her chin and pretended to watch the sunlight spreading down the trunk of a nearby tree. "Friends."

"Very well then. Let's get our equine nobleman hitched up to the chaise, shall we? It grows light, and I think it best to get out of London before the city awakes."

She nodded, dismounted, and stood watching as he approached Shareb, the mass of leather straps and buckles hanging over his arm. Sure enough, the stallion took one look at the harness, flung up his head, and backed away.

Ariadne crossed her arms over her chest. "He's not going to let you put that thing on him, Mr. Lord."

Ignoring her flippant taunt, he murmured softly and stretched out his hand toward the horse.

Shareb took another step back, broke out in a hard sweat, and turned his blinkered head to gaze beseechingly at his mistress.

"Oh, *poor* Shareb. . . ." Ariadne caught the cheek-piece of his bridle and pulled him toward her. Giving the veterinarian a long-suffering look, the big animal lowered his head and buried his face against his mistress's chest, keeping only his ears on Colin while Ariadne murmured and consoled. "It's all right, sweetie-heart," she crooned, threading her fingers through the sparse black mane. The small ears remained pointed at Colin. "That big, bad horse doctor is not going to hurt you. . . ."

"This big, bad horse doctor thinks it's getting late, my lady."

"He doesn't want to pull the chaise. Look at him. He's sulking, Mr. Lord."

"He's not sulking."

"Well, what do you call it then? Look at his face. He's *sulking*. I told you this was a foolish idea."

"Have you a better one?"

"Well no, but . . ."

"Then stop delaying and let's get him harnessed. Unless, of course, you don't really wish to reach Norfolk before the decade is out. . . ."

"Mr. Lord, you are the most irritatingly practical man I have ever met!"

"And you, my lady, are the slowest-moving fugitive I have yet to encounter. Now harness the horse while I hold his head."

"*Me*, harness a *horse*? I haven't the faintest idea how to harness a horse. Even on those rare instances when I did any driving, a servant always did it. Beneath my station, you know. I'll hold his head and *you* harness him."

"No, *you* harness him and *I'll* hold his head."

"You're giving orders again, Mr. Lord."

"Indeed I am. Here."

"I don't like it when you give orders. *I'm* running this adventure!"

"No you're not, you're financing it. Now harness the horse and let's get this escapade under way."

She had no time to protest further before he was thrusting the tack at her. Their fingers accidentally touched, and the heavy mass of leather fell to the ground with a thud.

Simultaneously, they both bent to pick it up. Brows rapping painfully, they jumped back and away from each other, he letting loose with a curse and she coming up with the harness.

"Sorry," she said, blushing.

"No, no, 'tis my fault. Are you all right, my lady?"

"Of course I'm all right, I have a very hard skull. Father used to tell me that all the time, you know—"

"And no doubt he was correct," he said, ignoring the sudden burst of angry color across her cheeks. "And I see that you have consented to harness the animal after all. They say that patience is a virtue, but I far prefer obedience. Especially when it comes to dealing with spoiled young noblewomen."

"*Spoiled?*" she retorted, drawing herself up to her full height. "You'll watch what you say to me, *Mr.* Lord! And I'll tell you right now that I prefer my servants to display a reasonable amount of respect. Had I known you were such a boor, I would never have hired you!"

"I am not a boar, I'm a man. Boars have tusks."

"What?"

He plucked the breastpiece and neck strap from her suddenly nerveless hand, shook it out, and, directing her to put it over Shareb's head, grinned innocently at her. "So, for that matter, do walruses."

"You are unforgivably impossible! Stop teasing me!"

"Am I?"

"You are, and I order you to stop it!"

"And I order *you* to put that harness on that horse under my tutelage, or I shall go back in the house, have my breakfast, and allow you to figure it out for yourself."

They faced each other, she holding the leather straps and glaring angrily at him, he merely looking at her with little crinkle lines of amusement fanning out at the corners of his eyes and the side of his mouth turning up in a lopsided, boyish smile that did dangerous things to her heart.

And Shareb-er-rehh—pricking his ears, arching

his neck, and sniffing curiously at the strange leather in her hands—was no help at all.

Sputtering and fuming, Lady Ariadne St. Aubyn began to harness her horse.

"Really, Tristan . . . I rather expected more from you than miserable excuses."

He gripped the edge of the table, hard, and leaned forward over his white knuckles. "They are not excuses, milord—"

"Sit down, Tristan.

"But you must believe me!"

"I said, sit down."

Sweating and terrified, he obeyed.

Clive sat regarding him calmly, dark, hypnotic eyes fixed unblinkingly on his face, the signet ring glowing dully on one long finger, every hair in perfect, impeccable place and his shoulders looking too broad, too magnificent, in the exquisitely cut black coat.

"Alas . . . I suppose I should've known better than to expect so much from one who seeks to pay off the gambling debts he owes me by amassing even bigger ones."

He sank a little lower in his chair, and only that dark, fixed stare held him upright and kept his suddenly nerveless body from sliding right down beneath the table.

"But sir, I'd been so lucky at the card tables, I really didn't think—"

"No, you are far too young and stupid to think. Which is why you have yourself in this mess, isn't it, Tristan?"

He was terrified; fear curled around his kidneys and rattled his heart within his chest. "I'll come up with the money I owe you, my lord, I swear it!"

Clive leaned back in his chair, a dangerous panther all in black, his eyes without compassion, pity, or soul. "Ah . . . and what brilliant plan have you now, my young friend?"

"I'll . . . I'll ask my father for my inheritance."

The earl regarded him with bored impatience. "And what shall you tell him, Tristan, when he asks you for what purpose you need the funds? Hmm? I suppose you might just come right out and tell him you owe me some money . . . to the tune of three thousand pounds."

He went white. He swallowed, his Adam's apple cutting into his crisply starched necktie, the thick lump of fear catching in his throat and hanging there. He clasped his hands beneath the table and forced his breathing to remain steady. His creditor was playing with him like a cat with a mouse.

"I suppose if you were a truly callous and enterprising young man, you could rather . . . shall I say, force your inheritance."

"F-force it, sir?"

"Why of course, Tristan."

"You mean . . . k-kill my father?"

Clive took out a cheroot, tapped it, lit it, and sat regarding Tristan through a lazy cloud of smoke. "Now, did I say that . . . Tristan?"

He stared into those black eyes, unable to speak.

The earl smiled darkly. "Did I?"

"No, sir, you did not. But—"

"Come up with the money, Tristan." *Clive tapped the ashes from his cheroot with studied elegance.* "You fancy yourself such an enterprising young man . . . I'm sure you can manufacture some clever scheme in which to do it." *He sat back in his chair, his eyes mesmerizing and blacker than the devil's soul.* "Because you see, Tristan . . . if you do not come up with the money, I can promise you that this Season in which you've brought about your own ruin . . ."

The earl smiled, evilly, and the blood ran cold in his veins.

". . . will be your last."

Will be your last . . . will be your last . . . will be your last. . . .

The words seemed to be in step with the mare's

steady trot, repeating themselves over and over and over in Tristan's mind.

Will be your last . . . will be your last . . . will be your last. . . .

That dreadful meeting had taken place two months ago and even now the memory made his mouth go dry with fright. With every mile the mare put behind her, with every person and beast they passed as he sought the Norfolk Road that would take him out of London and bring him to Burnham—*please God, let me get there before* she *does*—he felt that fear returning, its black tentacles curling around his spine and squeezing the air from his lungs.

For somewhere out there, was Clive . . .

Waiting.

Will be your last.

It had been all too obvious that his creditor had something far more dark and ugly planned for him than a mere debtor's prison. And what good would his inheritance, vast as it was, do him? Five months shy of his twenty-first year, he was too young to claim it anyhow. His hands tightened anxiously on the reins. He should never have told his father about his predicament, should never have expected the old man to react in any way but how he had, should never have put it past Ariadne to steal the one and only means he had of saving his own life. . . .

And maybe hers as well.

He gazed bleakly ahead through the mare's ears, watching them twitching back and forth, her creamy mane rippling on the light wind.

If only it was Shareb-er-rehh I had with me, not some common mare . . . if only I had Shareb-er-rehh. . . .

But he didn't have Shareb-er-rehh.

Ari did—and she already had a good head start on him.

He thought again of Clive's slow, saturnine smile of evil and foreboding, and urged the mare faster, into a canter.

He had to stop her.

But the rolling, triple-timed beat of the mare's hoofbeats made those final words even louder.

Will be your last . . .

Chapter 4

Her Ladyship managed such a socially challenging task as harnessing her own horse with surprising skill, and Colin didn't know which of the two nobles—the girl, or her equally highbred nag—seemed more indignant and incensed by the procedure. It was all he could do not to chuckle with mirth when he directed her to free the stallion's tail hairs from the crupper, an action that made her cheeks go pink with embarrassment and Shareb-er-rehh's head to jerk up with indignance.

Finishing, she turned, folded her arms across her chest, and stared at him with haughty triumph.

"Satisfied, Mr. Lord?"

He eyed her long and hard, until her composure began to falter. "Should I be?"

"Indeed you should. I have finished harnessing him."

He grinned and held out the driving bridle to her. "No, you haven't."

Dark eyes flashing, spine stiffening, she snatched the bridle and turned her back on him. Suspecting a conspiracy, Shareb-er-rehh eyed it with malice, backed up, and reared. Colin instinctively moved forward, but Her Ladyship expertly brought the stallion down with a quick yank on the reins.

Gripping the bridle's cheekpiece, she put her face as close as she could to the horse's blinkered head and stared into his dark eye. "I don't like this any more than you do!" she hissed, but in a voice that was clearly intended for Colin to hear. "Now, be good and stop your fussing!"

Instantly the big beast quieted, albeit with a surly look in his eye that belied his seemingly good manners. Then Her Ladyship reached up, deftly removed the hood and bridle, and gave Colin his first full view of the stallion's face.

His breath caught in his throat. The head was beautiful, classically sculpted, broad across the forehead with a white blaze starting just between the dark, intelligent eyes and widening as it spilled downward so that it encompassed nearly all of the fine, tapered muzzle.

"Handsome horse," he said, stretching his hand toward the stallion.

Shareb-er-rehh lashed out and nearly amputated his fingers.

"Loves compliments, doesn't he?"

"He loves his *dignity* even more."

"Yes, I'm sure he does. But he'll have to make do without it until we get to Norfolk. Please proceed."

"I have never been so insultingly treated in my life."

"And I've never had the liberty of having my horse harnessed and bridled for me. I find I rather like it."

She shot him a murderous glare, hooked an arm around the stallion's poll, and gently coaxed the bit into his mouth. Shareb-er-rehh stood chomping the metal, working it between teeth and tongue and eyeing Colin with as much malevolence as did Her Ladyship, but otherwise making no further protest as she pulled the bridle into place. Her tiny fingers buckled the throatlatch, pulled the stallion's forelock free from the browband, ensured the blinkers were adjusted over each eye. Then she walked briskly around the lathering animal, taking off her cap and tossing her hair over her shoulder as she swept past Colin in what could only be a deliberate attempt to tempt and taunt her human companion.

Her efforts found their mark. Colin caught the swirling scent of lavender, and with it an engaging blend of soap, horses, and femininity. Heat flashed through him, riding a wave of desire.

She was standing at the stallion's head, eyeing him with feminine triumph.

"I really think that we should make an effort to get along, if this trip is to be at all pleasant," she announced.

"I'm glad we are of like mind."

"Therefore, I expect you to show me a modicum of respect."

"And I would desire the same."

She smiled.

He gave her his most unsettling stare.

And she turned quickly away, stroking the stallion's nose and blushing furiously. "Furthermore, I've been thinking that *Mister* Lord simply will not do. It is far too ordinary, and not indicative of the great miracles I believe you are capable of performing with regard to healing animals. Therefore, I shall call you 'doctor' instead. Yes, *doctor*. Besides, if I go one hundred miles having to address you as 'Mr. Lord,' I shall wear out my tongue!"

"That would be a blessing," he murmured, picking up his trunk and shoving it under the seat of the chaise so she wouldn't see the twinkle in his eye.

"I beg your pardon?"

"I mean, that would be an unusual form of ad-dressing"—he looked up and gave an innocent grin—"me."

"Oh. I thought you said something else."

"Me? I would never insult my lady so."

"I should hope not. So, do you like your new title, *Doctor* Lord?"

"You flatter me, my lady, but veterinarians are not regarded as doctors."

"Indeed they are not. But you are *my* veterinarian and if I wish to consider you a doctor, I will. Therefore, you shall be *Doctor* Lord to me and Shareb." Her eyes sparkling, happy that she'd got-ten the upper hand in at least *something*, she put her hands on her hips and made a small circle around him, immensely pleased with herself and reminding him of a happy queen who'd just raised one of her subjects to the peerage. "Besides, you rather *look* like a doctor, especially when you wear your eyeglasses. By the way, where are they? You haven't forgotten them now, have you?"

"No," Colin said, his concentration swinging from her to the task at hand as he picked up the shafts of the chaise and brought it directly up be-hind the horse. The big animal stiffened and turned, regarding him warily. Already, the dark eyes were hard and flat, the ears back, the nostrils flaring with trepidation. The horse was no idiot, and obviously suspected what was to be asked of him. Colin tossed a blanket into the chaise. They'd be damned lucky if they weren't all killed. . . .

"Good. You rather look like a University grad-uate, all brainy and highborn with them on . . . I do hope you shall wear them often for me, just so I'm reminded that I have indeed purchased myself a veterinarian worthy of my stallion. I mean, at two thousand *pounds* you had better be worthy!"

"Perhaps next time you should shop around for

a bargain," he said drolly, as he directed her to back the horse into the shafts.

"Are you sporting with me, *Doctor* Lord?"

"Me, sport with you?" He widened his eyes and gave her his most innocent smile as he fastened the traces. "My lady, I would not dream of it. You are *far* too important a personage to make sport of, and I would be less than a gentleman if I were to insult you so."

"Good." She raised her chin and regarded him with a cool hauteur that was effectively destroyed by the mischief in her eye. "Because I would take great offense, I think, if you, a commoner, were to make sport of me without my knowing. That would be unforgivably rude and impertinent behavior on your part."

"Oh, yes. Unforgivably."

They stared at each other, both trying not to grin. Then her chin came down a notch, and he saw the helpless sparkle in her eye, the deviltry in her expression.

"So, are you going to wear your spectacles or not?"

"I only wear them for reading."

"You weren't reading when *I* saw you in them."

"I wear them during surgery, too. Or, for anything that requires strict attention to detail. Or when I'm tired. Or when—"

"Surgery!" She clapped a hand across her chest and went a bit green. "Do you mean . . . *cutting* things?"

"Not 'things.' Flesh. Skin. Muscle—"

"How utterly *ghastly*. Pray I shall never have to see anything more disconcerting than what you had to do to that poor, bloated dog yesterday! Imagine, stabbing it in the belly with a needle—"

"You should have stayed a bit longer," he couldn't resist adding, with a teasing grin. "The stomach tube procedure that followed was even more impressive."

She blanched. "*Stomach tube*?"

"Aye. A long, snakish thing of wire wrapped with leather. One must push it down the esophagus and into the stomach so as to relieve the excess—"

"Never mind, Dr. Lord, you may talk of such things *after* we eat breakfast! Which reminds me, would you like a black currant tart?"

As though on cue, the stallion's ears shot forward and he craned his neck and stared at Her Ladyship's pocket. Odd behavior, Colin thought, frowning. The little noblewoman reached into her coat, pulled out a thick wedge of paper-wrapped pastry, and, pushing aside Shareb-er-rehh's questing muzzle with her elbow, offered it to Colin.

He took it and thanked her, not realizing how hungry he'd been until the sugary, flaky pastry filled his mouth. The stallion eyed him flatly, one ear forward, one back; then it banged its head against Her Ladyship's shoulder, hard, at the same time that Colin felt paws against his knees and looked down to see little Bow, begging, drooling, and staring at him with desperate eyes. Hungry as he was, he broke the remaining pastry in half, gave the bigger piece to the dog, and, when he glanced up, noticed the stallion was munching something and regarding him with haughty triumph. He frowned. Dear God, he hoped she hadn't fed pastry to the horse. . . .

Early morning traffic was beginning to clatter past on the street beyond the buildings, and overhead, two chaffinches flitted amongst branches dressed in green. It was apparent that if they ever wanted to get out of London, he'd have to initiate the process. He made one final check of the harness, lifted Bow into the chaise—

And saw his employer giving something to her horse.

"What are you feeding him?"

"Pastry." She smiled lovingly at the stallion as it licked the last crumbs from her palm. "A black currant tart, to be precise."

"I forbid it."

She stiffened, a quick flash of anger firing her eyes. "Dr. Lord, you'll not *forbid* anything. Shareb *likes* pastry and ale—"

"*Ale?*"

"Yes, *ale*. Are you hard of hearing? Or do you forbid that, too, *Doctor*?"

"As a matter of fact, I do. As your horse's veterinarian I cannot allow him to have pastry and ale, no matter *how* much he enjoys them. Surely he can subsist comfortably well on hay, bran, oats, and corn, like any other horse—"

"Dr. Lord, you *don't* understand. Shareb-er-rehh is not 'just any other horse' and he deserves special treatment. Besides, I've been feeding him pastry and ale since he was a little colt. Now please, be reasonable . . . you're already forcing him to pull this dreadful chaise. The least you can do is allow him some small recompense to atone for this grievous assault on his pride."

Another wedge of pastry on her palm, Ariadne turned her back on him, held out her hand to the stallion once more—

And felt her wrist caught in the veterinarian's hard grip.

"I said, *no*."

He was no longer teasing her, and his tone was hard and commanding. She froze, staring at his fingers. How small and fragile her wrist looked, encircled by that broad, masculine hand; how white and dainty her skin was, how tiny her bones in comparison to the size of his knuckles, the breadth and strength of the back of his palm. She felt the warmth of his thumb against her pulse, the hard calluses of his hand against her flesh, and once again saw the mastiff, and this man next to her leaning over it, these very same hands coaxing the dog back to life. . . .

Her head jerked up and she stared straight ahead, her mouth set. "Dr. Lord. I did *not* give you permission to touch me."

He didn't let go.

Her voice rose. "Did you hear me, Dr. Lord? Kindly remove your hand from my wrist."

The pressure only seemed to tighten and tension crackled between them. "No more pastry," he ordered softly.

She set her jaw. Her breathing quickened, and a pulse began to beat in her ears.

"Your promise, my lady. *No more pastry.*"

Ariadne took a deep, steadying breath, slowly turned her head, and glared angrily up at him.

His eyes—those beautiful, gorgeous, striking eyes—were on her.

He was so close that she could see the starbursts of smoke radiating from the lilac depths of his irises, feel his warm breath touching her brow, sense the solid, unbending strength of his will and character. She noticed a curious, vertical dimple line faintly clefting his chin, threads of gold running through the fair hair that tumbled over his brow, the long, pale crescents of his lashes, the shape of his mouth.

His mouth . . .

Smiling coyly up at him through her lashes, Ariadne touched her forefinger to the corner of his lips.

"You have very beautiful eyes . . . Dr. Lord."

Her remark, combined with that single touch, was enough to stun him into shock, which was precisely what she'd hoped to accomplish. Quickly slipping out of his grasp and pressing home her advantage, Ariadne pushed the pastry into his palm, making sure her fingertips lingered against his skin a second or two longer than was necessary. His face going a dark crimson, he snatched his hand away, dropped the confection, and ground it into the dirt with the heel of his boot.

"Really, Dr. Lord," she said airily, dark eyes flashing with laughter and triumph, "I think you are being *most* extreme."

"Get in the chaise."

Shareb-er-rehh flung up his head and flattened his ears.

"But—"

"I said, *get in the chaise!*"

Giving him a victorious grin, she raised her brows and climbed delicately up into the vehicle. There she sat, head bent, smiling conspiratorially, and making a great pretense of straightening her sleeve. Colin, his blood pounding, set his jaw. Well, she might have scored a hit, the little imp, but she wouldn't win this battle.

No way in bloody hell.

Yet ... *did* she truly think he had beautiful eyes?

Damnation!

It didn't bear thinking about, for more reasons than he cared to count. Besides, if anything was beautiful, it—

He risked a glance at her.

—Wasn't him.

"You know, Dr. Lord, I think this is going to be a very exciting adventure, don't you?" she said airily, coaxing Bow into her lap and behaving as though the contact between them had never happened. "And oh, how *funny* it will be, that the whole countryside will be searching for a highborn lady dressed in the height of fashion when the *real* Lady Ariadne will be sneaking past under their very noses disguised as a boy! Isn't it grand, Dr. Lord? Am I not clever? And what do you think my Maxwell will say when he sees me thus?"

"I don't know your Maxwell. I have no idea what he'll say."

"Well, what would *you* think, Dr. Lord, if it was *your* betrothed who showed up on your doorstep dressed in a man's clothes?"

"I'd think she had the wrong doorstep."

"I'm serious! What *would* you think?"

"I suppose I wouldn't care how she was dressed, as long as I loved her and she arrived safe and sound."

"Have *you* ever been in love, Dr. Lord?"

"Not really."

"Have you ever *wanted* to be in love?"

"About as much as I've wanted scurvy," he lied, climbing into the carriage, picking up the reins, and already feeling his thigh catching fire where it touched hers.

"Be serious, Dr. Lord! This is important business we're discussing. You are a very handsome man, you know. Why, if you weren't one of the masses, and I'd met you before my dear, darling Maxwell, I might even take a fancy to you myself."

"And why is that?"

"Why is what?"

He impaled her with his direct gaze, trying to put her off-balance as she had so successfully done with him. "Why would you take a fancy to me?"

"I—" Color swept through her cheeks and she gave a trapped little giggle. "Dr. Lord, that is *not* a very polite question to ask a lady!"

"Regardless, I have asked it, and should you decide not to answer, 'twill be you who is being impolite."

"Very well then," she said, a bit huffily. "I would fancy you because . . ."

Her face went crimson, and she looked away.

"Yes?" he goaded, pleased to have turned the tables on her. "Because why?"

Her chin shot up and she stared straight ahead. "I have no wish to further this conversation."

"A pity. And here I thought I was going to be wonderfully enlightened as to why a beautiful young heiress might take a fancy to me. Such a cruel and unfair world, this! Never mind."

"Dr. Lord?"

"Yes, my lady?"

She was still staring ahead, back straight as a ramrod, hands fisted between her knees. "Drive on."

Chapter 5

$\sim\!\!\!\sim\!\!\!0\!\!\!\circ\!\!\!\sim$

The bit felt strange in his mouth and tasted of someone else. The straps that girded his body were alien and confining. The leather cinching the base of his tail was pinchy and uncomfortable, and the growing trepidation he sensed from both his lady and that impertinent blighter she'd picked up warned of something even more dire to come.

Something, most likely, that was bound to impact *him*.

His ears at half-mast, his eyes flat and hard, Shareb-er-rehh twisted his head to stare at The Enemy, his anger and jealousy mounting when he saw that the man's admiring gaze was on *his* human. He remembered the feel of those broad, soothing hands running over his withers, back, and flanks; there was something in the man's touch and manner that was immensely calming, immensely comforting, immensely attracting, and it had been all Shareb could do not to succumb to that powerful pull. Oh, if only the blighty knave would let down his guard for one moment, just *one-tiny-moment*, he could give him a nasty bite on the shoulder, the arm, a good kick in the leg that would make that limp he had now look mild in comparison. . . .

And then all thoughts of malice fled Shareb's cunning head as the man climbed into the chaise, picked up the reins, and urged him forward.

His worst suspicions were about to come true.

They wanted *him* to pull it!

Ariadne was quick to recognize the alarm and indignation in the stallion's eyes. "Really, Dr. Lord, I think this is a very bad idea. You're asking for trouble, I tell you."

"He'll be fine."

"No he won't. Pulling a chaise is beneath his dignity. Look at his face, you can see how angry he is. He gets very dangerous when he's angry—"

Colin tried again to urge the stallion forward, but he only hunched his back and froze, one hind leg coming up with dangerous intent. Ariadne couldn't prevent her smug smile; but then the animal doctor called a firm command, and this time Shareb-er-rehh moved ahead, not smoothly, not confidently, but in jolting, frightened rabbit leaps that made his tail snap out in the wind with each violent motion and nearly dislocated Ariadne's head from her neck.

"You are right, he possesses very unusual gaits," the veterinarian observed dryly. "I should think he is a most uncomfortable animal to ride."

"Very—funny—*Doctor* Lord," she managed, between the erratic jolts.

"How on earth do you sit to such motion?"

"Years of practice."

Ears flattened, Shareb moved forward, his head and neck at an unnaturally high angle, his lips pulled back in an angry grimace, his coat lathered with sweat. Despite the fact that blinkers hid his eyes, Ariadne knew the dark orbs were wild and ringed with white.

But he was moving, and Ariadne had to admit grudging admiration for the veterinarian's skill. Pulling a chaise was a lot to ask of an untrained horse, especially one which had been bred to do something entirely different.

Yes, I am glad I selected him to be Shareb's doctor, she thought, despite her earlier views to the contrary. *There is something about him, something I cannot quite put my finger on . . . something more than his gentle strength, his quiet demeanor, his dry humor. He is smart, strong, and sensible, and I feel safe when he is near.*

Now that was an odd notion. Safe?

Safe. But how long before she dared trust him enough with the truth about what Shareb *really* was?

Gait horse, indeed!

The jerky, jolting motion began to ease off as Shareb-er-rehh found his stride, and soon the stallion's head had returned to its proper angle and the powerful brown hindquarters were churning in a fast trot. The veterinarian guided him out of the little courtyard, and, shaking his head, Shareb moved into the street, his hoofbeats echoing loudly against the buildings that rose up on either side.

"Why, this is actually *fun!* Imagine, Shareb-er-rehh, pulling a chaise! My goodness, I never thought to see the day—can you believe how well behaved he's being? And here I thought we'd both be killed by now! Give me the reins, Dr. Lord, I want to try driving him!"

Such boundless delight was infectious. Colin chuckled, the wind on his face, buildings and glimpses of the silvered Thames passing in a blur as Shareb-er-rehh's fast, ground-eating trot sped them through London. As he'd predicted, Shareb wasn't so hard to manage, after all.

The horse was one thing.

Her Ladyship was quite another.

His mouth still tingled where she had touched it, her comment about his eyes still rang in his head, both awakening some unexplored part of his soul that responded to the attention and wanted more. He was unused to having a woman behave so boldly toward him, and he wasn't quite sure whether he liked it or not. Well, he thought he must like it, but he was unsure how to respond to it. Maybe the little flirt was just trying to upset his even keel. Maybe she was just trying out her own feminine wiles on someone she perceived as "safe." Or maybe she was purposely paying him back for winning the upper hand with regard to the two thousand pounds, or even harnessing the stallion. He didn't know. But what he *did* know, was that if she persisted on tormenting him so, he saw no recourse but to give her a taste of her own medicine.

And had no reservations about doing so.

Now, her thigh was pressed against his, her piquant face too close to his own as she gazed eagerly into his eyes, waiting for his answer. Such scrutiny was enough to send the blood pounding through his heart at a clip that, coupled with her childlike joy at breezing along through the streets of London, was totally disarming.

Now, he felt the pressure of her hand over his, her fingers tickling his knuckles as she playfully tried to pry the rein free. "Please, Dr. Lord, let me drive, it's *my* turn!"

"Not yet."

"Why not?"

"Let's put the city behind us, first. Then you may drive all you like."

"Now see here, he's *my* horse and I'm sure I can handle him!"

"Fine." He shrugged and handed her the reins. "Take him, then."

Shooting him a triumphant glare, she raised her chin and took the reins loosely in her hands. But her smugness was quick to change to worry as she realized her folly. Shareb-er-rehh immediately stepped up his trot. Her hands tightened around the reins. Shareb pulled harder. Her hands became fists. The stallion shook his head, fighting her. Her teeth sank into her bottom lip. Her knuckles went white, and she planted her feet against the floorboards as the stallion's brute strength began to pull her straight out of her seat—

"Fine day, isn't it?" Colin said mildly, leaning back in the seat and pretending an interest in the tangles of ivy that choked the wall of a passing house.

"Lovely," she managed, through clenched teeth.

"Got any more of that pastry?"

"There's a man for you, always thinking of his stomach."

Colin grinned. Most of the men *he* knew put other needs before their stomach's, but he kept the remark to himself out of respect for her gender, her innocence, and her status. And as for such "needs" . . . he was keenly aware of a tightening in his breeches at the closeness of the female who sat beside him. Damn him if he wasn't getting hard.

How on earth was he going to survive this trip to Norfolk?

He glanced over at her. Her cheeks were flushed with wind and the effort of holding the horse back, and her mouth was tight with determination. The stallion shook his head, trying to take the bit in his teeth and run.

"Having problems?" he asked tauntingly, raising a brow and enjoying her obvious distress.

"I told you he is not a carriage horse. And this is below my station, driving a horse while *you* sit there and enjoy the scenery. Not that the scenery in this particular area of the city is particularly *enjoyable*, mind you. Here, take him back."

Colin, grinning, pulled the sack of pastry out from beneath the seat. "I think I'd much rather eat my breakfast."

She all but stuffed the reins in his hands. "I said, take him back!"

"And how do you expect me to eat if I am to hold the reins?"

"I don't particularly care how you eat! Next you'll be asking me to feed you!"

Firmly taking the reins, he brought the stallion back under control. "Now, *there's* an idea. . . ."

She stared at him, eyes beginning to glint with deviltry. Or malice. It was impossible to tell which.

"Very well then, Dr. Lord," she purred. He raised a brow, wondering what she was up to as she took the bag, opened it, and peered within. "Let's see . . . we have apple . . . plum . . . black currant—"

"Plum's fine."

"Plum it is, then."

She reached into the bag and pulled out a thick, sugary wedge of pastry oozing globs of fruit filling. A slow, cunning smile curving her mouth, she held the pastry up to his lips. "Open your mouth, *Doctor* Lord—"

Colin had no choice but to comply, and opened his jaws exaggeratedly wide so as to avoid having her fingers touch his lips.

The chaise hit a bump and they did anyhow. Sweet, sticky fruit and flaky pastry jammed against his teeth, and with them, her fingers.

An electric charge rocked him at the contact.

She blushed, and laughed. "Ooh! Well, let's try that again. Say, *aaaaah!*"

God, help me, he thought, every cell in his body beginning to throb, to ache, to burn.

He shut his eyes, briefly, and again opened his mouth. This time she got enough of the pastry in that he was able to get a bite of it. One of Shareb's ears was straight back, listening, and immediately the horse slowed its pace.

Colin rapped the reins against the powerful hindquarters.

"Another bite, Dr. Lord?

"Just one," he managed, swallowing, "then give the rest to Bow."

She held the pastry up to him once again, her gaze fastened on his mouth, her little hand a hairbreadth from his lips. He caught the scent of horse sweat on her sleeve, the hint of lavender wafting from her skin. She was grinning a wicked grin, as though she knew just how difficult she was making his life, as though she knew just what she was about. In all probability, he thought wryly, she did.

God help you, little girl. You can't rattle me that easily.

"You know, Dr. Lord, you have a very nice smile, too. Do you realize that it's a bit crooked, and turns up a bit on the left side?"

Colin nearly choked on his pastry.

"I find it quite endearing. You should smile more often; it is such a direct contrast to that intent look you usually wear. Are you *sure* you don't have a lady friend? Or two? I cannot imagine someone as handsome as yourself spending your life all alone."

"This conversation is making me most uncomfortable."

"Why?"

"It just does."

"Don't you *like* it, Dr. Lord, when I compliment you?"

"I . . . am unused to such forwardness."

"But do you like it?"

He didn't answer, merely directing his gaze

straight ahead, a nerve twitching along his jaw.

"Do you like it, *Doctor* Lord?"

He turned his piercingly direct gaze on her, letting it rake heatedly over her face, down her neck, and to her bosom, where it lingered long enough to make her feel as though she wasn't wearing anything at all. Her throat went dry, and her face felt suddenly hot and damp.

"As a matter of fact," he said slowly, suggestively, as he raised his gaze back to hers, ". . . I do."

The striking, lavender eyes seemed to darken. Coloring furiously, Ariadne jerked her gaze away. Her hands were trembling.

"So . . . no more compliments?" he ventured, lifting one brow.

"Drive on," she snapped.

He chuckled, leaving her to squirm uncomfortably on the seat and wish there were ten miles separating their thighs instead of a mere two inches. She was uncomfortably aware of his male power and heat, the scent of his clean clothes and body, the way he kept gazing down at her and grinning that infuriating grin.

Five minutes passed. Ten.

She rubbed at her sore palm, raw where the reins had chafed it, and found the skin damp with sweat. The chaise hit a dip in the street and the doctor's thigh bumped her own.

She stiffened, and he glanced at her, watching her with a look of high amusement.

"Conversation," he said mildly, "can go far in transforming a long and boring trip into one that is far more interesting."

His deep voice sounded benign enough, with no hint of teasing or vulgar connotation. Conversation. Yes, that would take her mind off of how close he was sitting to her.

". . . How long do you think it will take us to

reach Norfolk, Dr. Lord?" she ventured.

His leg moved closer, just a bare inch, but enough to make her wish desperately for an escape route.

"Given the superb condition your animal is in and the speed with which he seems to enjoy traveling, I shouldn't think it will take long at all. In fact, we ought to be able to put a good fifteen or so miles behind us by the time we stop for the night."

"Twenty!"

"No. Let's not push him too much. Fifteen, and a good night's rest at a traveling inn for him."

"And maybe a bit of pastry, Doctor?"

He shook his head. "No pastry."

"But you feed it to your dog!" she protested, picking up the little mongrel that had been crouching under the seat and setting it atop her lap. "Why is it that Bow can have pastry and Shareb cannot? That's not fair!"

"The digestive systems of dogs and horses are two different things," he returned. "What is good for one is not necessarily good for the other. Can you not substitute something healthy—an apple, a carrot—instead?"

"Shareb doesn't *like* apples and carrots. He likes *pastry*."

"And I suppose Shareb is used to getting anything he wants?"

"But of course. He is Royalty, as far as horses go."

"Persist in feeding him pastry and some other nag will succeed him to the throne."

"*Doctor* Lord! You are *most* impertinent!"

He looked over and down at her and smiled. "And *you*, my lady, are simply a bit too used to having your own way."

She gaped at him, shocked that he had dared speak to her so.

"As is," he added, with a twinkle in his eye, "your horse."

"Really, Dr. Lord! You do not know your boundaries, do you?"

"Boundaries?"

"You seem to forget that our social standings are about as alike as . . . as . . . well, the digestive systems of dogs and horses!"

He laughed, quite impulsively for one she had thought rather reserved, and the action lit up his face like morning sunlight coming up over the sea. In that moment, Ariadne thought him quite beautiful indeed. She felt an aching, overwhelming urge to lean against him, to laugh with him, to let down her guard and enjoy him for the man he was. Uncomfortable with the feeling, and keenly aware of the heat of his long, hard, thigh, she pointed her chin at the clouds and refused to look at him.

"Well, you cannot blame me," he said softly, his eyes fond. "I'm having the devil of a time thinking of you as the grand lady when you've garbed yourself as the lowliest of stable hands."

She turned to him, her eyes gleaming conspiratorially. "It *is* a clever disguise, is it not, Dr. Lord?"

"Very clever." He nodded to a passing carriage driver. "But it didn't fool me."

"Yes, but *you're* not of the Quality, so I wouldn't have expected you to know who I am, anyhow. Thus, how could you be fooled? The important thing is that I deceive my brother. The authorities. Reward hunters." She touched his sleeve and leaned close, peering inquisitively, flirtatiously, up at him. "Do you think anyone will believe that I am a man, Dr. Lord?"

The stallion's ceaseless pulling was making his arms ache, but Colin turned his head to look at her.

Her eyes were bright, sparkling, and hopeful; her red hair bouncy and webbed across the flushed cheek she had turned toward the wind. There was no way, no way in hell, that that lovely face could be mistaken for anything other than what it was.

Strikingly, delightfully, female.

"Truthfully?" he asked.

Her eyes sparkled. "Truthfully!"

"No," he said, sobering. "They won't believe it."

Something in his beautiful eyes touched her soul and, taken aback, Ariadne looked away, fiercely stroking the little dog as she tried to get her suddenly racing heart back under control. Swift color caught her cheeks, and she was thankful for the cooling breeze against her face. Why was it that every time she tried to unnerve the veterinarian with her coy flirtations, he turned the tables and made *her* feel flustered and uncomfortable?

Keenly aware of his nearness, she looked off at the passing scenery. Already they were into the country; just ahead was a grove of trees, and beyond, a little pond with a flock of quacking mallards taking flight and leaving a long crescent of moving ripples in their wake.

She could sense the veterinarian's gaze upon her. Could *feel* it.

"Are you distressed, my dear?" he murmured, his voice holding a note of humor. "I can assure you that for the moment, your disguise is safe."

"The problem of my disguise, Dr. Lord, is not what is . . . distressing me."

"I'm here if you would like to share a confidence."

"Oh, no, I could never!"

"Well, if we are to be together for the duration of this trip, we might as well be friends. Friends do those things, you know. Share confidences."

"You have not shared any of yours with *me*."

"What would you like to know?"

She looked pointedly at him. "You said you have never been in love—"

"I was jesting."

"Well, have you?"

"That's a rather personal question, don't you think?"

"Perhaps. But if you tell me about *your* loves, then I shall tell you about my Maxwell."

"Well, I used to fancy an Irish girl."

"Did you, now!" She leaned conspiratorially close, though only Shareb and Bow bore witness to their conversation. "What was her name?"

He was grinning, remembering. "Doesn't matter."

"Oh, come now, Doctor, of course it matters!" She lowered her voice and pressed close, resting her fingers on his sleeve and peering up into his still-grinning face. "Tell me her name!"

"Orla."

"Were you in love with her?"

"Well . . . yes, I suppose I . . . admired her from afar."

"Why didn't you marry her?"

"I never got the chance to know her well enough."

"Why not?"

"You ask very personal questions, my lady."

"I know, Father used to say I pry far too deeply into other people's business. But since I'm paying you so much money, I should be able to ask you all the questions I like, don't you think? So tell me about this Orla. If you fancied her, why did you not marry her?"

His smile faded. Something in his face changed, and a shadow darkened his eyes. "I—changed my career."

"You have not always been a veterinarian?"

"No."

"What were you before?"

"A man who was paid good money to kill people."

She laughed, although his face was stern, perhaps even angry, and there was nothing teasing about his expression, nothing at all. "Come now, Dr. Lord! Tell me the truth!"

"That is the truth. I've no further wish to discuss it."

"But—"

"I *said*, I do not wish to discuss it!"

She stared at him for a moment, then her mouth snapped shut and she sat quietly sulking beside him, her feelings obviously hurt. Colin felt a wave of remorse. He hadn't meant to be sharp with her, but her playful queries had brought back memories he far preferred to forget. Not that *he* was still embarrassed or ashamed about the inglorious way his past career had ended, but there were others who most certainly were, and he suspected that this aristocratic, temperamental young pepper pot who placed such value on class wouldn't understand any better than the others—save his own mother—had. For some, unfathomable reason, the idea of her pitying and scorning him as Society had done filled him with sadness and despair.

"Dr. Lord? Did you hear me? I am talking to you!"

"Forgive me," he said, shaking his head and looking at her blankly. So much for her temporary sulkiness. "What did you say?"

"I asked you how you hurt your leg. Do you not think I haven't been wondering about your limp?"

He turned his gaze on her. "And do *you* not think I am a bit self-conscious about it, and therefore find it uncomfortable to talk about?"

"No, I did not think of that, and why *wouldn't* you want to talk about it?"

"Well, it *is* rather a private thing. . . ."

"Are you embarrassed about it, Dr. Lord?"

"Not of the limp itself. Of other things, associated with it—perhaps. But not the limp."

"Then tell me how you got it."

"Why are you so keen on knowing?"

"Nosiness. A desire to post it in the *Times*. So that I can hold it against you and wound you deeply. Why do you *think* I want to know? Because I suspect that it burdens you more than you'll admit, and I just thought it would relieve your mind to talk about it. Besides, *I* don't find it unattractive at all. It . . . adds character."

"Really, my lady."

"So are you going to tell me about your leg?"

Cocking his head as though in deep thought, he frowned and stared straight ahead. "My leg. A long extremity consisting of muscle, tissue, skin, and tendons enclosing one femur, one patella, one—"

Ariadne couldn't help herself. She leaned over and playfully cuffed his shoulder, and they both burst into laughter, defusing the tenseness of the previous moment.

"Don't make me laugh when I'm trying to be serious!" she protested.

"Of what concern is my poor leg to you?"

"I want to know how you hurt it!"

"I broke it."

"How?"

"I was shot."

"Shot!" Her eyes went wide and her mouth fell open. "You're jesting!"

"No, I'm not. I was shot. There. Are you satisfied?"

"With a *gun*?"

"No, with a cannon."

"A *cannon*!" She clapped a hand dramatically to her breast. "You must have been in the War!"

"Aye."

"Well, of course! Why didn't I think of that before? I know the army employs veterinarians—I mean, with all those horses in the cavalry, *somebody* has to know how to care for them!—but I had no idea that *you* were a military veterinarian, although that does explain your fine posture and that irritating way you have of issuing orders . . . I'm sorry, Dr. Lord, that I'm so nosy. I hope you don't regret telling me, now."

"Of course not. But I wasn't in the cavalry. And I wasn't in the army, either."

"Well, what *were* you, then?"

"Something I'm not, now. Something I don't want to think about, as the memories pain me. Let's talk about something else, if you don't mind."

"Such as?"

"Your stallion. He's no gait horse, is he?"

She blushed nervously and breezily waved off his question. "Oh, Dr. Lord, I don't wish to discuss Shareb . . . instead, let us talk about—about my wonderful Lord Maxwell. Yes! My darling betrothed. . . ." She sighed and closed her eyes, then opened them to gaze blissfully at the clouds. "I knew that he was for me the moment Papa brought him home to dine with us after they met at a Newmarket race meet. How dashing I thought him, how handsome and gallant! And do you know what he did? He stared at me—oh, I can still feel it right *here*"—she clapped a hand against her heart—"all throughout the meal, and then he made a toast to my beauty!"

The veterinarian raised a brow, and made a noise that sounded suspiciously like laughter.

"What, don't you think I'm a pretty woman, Dr. Lord?"

He stared straight ahead, his grin broadening.

"Well, *don't* you? My Maxwell told me I'm the Beauty of Burnham. He said that my skin is the fairest that he's ever seen, and that the color of my hair indicates a woman of spirit. And what do *you* think, Mr. Lord?"

"What happened to 'Doctor'?"

"Oh yes, that's right. You rather enjoy that, don't you?"

"Well, it is a bit unkind of you to bestow a title on me and then take it away."

"Of course, *Doctor* Lord. Now answer my question."

"Which was?"

"I want to know if you think me pretty."

He turned to her, and there was such intensity in his eyes, his stare, that she felt that long, heat-filled glance pierce her to the very core of her very soul. "No," he said softly, at last. "I don't think you are pretty at all. I think—"

Shocked at his rudeness, her mouth fell open.

"—that you are heartbreakingly *beautiful*."

He gave her the full force of his charming grin then, the wind ruffling the hair across his brow and the sunlight gilding his profile. Ariadne's mouth snapped shut and she jerked her gaze away, not knowing whether to be insulted or flattered.

I'll get you back for that, she vowed to herself. *Two can play at this game!*

"Well, you *did* ask," he offered, a teasing light in his eye.

"So I did. And if we are to be fair, I suppose *I* should admit something, too."

"By all means."

She looked down at the dog. A moment went by, another, and Colin watched her growing increasingly preoccupied with Bow's ear, twirling a long lock of curly hair there around and around her finger while her cheeks went rosy with color.

"Well?" he prompted.

She wouldn't look at him, but he could see the thread of a mischievous, blushy smile peeping out from beneath a loose fall of hair that had escaped from her cap. "Oh, how to say this—you know when you were unconscious, after Daniel hit you?"

His lips twitched with humor. "Not really."

"Well, no, of course you wouldn't, silly, you were out cold, but you know what I mean—" Her entire face was quite crimson now, and she was twirling the lock of Bow's hair faster and faster. "Well, when you were lying there on the ground, I had to . . . um, pick your head up so I could put my coat beneath it. Well, I didn't *have* to, but I wanted to, because the ground was wet and I felt sorry for you and—"

She glanced up at him, trying—and failing—to convey innocence. "Well, that's how I knew where the bump was, you see?"

He stared at her, an amused grin curving his lips, while she went scarlet and was forced to look away. Her words, and the knowledge that she had touched him as she had, was enough to make his own pulse begin to quicken. The tension must have communicated itself right down through the reins, for at the end of them Shareb-er-rehh suddenly began to fidget and tried to break into a canter.

He pulled the horse back, feeling it beginning to fight him. "My lady, I don't know what you're getting at."

"Well . . . I know I'm betrothed, but . . ."

Shareb began blowing hard, shaking his head—

". . . I could not help noticing that your hair was as soft and pleasant to touch as . . . well, as—"

She swallowed, looked up, and blurted, "my silk underthings from China."

Shareb-er-rehh exploded into a full gallop.

"Whoa!"

"Good heavens, Dr. Lord, what's *wrong* with him?"

"Whoa, boy! Easy!" A flock of pigeons burst skyward at the stallion's approach and Shareb went sideways against the shafts, stumbled, and recovered, hurtling down the street at breakneck speed. "Whoa, boy, *whoa!*"

With all of his strength, Colin managed to get the horse slowed down to a fast trot, then, after much fighting and coaxing, a panting, complete stop.

He blew out his breath, sat back on the seat, and turned his furious glare upon his white-faced companion. "Is *that* your big secret? The fact that you touched my hair?"

"No." She grinned, blushed, and looked coyly up at him.

"Then what is?"

"The fact that I want to touch it again. Just to see if it really is as silky and soft as I remember." She lifted her hand, stretched it halfway toward his head. "Can I, Dr. Lord?"

"You're betrothed."

"I just want to *touch* it. Nothing more."

They sat staring at each other for a long moment, until at last Colin felt his resolve weakening, his reason wavering, his thought processes clouding.

Her hand stretched closer.

"Just *touch* it, Dr. Lord."

He shut his eyes and nodded, wishing to God he had never agreed to take her to Norfolk, wishing to God he'd never met her, wishing to God he knew quite how to handle her bold actions and hoping to God she'd never stop. . . .

He was doomed.

Chapter 6

Ｗith trembling fingers and a pounding heart Ariadne touched the pads of her fingers to the veterinarian's silky, dark blond hair. He stared straight ahead, as though in physical pain, tension stiffening every muscle in his body. Sensing it through the reins, Shareb-er-rehh began to fret and prance, but Ariadne was aware of only the suspension of the moment, the movement of the doctor's throat, the quickening of his breath.

"I suppose I probably shouldn't be doing this," she said softly.

Shareb-er-rehh stamped and tried to bolt ahead.

Her fingers moved, absorbing the silk-and-satin feel of his hair, tracing the curve of his head, the shape of his ear. She had never behaved so outrageously, never felt so delightfully wicked, and the experience filled her with awe and power. Her eyes alight, her mouth frozen in a little half smile, she visually traced her hand's progress.

The veterinarian began to lean away from her, as though to escape her touch. She leaned with him, trailing her fingertips through his sleek locks, admiring their soft golden brown color, studying the way they framed his ear and lay against the back of his neck. Inadvertently, her fingers found the hard bump where Daniel had struck him.

He winced, then pulled away, his pupils very large and dark within their purple-gray irises.

"I . . . think this is most unseemly, my lady. Uh— you are, after all, uh . . . well, you're . . . betrothed."

"Whatever's wrong, Dr. Lord? You seem to be having difficulty constructing a coherent sentence."

"I . . . am having difficulty constructing a coherent *thought*."

She laughed, and gently smoothed the hair over the hard bump behind his ear. At last, she had won the upper hand!

"Are you enjoying this, Dr. Lord?"

"I am."

But Ariadne went too far.

"Your hair . . . it really *is* as silky as my . . . underthings, you know."

Recovering, he turned his full stare on her. "Well then, perhaps you should let me touch them, just to see if you're telling the truth."

Her hand shot back. "My *underthings*?" she cried, her face flaming.

"Well, yes, of course. You keep comparing my hair to them . . . therefore it only stands to reason that I should be the judge of their comparative silkiness, don't you think?" he asked, with deceptive innocence.

"That was unforgivably bold and rude of you, sir!"

He reached up, smoothed his hair back into place, and eyes twinkling, murmured, "If one plays with fire, then one can expect to get burned."

"My Maxwell would *never* have said anything so . . . vulgar!"

"I am not your Maxwell."

"Thank God!"

"And perhaps if he *had* said anything so 'vulgar,'

your hands might not be tempted to stray to someone else."

"How dare you!"

He merely grinned and picked up the reins, directing the stallion to continue. "Perhaps, my lady, you would be wise to keep those brazen hands to yourself."

His tone was condescending, infuriatingly parental. Incensed by the setback, and embarrassed to the marrow, Ariadne pursed her lips, shoved her hands between her knees, and directed her stormy gaze off over the shoulder farthest from her companion.

Play with fire and you're going to get burned.

Tightly, she spit, "I suppose you want an apology."

"Definitely not. It's not every day that I find myself stroked and admired by a beautiful woman. I daresay, it was a rather . . . nice experience."

"You can forget it ever happened."

"*You* can. As for myself, I will treasure the memory and hope it happens again."

Fresh waves of embarrassment coursing through her, Ariadne dug her nails into her palms and wished she could think of an appropriate, scathing retort. Beside her, the infuriating man began to whistle cheerily, the sound pleasant in conjunction with the smart beat of Shareb's trot. Ariadne swallowed hard. She looked down in her lap. Looked up at the veterinarian.

Found him watching her, grinning.

"I really do hate sparring," he teased, eyes twinkling. "Shall we call a truce?"

She shrugged and looked glumly away, feeling suddenly foolish for her behavior. He took her gesture for a "yes," and continued with his whistling. But Ariadne was not content to be ignored, nor was she one to remain angry for long. She gazed at

Shareb's glossy rump, his backswept ears, and remembered the stallion's reaction when she had tried to unsettle the veterinarian with her flirtatious gestures.

"Dr. Lord?" she said, over the sharp report of shod hooves against the cobblestones.

"My lady?"

"I cannot help but think that you were very anxious just a moment ago, and that you somehow managed to convey that anxiety straight down the reins and to my horse." She turned and faced him with a challenging stare. "Are you aware that you seem to have a way with animals?"

Colin frowned, thoughtfully. "You think so?"

She was staring at him, unnervingly, as though he held some great secret that scrutiny alone could uncover. "I find it very eerie, how my stallion just did that."

"Yes, well, something probably spooked him. Nothing more."

"Nothing spooked him, and you know it. And I also find it very eerie that he did not kick you when you were showing me how to harness him. He would have kicked anyone else, you know. And he's behaving admirably well for a horse who has never been driven. What do you have to say about *that*, Dr. Lord?"

He smiled and gazed ahead, negotiating a turn in the road. "I'd say that Bow probably told him to behave."

"I'm serious."

He shrugged, the sunlight refracting from gold strands in his hair. "Animals like me. I don't know why, they just do."

She thought of the effect he had on Shareb—and wondered suddenly, shamefully, what feelings those strong, capable hands would evoke if they were laid on *her*.

Heat flashed through her and a tingle shot up her spine.

Oh, dear God, what is the matter with me? Please, help me stop thinking such thoughts; he's a commoner, a veterinarian, someone far beneath me in class, breeding and status—please, God, save my desires for my rightful husband, and my marriage bed!

Shareb-er-rehh had settled into a comfortable trot once more, his hooves ringing hollowly on the cobblestones, his step high and smart, his small ears back, listening.

Eavesdropping.

"Nice day," Ariadne commented, trying to make benign conversation.

"Aye."

"Good that it isn't raining."

"Uh-huh."

"Did you *really* like it when I touched your hair?"

"I thought we were going to forget about that."

"Have *you* forgotten about it?"

"Well no, but—"

She twisted fully around on the seat. "You know, Dr. Lord, we're just going to have to find you a woman. Someone kind and sweet and good, as you deserve. I shall have to work on that. You and I will remain friends—we *are* friends, aren't we?— after I marry my dear Maxwell, and once this business of getting Shareb-er-rehh bred to Gazella is done, why then, we can see about finding someone to make your life less lonely. Yes, that is what we shall do."

A shadow darkened his eyes and he looked away, off over the hills that rolled away to the northeast.

"Don't you *want* someone to make your life less lonely, Dr. Lord?"

"What makes you think I'm lonely?"

"You told me yourself you've never *really* been in love. So reasonable deductions lead me to conclude that if you are not in love with someone, then you are alone. If you are alone, you must be lonely."

"I have Bow."

"Bow's a *dog*. What you need, Dr. Lord, is a *wife*."

"I am quite happy with my life the way it is."

"Are you? I think not. And I can tell when you're fibbing, you know. You look straight ahead and your jaw gets tense and Shareb-er-rehh starts acting up."

"I am not fibbing. My life is perfectly acceptable to me."

"And you are a blind man, Dr. Lord. Put on your spectacles and you'll see what it lacks! Do you want to spend the rest of your days in those lonely rooms in Chelsea all by yourself? Do you want to have a dog sleeping in your bed with you instead of a wife? Bring puppies, kittens, and foals into the world instead of your own children? Look me in the eye and tell me you'd prefer to keep your life just the way it is and *then* maybe I'll believe you!"

He couldn't.

"Go ahead, Dr. Lord!" She touched his arm and let a teasing, playful note come into her voice. "Look me in the eye and tell me that's what you want!"

"My lady, please," he said, staring straight ahead through Shareb's backswept, listening ears and trying not to laugh at her ceaseless cajoling.

"See? You *are* a lonely man. And as your friend it is up to me to do something about it. In fact— oh, I've just had an idea!"

"God help me."

"No, no, this is a *good* one!" She leaned close, putting her face deliberately near his so that her conspiring, excited eyes were just inches from his own and he felt he was drowning in the scent of lavender. "We shall stop along the way at my dear friend Lady Andrea's home. She'll not betray my identity, of course, and she has three lovely horses named Paccy, Magic, and Windy that you can befriend. But that is not all! Listen to *this*"—the piquant face leaned even closer to Colin's, the sweet breath feathering against his cheek, and he had to shut his eyes and grind his jaws together against the growing impulse to kiss that saucy mouth, those soft, pouty lips—"she has the nicest maid who will be just right for you. Kathleen, her name is, and she's lonely, too. I will have to introduce the two of you, and see how you get on together. Yes, that is just what I shall do!"

Infinitely pleased with herself, she sat back, clasped her hands between her knees, and gazed triumphantly at him.

"Aren't I a wonderful matchmaker, Dr. Lord?"

He turned and grinned at her, hoping to God she couldn't read the desire in his eyes. Not for some unknown lady's maid—but for *her*.

"Troublemaker, more like it," he said, but there was no heat in his voice. "I am rather . . . shy sometimes. The lass will probably find me boring and colorless."

"Oh, never. Any man who can save a dying dog, let alone get a horse that has never been driven to accept such a demeaning role with so little complaint could never be considered boring! The stories you could tell her! And your shyness is actually rather charming. At least, *I* think so." She paused for a moment, looking up at him, and making him heatedly aware of her steady, admiring gaze.

A long moment went by.

"Dr. Lord?"

"Yes?"

She was leaning close, eyes sparkling, face flushed. "I'll bet *I* can bring you out of that shyness."

He laughed. "Don't even try."

"Why not?"

"The consequences might be dangerous."

"Fiddlesticks. There's not a dangerous bone in your body."

"It is not my bones that I am referring to."

"Oh? Then what part of your anatomy should I beware of?"

"Never mind."

"Hmmmm?"

"My lady—"

She slanted him an amused, innocent look—but the bright sparkle in her eyes gave her away, and he suspected she was far less innocent than she let on.

He slanted her a look right back, one brow raised and a warning in his eye.

Ariadne colored and sat back, fanning herself with her hand and giggling uncontrollably. "Well!" she gushed, her face burning. "It must be these clothes; take me out of my proper attire and I behave like the most lowborn tart! Well, I shall apologize for being so vulgar, for though you are just a commoner, you are still a person. But I shall not apologize for feeling envious over whoever gets to be your lady, because you see, I *liked* touching your hair, and despite what you just said, I think you liked it, too."

Her bald honesty—unusual in a lady of the *ton*—was totally unnerving. And, coupled with her air of self-importance, amusing. He looked at her, grinned, and decided it was time to give her a taste of her own medicine.

Again.

"That aside, would you like it if I touched yours?"

"Touched *my* hair?" She jerked her head up and stared at him, appalled. "Oh, I don't think you should, Dr. Lord . . . I might like it, but my dear Maxwell most certainly would not."

Maxwell. That bloody name again.

"Yes, I can imagine he wouldn't."

"My Maxwell is a very dangerous man, Dr. Lord. If you even so much as *looked* at me with any passing degree of interest, he would call you out. He is a very deadly duelist, you know, renowned throughout Norfolk. It would not be wise to insult him. He is expert with both sword and pistol, and I would have grave fears for your life if—"

"I take it you have known this Maxwell bloke for long?"

"*Mister* Lord, show some respect for your betters!"

"Well, have you?"

She shrugged, threading Bow's ear through her fingers, over and over again. "He was an acquaintance of Papa's. A business associate, and a Jockey Club friend. And yes, we have spent considerable time together. Papa arranged our union, well before he died. My Lord Maxwell will make me a fine husband."

"Yes, of course. He certainly does have good credentials, doesn't he? I mean, not *everyone* is so matchlessly good with sword and pistol. It is a commendable, fabulously useful talent, one that every husband ought to have."

"Yes, yes, I quite agree—" She paused, frowning at the grin on his face. "Dr. Lord, you are making me feel that I am the butt of a joke I don't understand."

"Oh?"

"I think you're just jealous because *you* don't have Maxwell's talent."

"Yes, I am painfully inept with both sword and pistol," he lied.

"You speak as though that's *all* I admire about my Maxwell!"

"Oh? You mean there's more to admire?"

"Well of course there is," she said, indignantly. "He's incredibly handsome, kind, astute when it comes to judging horseflesh. In fact, he has Black Patrick, the fastest racehorse in England, in his stable. That is"—she glanced at Shareb-er-rehh, then quickly away—"the fastest *tried* racehorse in England. Oh, and he's rich, but that doesn't matter, because so am I."

"So he has lots of money, a fast horse, and can kill people in duels. Sounds like a prime catch. I wish you every happiness, my lady."

"The sarcasm in your voice leads me to believe otherwise."

"And when is this monumental union supposed to take place?"

"When I complete the necessary mourning period for my father."

"Oh," he said, and seeing the shadow that suddenly darkened her eyes, added, "I'm sorry."

She shrugged and pretended a great interest in the dashboard of the chaise. Wordlessly, Colin reached out and laid his hand over hers. But she quickly snatched her hand free, holding Bow close to her chest and hugging the tiny dog more fiercely than was comfortable for her. Bow never protested, only tilting her head back to lick the girl's chin.

It was obvious that if she was grieving, she wanted no comfort. And, really, he shouldn't have thought he could give her any. She was out of his realm, beyond his reach. *Taken*. Her life was a neat and tidy package, cut to pattern by others and sewn up by herself. She had all she wanted, all she deserved—and he was happy for her. But still, there was a part of him that couldn't help but think, *If only I'd met her when I was the man I once was, I could have had a chance at her.*

But he was no longer that dashing hero and never would be again.

Now, he was only an animal doctor of modest means, and she, a high society beauty who would despise and pity him if she were to learn of his fall from grace. He could not have her. Better not to let himself even think it could be otherwise.

It couldn't.

"You've grown awfully quiet, Dr. Lord."

"Forgive me." He grinned. "I was trying to think of a way to polish up my skills with sword and pistol before we reach Norfolk."

She looked at him, saw the cajoling light in his eye, and laughed.

"I'm sorry, Dr. Lord, if my touching your hair bothered you so. I never meant to make you angry, upset, or distressed. And if you really want to, you *can* touch my hair. . . ." She leaned close, her eyes sparkling with conspiracy, and grasping one of the red locks that had fallen loose from beneath her cap, held it out to him. "I'll not tell Maxwell."

"I think it best if I do not."

"Don't you like my hair?"

"It has nothing to do with whether or not I like it. It has everything to do with the fact that you are promised to somebody else, that it's unseemly, and it's—it's not good for me."

"Not *good* for you? Is this another one of those pastry dictates, Dr. Lord?"

He shot her a confused look.

"What I mean, is"—she shrugged, for her words

had made perfect sense to her—"how can touching my hair be bad for you?"

"I don't want to go into it."

"Is it because I had to cut it, and I'm no artist with a pair of shears?"

"No."

"I know. You don't like red hair."

"On the contrary, my lady, I adore red hair."

Her eyes gleamed. "Hmm. Well, then it must be because I have it stuffed up under this cap. Not at all styled in a fashionable way. That's the reason, isn't it, Dr. Lord?"

"No, that's not the reason at all. The reason is that I am a man, with normal, healthy, base appetites, and touching your person may very well inflame something that is better left dormant."

"Do I inflame you, Dr. Lord?"

"Lady Ariadne, *please*."

"Well, do I?"

"You make my head ache. That's what you do."

"I can kiss it and make it better, you know."

"You're a damned flirt," he said, but not unkindly.

To his surprise, she let loose a peal of high laughter, and put her hand on his arm. "Yes, Dr. Lord, I suppose I am. Now what do you say we start looking for a place to stop for lunch? My stomach's growling and I'm sure yours is too."

He felt her thigh pressing hotly against his.

Caught the fading scent of lavender on her skin, sweet black currant on her breath.

And knew he couldn't get away from her soon enough.

"A grand idea," he said wryly, and clucked to Shareb to pick up his speed before he could give in to her playful request—and touch *more* than just that fiery red hair.

Chapter 7

‹~~~∞∞~~~›

The stallion came up lame several miles later. Colin felt the sudden lurch of the reins through his hands, the quick stumble before the horse recovered himself. He pulled back to get the horse to halt, but Shareb-er-rehh only shook his head, fighting him and staggering a few last steps before finally answering the pressure on the bit. He stopped, shuddered, and dropped his head dejectedly as Colin and Ariadne leapt simultaneously from the chaise.

"Shareb!" Ariadne cried, racing to his head.

The stallion raised his foot and held it up beseechingly, his eyes large, wounded, and hurt.

"Shareb! Oh, Shareb, sweetheart! Dr. Lord, his leg!" She was close to tears. Shivering in pain, Shareb put his face against her chest.

Colin put one hand on the stallion's hot and sweaty shoulder, and ran the other down the long foreleg.

"That bandage is going to have to come off, my lady."

"Oh no, I can't take it off, it's on there to conceal—"

"Hold his head, then, and *I'll* take it off."

105

She bit her lip, about to protest. Colin knelt down, his shoulder close to the stallion's, his hands quickly unwrapping the thick, unnaturally heavy bandage.

He removed it and looked up at her, his gentle eyes suddenly angry. "Why on *earth* do you have weights wrapped in this bandage?"

The stallion shifted his weight, regained his balance, plaintively raised his foot once more.

Sheepishly, she looked away. "To . . . disguise his gait."

Colin made a noise of disgust and flung the hot, damp bandage to the grass at the side of the road. The stallion's leg was long, fine, and straight, the bones strong and well formed. It was the leg of an aristocrat, but all he was concerned about was locating the injury. He checked the carpus, ran his hands down the long cannon bone, palpated the flexor tendons in search of a blown tendon.

Nothing.

"What is it, Dr. Lord?" she asked anxiously, hovering over his shoulder. Her voice sounded perilously close to tears. "Is he all right?"

He palpated the splint bones.

Nothing.

Searched the joints for swelling.

Nothing.

"Dr. Lord? Please, tell me, is he all right?"

"So far," he answered, and moving his hands down to the stallion's white-ringed fetlock, gently picked up the animal's foot.

"What are you doing?"

"Looking for a nail, a stone, or a bruise on the sole."

He pressed his thumb against the tough triangle that made up the hoof's frog. The stallion didn't flinch. He examined the hoof wall; aside from some caked mud, it was strong and healthy.

Gently, he let go of the stallion's hoof.

Shareb stamped it down on his toe, hard.

"Ouch!" Grimacing, Colin pushed hard on the animal's shoulder to get its weight off his foot. The stallion stumbled, and drove his head into the cradle of his mistress's arms. One ear remained on Colin, and he had the strangest feeling that the animal was laughing at him.

"Oh, Dr. Lord, I *knew* it was a bad idea to hitch him to that dreadful chaise, now he's lame, he's injured, and what if he's broken something and has to be destroyed—"

"He's fine," Colin said, wryly. He grasped the bridle and tried to pull the noble, cunning head around so that he could stare into the stallion's dark eye, but Shareb jerked away, his ears flat back.

"He's *not* fine, he's in *pain*! His leg hurts, Dr. Lord, and you must do something!"

"I can't find anything wrong with him, my lady."

"But he's *lame*!"

"I can see that." Colin stared at the stallion's leg, then, frowning, walked around to look at it from the front.

"Well?"

He straightened up, and stared into the stallion's eyes.

Shareb turned his face away, and hid it against Her Ladyship's chest.

"There's a coaching inn just up the road," Colin said. He unhitched the stallion and picked up the shafts of the chaise. "You lead him. We'll stop, give him a rest, have something for lunch. If he's indeed injured, I should find some swelling by the time we return."

"What do you mean, *if*? Of course he's injured, look at him!"

But Colin didn't reply.

He was beginning to suspect that Shareb-er-rehh was a hell of a lot smarter than he'd given him credit for.

The coaching inn, a rambling, whitewashed building with a swaybacked roof, was nestled in a bed of daisies, grass gone to seed, and shrubbery through which two robins chased each other with merry abandon. Roses made pools of scarlet against the walls and sills, and a sign in front swung gently in the breeze, proclaiming the establishment to be the "Hungry Horseman."

"Oh, good," Ariadne said, breathing a sigh of relief. "It has windows."

Pulling the chaise while the horse limped along beside him, Colin followed her gaze. An ancient hound slumbered on steps splashed with sunlight, and an old mare with one hind leg propped beneath her was tethered just outside. Upon noticing Shareb-er-rehh, she turned and whickered softly.

Up went Shareb's head, and his ears along with it.

"Windows," Colin said, as the stallion began to prance and blow and arch his neck. "I should think the food would be of more importance than the windows."

"Oh, no, Dr. Lord. It *has* to have windows. I have to be able to see Shareb-er-rehh from inside. What if someone should try to steal him?"

"I daresay they'd lose their fingers in the attempt."

"Oh, stop!" she said, playfully. "I told you, he's a very sweet horse, just angry because you denied him pastry and ale. Now come. Let's get something to eat. My treat, of course."

She went on ahead of him.

"Uh . . . my lady?"

"Yes?"

"If you wish your ruse to succeed—" Colin rubbed his jaw, and looked thoughtfully at her shapely legs. "Try not to walk so ... well, try to walk like a man."

"Like a man?"

"Your hips, my lady. They—tend to swing a bit."

"Very well then." She let go of Shareb's reins. "Shall I walk like this?" Apishly hunching her shoulders and letting her arms hang stiffly at her side, she walked awkwardly toward the stairs, where she turned and shot him a look of high amusement.

"Never mind," Colin said, putting the shafts of the chaise down and taking the stallion's head. Stiffness clawed through his leg as he led a protesting Shareb-er-rehh a safe distance away from the mare and looked for a place to tether him. "This is never going to work."

"Yes it will, I shall *make* it work." She glanced at Shareb-er-rehh, and her face lit up with excitement. "Look, Dr. Lord! Shareb's not limping any more!"

"Yes, war wounds tend to disappear when there is a fair lady to impress."

His comment went right over her head. "We'll stop here for a nice, leisurely meal and maybe when we come out, Shareb will be all better. Come along, Doctor!"

Colin tied the stallion, casting a dubious glance over his shoulder to check the animal one last time as he went to join Ariadne. Shareb-er-rehh caught his glance, and lifted his left front leg to show that he was still lame.

But the horse had erred.

It had been the *right* that had supposedly been injured.

Colin grinned, and the stallion, realizing his mistake, turned sheepishly away before guiltily putting his foot down.

"Think he'll be all right, Dr. Lord?"

Colin turned his back on the horse and passed the mare as she perked up her ears and swung her rump toward the stallion in saucy invitation.

"Aye, my lady. I'm sure of it."

The ceiling was thickly beamed and ancient, the walls painted in shades of oxblood and hung with prints of fox hunts and racehorses. Laughter came from a group of locals near the hearth, but the two travelers preferred instead to take seats beside the window, where Ariadne could keep an eye on her horse. There, they lunched on steak and mushroom pie, thick, crusty bread, cheese, and a flagon of rich, foamy ale. Or rather, Ariadne did. Halfway through the meal, she noticed her companion's appetite had not led him to touch the beef.

She stared at him in puzzlement. "Is the pie not to your liking, Doctor?"

He offered a rather sheepish smile. "I do not eat meat."

"Why not?"

"It's animal flesh. I . . . I just can't. Not anymore."

She frowned a bit, studying him. Then she put down her fork and knife, propped her chin atop her hands, and stared long and hard at him. "You are a very unusual man, Dr. Lord."

He shrugged, broke off a piece of cheese, and ate it, grinning at her all the while.

Her gaze went to his unfinished glass of ale. "I see you don't drink much, either. What sort of an Englishman are you, anyhow?"

"A sober one."

"Indeed."

"My tolerance for alcohol is remarkably low," he added.

"Really? Mine's not. Hand me your glass, Dr. Lord. Better yet, be a gentleman and order me another."

She swept up his glass, shot him a challenging glance, and raised the drink high. "To . . . friendship."

"Aye." He picked up his cheese and smiled. "To friendship."

She laughed and downed the ale in three unladylike gulps. Their gazes met, and she blushed prettily. "You know, Dr. Lord . . . I'm really enjoying your company. I take back my earlier words, about wishing I hadn't hired you to be my veterinarian. I'm very glad that I did, even if you *can't* figure out why Shareb is lame. Now, if you don't want it, may I have your beef?"

He looked at her, one brow raised, and she giggled in embarrassment.

"Well, if I'm to dress like a man, I might as well eat like one."

Three miles ahead of them, Tristan, Lord Weybourne, sat in a similar public house, nursing a cider and staring gloomily into the clear, amber depths of his glass. He, too, had positioned himself near a window, where he could watch the traffic passing on the Norfolk Road and be on the lookout for the bay stallion.

The bay stallion.

All that stood between him and total ruin. And all that carried Ariadne to a nightmare she couldn't even begin to imagine.

His mind wandered back over the years, to the time when Papa had brought him to see his first race. He had never forgotten the thrill of seeing those mighty steeds galloping toward the finish line, thundering past with such force that he could feel the vibrations rocking his chest while the crowd went wild with excitement around him. Maybe the fever had started then—Papa certainly must have seen it, for he'd turned, looked steadily into his eyes, and warned him about the allure of the racetrack. But he hadn't listened, of course. After all, he, Tristan, had picked the winner of three out of four of those races. He had a talent. What did Papa know, anyhow?

And as he grew older, he realized while spending his mornings observing the Norfolk Thoroughbreds galloping around his father's pastures, and his weekend afternoons at the races at Newmarket, that such a talent should not go to waste.

Age and maturity had not cooled the fever. He had found friends to share his interest, older, equally highbred friends who didn't mind that he was the youngest of the lot. After all, he was the future Lord Weybourne. He was bored, he was titled, and he knew horses. And the races! He would win some, lose some, win a little more, gamble a lot. And the fever had spread—to the gaming tables, to the boxing matches, to the cockfights. He couldn't remember when his gaming had begun to worry him. Maybe when he'd begun to realize that he was losing more than he was winning. When he knew he was in trouble.

And still, he could not stop.

Too proud, too ashamed to confess his dilemma to his father, he had gone to Clive Maxwell for help . . . again . . . and again.

And now he was in over his head.

He should have listened to Papa, dear, wise Papa, who had spent his life developing a horse that could outrun anything but the wind. His father had known more about racehorses than Tristan would *ever* know. Oh, how foolish he'd been! If only he'd gone to him before the debts had mounted, maybe things would have turned out differently. Maybe Papa would still be alive; maybe Ariadne wouldn't be on the run with the last of the Norfolk Thoroughbreds; and maybe he wouldn't have a death threat hanging over his head.

He put his hands over his face, remembering his father's horror when he'd told him about Clive, and just how evil the man really was. And now Ariadne was involved, and heading for her own demise as surely as he had engineered his own.

God help him, he had to stop her. It was too late to save himself—but not his sister.

Picking up his cider, he gazed bleakly out the window, scanning the passing horses for Shareb-er-rehh's glossy bay coat. A damned common color, even if the horse himself was uniquely spectacular. But in the past quarter of an hour, no less than seventeen bay horses had passed, three in the last two minutes alone. One had been a smart, glossy-coated hack. Not Shareb-er-rehh. Another had been a stout Shetland pony hitched to a cart, with an old farmer at its head. Not Shareb-er-rehh. The most recent was a rangy, deep-chested, high-stepping carriage horse with bandaged legs and a light blanket over its back, pulling a chaise with a man and his young son in it.

Definitely not Shareb-er-rehh.

Swearing in frustration and rising anxiety, Lord Weybourne put his head in his hands and ordered another cider.

"Really, Dr. Lord . . . I think that if one has to *work*, one should have a job like yours. Your day must be so very interesting, treating sick animals and saving their lives. I mean, all you had to do was *touch* Shareb's leg, and the limp went away, just like that! I think you are wonderful."

"Thank you."

"As well as handsome."

He grinned, shook his head, and looked away.

They had been back in the chaise for an hour now, and the late afternoon sun slanted down through the trees and dappled Shareb-er-rehh's glossy rump as they trotted along the Norfolk Road. Sweeping green hills, bright with crops, climbed away to the right and opposite, fenced pastures dotted with sheep and cows met the eye for as far as it could see, until the horizon finally dropped handfuls of clouds upon the distant rises.

"Your praise is very much appreciated, but I did nothing to make your horse's lameness go away," Colin said.

"Do you think it was the bandage, then? The weights?"

"No, I think you have a confoundedly smart horse who has no desire to pull a chaise."

"You mean, the lameness was all an *act*?"

"Aye, and a very good one. Even had me fooled—'til he forgot which foot was supposed to hurt."

"Oh, no, Shareb would *never* do something deceitful like that! He's an angel."

"Yes, and so was Lucifer."

"Dr. Lord, *really*. I would expect you to exhibit more loyalty and respect toward your patient! And to compare my sweet and innocent horse to the Devil. . . . That is very mean." She raised her voice and called, "Isn't it, Shareb?"

As if in agreement, the stallion tossed his head.

They continued on for another quarter mile, and the doctor's reluctance to be drawn into a conversation about her dear Maxwell, combined with boredom and an overindulgence of ale at the coaching inn, began to weigh on Ariadne's eyelids. She looked up at him, wondering what he had *re-*

ally done to cure Shareb's poor, hurt leg. Surely, he must have worked some sort of magic. First the dog, then Shareb. . . .

And that shoulder of his, so very close to her own, was looking pleasantly inviting.

Lud, she was as drawn to him as animals seemed to be.

"Dr. Lord?"

"I am beginning to dread that tone of voice. . . ."

"I think I ate and drank too much back there, as I am just getting so-o-o-o sleepy. . . ." She yawned prettily, and eyed that safe, solid shoulder. "Perhaps if you tell me about what your horse was like, it will help me to stay awake. Was he as special to you as Shareb is to me?"

A shadow darkened the veterinarian's eyes, and he smiled wistfully. "Yes. He was . . . very special."

Ariadne said nothing, trying to keep her heavy eyes open and her mind off his shoulder. She wondered if he would mind very much if she leaned against him and went to sleep.

"What was his name?"

"Ned."

"Ned. What a gentle, simple name." She yawned, again. "I'll bet he was much better suited to pull this chaise than my Shareb."

"Yes, I'm afraid he was. Much easier on my arms and shoulders."

"Is Shareb still pulling?"

"Pulling?" The veterinarian grinned. "I'm beginning to suspect this animal is not a riding animal, but a plow horse. He is devilishly strong and hard on the bit."

She tightened her hands in her lap, grateful that he hadn't hit upon the truth about Shareb. Especially since they'd taken the weights out of the bandages and Shareb's stride had returned to the long, fluid trot that was putting the miles behind them with telltale speediness. She figured their secret was still safe, though.

That is, as long as the doctor never saw him in a full gallop. . . .

"I'm sorry," she said. "Do you want me to drive for a while? I promise to try harder this time to control him."

"No. I'm fine, really. Sit back and enjoy the scenery."

She tried, but could not, for the scenery two inches from her body was far more interesting than that of the surrounding countryside. Emboldened by the ale, feeling unrestricted without her identity and the clothes that would have proclaimed it, she gazed up at her companion's high, intelligent brow, the sweep of sunlit hair that fell over it, the shape of his nose and the intent keenness of his eye. Too bad he was a mere commoner; his profile was nothing short of aristocratic.

"Dr. Lord?" The motion of Shareb's powerful trot jouncing the chaise was making her all the more sleepy.

"Yes?"

"I think I should not have had so much ale."

He looked down at her, suddenly concerned. "Are you ill?"

"No, merely tired. I mean, I usually do take a nap in the afternoon, because I keep very late hours—town hours, you know—but between this sunshine, the motion of the chaise, a decided lack of sleep and now, the ale . . . well, I hope you can forgive me if I am not quite awake."

"There is nothing to forgive."

She reached up and lightly laid her palm against his shoulder. The muscles there were tight and hard.

"Dr. Lord . . . would you mind terribly if I laid my head against your shoulder and went to sleep?"

"We could stop at an inn, if you like."

"No, no, we shall do that tonight. I want to put London—and my brother—well behind us. Besides"—she covered her mouth, trying to keep her yawn to ladylike proportions—"that's not what I asked you. I asked if you'd mind."

"No . . . not at all," he said, a bit tightly.

She smiled her thanks, curled her arm around Bow, and carefully lowered her cheek to the veterinarian's shoulder. He had taken off his coat, and his shirt smelled of soap and clean wind. She sighed in contentment. But her face had no sooner touched the soft fabric when the chaise hit a bump, painfully smashing her teeth together. She tried again, settling her cheek against the hard muscle. Closing her eyes, she could feel the heat of her companion's body, hear the comforting, thumping beat of his heart. She smiled, and sighed. . . .

And began to drift into slumber.

The chaise hit a rut and her cheek slipped from his shoulder. Blinking in annoyance, she stared gloomily ahead, growing more perturbed by the moment.

And then the doctor's arm went around her back, pulling her close to his body and coaxing her head down into the cup of his shoulder. Ariadne closed her eyes, feeling his warmth and strength surrounding her, hearing his noble heart beating beneath her ear, knowing that he would keep her safe while she slept and never let anything happen to her.

She felt her body twitch, grow heavy. And then, with a sigh, she smiled against his shirt, rested her hand against his thigh, and went to sleep.

Suddenly, all was right in the world.

The traffic had thinned out the farther they got from London, and they passed nothing more than a team of draft horses that Shareb ignored, a fast-trotting mare who elicited enough of the stallion's interest that Colin had to touch him with the whip to keep his mind on business, and an old shepherd who, with the help of a faithful dog, was bringing home his flock for the night. The sunlight was rusty, the shadows long and reaching by the time Colin finally decided to start looking for a place to spend the night.

Her Ladyship was still asleep, her cheek nestled in the cup of his shoulder, her little hand lying innocently across his knee. For the hundredth time in the last hour, he looked down at her, and felt his heart skip a beat.

She fit within the circle of his arm as though she'd been made to it. Her cap was perched loosely on her coppery hair, and she smelled sweet and warm. She did not snore. She did not twitch. She merely lay there against him, soft and lovely and painfully beautiful.

Damnation, how I envy you, Maxwell!

He could not take his eyes off her. Now he knew what the poets spoke of when they praised the fairness of her sex, now he understood the leaping of the heart, the singing of the soul, the aching, frustrating need and want that accompanied total infatuation. His chest tight with feeling, he looked down at the top of her nose and fair cheek, and after a moment of long, careful hesitation, bent down and kissed her brow.

Her skin was smooth and sweet and soft. He looked up—

—and saw two pretty girls standing at the side of the road with their ponies, giggling and pointing at him.

"My son," Colin said, blushing furiously.

Their high laughter followed him.

"Bollocks," he swore.

Shareb-er-rehh snorted.

"Yes, you would think it's funny, damned horse!"

Her Ladyship stirred, stretched, and opened her eyes. But she did not lift her head from Colin's shoulder. "What's so funny, my good doctor?" she said, sleepily.

"Nothing."

"I don't talk in my sleep or anything, do I? Or, God forbid, drool. That would be quite ghastly and embarrassing, drooling."

"You did not drool. And if you talked in your sleep, you spoke to yourself, because I did not hear you."

"Mmmmm." She closed her eyes and belatedly Colin realized he still had his arm around her back and shoulder. He leaned back and tried to pull his arm away.

"Dr. Lord . . . please don't. I'm so comfortable. . . ."

"This is unseemly."

"Only if I deem it so. And I don't. So please, let your arm stay where it was."

He shrugged, allowing her to take his arm and pull it about her like a blanket. Tightness coiled in his loins, and he mentally counted off how many days, how many more hours, he would have to put up with this sweet torture. How much more could he take before he finally broke? How far would she push him before he said or did something he would regret?

He looked down at her, but she was asleep once more.

"Heaven help me," Colin said, and drew her close.

In a few days, she would belong to Maxwell.

But for the moment, she belonged to him.

Chapter 8

"I'm sorry, sir, but I only have one room left. You might try Mrs. Downing's place back up the road a mile or two—sometimes she has a few extra rooms, and would probably be able to take you in. On second thought, your horse—be it a mare or a gelding?"

"Stallion."

"Oh, then forget *that*," the innkeeper muttered, waving his liver-spotted old hand in dismissal. "Won't put up a stallion, Mrs. Downing won't. Husband got killed on one and she won't have one in her stable. Says they're too wild and unpredictable." He straightened up, put a hand on his hip, and, with a twisted grimace, jerked the crick out of his back, allowing Ariadne to see beyond him and into the tavern. It was dark, gloomy, and low-ceilinged, with great beams and rafters darkened by centuries of pipe smoke; quite ordinary as taverns went, with lanterns cutting swaths of cheer through the smoky gloom, maids rushing around with plates of food, groups of men engaged in lively conversation. The pungent scent of smoke and greasy meat hung in the air like a fog. "Well, it's up to you, sir," the man said, impatiently. "I

121

have one bedroom left, take it or leave it."

Ariadne saw her companion reach up to palm his brow and rake his hand back through his hair, making it stand on end before it tumbled haphazardly back into place. Her companion was tired—she could see it in the lines around his eyes, the pale cast to his skin, the grimace of pain he'd tried to hide when he'd stepped down from the chaise and walked up to this coaching inn. He all but dragged his leg behind him.

"Thank you, but I think we'll continue on and see what's up the road a bit," he said, rubbing the back of his neck and turning to leave.

Ariadne caught his arm.

"Nonsense," she said, counting out some coins and pressing them into the innkeeper's hand. "This is the third coaching inn we've tried tonight, and yours is the only room to be had. My poor . . . brother is very tired. We'll take the room."

"But—"

"Now *Colin*, don't argue with me. I'm right this time, and you know it. Sir? If you'll be so kind as to show us where your stable is so we can tend to our horse?"

"Let me get the ostler and he'll tend to it—"

"That is very kind of you, but we would prefer to do it ourselves," Ariadne said.

The innkeeper knotted his receding brow and regarded them thoughtfully, then dropped the coins into his pocket. Turning, he cupped his hands over his mouth. "Meg! Guests! Show 'em where the stable is, would you?" He turned back to them. "Take care of your horse, and by the time you get back in I'll have a good supper on the table, waiting for you."

A serving maid, wiping her hands on her starchy apron, sauntered around the corner, looking over her shoulder and laughing at something someone had said back in the kitchen. She was buxom and pretty in a rustic sort of way, with yellow curls tumbling about her shoulders and blue eyes that were alive with humor.

She shot a ribald report back to the unknown person in the kitchen.

And then she saw Colin Lord.

The narrowing of the eyes, the sudden, silky smile, the passing of the tongue over the curving lips—Ariadne saw it all, and was filled with a sudden, unreasonable, sense of anger and possessiveness.

"Right this way . . . gentlemen," the woman said huskily, casting a long, assessing look at Colin that was almost insulting in its intensity, let alone vulgar. Then she picked up a lantern and glided past him, looking coyly over her shoulder to make sure he was following.

It was all Ariadne could do not to reach out and lay her hand on his arm to proclaim that he belonged to her. Then she remembered she was pretending to be a young man and common sense won out. Such behavior would be highly inappropriate, and suspect. And the animal doctor! Totally unaware of and completely oblivious to the serving maid's interest in him, he merely took off the spectacles he'd donned earlier, pinched the bridge of his nose, and followed the woman out of the inn.

"Methinks you have an admirer," Ariadne spit nastily as he put the spectacles back on.

"I beg your pardon?" He stopped and looked at her in confusion.

Ariadne jerked her head toward the serving maid, who was several strides ahead of them and rolling her hips exaggeratedly as she walked. "I sincerely doubt that brazen display is for *my* benefit!"

The doctor frowned, looking more confused than ever. "Oh. Her. I hadn't noticed."

Ariadne grabbed his arm and yanked him forward. "Never mind. I swear, Dr. Lord, you're as blind as a bat sometimes!"

They followed Meg outside and across the drive to the darkened stables. The wind had become gusty, the summer air heavy and charged. Crickets cheeped from the grasses and, as they approached the stable, a cat crept out of the darkness and wound itself around the veterinarian's ankles, mewing plaintively and gazing up at him with adoring, feline eyes. He reached down to pick it up while Meg unlocked the door.

"Looks like rain," Meg grunted, wrestling with the latch. Then she spotted the tortoiseshell cat in Colin's arms, and her eyes widened with surprise. "Well, would ye look at that!" she exclaimed. "Gemma here *never* goes to anyone, 'specially strangers!"

"Dr. Lord has a way with animals," Ariadne said flatly.

"I should say he does," Meg murmured, letting her gaze wander up and down Colin's body in a heated caress that he, still petting the cat, never even noticed. "Bet he's got one with the ladies, too."

That comment did catch his attention. He looked up and, despite his fatigue, managed a broad, engaging smile that made Ariadne bristle in annoyance and feel like a third wheel. He stood cradling the cat in his arms as the servant dragged open the door, then, giving the feline a last fond rub behind the ears, carefully put it down and went to get the stallion. The cat ran after him, following worshipfully at his heels, meowing, and nearly tripping him.

"What happened to yer brother?" Meg asked Ariadne, leaning against the stable door while they waited for Colin to return with Shareb-er-rehh. "Such a pity, that limp."

"He was in the War."

"Fine-lookin' man. Too bad he's a cripple."

Ariadne stiffened and, eyes flashing, bestowed a withering glare on the other woman. "He is *not* a cripple. He's capable and confident and I'll thank you not to demean him so."

"Don't get so huffy, little boy, I was merely making an observation," the wench said, her voice a husky, sultry thing that grated on Ariadne's nerves. "In fact, ye can tell yer handsome sibling that I rather fancy him . . . limp or not."

"Yes, well, you can fancy him all you wish, but he's taken. He already *has* a lady friend."

Now why on earth had she said *that*? The other woman laughed, obviously unfazed.

"Is that so? Well, I'm sure he won't mind . . . another."

There was nothing that Ariadne, in her role as "little brother," could say without drawing suspicion to herself, and so she raised her chin and bit her tongue and dug her nails into her palms to keep her angry retort at bay. She hated herself for feeling so possessive about someone who didn't belong to her, and it rankled. She had no claim on Colin Lord. For heaven's sake, he was just a servant! Yet why did she feel this red shaft of jealousy?

Self-disgust filled her. Papa had picked out Maxwell as a husband for her, dear, wonderful Maxwell, and she had no right to even *think* of anyone else. What would people say if they could know the direction of her thoughts? Lady Ariadne St. Aubyn fancying a lowly *veterinarian*, of all things! Heavens above, she'd be ostracized.

Shareb's smart hoofbeats heralded his approach

and Colin had barely gotten him into the stable and unhooked from the chaise before the skies opened up in earnest, the rain hammering against the roof at a volume that made even talk impossible. As the other horses turned their heads to watch his arrival, Shareb-er-rehh's sulky attitude immediately vanished, as though he'd been humiliated by pulling the vehicle and had just been released from a terrible burden. He whinnied softly, and each horse in the stable stared at him as he passed, tail high, neck arched, nostrils flaring with self-importance.

Ahead, Meg walked with the lantern, leading them down the gloomy aisle, occasionally glancing over her shoulder to smile invitingly at Colin. She had regarded Shareb-er-rehh's blanket and bandaged legs rather dubiously, and Ariadne hoped that the disguise did not call suspicion down on all of them.

She saw Colin watching her from above Shareb's withers.

"Go inside, little brother. I'll see to the horse."

And leave him to Meg, who was watching him like a hawk after a rabbit? "No. I'll stay and help."

He merely grinned, causing her to suspect that he knew *exactly* why she chose to stay. It was infuriating.

Meg paused outside an empty stall and jerked her head to indicate that it was available for the stallion's use. As the veterinarian led Shareb inside, the woman let her eyes rake appreciatively over his back, his face, his form. Again, Ariadne felt the hot lance of jealousy.

She raised her chin. "We have no further need of your services, save for supper and a good breakfast in the morning. Good-night."

Meg looked startled, then indignant, at Ariadne's unexpectedly haughty tone. "My, such airs," she commented, and, giving Colin a last, inviting look that he ignored, turned on her heel and strode angrily out of the stable.

Ariadne went into the narrow stall. The veterinarian was removing the harness, looking down at Shareb's sweat-dampened hide, and smiling a private grin.

"Care to tell me what you find so funny?" she snapped.

"Not really."

She reached up and straightened the blanket into which was sewn more money than he'd ever see in his lifetime. "Here we go, more secrets."

"Forgive me, my lady, but you seemed almost . . . jealous."

"What, of that overblown rose? Hardly!"

"She didn't look so overblown to me. In fact, I thought she was rather pretty." He grinned, taunting her. "Such lovely hair . . . probably as silky to the touch as"—he removed Shareb's bridle and shot her a teasing look—"your silken underthings from China."

"I have no wish to talk about my underthings, thank you. Nor do I care to discuss that hussy's *hair*."

"You really think she fancied me?"

"Well she did issue you an open invitation to her *bed*. Maybe you ought to take her up on it, might do you some good."

"Think so?"

"*No!*"

He raised one brow; then, his eyes twinkled, and his mouth turned up in that helpless, crooked grin that she didn't know whether to love or hate. Ariadne swung away, her face flaming, and busied herself with unbuckling the harness. "Very well, then," she admitted, sullenly. "Maybe I *was* a little bit jealous. I mean, angry. But I disliked that woman, and I disliked the way she was looking at you. She had no right."

"And you do?"

"I'm . . . *paying* you!"

"Oh, that's right. You own me. How dreadful of me to have forgotten."

"Dr. Lord."

"Yes?" he said, innocently.

"Mind your impertinent manners."

He laughed, tied the lead shank to a ring bolted to the wall, and put the harness in the chaise. "Yes, my lady," he said in an exaggeratedly grave, deep voice. "Anything you say, my lady." He scowled down at her until her frown faded to a helpless grin, then offered his elbow with a gallant flourish. "Come, let Shareb and Bow have their suppers and let us go have ours, and perhaps after a good night's sleep we'll both feel better in the morning."

"Oh, Dr. Lord. How *do* you put up with me?"

"With patience and delight," he said honestly, and then, before she could question him on such a remark, he led her out of the stable and through the rainy darkness.

Supper was a fine steak and kidney pie served with roast potatoes, parsnip, and swede, accompanied by a loaf of hot, freshly baked bread, creamy butter, a wedge of aged cheddar, and plenty of ale to wash it all down. Respectful of her companion's aversion to eating flesh, Ariadne traded her vegetables for his slab of pie. She held off the spirits this time, and when Meg brought deep dishes of apple cobbler topped with cream for dessert, she set her mind to thinking up a way to sneak her portion out to the stable so she could give it to Shareb-er-rehh.

God forbid if the stallion didn't get his nightly

dose of pastry and ale. He'd be an absolute *demon* come morning.

She pretended to toy with the cobbler, and shot a quick glance up through her lashes at the veterinarian. His face was golden in the glow from the lantern, his hair rumpled from his habit of raking it back off his forehead, but tired as he looked, those clear, keen eyes of his were alert and awake.

And on her.

He smiled, and looked at her over the rim of his tea cup. "Don't even think about it."

"Think about what?"

"Taking that cobbler out to the horse."

She widened her eyes and, with a guilty little laugh, plunged her fork into the crumbly topping. "Be serious, Dr. Lord, do you think I could just put it in my pocket? What a mess it would make, with all this cream and sticky juice." She smiled innocently up at him. "Why, I'd soil my clothing!"

He looked at her for a dubious moment before sighing heavily and shoving his half-finished cobbler away. Then he took off his glasses, rubbed his eyes, and sat staring down at the table as though in a daze, too tired to trade banter with her.

"Dr. Lord?"

He looked up, trying to look more wakeful than he really was. "Yes?"

Ariadne took a bite of her dessert and dabbed delicately at her mouth. "Is it past your bedtime?"

"Forgive me, my lady. It's been a long day."

Both of them looked down at their dessert bowls, thinking about the bedroom that awaited them upstairs, and neither quite willing to bring up the subject of sleeping arrangements. A minute dragged past. Two. Ariadne glanced up and saw that the doctor's head was drooping, his beautiful, long lashes starting to slip down over his eyes, and that he was fast on his way to falling asleep in his chair.

"Dr. Lord!" she said, sharply.

He jerked his head up, blinking.

Ariadne got to her feet. "Despite the fact that both of us feel rather awkward about this situation—"

"Well, one of us does, anyhow—"

"I see no reason to delay it any longer. Come, let us go upstairs. If we both sleep with our clothes on and don't share the bed, there is nothing unseemly about it."

But Colin wasn't thinking about the unseemliness of the situation. He was thinking how lovely and desirable Her Ladyship looked, and wondering how the devil he would be able to pass a night with her in the same room, not just *any* room, but a damned bedroom, for God's sake. He rested his elbows on the table, then reached up to knead his aching nape, trying to massage away the stiffness caused by Shareb's ceaseless pulling.

She was already on her feet, beckoning him with a practiced motion of her hand to rise and follow her. Too tired to protest, Colin got up, threw down his napkin, and limped painfully after her. They passed the landlord's old dog, sprawled before the hearth, and headed for the stairs, she marching like a general and he dragging his leg behind him. The other patrons had long since gone to bed, and each step creaked loudly beneath them.

At the end of a short corridor was their room, and with no small degree of trepidation, Ariadne pushed open the door. The chamber was small, cozy, alarmingly intimate—and dominated by the bed.

She swallowed hard, trying to maintain her bravura and poise, and glanced at her companion. He was staring at the bed and she could see the fine sheen of perspiration that suddenly glistened on his brow before he abruptly shoved his hands in his pockets and made as if to storm past her.

"I think it best if I sleep in the stable."

She sidestepped so he couldn't pass. "No, no, Dr. Lord, I should."

"Nonsense. You're an earl's daughter, for God's sake, you can't be sleeping in a damned stable."

"The good Lord not only slept in a stable, He was born in one. If He can sleep in a stable, then so can I. You stay here, and take the bed. You're far more tired than I am."

"No, I must protest. As a gentleman, I insist that you take the bed."

"As your employer, I insist that you do."

"You hired me to look after your horse. Therefore, I will sleep in the stable with Shareb and Bow, and I'll hear no more argument on the subject. Good night, my lady. I shall see you in the morning."

He strode past her in a gait that belied the pain his leg must be causing him, leaving her staring indignantly after him with her jaw agape. In his wake, the room suddenly felt lonely, empty, and cold, and Ariadne waited just long enough to hear his tread on the stairs before she went marching after him.

"Dr. Lord," she cried, watching his broad back as he went down the stairs, "you'll not have the final word about this!"

"I just did."

"You just think you did! I shall not let the matter rest here, do you hear me? I won't!"

She ran down the stairs after him. He pushed open the door and let it slam back in her face as he went out into the rainy night.

She jerked it open. "Dr. Lord!"

He turned, wagged a finger at her. "Go to bed!"

"Don't you tell me what to do!"

"I'm telling you, and you'll do it." He turned

and kept walking, his boots sighing over the wet grass.

She hurried after him. "Fine, be that way! We'll *both* sleep in the stable, then!"

He pulled open the door of the stable and stormed past their chaise, the stalls, the cat that was curled sleepily atop a bale of hay, until he was just outside Shareb's stall. He took off his coat, tossed it to the straw, and sat down on it. With his legs thrust out before him, he leaned his back and head against the wooden door and prepared to sleep.

"You can't sleep like that," she said, standing above him with her hands on her hips.

"Watch me."

He shut his eyes and turned his face away from her.

She squatted down in front of him and pulled off his glasses.

He would not open his eyes.

"Lady Ariadne, *please*. You are beginning to anger me."

His tone was tense and hard, unlike anything she had heard him use yet, and it cut her to the quick. The playful smile faded from her lips and Ariadne, brought up short, could only remain unmoving, torn between going quietly away or standing her ground. But oh, God help her, she had no wish to go back to that lonely, upstairs room. She wanted to stay here, in this warm, cozy stable, where the scent of hay, grain, and horses lent it a homey, comforting ambience that would be sadly lacking in that small upstairs chamber. She waited for an apology from the veterinarian. None came. Hurt, and feeling suddenly unwanted, she sat down in the darkness beside him, her shoulder and hip a mere two inches from his. He made no sound, and she could feel the tension emanating from him. It was too late now to retreat back to the bedroom.

Childlike, Ariadne wrapped her arms around her knees and squeezed tightly, trying to keep her emotions under control.

"Dr. Lord . . . I don't want to be alone up there in that tiny room when the only two souls left in this world who are dear to me are sleeping out in a stable. Besides . . . I feel responsible for you and your well-being—"

He chuckled without humor. "*You*, responsible for *me*?"

"Well, yes—"

"Imagine that."

She hugged her knees in the darkness, feeling suddenly cast out, lonely, and foolish. Tears stung the back of her eyes, slipping down her cheeks and falling softly atop her kneecaps. She bent her head and squeezed her arms tighter, willing herself not to cry.

And then, unexpectedly, he reached out in the darkness, pried her clenched fingers out of her upper arm, and clasped her tiny hand within his own.

Ariadne froze, her hand a rigid block of wood within his.

She felt his thumb caressing the inside of her palm, the warmth of his fingers covering the back of her hand. She trembled inside, unsure of whether to jerk her hand away or not and feeling suddenly trapped and panicky. Over and over his thumb moved, the motion no longer invasive, but now calming, soothing, until she wanted to bury herself against him like a little child and release her pent-up sobs. But she could not do such an unspeakable thing and so instead, she held his hand, gingerly at first, then as though it was a lifeline, and sat listening to the rain tapping gently against the roof, the crickets chirping in the dim recesses of the stable, the hoot of an owl somewhere off in the night. It was dark, but no so much that she, just turning her head, couldn't see the dim profile of her companion's face. His eyes were open and he was staring into the nothingness.

His glasses were beside her hip. She folded them and set them carefully on the straw a safe distance away. "I'm sorry, Dr. Lord. I didn't mean to ... anger you."

"No." His voice was very soft, almost fond. He squeezed her hand, briefly and quickly. "You haven't, my dear."

My dear. The words sent a flood of warmth through her, and she pressed her arm to her ribs to control the intensity of the sudden, tingly feelings they evoked.

"I like it, that you called me that," she whispered, shyly.

"Called you what?"

" 'My dear.' "

"Forgive me," he said, his eyes slipping shut. "I must be more tired than I thought. We both know there is nothing 'dear' about you at all, now, don't we?"

"If you're trying to goad me, it will not work. I know by now that you're just teasing."

"Mmmm." He smiled without opening his eyes. "And as I am very tired, you will also know that I'd be quite happy if you'd go away now and allow me my rest."

"And if I remain quiet, instead?"

"We're talking impossibilities here, I take it."

"I'll consider it a challenge."

"Very well then. Stay if you like."

He shifted a bit, trying to make his leg comfortable, and she remembered the serving maid's mean comment. *Cripple.* A fierce sense of protectiveness rose within her and, for once, she cursed her genteel upbringing. Had she been the lad she was masquerading as, she would have slapped the chit across the face.

"Does your leg pain you, Dr. Lord?" she murmured, suddenly concerned.

"I knew the silence couldn't last."

"Just answer this one question and I shall be quiet."

He chuckled. "Leg's fine," he said, and in the darkness, she could see that he'd closed his eyes and tilted his head back against the door. "Or, as good as can be expected given the weather. In truth, 'tis my shoulders that are on fire."

"From Shareb's pulling?"

"Aye. He's a strong horse, that one."

She said nothing, only holding his hand in the darkness. Gradually, she found herself thinking of that hand itself, and growing acutely aware of the rough texture of the palm, the warmth of the skin, its sprinkling of fine hairs and the shape of the knuckles. She wondered if he was making similar observations about *her* hand.

"I'm sorry about that," she said.

"You have no need to be."

"Well, he's my horse, and I feel rather guilty. . . . I suppose we should be thankful he even consented to pulling the chaise, considering he's never done so before and surely did not enjoy it. Beneath his dignity, you know. But then, as I've said, you *do* have a way with animals, Dr. Lord, and perhaps that is why he behaved as well as he did."

He said nothing, only the sound of his breathing disturbing the quiet of the stable. She pulled her hand out of his and of its own accord, it crept up to touch his shoulder. The muscles there were rock-hard beneath her fingers.

"Can you sleep, Dr. Lord?"

"I . . . don't know."

She innocently misinterpreted his comment as

referring to the pain in his shoulders when in truth, it had more to do with the proximity of her body to his—and the effect it was having on him.

"You're an animal doctor," she said quietly, her hand still lying against his shoulder. "If someone brought a horse to you that was stiff and sore, how would you treat it?"

"Liniments, a good rubdown, and a warm blanket."

"Oh." Ariadne was glad of the darkness; it concealed the sudden trepidation that must have been written all over her face. She cleared her throat, and even though he couldn't possibly see how embarrassed the thought alone was making her, she felt her face going hot with color.

Liniments, a good rubdown, and a warm blanket.

She couldn't. No. It wasn't proper. . . .

He sighed and stretched his leg, drawing his breath in sharply.

She couldn't!

He pulled the leg back up, trying to get comfortable.

God help her. "I . . . may not have liniment, but I . . . *can* give you a—a, uh—rubdown and a blanket."

He was quiet for so long that she thought he must not have heard her. Then she saw him turn his face toward her in the darkness, one fair brow raised. "You would do that, for me?"

"I would . . . if you do not tell my Maxwell, that is," she added, hurriedly.

He was silent again. *Too* silent, as though her words had made him angry. At last, he let out a heavy sigh, rolled over, and stretched out on his stomach in the hay, the side of his head resting atop his crossed wrists. "Very well," he murmured. "Be about it, then."

"But"—she stared at those broad shoulders,

curled her hands into fists, and drew them protectively up against her bosom—"I don't know what to do!"

Hay rustled as he positioned himself more comfortably. "I suppose it would be useless to ask if you've ever kneaded a loaf of bread dough?"

Her silence was answer enough.

"Never mind," he said quietly, fondly, and folding his coat into a pillow, propped it beneath his forearms.

"No, I won't 'never mind,' " she retorted, suddenly feeling quite foolish—again. "You're hurting, and I can't bear the thought of you tossing and turning in pain all night." She moved closer, sitting as close to him as she could get, until her thighs were pressed right up against his torso and the heat of him warmed the entire side of her leg. Panic—and something else—rocked her. She swallowed hard and, with an effort, found her voice.

"I want you to know that we're just f-friends, and that nothing is to come of this," she announced shakily, wondering if she was trying to convince herself or him. "If anyone were to learn about this, I'd be shunned and banned from polite society."

"My lady, I fear that your actions over the past two days will have already accomplished such a banishment," he pointed out. "But if it will make you feel any better, your secret is quite safe with me."

"You're sure."

"I give you my word on it."

"V-very . . . well, then."

He chuckled, and relaxed.

Waiting.

Swallowing hard, her nerves making a wreck of her composure, Ariadne stretched shaking hands toward that strong, lean back.

And knew—the moment her fingers touched his

shoulders—that she'd made a mistake, for what was between them was something that threatened to be far more than *friendship*. She felt his warmth, his power, his pull, the sudden gallop of her heartbeat. Oh God. She shouldn't be doing this, it was wrong, wrong, wrong! But she couldn't stop. Not now. Not when her hands were already on his shirt, her fingers already probing the stiff muscles beneath the soft fabric, her palms skimming hesitantly, confidently, boldly, over the sheaths of power that muscled his back and loving every bump, rise, and plane they encountered. Blindly, she shoved away thoughts of wrongdoing and concentrated on her task, kneading the soreness from his muscles, telling herself over and over that she was only tending to a friend while her face flamed and her heart pounded and the breath came hot and harsh through her lungs—

Maxwell's face reared up in her mind.

"Mmmmm, that feels good," the veterinarian murmured, just when she would have snatched her hands away. Guilt flooded her, to be replaced with admonition for behaving like such a frightened ninny, and, with renewed determination, Ariadne bit her lip and continued her ministrations. She was no coward! And she would prove it—if not just to Colin Lord, then to *herself*.

Her fingers strayed, following the knobby, upward direction of his spine, his neck, until the ends of his hair kissed her knuckles. Gently, she stroked the warm, silky locks that followed the curve of the back of his head, wondering at the feel of them against and through her fingers. Again she thought of Maxwell. Again—angrily this time—she shoved the thought of him aside. Then Dr. Lord made a contented, sighing sound and Ariadne promptly forgot Maxwell, her station, and any guilt of wrongdoing because suddenly all was right in her world and nothing else mattered, nothing at all. Shutting her eyes, her fingers trailing through his hair, she listened to the rain beating gently against the roof while the stable slumbered around them.

"Your ministrations are quite soothing," he murmured, as she kneaded the back of his neck, the base of his shoulders, and then, ran her palms out over the stiff, hard muscles of his back and arms with increasing skill and confidence. "I think I could go to sleep, like this."

"I thought that was the idea." Her hands found the powerful muscles of his upper shoulders. They seemed to be carved from stone, and as she began to knead them with her fingertips and sides of her thumbs, he winced, as though in pain. She nearly jerked her hands back. "Does it hurt?" she whispered, not daring to call up her voice for fear he'd hear its hoarse trembling.

"A bit. But you're doing admirably well for someone who has never given a rubdown before."

"If so, it's only because I *have* watched the stable hands giving them to the racehorses after a hard workout—"

She winced and sucked in her breath at the errant slip of her tongue, but in his fatigue, he never noticed. But did he notice other things? Like her rapidly beating heart? The hot dampness of her hands? The nervousness that must be apparent in her voice? Thank God he couldn't see her face. *I'm not doing anything wrong!* But if she wasn't doing anything wrong, then why did she feel so hot and flustery? So nervous, quivery, and skittish? She swallowed hard, bearing down on the heels of her hands, her fingertips, putting her weight into the gentle massage and pushing at the stiffness she felt beneath her fingers until he gave a slight groan of pain.

"I'm sorry!" she gasped, easing up on the pressure.

"No, my lady. You could never hurt me."

For a long moment she said nothing, merely gazing down at the back of his head, his ear, and her hands, lost amidst the folds of his shirt where it spanned his broad and powerful shoulders. Then, gently placing the heels of her hands against the knots of muscle, she leaned down until her lips were inches from his ear and whispered, "Ariadne."

"Sorry?"

"Ariadne. It is my name. I give you permission to use it." She gave a nervous little laugh. "In trade for your permission for me to use *your* Christian name, as well."

She felt the sudden threads of tension in his shoulders, heard the slow release of his breath. He was so close that she could easily lean down and bury her lips in those silky locks.

"Ariadne," he said, his voice muffled against the coat as he tried the sound of it out on his tongue.

"Colin," she returned, doing the same.

"Yours is a pretty name," he murmured, and she could just see that his mouth was turned up in the softest of smiles, his lashes lying against his cheeks. "I like it."

"A bit difficult to say though, don't you think?"

"Ah-ree-ahd-knee. The young beauty who led Theseus out of the maze with the ball of string."

"The very one."

"Dare I dream I am Theseus?"

Something hitched in her chest, but his was a question best left unanswered. It was obvious that he was growing more than fond of her, and despite her earlier flirting with him—which she was now beginning to regret, because it *had* been mean and unfair—she had no desire to lead him down a path that would only be a dead end. That would be cruel, and she was beginning to care for him far too much to hurt him so.

And yet . . .

"You have a nice name too . . . Colin. It may take me a while to get used to calling you anything but 'doctor,' but I will manage." She sighed and smiled, keeping her hands moving in gentle, firm circles over his back, shoulders, and upper arms. And nice arms they were, too: strong and well formed, with a natural grace and beauty of definition. Unbidden, she thought of what it would be like to go to bed every night held safely within them, with those beautiful eyes looking up at her in the darkness and her name—*Ariadne*—a gentle, whispered caress on his lips.

A deep, blooming ache gripped her heart—for some things, of course, could never be, and should not even be thought about.

Thank God he could not see the sudden moisture in her eyes. She smoothed his hair back from the side of his brow, over and over again until his eyes drifted shut, his breathing grew heavy, and his lashes lay heavily against his cheeks once more. He would make a good husband for some lucky woman, she thought, with no small degree of wistfulness and pain. And a good friend, as well. How very special he was, this kind, gentle man whom animals loved and trusted. Maybe it was time *she* dared to trust him, too. . . .

And tell him the truth about Shareb-er-rehh.

Tomorrow.

"Sleep now, good doctor," she whispered, as she felt the last stiffness fading from his body, until she felt him slipping away beneath her hands, until she knew she had brought him beyond pain and into sweet, peaceful slumber. She gently pulled his coat out from beneath him and spread it over his back. Then she gazed down at him, a huge lump filling the back of her throat as she put her lips beside his still cheek.

"Dr. Lord?"

Nothing.

She smiled then, listening to his quiet breathing, letting her hand rest on the side of his head. Then—very slowly, very carefully—she closed her eyes, leaned down, and buried her lips in his hair.

It was sweet-smelling and clean, like silk against her face.

She took a deep, shaky breath, and pressed a kiss against his temple.

"Good-night, my sweet friend."

Chapter 9

Colin came awake to the sound of rain tapping against the deckhead above. He lay there in the darkness, waiting for his servant to come in and tell him the ship's position, its course, the direction and strength of the wind. He sat up, blinking away his dream while consciousness returned and he felt the customary despair, the heavy plunge of his spirit at the cruel realization he was not in his cabin aboard HMS *Triton*. He was land-bound and the sound he heard was nothing more than the dull tattoo of rain against a roof.

He wondered if he'd always come instantly awake at four in the morning, wondered if the memories would ever go away, wondered if he'd ever be able to get the sea out of his blood.

He suddenly realized just where he was—and whom he was with.

She lay beside him, deeply asleep—as most people were, at four in the morning—her spine pressed intimately against his chest, her hand gripping his, her breathing soft and slow in the darkness. His blood ignited, bringing on an erection made all the more excruciating by the fact that his manhood was already pressing into the softness of

143

her backside. The sweat popped out on his brow, ran down his temple. Taking a deep, unsteady breath, Colin carefully pulled his hand out of hers and eased away from her.

He stood up, trembling, aching, needing, *wanting.*

Dear God. Give me strength. . . .

His head bent, the heel of his hand pressed to his forehead, he stumbled down the long, dark aisle, pulled the door open, and turned his hot face up to the cool, drenching rain that poured out of the night.

"God help me," he said aloud, his fists clenched, his body rigid, the water streaming down his cheeks. He shook his head and squeezed his eyes shut, baring his teeth in pain. "God, I just can't resist her much longer. Please, help me. I *beg* of you, help me, give me strength, take this temptation away. . . ."

The rain came down harder, beating like shot against his forehead and upturned face, soaking his hair and plastering it to his scalp. Water ran down his neck, his nose, pummeled his brow and cheeks and eyelashes.

"Ariadne," he whispered in anguish, and began to walk, away from the stable, away from *her*. His breeches pressed against his hardness, making each step an exercise in discomfort. He heard the door creak behind him and little Bow came racing out, streaking ahead of him through the darkness after a barn cat.

Walk, and it won't hurt as bad. Walk, and put her out of your mind. You cannot have her. She's promised to another. It's not to be, dammit, the wind blows from a different quarter.

He walked faster, head bent, the rain streaming down his cheeks, dripping off the tip of his nose, beating against his bare head and soaking the back of his neck. Gravel crunched, then mud squished beneath his boots as he crossed the drive and headed up the footpath that traversed the gentle hills. He leaned heavily on his good leg, mercilessly abusing his bad one until the latter screamed in protest, but he walked faster, damning the fates that had made him look up the other day and see *her* sitting so coolly astride that damned horse, the fates that had laid him out cold at her feet, the fates that had thrown the two of them together and would only rip them cruelly apart in the end.

God, it *hurt*. Knowing his doomed fate hurt more than just about anything he'd ever encountered or ever expected to encounter—

Except for the day he would meet that unknown bastard, Maxwell. The day he would hand her over to him would likely tear him apart.

Oblivious to the pain in his leg, oblivious to the slowly lightening sky, he pushed himself onward. He didn't see the dog racing off into a wet tangle of blackberry bushes after a hare, didn't smell the musky fragrance of blossoming wildflowers and wet grass, didn't hear the birds coming awake around him, nor notice the sky to the east going pale gray with the coming of dawn. He could only think of *her* back there, asleep, could only relive the sweet bliss of drifting away beneath her touch last night only to wake up with his rock-hard erection pressing into the luscious softness of her backside.

Didn't she know what she was *doing* to him?

He passed a mist-shrouded field, gray beneath the still-dark skies, where several cows stared at him as he passed. One of them raised its head, let out a long, lonely call, and began to walk after him, separated only by the fence. Sure enough, the rest of the herd began to follow, all stumbling along placidly through the mud, swishing their tails and trailing in his wake.

He kept walking, too full of anguish to notice them, his chest so tight with distress and emotion that it hurt just to breathe. He thought about leaving her and returning to London. He thought about how many other women there were in the world, and how his way of life and, yes, his attitude, were really all that kept him from meeting someone he might ache for and desire as much as he did his fiery, flame-haired employer. For five years he'd been a recluse, throwing himself into his new career as emphatically as he had his old one; for five years he'd felt his purpose in life was to ease suffering, a small atonement for the lives he had destroyed in the name of *war*; for five years he had used his shyness around women as an excuse not to get close to any, for fear that they would see him as a ruined hero and reject him. For five years he had filled the emptiness in his heart by taking refuge in solitude and his profession.

And then he had met Lady Ariadne St. Aubyn. Her charm, her bubbly playfulness, her carefree attention to him made him aware, in painfully striking clarity, of all that he had been denying himself.

You can't have her, he told himself with the same phlegmatic, practical stoicism that had saved him from life-threatening despair after the courtmartial. *She belongs to another, and you are only wasting energy by pining for her. There are other women out there. She has merely opened a door, shown you that there is more in life than just being the finest veterinarian you can be, that you need someone to love and be loved by as much as the next person. . . .*

Then why didn't he tell her about the courtmartial? His own noble blood? Why did he hold back when she wanted to know about his old life? After all, *he*'d long since accepted and come to terms with what had happened to him—it was the rest of the world who could not accept what he had become.

He trudged along through the wet grass, the fragrance of clover and damp earth filling his senses. God, how he wanted to share with Ariadne the pain he'd felt when his former career had come to its abrupt and untimely end; how he wanted to tell her what had *really* happened, so she might know that he'd been a hero once, and worthy of her. But he couldn't. Because she, like his peers, like his former friends, like the rest of the world, would only pity and despise him, and he couldn't bear the thought of that bright smile fading away when he revealed what had happened to him. She was young. She was class-conscious. She had not yet learned, might not ever learn, given her privileged status, that it was the person inside that counted.

He might have fallen from glory, but he was still the same man he had been.

A better one, probably.

The rain began to let up, the droplets fading to cool mist against his face. A flock of honking geese winged overhead, and still he pressed on. He thought of Orla, and tried to recall her dark hair and wise eyes that had seen too much, but her face was lost to time and all he could remember was the little pirate ship, the all-women crew of which she had been a part, and their lady-captain, his cousin Maeve, who'd found her own true love in the arms of his philandering admiral, Gray.

They were painful memories to ponder. Especially when he considered what had happened after he, Colin, had brought them all back to the Caribbean . . . and the storm had hit, changing his life forever.

Now, Orla was an ocean away, far beyond his reach. But even the brief flame he had felt for the Irish girl was nothing compared to the raging fire that burned in his heart and blood at the mere thought of Lady Ariadne St. Aubyn.

He ought to leave her. He ought to run, to flee, while he still had a heart beating within his breast.

You have very beautiful eyes, Dr. Lord.

He ought to get as far away from her as he possibly could, and as quickly as possible.

You have a very nice smile, too.

Yes, far away . . . and fast.

You're a very handsome man, Dr. Lord.

He dug the heels of his hands into his eyes, pressing hard. He couldn't leave her, of course. He was a man of honor, had given his word to stay by her side, to protect her and safeguard the well-being of the stallion. He could last just a few more days, couldn't he? Besides, what he felt for the lovely heiress was nothing more than infatuation born out of his own loneliness. It would go away, as soon as he saw her safely to Burnham and returned to London.

It *had* to.

Soaked to the skin, he walked until gray light revealed the patchwork fields and hills, the fences and hedgerows and the muddy, rutted path on which he walked. He whistled for Bow and, turning, strode back the way he'd come, resolved to be strong where *she* was concerned, resolved to put some distance between them for the sake of his own heart, resolved to be practical about the matter, as he was about everything else in his life, and not let a bit of whimsy fill him so full of anguish.

The world had awakened during his absence. He heard the old sheep dog barking in the drive long before he came down the last hill and saw the coaching inn in the distance, people already moving in and out of the barn, travelers coming and going, and Meg hauling twin buckets from the well and carrying them into the inn. A curl of smoke rose from the chimney, dark against the thick, misty air, and his stomach growled at the thought of breakfast.

She was nowhere in sight.

A pair of matched grays hitched to a fine carriage stood in the drive, their coats streaked with rain, their eyes on Colin. As he passed they, like the cows, tried to follow him. A groom pulled them back. With Bow at his heels he slipped into the barn, his eyes helplessly drawn to that place where he and Ariadne had spent the night. But there were people up and about the stable now, horses being led in and out, and the place where he had slept and dreamed and ached for a woman he could never have was marked by nothing more than a flattened patch of straw.

Passing their chaise, which had been pulled over to the side of the aisle, Colin peered into Shareb-er-rehh's stall.

The stallion was gone.

A rush of fear and alarm swept through him and he whirled, only to collide with Meg.

"Ah, Mr. Lord! Your little brother asked me t' give ye a message—said the horse needed exercise and he was going t' take him out for a gallop. Said he'd be back in an hour...."

"Oh." Colin sighed with relief, and wiped the rain from his face. "Yes, well, uh, thank you."

Touching his arm, Meg tilted her face up at him. "An hour ain't so long, you know." She winked. "But long enough to take a little *ride* of our own. What do ye say, handsome?"

Colin smiled, his mind groping for a suitable but polite excuse to decline. Though it would probably do him a world of good to take a tumble with Meg, he just couldn't do it. Didn't *want* to do it. He shook his head, and made some excuse that sounded implausible even to his own ears, leaving Meg to stare at him as though he'd grown a third eye.

"Ah, Mr. Lord. 'Tis heartier fare I'm offering ye, but maybe there's some truth that the way to a man's heart is through his stomach. Maybe next time, hmm? Come, follow me. Uncle Rodney's serving breakfast, and that's the least I can give ye."

He followed her out of the busy stable, passing horses being brought out and harnessed, the matched grays, and an old, swaybacked bay gelding that had just been driven into the little yard. Its coloring and markings mirrored Shareb's, but any similarity stopped there. The animal's head was lowered, its nose hanging near the ground, its eyes half-closed, and its entire body broken and defeated.

"Hey, boy," Colin murmured, and put out his hand to touch the drooping head.

Unlike the fiery Shareb-er-rehh, this sad, gentle creature took a weary step forward and placed its muzzle in his palm. Its sides expanded in a deep sigh, and it was then that Colin noticed the cruel sores beneath the harness, the rawness about the animal's poor mouth. *Oh, God,* he thought, his heart constricting, and laid his hand against the old beast's rain-soaked neck.

You have healing hands, Delabere Blaine had once told him, upon noting the eerie way that animals behaved around him. But even healing hands could do nothing to take away cruelty and the pain of abuse.

"Hey, you! Yeah, you! Git away from my horse, ye hear?"

He looked up as a fat, pox-scarred man waddled toward them. Out of the corner of his eye, he saw Meg standing on the inn's steps, hands on her hips, head cocked, watching. Not wishing to make a scene, Colin gently stroked the gelding's thin neck and said mildly, "You might try a little kindness where your horse is concerned. He'll perform far better for you."

"I'm kind as the day is long," the man puffed, glaring hatefully at the poor old gelding. "Damned horse, paid enough money for 'im and 'e's sick. Won't go. And here I gotta be in Norwich day after tomorrow an' this damned thing ain't fit for nothin' but dog food. Damned farrier's supposed to be along any minute t' have a look at 'im. I'm tellin' ye, though, if he can't do anything for the stinkin' beast, I'm sending 'im off to the slaughterhouse!"

"Mr. Lord?" Meg called saucily. "Coming?"

Colin's worried gaze remained on the gelding. He touched the soft white-and-pink muzzle and felt the animal's warm breath against his fingers. "Perhaps I could help," he suggested, keeping his tone steady and mild in an attempt to defuse the owner's ill temper. "I'm a veterinarian."

"A what?"

"Veterinarian."

"What the hell is that?"

Colin smiled, and stroked the gelding's sagging neck. "An animal doctor."

"There ain't nothin' you kin do that me own farrier can't," the man growled. "I don't need no university-educated know-it-all telling me how to treat me horse."

Colin sighed. Maybe, just maybe, one of these days he'd learn that he couldn't fix the world. "Have your farrier treat him, then. But if my advice means anything to you, try putting a pad of sheepskin right here"—he gently lifted the saddle of the harness and indicated a raw spot, just behind the gelding's withers—"to keep the leather from chafing his back. He has harness sores, and they hurt. No wonder he won't go for you."

The man stared at him, and, wordlessly, Colin

gave the poor animal's nose a last stroke. But as he turned and walked away, the old horse let out a long, plaintive whinny, trying to call him back. The sound tore at Colin's heart. Steeling himself, he kept walking. The gelding whinnied again.

You can't fix the world.

Meg was holding the door open for him, and as he stepped inside, a notice displayed boldly across its front caught his eye and pushed thoughts of the old horse to the back of his mind.

WANTED: Any information leading to the whereabouts of Lady Ariadne St. Aubyn, daughter of the late Earl of Weybourne, who disappeared on Sunday last. . . .

"Bloody hell!" he said under his breath. "She *wasn't* exaggerating!"

"What?" Meg asked.

His smile was quick and false. "Oh—uh, nothing. Friend of mine told me about this—um, this fugitive, but I suppose it's such a singular story you have to see something like this in order to believe it, eh?"

"I suppose. Whole countryside's talkin' about it, though. Can ye imagine? Fifteen hundred pounds to return the girl—an heiress, no less!—an' the stallion to her brother. Must be one valuable horse indeed. . . ."

Sudden sweat ran down Colin's back, his heart pounded in his ears, and it was all he could do to retain his composure as he followed Meg into the inn. It was a far different scene than it had been last night; this morning patrons were laughing and drinking and sitting elbow to elbow at the dark, polished tables. Smoke and the nauseating scent of frying pork clogged the air. Colin found a chair and stared desperately out the window, where green hills dotted with sheep rolled away to the horizon.

He fisted his hands beneath the table. *Come back, Ariadne. We have to get out of here, now.*

Meg set a plate and a pot of tea before him. He shook his head and waved them away. "No, no. Ale. Strong, dark, with plenty of bite to it. Ale."

"Mr. Lord, are you quite all right?"

He raked his fingers down his face. "I'm fine. Bad night. Didn't sleep well. Take this away, please, I can't eat it."

"But it's fresh bacon, surely—"

"For God's sake, woman, take it away and bring me a plate of eggs and toast instead!"

Forgetting the teapot, she hurried off, leaving him to sit there in his soaked clothes. By the time she returned Colin had gotten his composure under control once again. He guzzled the ale, shoveled the eggs into his mouth, and sopped up the yolks with the toast. Something touched his feet and he looked down to see the tortoiseshell cat slamming its torso against his ankles and purring in high delight.

He waited until Meg's back was turned, then scooped up a bit of egg yolk on his finger, put his hand beneath the table, and let the affectionate feline lick it off.

The door opened, and Ariadne walked in.

He grabbed her sleeve as she approached, hauling her so close that her startled face was mere inches from his. "Where the hell have you been?!" he demanded, beneath his breath. "We can't stay here, not now—"

She stared at him, properly affronted. Then, with that casual, haughty elegance she could command at the bat of an eye, she shook him off, moved around the table, and sat down across from him, her eyes sparkling with humor and the love of what surely, to her, must be the ultimate adventure. "Really, *Doctor*, do you think I did not know?

They were banging that notice onto the door at an hour unfit, even, for the roosters. Made enough racket to wake the dead. Now where's that foolish maid? I could go for some tea and toast."

He glanced over his shoulder then leaned forward, hoping no one had recognized her. "Ariadne, keep your cap on and your head down. Don't meet anyone's eyes. Just sit there, don't say a bloody *word*, and for God's sake, keep your coat closed!"

"Really, Colin, I have no plausible reason to open it."

"Damn it, it's not funny!"

"No, the situation is not." She reached over and touched his nose. "But your concern is." Grinning, she picked up his cup and angled her head toward the untouched pot of tea.

Rolling his eyes, Colin picked up the pot and filled the cup with the steeped brew, keenly aware of her eyes on his face.

She grinned and lifted her hand in an imperious motion for Meg to bring her some toast. "I have been on the run for several days now. I have seen these notices all over London. I expect to see them all the way to Norfolk, and I'm certain with increasing frequency." She smiled sweetly, and leaned back as Meg set toast, butter and a pot of marmalade before her. "But I know, the shock of seeing one for the first time is rather distressing, is it not? By the way—"

She reached into her pocket, and grinning, came up with his spectacles. "Look what I found in the hay this morning."

The memories came flooding back.

"Sleep well, Dr. Lord?"

So, they were back to *this* again. She, virginal and frightened by night, bold and flirtatious by day. He couldn't keep up with her, let alone understand her. Grinning helplessly, Colin propped his jaw on the heel of his hand and let his gaze bore into hers.

She giggled beneath his twinkle-eyed scrutiny and toasted him with her teacup. "I've never put a man out before," she said, watching him from over the rim. "I say, I must have the magic touch!"

"Lady Ariadne—"

She didn't let up. "I watched you sleep, you know."

He tried to scowl, but she merely giggled.

"You made a charming sight. I hope you don't mind. But it was rather fascinating, watching you. I mean, I've never watched a man sleep before."

He abandoned his attempt at intimidation and instead picked up a piece of toast and buttered it for her. "Let me guess," he said wryly, "*I'm* the one who drools. Who talks in his sleep."

She laughed, opened his glasses, and leaning over the table, slid them onto his nose. "To be honest, good Doctor, I really didn't notice. And if I did, I am not so sure I would embarrass you by telling you."

"Marmalade?"

"Yes, please. And lots of it, if you don't mind."

He spread the jelly thickly over the toast then handed it to her. Still grinning at him, she took a bite out of it, crunching happily and studying him pertly from across the table. She was the only person he'd ever met who could reduce his composure to pudding; not even his admiral, not even *Nelson* had been able to shake him. But this girl—this playful, saucy, flirtatious little noblewoman—she could reduce him to a bucket of guts without even trying, just by paying him too much attention in all the right places.

Wishing he could ignore her, knowing he could not, he picked up his mug and brought it to his lips.

"You're a very handsome man, you know."

He looked up, glaring at her through his spectacles.

"Oh, *Colin*, you are so refreshing after the pampered blades of London! So artless, and totally unaware of yourself . . . really, it's a pity that you're not of the Quality, and that I didn't meet you before Papa promised me to Maxwell, because you really are a lot of fun and I quite enjoy your company. You know, I might even keep you on as my personal veterinarian after I get married. I'd pay you well, Colin, I swear I would, and I just *know* that Maxwell won't mind!"

"How was your ride?" he said tightly, trying to change the subject.

"My ride?"

"Yes, your ride. Meg told me you took Shareb-er-rehh out for a gallop."

She grinned and stretched her hands over her head, totally oblivious to the pain she had just caused him with that single word—*Maxwell*—totally unaware of the charming sight she made in her shirt, cap, and breeches. "Ah, it was exhilarating! Shareb-er-rehh is all set to go, happy as a lark this morn because I gave him some pastr—I mean, breakfast and now the sun is starting to break through the clouds, and you know something, Dr. Lord, I think it's going to be a positively *grand* day!"

Just then, a terrified, inhuman scream split the air.

Colin bolted to his feet, nearly upsetting the table, his face draining of blood.

"Lud, what on *earth* was that?" Ariadne gasped, clapping a hand to her chest.

But Colin threw down his napkin and, heedless of the angry protests, shoved his way through a group of milling patrons in his haste to reach the door. As he charged outside, the other diners rose to their feet, their chairs scraping and silverware hitting their plates.

"What is it?"

"Dunno. Something going on outside!"

"Cor, what a bloody awful sound—"

Ariadne ran to the door to see what the commotion was all about, but the other patrons were there before her. Again that chilling scream rent the air, deep and raw and awful. She felt the hair rise on her nape and her blood running cold as she shoved her way through the crowd and halted in her tracks on the doorstep just outside.

Her hand went to her mouth in horror.

In the space of a moment, she saw it all. An old, broken-down bay horse, harnessed to a cart and screaming in terror as a man beat it about the ears with a stick and another man, holding a bucket and some sort of knife, tried to get close to its neck.

And the veterinarian. *Her* veterinarian, striding angrily down the lawn toward the frightened animal, his fists clenched and his back stiff with rage.

"Colin!" she cried. Then, she broke from the crowd and raced headlong across the lawn after him. "*Colin!*"

He never stopped, his angry, hitching stride carrying him toward the horse at a speed she would never have thought him capable of attaining. Breathless, she caught up to him and grabbed his arm. His jaw was set, his eyes hard and furious behind his glasses.

"Colin, you can't just *interfere*—"

He shook her off, shoving his way through the small group that surrounded the horse until he reached its head.

"Excuse me," he ground out, with tightly suppressed fury, "but may I please offer a bit of advice here?"

He caught the gelding's bridle, and Ariadne saw the poor, suffering animal turn its face against his chest in grateful relief.

"Who the hell are you and what do you think you're doing, you blighty bugger?" the farrier cried, raising the scalpel as Colin came between him and the horse. "Get out of here and mind your own business; I've got work to do!"

Cradling the gelding's head in the curve of his arm, Colin turned blazing eyes on the farrier. "There is no need to practice phlebotomy on a horse with the mere complaint of harness sores. Take your damned scalpel and bucket and get away from him."

People came running from the inn to surround the horse. An awed murmur rippled through the crowd like lightning through thunderclouds.

"Who the hell are *you*?" the farrier persisted.

Filled with pride and admiration, Ariadne stepped forward. "He is Colin Lord, London veterinarian, and if says the horse doesn't need to be bled, he doesn't!"

"Well, *I* say he does, and I damn well ought to know!"

"He does *not* need to be bled! No animal does!" Shielding the gelding's face from the enraged farrier, the veterinarian turned beseeching eyes upon the horse's shocked owner. His voice was shaking, unsteady with rage. "Look, mister—please. Let me treat him. For God's sake, I won't charge you a damned penny—"

The farrier flung his bucket down in the mud. "You questioning my skills? You think I don't know what I'm doing? Who the hell do you think you are, to just come in here and tell me how to do my job? Huh? You tell me, you bastard!"

The crowd stirred uneasily, anticipating a fight.

"*Tell me!*"

"He's going to hit him," whispered the reedy, gog-eyed man beside Ariadne, jerking his head toward the farrier. "You can't push John Beckett too far, I tell you!"

"Nah, he won't hit a lad with glasses," another hissed back.

"Ye want to make a bet? Glasses or no, I've seen John take out far stouter men than that one. My money's on Beckett."

"And *mine's* on the veterinarian!" Ariadne cried. "Don't let him hurt that poor horse, *Doctor* Lord! You hear me? *Don't let him!*"

Her shrill cry sent the farrier over the edge. Scalpel raised, he went for the gelding's jugular, and from her close vantage point, Ariadne saw it all.

The perfectly cool expression on the doctor's face. The absence of hesitation as he stepped protectively in front of the gelding. The quick, upward flash of his fist.

And the farrier, crumpling to the wet gravel, his nose spraying a fan of blood.

Colin stepped back, pushing the spectacles up the bridge of his nose and shouldering the horse away with him.

"Huzzah for you, *Colin!*" Ariadne shouted, caught up in the moment and jumping up and down as the crowd went wild around her. "Give the blackguard what he deserves!"

The farrier stumbled to his feet, one hand covering his bleeding nose, his eyes red with rage. "You hit me!" he roared, flinging down the scalpel. "Damn yer eyes, ye bloody hit me!"

"Yes, and I'll do so again if you so much as come near this animal with that scalpel." Still holding the gelding, Colin turned to the shocked owner. "Sir, please. I'll buy the beast from you. How much do you want for him?"

"Well, I—"

"Twenty pounds? Thirty?"

"You bloody HIT me!"

The farrier hurled himself at Colin and in the space of a heartbeat Ariadne saw her veterinarian draw a breath, glance heavenward in a plea for divine patience, and then whirl to drive his fist into the farrier's jaw with such force that the man's head rocked back, his knees buckled, and he fell sprawling on his back in a fresh pile of dung.

And this time, he did not get up.

The crowd, shocked, went dead silent as Colin turned calm, patient eyes upon the horse's owner. "Sir? You were saying?"

"T-t-twenty pounds," the man stammered, backing away. "Twenty pounds and he's yours."

The veterinarian smiled. "Done."

Chapter 10

Shareb-er-rehh soon found that being tied to the chaise and neglected while the decrepit old nag that now pulled it got all the attention was far less tolerable than the degradation he had suffered in his previous role as carriage horse. Jealous and bored, he plodded along beside the chaise's right wheel, his ears back, his eye on the man who sat beside Lady A.

He didn't like the way the man's admiring gaze was constantly on Her Ladyship, didn't like all the attention he paid to the new horse, didn't like the way he teased Lady A when she became a bit stuffy. And now, instead of reprimanding him for his impertinence as she had done earlier, she laughed right along with him. The blackguard. Just who did he think he was, coming along and stealing *his* human?

Her hero-worship for the blighter was worse than ever, thanks to that little scene in the stable yard. And his regard for *her* was growing by leaps and bounds.

Something had to be done.

Letting the chaise get slightly ahead, Shareb stretched out his head toward the man's shoulder, pulled his lips back—and saw two mares approaching at a fast trot.

He had his priorities. Quickly pulling back, he flung up his tail, snorted, and began to prance, putting on a show guaranteed to turn their pretty heads.

Sure enough, they noticed him.

They were lovely, matched chestnuts with white accents, and the near one had a look in her eye that was lustily inviting.

What he wouldn't give to nibble on *her* mane. . . .

He was magnificent and he knew it. Angling his body so that they could view his masculine splendor, arching his neck and his tail, prancing in place and calling softly to them, he never noticed that the old nag pulling the chaise had stopped to relieve himself.

And when the chaise stopped, Shareb-er-rehh's proud chest smashed painfully into the wheel.

He squealed in humiliation and the mares passed, laughing amongst themselves.

"Oh, Shareb!" Lady A turned in the seat, her heart in her eyes and her arms outstretched. "Are you all right, sweetie? Oh, Shareb, *baby*—"

Trembling, he went to her, burying his head against her chest as the sweat broke out along his neck.

"Nothing but injured pride, my lady," the man said dryly. "He's fine."

"Yes, but if you hadn't bought that stupid nag, it would not have happened!"

"If I hadn't bought *Thunder*, your disguise, and that of your stallion's, would become curiously suspect, not to mention, useless. The authorities, indeed, every money-hungry reward hunter from here to Norfolk, are on the lookout for a bay horse and a young, flame-haired woman. Thunder is a necessary complication to your ruse."

She kissed Shareb's nose and said indignantly, "I fail to see how."

"No one is going to be looking for *two* bay horses, similar in size and color—"

"*Dr.* Lord, how can you even *compare* that ugly old thing with my magnificently beautiful Shareb? They are night and day! The only saving grace about that nag is that he obviously *enjoys* the demeaning role of carriage horse. Thus, it frees Shareb from the task, and has allowed me to put the hood and blinkers back on his head."

"So stop complaining."

"I'm not."

"You are."

"Dr. Lord, sometimes you are too uppity for your own good. Acting better than you are. Such behavior is highly inappropriate."

"And how would you like me to behave?" he asked, raising a brow and secretly wondering if now would be the right time to tell her about his own fine *pedigree.*

"Appropriately."

"And what is appropriate?"

She sniffed. "Suitably subservient."

"Yes, Your Highness."

"Don't get smart."

"Of course not, Your Highness."

She laughed and playfully swatted him with her cap. Then she coaxed Bow into her lap, and as he, grinning, urged Thunder on once more, she leaned back in her seat to watch him.

She was studying him with admiring, worshipful eyes—just as she'd been doing since he'd stepped in and rescued Thunder from the farrier. It was unnerving. Disconcerting. Bloody hell, how was he going to endure this? He looked away, pretending indifference, but out of the corner of his eye he saw her still watching him from beneath her cap. He could see her red locks, her pouty mouth, the bored, restless look in her eye.

She sighed.

He didn't say anything.

She began kicking her foot against the bottom of the chaise.

"Would you like to drive?" he asked, trying to think of something to amuse her.

"No." She sighed again. "I would not like to drive. I would like to talk about . . . last night."

"That's unfortunate, because I do not."

"Don't be a prude, Colin. It's not as though anything *happened*."

She drew her legs up, turned on the seat, and then startled him by lying back until her shoulders were against his thigh, her head in his lap.

Colin went stiff.

"My lady, *this* is not appropriate," he said, his light humor vanishing.

"What, do you mind so very much?"

"It's not that I mind, but—"

"Then what is the trouble?"

"You're betrothed."

"Yes, but I'm not doing anything wrong. Besides, I am most comfortable, you're a very handsome man, and I enjoy looking at you."

"You *shouldn't* enjoy looking at me; you belong to somebody else."

"Not yet. Until I'm married I may look at anyone I please. And right now, I find it immensely pleasing to look at *you*. It's unfortunate that you don't like to look at *me*."

"What makes you think I don't?"

"It's obvious."

"So, I behave within the confines of propriety. There is nothing contemptible about that."

"No, but how utterly *boring*. So, good Doctor, are you saying you do or don't like to look at me?"

"I'm not answering that."

"Well, do you or don't you?"

"I . . . do."

"Would you like to look at me now?"

"No. I'm busy."

"No you're not, you're afraid of me. I intimidate you, don't I? Admit you're afraid of me, Colin."

"I'm not afraid of you."

"All right then, admit that you're attracted to me."

She was looking up at the underside of his chin, and thus, saw the slow grin he was helpless to prevent. "I'll admit no such thing."

"Well, are you?"

"Am I what?"

"Attracted to me."

"Any attraction I feel for you is a useless emotion."

"So. That doesn't mean you cannot have it. Are you attracted to me, Colin?"

He set his jaw.

"Come now." She reached up and tickled the underside of his stubbled chin. "*Are* you?"

"What do you want me to say?"

"I want you to say that you are, of course."

"All right then, yes, I'm attracted to you."

"Would you like to *touch* me?"

"Ariadne, this conversation is doing neither of us any good—"

"That's not what I asked." Smiling, she reached up, pried the rein from his left hand, transferred it to his right, and tried to bring his fist down to her lips. He fought her, jerking his hand free with a muttered curse. She laughed and caught it once more.

"Stop it!" he commanded, growing angry.

"But Colin, Doctor, dear, sweet, *Doctor*, I am only playing."

"I damn well don't consider it play!"

"I do."

"I *don't*. Now get up, and act like a lady."

Ariadne understood his anger, knew it was born out of fear of, and resistance to, what he felt for her. He was not the first man she'd gone about trying to bedevil to distraction, but he was certainly one of the few who could hold out so long against her flirtatious teasing, and the more he resisted, the more she was determined to get to him. Her skittishness in the stable last night was now just a dim memory and, in the full light of day, seemed quite ridiculous and unfounded. Colin Lord was harmless. Besides, if he had any plans of compromising her, he would have done so last night.

No, there was no harm in teasing him. The man needed to learn to have some fun!

"Dr. Lord, I cannot act like a lady when I am masquerading as a man."

"Yes, well if you were serious about your *masquerade*, you wouldn't be lying there with your head in my lap!"

"I *want* to lie here with my head in your lap, and look up at your face, silhouetted against the blue sky and clouds, and watch the sunlight dry your hair."

"I suppose you get everything you want."

Ariadne looked up at him, her handsome, strong hero, savior of animals and defender of their rights, the man she had gazed upon long into the night, the man who filled her head with wicked thoughts of kissing and touching and, well, other things a lady should not be thinking about, the man who could make her skin tingle and her heart race with just one glance from his oddly beautiful eyes.

Wicked, wicked, Ariadne. She wanted him to touch her. Wanted him to kiss her. Wanted . . .

She sighed in despair. "No," she said, softly,

reaching up to run her finger along the underside of his jaw. "I *don't* always get everything I want."

He kept his gaze straight ahead. "Do you want this marriage to Maxwell?"

She didn't answer, merely gazing up at him with sad, suddenly wistful eyes as she traced the bottom of his jawbone. The skin was rough, stubbly, the tiny bristles picking up the glare of the sun.

"Do you?" he repeated, his voice tight.

"I ... well ... well, yes, of course I do. Why wouldn't I?"

She saw his lashes fall as his eyes closed, briefly. "I don't know. It's just that as your *friend*, I thought it my duty to warn you that marriage is not a commitment to be entered into lightly."

"No. Indeed, it is not. But I am an heiress, and my father promised me to Maxwell. My life is pre-ordained. I have to marry him. It's what he wanted."

"Yes, but is it what *you* want?"

He bent his head and turned his clear, lavender eyes on her, and the look of raw longing and desire she saw there went straight to her heart. The color faded from her face, and she suddenly felt confused, afraid, trapped. Of course she wanted to marry Maxwell! There had never been any question about *that*.

Yet why, suddenly, did the thought fill her with a strange anxiety, a doubt that she didn't understand? Why did it make her feel helpless, unhappy, and trapped?

"All brides get cold feet," she snapped, unable to look him in the eye. "I suspect it's quite normal."

He looked back up, a shadow darkening his beautiful eyes and anger tightening his jaw. She sensed him mentally withdrawing from her, pulling within himself, and, as it had last night, the feeling left her scared and lonely. She didn't like it, and reaching up to take his hand, pulled it down until his tight fist rested against her lips.

"Colin?"

"What?"

"Did I say something wrong?"

"No."

"You're being short with me. I hate when you become aloof and distant."

He did not respond.

"Your eyes are just as beautiful when you're angry, you know."

"Stop it, Ariadne."

"No, I won't stop it. Unless you give me just a *tiny* smile."

"I said, *stop it*."

"A teeny, tiny smile. . . . Come on, Doctor! Show me that crooked grin."

Again he didn't respond, only looked away with eyes full of pain.

Ariadne sighed, wishing she knew what she'd done to make him retreat into himself so. "You know how a moment ago, we were talking about things we want. . . ."

"Yes."

"And how I told you it was so fascinating watching you sleep—"

He bent his brow to his hand.

She moved her lips against his clenched fist, intently watching his increasingly distressed expression. "Well . . . can I put you to sleep again tonight?"

"No."

"Why not?"

"Because I suspect that sleep is something I will find quite damnably elusive."

"Because of me?"

He didn't answer.

"Because of me, Colin?"

"Yes."

"How about if you put *me* to sleep, then?"

"Equally dangerous."

"Why?"

"I don't think we should be sleeping near each other. Last night proved that."

"Well, we can't very well sleep apart. You're supposed to be protecting us. So therefore we have to sleep near each other, don't you think?"

He sighed. "My lady, let us cross that bridge when we come to it."

"I wish we would come to it now, because I very much enjoyed sleeping together last night. I felt so . . . so *safe*, Colin. As though nothing could ever happen to me as long as you were near."

"We weren't *sleeping together*."

"Well, we were sleeping *next* to each other."

"And don't let appearances deceive you," he added. "I'll do my best to protect you and Shareb, but I am not infallible."

"Oh, Colin, stop being so self-deprecating. I saw the way you laid that farrier out cold. You were magnificent, wonderful! And you fight dreadfully well for a healing man. Did you learn how to do *that* in the War, too?"

"You might say that."

"Did you get in fights very often?"

"Often enough."

"Fistfights?"

"No."

"What kind, then?"

"I'd rather not talk about it."

"Why not?"

"Ariadne, *please*."

"Well, I cannot imagine what the big secret is. . . ."

"Yes, and it's better that you don't. I find it painful to discuss. Talk about the weather if you like, ask me questions about my career as a veterinarian, but do not query me about my past."

His hard tone forbade further prying. What was the big mystery? What had happened to him that was so painful he refused to discuss it? Ariadne sighed, her gaze playing over every curve of his face. His eyes were distant, dark with remembered anguish, and she had a sudden, unexplainable urge to take him in her arms and comfort him. Instead, she reached up, played with the hair that fell over his brow, ran her finger playfully down the indentation of his temple.

"Colin?"

"What?"

"Can I tell *you* a secret, then?"

Her conspiratorial tone raised a reluctant smile from him. "I suppose you will whether I wish you to or not."

Her eyes were dancing. "I kissed you good-night last night, you know."

He sighed and kept his gaze between Thunder's ears, but his grin was spreading.

"Did you know that?" she asked, still touching his face. "That I kissed you?"

"I was not aware of it."

"How do you feel about my telling you, now?"

"Embarrassed."

"Why?"

"Because."

"You've never been with a woman before, have you, Dr. Lord?"

He went stiff, and the color fled his face. "That is *not* a subject a young lady of high birth and breeding should be discussing!"

She grinned, her eyes sparkling. "You haven't, have you?"

"None of your business."

"Come now, Colin, you can tell *me*. . . ."

"I said, it's none of your business."

"How many women? Two? Three?"

"Ariadne—"

"Five?"

"Several."

"Did you bed them?"

"Bloody *hell*, Ariadne!"

"Well, did you?"

"Yes, damn it, I bedded them, what do you think I am, a bloody monk?"

Giggling at his embarrassment, she unfolded his hand and traced his palm with her fingernail. His body jerked beneath her, and his lap felt suddenly hard and stiff against the back of her head. She felt an answering surge of heat deep between her legs, and a shortness of breath that was altogether frightening.

Intriguing.

"Colin?"

"Don't ask me any more questions," he said hoarsely. "Please, no more bloody questions."

"One. Just one."

"No."

"One!"

"*No!*"

Still holding his hand, she dragged her thumb across his palm, finding it hot and damp, and loving its warmth, strength and texture. His were strong hands. Healing hands. She saw the tenseness coming into his jaw and guessed that the blood was rushing through his body, just as it was with hers.

"Here goes. Here's my question. Ready?"

He dropped his brow to his hand and shook his head.

"Last night," she said, watching his face, "I kissed you. That is no big secret, because I already told you. But Colin, I—I have a confession to make.

Maybe it started when I first saw you, down on your knees on the cobblestones and saving that poor dog. Certainly, it has grown stronger, this fondness I have for you, with every kind thing that you do, with every witty thing that you say, with . . . well, with just *being* around you. And I know I'm not supposed to want this when I'm engaged to be married to my dear Maxwell, but since I have yet to speak my vows I see no harm in it—"

"Ariadne, *what* is your point?"

She smiled, suddenly nervous, but knowing it was too late to back down. "I want you to kiss me."

"You want me to kiss you."

"Yes, that is what I said."

She could feel the tension flowing into his body, could feel that stiff, masculine part of him growing rock-hard beneath the back of her head. She wondered what it looked like, that wicked, manly thing that was only to be seen by blushing brides and *un*blushing prostitutes. She pushed her head down against it, and he clenched his teeth on a moan of pain.

"Colin?"

He was breathing hard, his eyes bleak, angry and helpless.

"Colin, stop the chaise."

He ignored her and urged Thunder on faster. Behind them, Shareb-er-rehh broke into a trot to keep up.

"Colin, *stop* the chaise. That's an order."

She lifted her hand and grabbed the reins, pulling back on them. The old horse faltered and came to a halt.

"For God's sake," the veterinarian said, and, releasing the reins, bent his forehead to his hand. "Must you do this to me? Must you torment and tease me and put me in a state of—"

"All I want is a kiss. A simple, harmless, ki—"

He looked at her then, turning such a look of pure fury and desire on her that she wanted to melt right down into the floorboards of the chaise to escape the force of it. She had pushed him too far.

And now, he was going to teach her a lesson.

"A simple, *harmless*, kiss," he murmured with dangerous softness, and she felt her flirtatious grin freezing to her mouth, her heart beginning to beat a panicked tattoo within her breast. Wide-eyed and unable to move, she watched his head lowering to hers and blocking out the sky above, felt one arm going behind her neck and lifting her face up to his, the other hand pulling free of her suddenly boneless grip and drifting up to caress the hot skin of her throat, to pull at the closure of her shirt, with an intent that was all too obvious.

Ariadne began to panic.

"I'm sorry, Colin, I was just t-teasing—"

"I've had it with your teasing, Ariadne. One of these days you're going to push somebody too far. It's about time you learned that kissing can be about as *harmless* as setting a spark to gunpowder!"

And then, before she could protest, cry out, or even raise her hand to slap him, his mouth came down hard upon hers, forcing her head down and back against his rock-hard thigh. His tongue thrust between her lips and plunged into her mouth, one hand anchoring her head by the jaw, the other moving alarmingly toward her breast. Whimpering in fear and rage, she tried to pull away, backward, sideways, anywhere, but there was nowhere to escape. His tongue invaded deeper. She couldn't breathe. She opened her eyes, saw only his brow and his eyes and his hair. His hand—warm, coarsely textured, skillful—slid beneath her shirt and found one breast, the calluses of the palm grazing the sensitive nipple, his fingers tweaking, squeezing, stroking until she felt the rage and fear beginning to melt into need and desire, until dampness began to flood the hot junction of her legs, until her world began to spin and pulse and go dark around the edges.

And then, with no warning, he released her and left her reeling.

Shaken, Ariadne fell back against his thigh, the breath whooshing into her lungs as she stared dazedly up at him. One hand fluttered weakly at her breast, trying to calm her pounding heart.

"C-Colin?"

He impaled her with a glare that was hot, dark, and full of warning. "That is just a *taste* of what happens when you push a man too far!" he said hoarsely, snatching up the reins. "You wish to taunt and tease me? Well, keep at it, then, but I'll not answer for the consequences. Do you understand me, Ariadne?" He leaned threateningly down, eyes blazing, his breath hot against her cheek. "*Do you?*"

"Yes," she breathed, staring fixedly at his mouth and touching her fingers to her lips. "I . . . understand."

"Good," he muttered, turning away and willing the fire in his blood to die down.

"But I wonder if you could, before we set out, kiss me one more time, Colin? Just to . . . be *sure* that I've learned my lesson?"

She reached up to touch his cheek—and in that moment Colin knew that his attempt to scare her into leaving him alone had recoiled like a gun slamming inward on its tackles. Angrily thrusting her hand away, he leapt from the chaise and hauled Shareb's tack out from beneath the seat, bridling the stallion and all but flinging the saddle onto his back before tightening the girth with such quick, sharp, movements that the angry horse swung fiercely around and struck him, hard, with his teeth.

He gasped and, grimacing, clasped a hand to the shoulder, shutting his eyes in pain.

"Colin!" she cried, leaping out of the chaise.

"Stay in the chaise," he said hoarsely, breathing hard and leaning his brow into the curve of his arm. "Just stay in the bloody chaise, don't move, and in God's name, don't *ever* ask me to kiss you again."

Chapter 11

⌒⟋ᷜᷜ⟍⌒

Ariadne came to her senses just as the veterinarian swung stiffly aboard Shareb-er-rehh.

"Colin, *don't!*"

Too late.

With a shrill cry, the stallion exploded up and outward, his body twisting, writhing, and coming five feet off the ground before his back heels kicked out in a savage, jarring thrust that sent the animal doctor halfway over his neck.

"Shareb!" she screamed, racing forward.

The stallion hit the earth and reared straight up on his hind legs, higher, higher—

"*Shareb!*"

—and began to go over backward.

Horrified, Ariadne saw it all. Colin, falling from the horse, rolling out of the way a split second before Shareb's big body crashed down into the dirt, and Shareb—landing on his back, his legs flailing, his frightened squeals piercing the air, before he lunged to his feet and stood there, shaking and trembling and blowing hard through his nose.

Ariadne loved her horse—but it was the veterinarian that she ran to.

"Colin! Colin, are you hurt?"

He was lying on his back in the road, his lips parted, his eyes staring up at the stallion. His face was pure white.

"*Colin!*"

As she fell to her knees in the dirt beside him, he moved his head and looked dazedly up at her. "I . . . guess that was a bad idea."

She burst into tears, cradled his face in her hands, and buried her forehead in the warm curve of his neck. "For God's sake, he nearly crushed you, you could've been killed, don't you know he has never been ridden by anyone but me, will not tolerate another soul on his back, for heaven's sake, Colin, *he could've killed you!*"

"Kind of you to warn me beforehand," he drawled, pushing himself up on one elbow. She thrust out her hand to help him up, but he merely glared at it, then at her. "If you don't mind?"

Ignoring her hand, he got painfully to his feet. Then he brushed the dust from his clothes and, turning his back on her, limped toward the stallion, leaving Ariadne with her hand still outstretched and her face going crimson with shame and embarrassment.

Shareb saw him coming and shied away, his eyes wild, angry, frightened.

"Easy, there. Easy. . . ."

Colin put a hand out to the shuddering beast. Again, Shareb bolted, but not before he managed to snare one rein. The stallion reared high once more, legs pawing the air, hooves flashing dangerously close to his head. Colin jerked down, hard, and Shareb plunged to the earth, shied, and nearly tore the bit out of his mouth.

"*Easy!*" he repeated, firmly, and laid his scraped palm against the animal's hot, lathered, neck.

Instantly, the horse quieted. His head drooped, his sides heaved, and he stood there, trembling and shuddering and refusing to look at the man who held him.

Colin heard Ariadne coming softly up behind him. She wouldn't look at him either, but merely patted her horse, her dusty face streaked with tears and her skin a bright pink. "He's embarrassed," she interpreted, meekly. "He's sorry."

He, or you? Colin wondered.

Shareb lifted one front leg in agreement.

"Yes, he looks very contrite," Colin snapped, his voice cold and angry. He was still shaking inside. Keeping his hand on the horse's glistening hide, he passed the reins to his tiny employer. "Hold his head while I make sure he didn't injure himself."

"But what about you?"

"Just hold him."

Her throat tight, Ariadne took the reins and watched quietly as he stroked the stallion's neck a few more times to steady him. Guilt and shame filled her. The fall had hurt the animal doctor; she could see that in the tightness around his mouth and the way he was dragging his leg, but he was too concerned about the horse to worry about his own injuries. She bent her head, and kicked at a stone poking out of the dirt. She should never have asked him to kiss her, should never have tried to satisfy her own curiosity and wicked longings, should never have flirted so shamelessly nor pushed him as far as she had. She glanced up, watching him, her eyes remorseful as he ran gentle hands down Shareb's fine legs, limped painfully to the stallion's far side, and repeated the process there.

"Colin, are you hurt?"

He was kneeling down, inspecting Shareb's up-lifted foot. "I'm fine. Though I daresay your saddle didn't fare as well."

"I don't care about the saddle. I care about *you*."

He didn't look up, though she saw a muscle ticking in his jaw as he carefully examined the stallion's foot. He was vexed with her. Not just vexed, but furious.

He stood, raked his hair back over his brow, and, laying a calming hand on the stallion's throat, gazed levelly, angrily, into her eyes.

"You shouldn't care about me, Ariadne. You shouldn't care a damned bit about me, because you and I are on different paths and the two of them shall never mesh."

"I care about you as a *friend*."

"Be that as it may, your behavior transcends *friendship*."

"But it is totally harmless—"

"You *think* it's harmless. You think it's flirtatious and funny that you have my desire at your mercy, and my insides so twisted up I don't know if I'm coming or going. You know I'm attracted to you, but I dislike your little game. You may think it amusing, my lady, but you are not the one having to suffer the pains of deprivation, you are not the one being teased and tempted, you are not the one who has to exert all the will in your body not to do something you'll later regret."

"Colin!"

"Now get in the chaise, and I don't want to hear another word about it."

"How dare you talk to me like that!"

"Get in the damned chaise!"

She jerked her chin up and glared at him, her embarrassment at having been put in her place offset by anger that he dared exhibit such impertinence and disrespect.

Her face hot with shame, she glanced away— and at the side of the road, saw a flock of sheep lining the perimeter of a stone fence, gazing at the animal doctor's back with wide-eyed, ovine adoration.

She stared in astonishment.

The veterinarian turned his head to follow her gaze. The animals pressed themselves against the fence as though trying to get closer to him. One let out a soft bleat, then another, and then the rest of the flock followed suit, until the whole group was bleating and baaing.

"Colin?"

He was still gazing at the sheep, beginning to smile a little.

"*Colin!*"

He turned then, shook his head as though to clear it, and looked away. Ariadne stared at him. Again, she sensed the eerie pull that animals felt toward this gentle man, and had a sudden, strange feeling of standing on the fringe of a circle she could never be a part of. Again, she saw him falling from Shareb's back, and the thought of him lying dead, his neck broken, his body crushed, sent a shaft of icy terror and grief straight through her heart. Impertinence aside, he was becoming very dear to her, this man. If anything had happened to him . . .

Swallowing her injured pride, she reached up with both hands, smoothed his hair back from his temples, and thumbed away a smudge of dirt from his cheek.

"You're hurt, aren't you?"

His eyes suddenly desperate, he caught her wrists in his hands and took a step backward. "Don't touch me, Ariadne. *Please.*"

"But you're hurt."

"I'm fine."

"No, I saw Shareb get your shoulder when he bit you. Let me see it."

"I said, I'm *fine.*"

"Colin, for heaven's sake, I only wish to see what Shareb did to you. After all, I've paid good money for you and am merely protecting my investment."

"Ah, so now I'm an investment."

His tone was light, but she sensed the tension in it, and the struggle he was waging within himself to deny her. And still, he was holding her at arm's length, his eyes warning her away, his strength preventing her from stepping any closer.

Ariadne got the message. With a sigh, she pulled her hands from his, her heart hurting.

"I'm sorry, Colin. You have asked me not to touch you, and so I shall not." Trying to regain some of her dignity, she turned her head so she wouldn't have to look into those beautiful, lavender eyes. "You must think me a terrible hussy."

"No, Ariadne. The curiosity of youth can be forgiven. It is the weakness of those of us who are old enough to know better that cannot be."

Guilt and shame prevented her from meeting his gaze. "No, you are wrong. You are a gentleman, trying to ease my distress, but you are wrong, Colin. I should not have asked you to kiss me. You are a man and men are weak and unable to help themselves. Besides, you're a commoner, beneath me. If anyone were to find out we kissed, I would be ruined. I deserved to be set in my place and I thank you for doing so."

She raised her chin, trying to command hauteur and failing miserably. Her hands were trembling, her nerves quaking, and she had the awful feeling that he could look into her eyes and read every one of her wicked, wanton thoughts. She looked down, pretending a sudden interest in the fabric of her sleeve. "I suppose I shall go straight to Hades for admitting this, but I think I feel drawn to you just like these animals. That's all it is, isn't it? Animal attraction. Nothing more. I am helpless against it. Just like Shareb, just like Thunder, just like"—she gave a little laugh and jerked her head to indicate the flock of sheep—"like those stupid beasts over there."

She set her jaw to keep her mouth from trembling and toyed with a thread on her sleeve, feeling his heavy gaze upon her. A long moment passed. At last, she heard him clear his throat and then his warm hand tentatively grasped hers. "Ariadne."

She swallowed, hard. "What?"

"There is nothing to forgive."

She turned, and looked up at him. Her heart ached with guilt, with want of touching him, holding him, and yes, kissing him. But she could not tell him that, could never tell him that. Instead, she reached up and hesitantly touched his hair, his beautiful, silky, shining, hair. "Oh, Colin . . . I—well, I know you don't think you're an attractive man, but . . . but you are, and maybe some of the things I've done have been because I could not help myself. I did not do them out of a devious wish to torment and tease you."

"I know."

"Do you?"

"Of course. You're . . . young. But no good can come of it, Ariadne. You said it yourself. We are as alike as"—he grinned, more charming than he had a right to be, more handsome than she remembered Maxwell as being, and she felt her chest constrict with a raw, unfulfilled ache that twisted her heart like a dishrag—"the digestive systems of the dog and horse."

"Oh, Colin. . . ."

With a forgiving little smile he held out his arms, and she went into them, their hard, gentle strength pressing her close to his heart. She shut her eyes over a film of tears, the clean scent of his shirt and skin filling her nostrils, his heartbeat thudding beneath her cheek. *I don't want Maxwell,* she thought, desperately. *Dear God help me, but I want you.*

But that was impossible, and as she sensed the stiffness in his stance, she realized she'd stayed within his embrace a second longer than what either of them might have considered proper.

"Your shoulder," she said, shakily, pulling back and pushing a stray lock of hair out of her eyes. "I'm sorry, I hope I didn't just hurt you—"

He grinned, trying to lessen the awkwardness of the moment. "Not that you could. That fool horse of yours, on the other hand ..."

"I think you should let me look at it. I feel horribly guilty—I mean, if it weren't for me, Shareb would never have bitten you."

"Shareb has been itching for an excuse to bite me since we first met. Don't blame yourself."

"Let me look at it. If only to satisfy my own conscience."

He frowned, but her hands were already at the closure of his shirt. She tilted her head back and looked up at him. "Please, Colin?"

He shrugged in answer and looked away.

With trembling fingers, she undid the top buttons of his shirt. She drew it down and off his shoulder, her hands tender, gentle, shaking, barely grazing his skin as they moved over his collarbone and to the bruised area.

He shut his eyes and drew a ragged breath, and beside them, Shareb twisted his neck and watched.

"He says he's sorry," Ariadne said quickly, trying to take their attention off what she was doing.

"Does he, now?"

"Yes. He says he's not *happy* about having to apologize, but since you did not punish him for trying to kill you, he thinks he should act with reciprocal gentlemanly behavior."

Colin looked at the stallion.

Shareb bared his teeth.

"How magnanimous of him."

"Yes, I rather thought so, myself."

"And what does Thunder think of all this?"

"Oh, Thunder doesn't think," she said, dismissing the ugly old gelding with a casual wave of her hand. "He's just a horse."

"And Shareb is not?"

"Well of course he is, silly, but he's *special*."

He looked down at her, his eyes soft. "My lady, all of God's creatures are special, no matter what their looks, their character . . . or their breeding."

Roses bloomed in her cheeks, and his gentle reprimand made her feel small and mean. Unable to meet his eyes, she looked at her hand. He was wrong, of course. Thunder, with his nondescript pedigree and poor conformation, was nothing but a worthless nag whose only value was in rescuing Shareb from having to pull the chaise. Such an animal held little if any significance in the whole scheme of things. But she sensed that the old horse was important to the veterinarian, and she did not want to hurt his feelings by protesting otherwise.

She glanced at the broken-down nag. It had dark, soft eyes, and was gazing at her with infinite sadness.

Lud, it was uncanny, the way the ugly old thing was looking at her. Almost . . . accusingly.

"I suppose," she agreed, and unable to face the gelding's mournful eyes, turned her attention to the animal doctor's shoulder. She felt his breath in her hair as he bent his head, trying to see the spot where Shareb had struck him. Her fingers began to tremble madly, and she heard the old horse take a step or two forward, as though it wanted to protect its savior.

Ariadne pulled the shirt away—and knew she'd

made a mistake as soon as his chest was bared to her gaze.

She saw the soft, sparse hair there, light brown and tickly against her fingertips. She saw slabs of muscle, sharp and defined across his chest, flat and tapered where they embraced his ribs. She saw his chest rising and falling with his breath, saw the pulse beating at the base of his throat—and saw the purple bruise in the cup of his shoulder where Shareb's teeth had broken the blood vessels.

She looked up at him, her eyes very wide. "Ouch," she said.

He smiled, tentatively, though she sensed the tension in his body, the emotions that raged through him at her soft touch. "Ouch."

She held his gaze for a long moment. Then, she lifted her hand, put her lips against her palm, and turning it outward, pressed it tenderly against the injured area.

"Ariadne." He shut his eyes, shuddered, and took a deep, steadying breath. "You ... said you would not touch me."

"I lied."

"But—"

"This is my way of kissing it and making it better."

He opened his eyes, and in them was a desperate plea. Whether it was for her to keep her hand there or remove it, she did not know. Did not care. Did not *want* to care. . . .

Softly, she said, "I can feel your heart beating, Colin. Thump-thump, thump-thump, thump-thump." Her thumb softly grazed his chest and the sudden moisture in her eyes made the fleecy brown hair there grow shimmery. "A few more inches, and Shareb would have crushed you and silenced that heartbeat forever. You have become very dear to me, Colin. I don't think I could've borne it, if Shareb had fallen atop you."

"Indeed, I don't think I could have, either."

"Well of course not, you'd be dead!"

"Precisely."

She looked up at him and found those gorgeous lavender eyes perusing her with fond amusement. The depth of naked desire she saw in his face unnerved her, and, recovering herself, she snatched her hand away from his warm flesh, closed his shirt, and fumbled with the buttons. Every fiber of her being wanted to go into his arms and beg him to kiss her once again. The pain of denial was real, and unbearable. How unfair, this attraction for a man she could never have and should never want. But as she'd told him—*life* wasn't fair.

"Come on," she said, giving a false little laugh to disguise the ache. "You ride in the chaise and I shall travel aboard Shareb. That way, I won't be tempted to touch you and you won't be tempted to touch me in return, and nothing can happen between us, right?"

"That is the wisest idea you've had all day," he said, his gaze lingering on her face for a long, searching moment. Then he turned abruptly and climbed back into the chaise. But as he picked up the reins and clucked for Thunder to move, his countenance mirrored the raw agony of separation that she also felt in her own heart. She cried inside at the fates that had separated them by class and circumstance.

Tristan, Lord Weybourne, pushed open the door to the coaching inn, shoved his way through the crowded, smoke-filled room, peeled off his gloves, and threw himself down at the nearest table. His throat was dry with road dust, his stomach churned with emptiness, his fine clothes were damp with sweat, and he was nursing a headache of thunderous proportions.

Putting his elbows on the table, he dropped his head to his hands and kneaded his aching temples.

"Hello, handsome."

He looked up and into the face of a buxom serving maid.

"Name's Meg," she said brightly, tucking a yellow curl behind her ear. "What'll it be today, luv? A good pint of ale? Something to fill yer stomach and stick to yer ribs?"

"Ale, and whatever's on the menu."

She nodded and wound her way through the patrons, deflecting a groping hand here, saucily responding to a gibe there. A moment later she was back, a plate in one hand and a foamy mug in the other. "Should've been here a few hours ago," she said, setting the food before him. "Missed all the excitement, ye did!"

Tristan didn't bother responding to her obvious lure to draw him into conversation. His mind was elsewhere.

The woman persisted. " 'Twas quite the scene, I tell ye! Some fellow calling himself a veteran"—she frowned, cocked her head, tapped her tooth with a long nail—"vettanar—Oh, never mind, it don't matter none. Animal doctor! Aye, that's what he was, an animal doctor. Had breakfast here with his little brother, then went outside an' laid John Beckett out senseless! And all for bleedin' a horse. Can ye imagine?"

"No," Tristan said flatly. He lifted his mug, and the cool, foamy liquid slid down his dusty throat. By his calculations, Ariadne was probably a third of the way to Norfolk by now. Pain and terror washed through him at the thought, and he felt a fresh wave of cold sweat break out along his spine.

By God, he *had* to catch up to her and that horse before—

"Oh, 'twas something to see, it was! Such a quiet and gentle-looking man, who would've thought he had such fire in him? Some people, ye never know. . . ."

"No, I suppose you don't. If you'll please excuse me—"

"Had a fine-lookin' horse with him though, and now he has two. Matched bays, though the broken-down old gelding he saved from the bleedin'—now what did he call it? A flu-bottomy. Aye, that's what it was, *flu-bottomy*—can't hold a candle to that fiery stallion he came in with. Gorgeous horse. Simply gorgeous."

Something clicked in Tristan's brain. He set the mug down and looked up, his eyes narrowing. "Fiery stallion?"

"Oh, aye. Grand-looking animal, though ye couldn't see much of it beneath all the trappings they had on it. Legs all bandaged up, blanket on its back, and the strangest hood on its head, covering most of its face an' little cups over its eyes. Big chest, though. Long, long legs, rather like a racer's—"

Rather like a racer's.

Tristan's hand shot out and grabbed the maid's arm.

"Did it have a white blaze down the front of its face?"

She knuckled her brow, thinking. "Well, now . . . aye, as a matter of fact, it did. Couldn't see much of it, though, what with that hood they had on him, but aye, I do recall 'e had a white muzzle—

"How tall?"

"Oh, maybe fifteen, fifteen an' a half hands?"

"His eye—" Tristan was gripping the maid's

arm almost cruelly. "Was his right eye ringed with white?"

"Oh, don't know about that, luv, 'twas dark last night when they got here and what with all the excitement this morn, I really couldn't tell ye. Only caught a good look at the horse this morning; the little brother was up at dawn and took it out for a hard gallop. Runs fast, that horse. *Real* fast. The laddie came back and fed it a piece of apple pie and then—listen to this!—shared a mug of ale with it. Imagine, a horse that craves apple pie and *ale*! I've never seen the like—

Tristan leapt to his feet, grabbed his hat, slammed a coin down on the table, and, nearly knocking over an incoming traveler, ran for the door. "Which way did they go?"

She folded her arms and pointed up the road. "North. Toward Norfolk."

Chapter 12

After spending eight miles alone in the chaise, Colin found that physical separation from Her Ladyship was no release from temptation or torment, and as storm clouds began to sweep in from the west and low, angry rumblings of thunder sounded from far off in the distance, he felt the weather's growing turmoil reflected in his own heart.

Granted, he did not have to suffer the exquisite anguish of having her leg bumping against his with every movement of the horse, didn't have to counter her bald compliments, didn't have to inhale her sweet scent or fight the impulse to kiss her pouty pink lips, but torture could—and did—come in many forms, all of them equally painful. It came in watching her sit astride that bold stallion of hers with all the elegance and dignity of Joan of Arc. It came in gazing at the taut curve of her buttocks, and watching the play of her muscles beneath the riding breeches; it came in listening to the sound of her laughter, fantasizing that her smile really *was* for him, and biting back the unreasonable jealousy he felt every time she mentioned the name *Maxwell*.

"I am damned," he muttered, tearing his gaze

from her stiffly elegant back and glaring over Thunder's tail and plodding haunches. "Damned and double-damned."

Bow put her paws on his chest and licked his face, and one of Thunder's ears went back, listening. Even Shareb-er-rehh, walking just ahead of them, turned his head, the white ring around his right eye lending him an expression of high amusement.

"Colin?" She pulled the stallion up, allowing Thunder to catch up with them. "Did you hear me? I do wish you could coax some speed out of that stupid nag. We shall *never* get to Norfolk at this rate!"

"Thunder is old, tired, and sore. I don't wish to push him."

"Yes, well if he ends up being responsible for Shareb's loss and my capture, don't expect that two thousand pounds."

Overhead, thick, dark clouds were sliding in over the hills to the west, the late afternoon sunlight painting slivers of orange against their ominous black bellies. A gust of wind rustled the leaves of a nearby oak tree, and from off in the distance came the low grumble of thunder.

Colin raised a brow at her petulant words and slanted her a chastising look. Immediately, her face went pink with embarrassment. "I'm sorry, Colin—there I go, sounding mean again. I hope you can forgive me, but the deprivations of this adventure are contriving to wreak havoc on my nerves."

"Of course."

"Don't you think we should find a place to wait out the storm, and possibly stay for the night?"

Colin's leg was throbbing incessantly. He reached down, kneading the deep ache with his fingers as she rode just beside the chaise.

"Colin? Did you hear me?"

"Yes, of course. I was just thinking, that's all."

"About what?"

"About . . . tonight's sleeping arrangements and what to do about them."

"Oh. *That*." Her cheeks reddened a bit, but the familiar sparkle lit her eye. She reached down to poke his shoulder with her crop. "You mean you're not going to let me play with your pretty hair again, Doctor?"

"We already discussed that. No touching."

She ruffled his hair with the end of her crop. "I wouldn't dream of it."

Grinning, he deflected the whip with his elbow. "And what do you call that?"

"You didn't say I couldn't touch you with my crop."

He shook his head, torn between exasperation, desperation, and desire.

"Or," she continued, kicking her foot free of the stirrup iron and resting her toe on his shoulder, "my boot."

"Stop flirting."

She giggled. "I'm not."

"You are."

She put her foot back in the iron and gaped at him with exaggerated shock. "Really, Colin, that is *not* gentlemanly, to accuse a lady of that! Although it is, of course, true. I cannot help but flirt, though I suppose I shall probably roast in the fires of hell for my wickedness."

As if in answer, a long, low rumble issued from the incoming clouds, and Ariadne instantly sobered. She frowned, looking at the green pastures as they grew dark and silent with the approach of the storm. Even the air seemed tight with tension, and now, a gust of wind drove across the land, pulling tufted ripples from the surface of a small, nearby pond. Little Bow whined and hid her face in the cup of Colin's shoulder.

"Yes, I think you're right," he said, cradling the shivering little dog to his chest and soothing her with gentle fingers in her fur. "We'd best look for a place to stop now, before the storm is upon us."

"Not a coaching inn, I hope! Oh, how I despise them; someone will surely recognize Shareb and me, I just know it. And my horrid, degenerate, wastrel of a brother . . . he's out there, Colin." She waved her crop to indicate the darkening hills, the road ahead and behind them. "He's out there, and he won't stop until he finds me."

Again, the thunder rolled, deep and dark and ominous.

"Yes, I've been giving considerable thought to the problem of Shareb-er-rehh's disguise. To be safe, I think it's time to alter it a bit, just in case any of the people we've encountered have put two and two together and realized he's the horse the whole countryside is searching for."

"Alter it? How?"

"With some mud or grease to cover that white blaze of his. And maybe some dye around his fetlocks, to conceal the white coronets and stocking and make his legs appear solid black."

"Dye? *Mud*? On my noble Shareb?" She gave a little laugh. "Oh, Colin, that would be horribly degrading for him—"

"He'll survive."

"But—"

Another long, warning growl of thunder came from over the hills, and the sky went the color of ink as gusts of wind drove Shareb's sparse mane over Ariadne's fists. The stallion began to snort and blow, nervous about the approaching storm.

"Don't look so woeful," Colin chided, "it will only be temporary. But in order to get that horse safely to Norfolk, we must constantly alter his disguise. After all"—he gestured to the empty road behind them, and the black clouds that were bearing down on them—"you don't know who may be tracking us."

She nodded, seeing the wisdom of his decision. "Very well then, let's be about it."

That afternoon they found a printer in the next village they came to. While Ariadne waited anxiously outside, Colin—ignoring the raised brows of the proprietor—purchased a large quantity of black ink, which the kindly man supplied to him in a wooden bucket. After carefully placing it on the floor of the chaise, Colin jumped in and sent Thunder hurrying on, hoping to find refuge before the storm hit.

They found a pub up the road which had a barn and stables attached.

Colin made arrangements to stable the horses and returned to the darkening paddock, where Lady Ariadne waited with a fretful Shareb-er-rehh.

"Time to get this disguise in place," he said cheerfully, trying to banish both the darkness of the day—and the darkness in her face. It was obvious she was none too happy about putting ink, or mud, on her beloved horse. Well, he wasn't either—but some things were for the best.

"And just how are we supposed to get *ink* out of Shareb's fetlocks, once we get him safely to Norfolk?" she asked, sulkily, as Colin led the horse beneath the shelter of a lean-to and placed the bucket in the dirt beside him.

"Have no fear, my lady. I have a special soap in my trunk that removes just about anything."

"Yes, and it will probably remove his hair as well. I'm warning you, Colin, that if Shareb suffers any discoloration or ill effects from this—"

Colin had already removed the leg bandages and was looking at Shareb's long legs. A true bay, the horse's black stockings started at the knees and hocks and ran down to the hooves—where they were broken by distinctive bands of white in the form of tiny coronets on the front legs, and on this right rear one, a half boot. All would have to go, so that the legs appeared totally black. He dipped a rag into the ink and touched it carefully to the white anklet.

"I promise you, Ariadne, it *will* come out. Now, please hold him, would you? I don't like the way those ears of his are coming back. . . ."

"Yes, and *he* doesn't like the indignity of what you're doing to him."

"Too bad," Colin said, working the ink into the white half stocking. "He'll just have to suffer until further notice."

But if he had to suffer, Shareb-er-rehh had no intention of doing so alone. He had already suffered the humiliation of having to pull a chaise. He had already suffered the insult of coming second to the other horse in that man's attention. He had already suffered the indignity of grease and mud applied to his face, and its stench was now making his nostrils pucker. Shareb-er-rehh did not like to suffer, and until Lady A had met this insufferable blighter, had never had to. Now, he stood still as a stone while the veterinarian applied the ink to his feet, hating the man as he had never hated him before. He felt the cool liquid seeping through his fetlock and into his skin. He felt the tickly touch of the man's fingers, felt the despair in Lady A's stance.

And knew that this latest degradation could not be tolerated.

The veterinarian moved to his other rear leg.

I could kick him, he thought. *I could kill him with*

*one little love tap, right between the eyes as he bends
close to my hoof. Boom. Easy as that. . . .*

No. Killing was a bit extreme.

*Or I could slam my foot into his kneecap instead, and
render him unable to walk. . . .*

The veterinarian picked up the bucket of ink and
moved to his forequarters.

He turned his head, pretending placid acceptance as the man knelt at his left front foot and
went to work on the notch of white that separated
his hoof from the black stocking. He saw Lady A
holding the lead rope in slack hands, stifling a
yawn. He saw the veterinarian's striking light hair,
which so entranced Lady A.

And he saw the bucket of black ink.

Easily within reach.

Ah, revenge. Sweeter than sweet.

The veterinarian was dabbing the ink around
his fetlock now . . . reaching into the bucket for
more . . . looking up to grin at Lady A—

Shareb-er-rehh acted.

His head snaking out like a striking adder, he
seized the bucket in his teeth and before Lady A
could even utter a shriek, had it turned upside
down on the beautiful gold hair that she so fancied.

"*Shareb!*" she cried, leaping back from the
splashing river of ink that made its way toward her
boot. And then, her hands flew to her mouth and
her eyes went wide. "Colin!"

The veterinarian stood slowly up, the ink running in rivulets through his bright hair. He took a
deep, steadying breath. Then, he reached into his
pocket, found a handkerchief, and slowly wiped
his face dry.

Only then did he turn to look at the stallion.

Shareb-er-rehh stood regarding him, as amused
and innocent as a mischievous colt, ears pricked

forward, head high. He lifted his head, peeled his lips back, and whickered in delight.

Ariadne began to laugh. Shareb had repaid indignity for indignity, and the veterinarian looked fit to kill. She saw his chest rise on a deep, angry breath before he slowly let it out. He glared at the horse. Shareb gave another horse-laugh. Then, Colin moved wearily to his sea chest, retrieved a comb, and began to draw it through his hair.

"What are you *doing*?" she asked, her laughter fading as he dragged the blue-black ink through those beautiful golden locks that had escaped the onslaught of ink.

"Might as well make it uniform," he muttered, and, with a helpless sigh, finished the job.

Colin heard the fiddle long before he and Ariadne entered the pub, and its haunting melody was enough to make him forget all about the humiliation that the stallion had dealt him.

Inside, the room was teeming with travelers, all laughing and drinking and hoping to escape the deluge that was about to pour out of the heavens. A fire crackled in the hearth, a game of backgammon was in full swing with a dozen people clustered around one table, and the air was thick with the pungent scents of smoke, sweat, and grease. The din was so loud that he couldn't hear himself think.

But still, he heard the fiddle. Though he wished he did not.

"Oh, listen!" Her Ladyship exclaimed in childish delight. She pointed to the old man who sat in a stool near the hearth, the instrument against his cheek as he pounded out a rollicking old sea chantey. "Isn't he grand?!"

Colin smoothed the nearly-dry hair off his brow, his hand shaking. The music went straight to his heart, choking it with a deep, raw ache that spread to the farthest reaches of his very soul. He didn't have to see the tattoo on the old salt's arm, didn't have to spot the out-of-fashion queue hanging down his back, didn't have to recognize the chantey he pulled from the willing old fiddle, to know the man had been a sailor.

Pain swept through him and memories that, even after five years, were still too fresh and raw to be delved into. *She*, walking just behind him, was never aware of it. But the old fiddler was. He looked up after finishing the tune, and as the tavern erupted in applause, cheers, and loud calls for more, his foxy old gaze caught Colin's and something deep and unspoken passed between them.

The old man knew. Maybe it was in the way that Colin walked, maybe it was in his military bearing, maybe it was just the look on his face as the two stared at each other. Maybe the old man had seen him piped aboard some ship five, maybe ten years ago, with ceremony and respect, and remembered his unusual lavender eyes and blond hair—*no, no, your hair is not blond now, damn it, it's black, BLACK!* Colin let out a slow sigh. Perhaps the old man simply sensed a kindred spirit who would never again feel the freedom of sea and wind and sky but would never stop longing for it. Nevertheless, he *knew*, and as Colin passed, the old man touched his forelock in a gesture of respect.

"Evenin', Cap'n," he said, soberly.

Colin gave a brief nod, and hoped the man's words had been lost on Her Ladyship.

They had.

"Dr. Lord, I find this establishment *most* disagreeable!" she hissed, pressing close to him. "It reeks of sweat and smoke, the din is horrific, and I'm worried about Shareb."

As if to punctuate her remark, thunder rolled

from the heavens outside, though the brunt of its roar was lost amidst the noisiness of the tavern.

"Yes. . . ."

"Colin?" She caught his sleeve and peered up at him. "Are you well?"

He gave a pained grin and turned his back to the fiddle, wishing he could turn his back on the memories it evoked, as well. "Yes, I'm fine," he assured her. "And stop worrying about that damned horse."

"I cannot help it!"

"Do you want me to go out and hold a parasol over him to shield his noble head from the threatening raindrops?"

"Oh, very funny. I think you're still angry with him for dumping the ink over your head. And, I *still* think he should've been put in their stable, not out in a paddock!"

"You heard the man, the stable is full. He'll be fine in the paddock, and there is shelter for him. Besides, we shan't tarry long here."

"Colin, I really wish you'd tell me what has upset you so. If it's your hair, I'm so sorry, even if I *did* giggle . . . when we leave here we can stop at a brook somewhere and I'll wash the ink out—"

"I'm not upset."

"You are. I can see it in your eyes, even though you're trying hard to hide it. Is it anything I've done? I mean, I have been so very good, and have not even touched you for the past hour!"

He looked down at her. Her bright eyes were worried, her piquant little face distressed. "No, Ariadne," he said, softly. "It's not you. It's not my hair. It's just . . ."

"Just what?"

He guided her toward an empty table near the fire, where the heat would dry the last, lingering dampness that still clung to his locks. "Ghosts from my past."

He slid behind a group of travelers involved in a dispute about the benefits of horse versus cow manure as fertilizer, and onto a bench seat along the wall. Outside, the lightning flashed purple through the windows and glazed the rolling hills, and when the resounding clap of thunder came, the inebriated patrons of the tavern cheered and whooped in delight. Through the yelling and sounds of tankards being slammed down on the tables, came the strains of the fiddle—haunting, sad, remembering.

She took the seat across from him, perching on its edge with stiff-backed, ladylike grace, and stared at him.

He looked at her and raised a brow.

"I worry about you," she said, in response. "You are so very . . . aloof, sometimes. And when your eyes look sad, I can't help but be sad, too." She reached out and touched his hand. "I'm sorry if I hurt your feelings with my remark about your horse being a decrepit old nag. I know it—*he*—is very special to you, and I should never have said that."

He smiled, helpless against her natural charm. "My lady, you have done nothing wrong. Don't trouble yourself over me."

"Truthfully, I think you are a very gallant hero for stepping in and saving the animal as you did. You have won my eternal and undying admiration."

The emphatic character of her words brought the smile into his eyes at last. "Eternal and undying."

"Forever."

He raised a brow, which had not escaped the stain of the black dye. "My lady?"

"Yes, Doctor?"

"I suggest you slouch a bit, as you are attracting the attention of the poor fool sitting ten feet behind you."

"Oh!"

Her eyes glinting with conspiracy, she slid down in her seat, tucked a lock of red hair up under the cap, and duplicating him, lazily placed her arm over the back of the adjacent chair. "Better?"

"Much."

"Lud, next you'll be telling me to belch and scratch!"

"Well, since *you* thought of it, it probably wouldn't be a bad idea. . . ."

"*Doctor* Lord!" She grabbed up a napkin and playfully tossed it at him. "What an utterly heinous suggestion!"

He laughed, enjoying her exaggerated shock, and she laughed right along with him. Their gazes met, held, and the unspoken attraction that passed between them caused them both to look away. Colin cleared his throat, wiped up a ring of moisture off the table with the napkin; Ariadne thrust her hands into her lap and glanced out the window.

"Colin, I don't think I like you in black hair. It doesn't . . . fit."

"Well, on the bright side of things, at least *I'm* in disguise along with you and that damned horse."

"Speaking of which, are you sure they'll be all right out there?"

He followed her gaze. Thunder, being a gelding, had been safely turned out with the other horses who had arrived too late to be given space in the stable, and stood happily munching hay with a crowd of mares to whose allure he was totally oblivious.

Too bad the same couldn't be said of that damned stallion.

Shareb-er-rehh, confined to a small paddock

with a lean-to shed, had thoughts for nothing *but* the mares. His fine head high, his nostrils flaring, and his tail streaming behind him, he made a magnificent sight as he galloped back and forth along the fence that separated him from the other horses. As they watched, he let out a long, piercing scream, skidded in the mud at the end of his short space, wheeled, reared, and raced back the way he had come.

"Oh, look at him, Colin!" Ariadne said, leaning over the table so she could see out the window. She paid no attention to the maid who brought them tea, a tiny pitcher of milk, and cakes. "He's showing off for those mares!"

Lightning flashed down, splitting the sky and washing the paddock and buildings in violet. The clouds grew darker. Blacker.

The rain would come any minute now.

"I'm afraid, my lady, that it is not just the mares he is trying to impress, but a rival for their attention." Colin sniffed the milk to ensure its freshness before pouring some into each of their teacups, then pointed toward another paddock, opposite the stable. "Look."

There, also confined, was the real reason for Shareb's challenging display; a huge, glossy red-chestnut steed with fire in its eye and fury in its stance.

Another stallion.

Colin sipped his tea, thankful for the fence that separated the two horses.

"Yes, but look at Shareb! Isn't he beautiful? It's the desert blood in him, you know. He wants to fight. He is pure fire, pure magnificence. Everything a horse should be."

Desert blood?

Lightning flashed down again, and the two stallions screamed threats and challenges to each other across the small field that separated them. Inside that field the mares lifted their heads and began to mill nervously:

Thunder kept on eating.

Now the red stallion began to prance and pace the length of his fence, calling insults to Shareb. Shareb responded with a shrill scream. Then his ears swept back, he galloped across his paddock—

And a brilliant flash of lightning forked out of the clouds.

The timing couldn't have been worse. Colin saw it all: Shareb, bolting sideways as the resulting crack of thunder split the sky just overhead, wheeling, then plunging straight for the fence, where he paused for only the briefest of seconds before leaping the tall enclosure like Pegasus on the wing; then, without breaking stride, he tore across the grassy field and bore down on his rival at a speed that nearly burned the grass up beneath his hooves.

"Stallion fight!" shouted one of the patrons, and everyone ran toward the door on a mass exodus.

Colin was already on his feet and racing from the tavern. With Ariadne hot on his heels, he ran toward the paddocks, knowing he'd never make it in time. Shareb's challenging scream split the air, and he saw the stallion hurl himself straight into the chestnut's fence, heard the horrible crash of breaking wood and the other horse's enraged squeal as it rose to meet Shareb's attack. There was the awful sound of heavy bodies slamming together, hooves hitting flesh, squeals and screams and angry whistles, and over it all, the boom of thunder at close range.

"Get that damned bugger off my horse!" a balding man cried, running past them with a pitchfork. "So help me God, I'll kill him!"

He paused, drew back his arm to hurl the pitchfork—and faltered as a tiny ball of salt-colored fur flung toward him.

Bow.

But Colin had no time to grab his pet, no time to warn Ariadne back, no time to respond to the enraged man trying to fend off the suddenly vicious little dog. The stallions were fighting with savage, murderous fury, and the chestnut was getting the worst of it.

"Colin!" he heard Ariadne cry. "Get them apart!"

He raced past the mares, their heads thrust over the fence as they happily watched the two stallions fighting over them. He grabbed up a broken piece of fencing and, heedless of the danger, dived between the two enraged animals, brandishing the wood like a club.

The chestnut, already losing the fight, bolted away to the side, his neck streaming blood where Shareb's teeth had found purchase. Colin threw down the board and made a wild grab for Shareb's halter—but the stallion's blood was up, fire was in his eyes, and, without breaking stride, he turned, crashed back through the fence, and with lightning glowing against his flying body, galloped out of the broken paddock—

—and straight toward an elegant gray horse just entering the yard, whose handler screamed and fled as Shareb charged toward them.

In horror, Colin realized the newcomer was a mare.

There was nothing he could do to stop it, and he saw it all. The mare, flinging up her head in alarm as the mighty stallion bore down on her at a speed Colin would never have believed had he not seen it with his own eyes; her handler, fleeing for his life; and Shareb, teeth bared, neck outstretched, mud and grass and thunder flying from his hooves.

Shareb gave a piercing scream, nipped the mare's rump as he galloped past, and, tail high, thundered out of the yard and down the road at a speed so intense it was almost frightening. The mare, whinnying like a barmaid in love, went charging off after him, lead shank flying.

"Colin! Colin, *do* something!" Ariadne cried, racing up to him with Bow in her arms.

But there was nothing that he could do. The stallion was gone. The landlord was barreling toward them, already screaming for recompense for the damage to his fence. And now the first drops of rain were beginning to pelt the earth, gathering in force, frenzy, and fury, and Colin found himself stuck with a geriatric gelding, a yapping dog, and some thirty men who were all staring at Ariadne's distinctively lovely chest.

He turned, and looked bleakly at Thunder.

The gelding was still munching his hay.

"Time to go," he said, and, spinning Ariadne around and shoving her toward the barn, ran to get the horse.

Chapter 13

The long legs. The unusually deep chest. The sloping, powerful hip, the great layback of the shoulder, and the speed.

Especially, the speed.

After witnessing that blistering display of pure lightning out of the courtyard, Colin now knew the truth. Shareb-er-rehh was no high-stepping riding horse. He was no carriage horse, pleasure horse, or lady's pet.

He was a racehorse.

A damned *fast* racehorse.

And now, an hour and a half after he'd made his blazing escape, he was still missing.

With Colin leading Thunder and Ariadne walking on the gelding's other side, they tried tracking the stallion by his fading hoofprints, Ariadne gripping Shareb's lead shank like a nun with her rosary beads, both of them huddled in their coats and neither of them saying much. Bow, her coat wet, tangled, and muddy, trotted at Colin's heels; every so often she, like Colin, shot a worried glance at Lady Ariadne. The little noblewoman's face was white and strained, and only the dictates of her breeding and upbringing prevented her from giving in to the tears Colin knew lurked just beneath the surface.

It was that same threat of tears that kept him from confronting her.

No gait horse at all, but a race*horse.*

It hurt and angered him that she had lied to him, and not trusted him. Who did she think she was fooling? How long had she expected to keep a horse like that hidden under a disguise?

But the raw misery on her face was enough to do him in, and for now, he'd hold his tongue.

She paused for the tenth time in as many minutes to cup her hands over her mouth and call the stallion.

"Shar-e-e-e-e-e-e-eb!"

Colin stopped, too, listening to her voice echo emptily over the green hills.

"Shar-e-e-e-e-e-e-eb!"

Nothing.

"Come, Ariadne. Let's keep moving."

Ignoring him, she called the stallion one last time, her voice rising in desperation and cracking under the strain; then she wiped at her eyes, jerked her chin up, and trudged along beside him.

"He's gone, Colin," she said miserably. "Someone must have stolen him and turned him in for the reward. If he was out here, he would have come for me."

"Now, now," Colin said soothingly, walking just to the side of the long, muddy puddles that pooled in the wheel ruts. "We still have another two hours of daylight. And *I'm* not ready to give up."

She shot him a watery look. "Oh, Colin . . . I don't know what I would do without you."

"You'd still be dillydallying in London," he teased, trying to coax some humor back into her. Bravely, she tried to smile, but he saw her face crumple, and she looked quickly away before he could witness her loss of composure.

They continued on. A black-and-maroon mail coach thundered toward them, its wheels spraying great arcs of muddy water as it tore through the puddles, the scarlet-clad guard clinging for dear life to the back of the coach; then the vehicle was past, the team of horses that drew it sending up great clods of muck from their galloping hooves

Silence, and the sound of the rain once more.

Colin stole a sideways glance at his companion. The lead shank drooped from her hand, her feet dragged in the mud, and her eyes were vacant and staring. Gone was the piquant vibrancy of her personality, the sparkle in her eye, the saucy, snappy spirit that had so captivated him.

"We'll not find him tonight, Colin," she said bleakly, pointing at the empty road ahead of them. The mail coach had obliterated most of the stallion's tracks, and what was left of them were fading. And then, as though nature itself was against them, the skies opened up and the rain came down in cruel, slashing torrents that ran like tears down Ariadne's cheeks. Maybe they *were* tears; at that point, it was impossible for Colin to tell.

Moments later, all that was left of Shareb-errehh's tracks were washed away into puddles of mud.

Ariadne stopped and bowed her head against the rain, her shoulders slumped in defeat as the torrents beat cruelly down on the back of her head and neck.

For Colin, it was too much. Blinking against the deluge that slashed his face, the thin streams of ink-stained water that stung his eyes, he took off his coat, tenderly wrapped it around her head and shoulders, and fashioned a sort of hood out of it to protect her from the rain as she stared miserably up at him. Then he took Thunder's bridle in one hand, drew the noblewoman into the protection of his other arm, and, half-carrying her, ran as fast as his bad leg would allow to a grove of oak trees.

There they stood, relatively sheltered by the canopy of leafy branches above their heads. Around them, the rain came down in thunderous torrents, then white sheets of fury, beating against the earth with such force that steam began to rise from the grass. The drumming roar obliterated all sound, and, instinctively, Ariadne huddled closer to the veterinarian, seeking shelter beneath his arm.

She looked up at him. His hair, blue-black and glistening, was plastered to his head and curling loosely at its ends. Water dripped down his brow, clumped on his lashes, trickled down his cheeks. His wet shirt clung to his body, emphasizing the muscles of his arms and chest.

Even soaked, even black-haired, he was beautiful.

He sensed her staring and glanced down, an encouraging little smile playing about his mouth. She smiled hesitantly back and moved closer to the steamy warmth of his body. He made no protest, merely watching the mad torrents bombard the earth around them and keeping his arm wrapped securely around her shoulders. A part of her wished he would keep his arm there forever, and, closing her eyes, she laid her cheek against his wet shirt. Somewhere out there in the rain was Shareb; but sheltered by Colin's body, comforted by his presence, Ariadne's fears began to subside, and as she'd done when she had first seen him saving the mastiff from bloat, she relinquished her fears and placed all her trust in him. They would find Shareb. The doctor would make sure of it.

She opened her eyes. The roar of the rain faded to a dull thrum, then individual spatters against the leaves, leaving the exhausted earth to catch its breath in gratitude.

The veterinarian's arm was still around her shoulders. She knew she should step away now that the rain had tapered off and his gallant protection was no longer necessary. But she did not move, and neither did he, and at last, the rain was only a soft, lulling drip as it trickled from the leaves overhead.

From somewhere near, a songbird called, then another.

And still, Ariadne did not move.

She laid her palm against his chest, then her cheek against the back of her palm, and stared off over the green, green hills. Beneath her hand, she felt his heart beating.

"Colin."

He cleared his throat. "Yes, my lady?"

"You are very gallant, giving me your coat as you did."

He leaned his head back against the tree trunk, letting the raindrops splash against his upturned face and smiling with the enjoyment of the sensation. "Oh, I think any gentleman would have done the same."

"I know plenty that would not have," she returned. She studied the intricate weave of his shirt, thought of the strong body it clung to, listened to and loved every precious beat of his heart. God help her, but she wanted to peel the wet shirt off of him and bury her lips in the downy hair that pelted his chest; God help her, but she wanted to stand on tiptoe and kiss the damp skin at the base of his throat; God help her, but if she never saw Maxwell again, she really wouldn't care as long as she could be with Colin Lord.

"Colin?"

She felt his heartbeat quickening beneath her palm. "Yes?"

"Do you think it's wrong, that we're standing

here as we are, with your arm around me and me enjoying every moment of it?"

"You're not the only one enjoying it, Ariadne."

She colored a bit, and looked earnestly up at him. "*Is* it wrong, Colin?"

"I don't know. Hell, I just don't know. Wrong it may be, but it feels *right*."

"Yes. . . . I guess that is what I was thinking, too. That it feels right." She sighed, and inhaled deeply of his clean, wet, male scent. "You are very dear to me, Colin. I only wish . . ."

His arm curled around her back, and she felt his gentle hand against her shoulders, pressing her body closer to his. "You only wish what?"

"I wish that . . . things could be different, I guess. That you were Maxwell. I—oh, Lud, I know that sounds terrible, but I don't know any other way to put it."

He said nothing, only holding her tightly and allowing her to continue. Rain dripped from the trees, and the grass sparkled in the brightening, late afternoon sunlight.

"I let him kiss me once," she said softly, remembering. "It was out in the garden at Lady Andrea's last soiree. We sneaked out for a breath of fresh air after a particularly strenuous round of dancing. He put his lips against mine, and he kissed me. But you know something, Colin?" She looked up at him, her eyes confused, sad. "I kissed him, but it didn't make me *feel* anything."

He gazed down at her, his face troubled. A drop of rain fell from the leaves above, hit his eyelashes.

"I would have thought that since Maxwell is to be my husband, that his kiss should have made me feel happy, thrilled, eager for more. But it didn't. It was—cold." She stared into his face, her eyes wide, desperate. "The kisses of your future husband are not supposed to make you feel cold, are they, Colin?"

Carefully, he said, "I shouldn't think so."

She laid her cheek against his wet shirt and stared dismally off over the darkening hills. "I suppose that if I had nothing to compare Maxwell's kiss to, I wouldn't be so worried. Perhaps this whole matter would not trouble me so much if I hadn't kissed *you*. When *we* kissed, it was entirely different from when I kissed Maxwell. With you"—she blushed, and gave a sad little smile—"it was . . . different. I wanted more."

Beneath her cheek, his heart was beating fast. Faster. He swallowed hard and as she pulled back to look at him, he gazed down at her, his eyes holding hers for a long, searching moment before his hand came up to gently caress her cheek.

"I'm sorry, Colin. It may be horribly vulgar, but I have always been one to say exactly how I feel. I don't mean to embarrass you."

"No, no. I am not embarrassed. Actually, I'm . . . rather flattered."

She looked up at him. "Are you, Colin? Are you truly?"

"Well, of course. It is not every day that a lonely old sod like me hears a beautiful lady confess that she finds his kisses exciting."

"You're not an old sod! For heaven's sake, you're what, twenty-five? Twenty-eight?"

"Thirty-three."

"Well, you look younger. It's the spectacles, I think, even though you don't wear them very often. Or maybe it's your youthful face, or your teasing grin. Plus, you're not paunchy like so many other older men—"

"For God's sake, Ariadne, I'm not an older man!"

"Well, I didn't mean it *that* way," she said,

quickly. "How is it that here I'm trying to tell you that I enjoyed your kiss more than I did my future husband's, and we get into a row about older men?"

"Truly, I don't know. But what I *do* know is that if your future husband were to see you standing here with your cheek against my chest, he would be inclined to call me out."

"Oh, no, Colin, I would never let you duel over me. I'm not like some of those other women who like to have men fighting over them. If you ever got hurt—"

He sighed, his eyes twinkling. "First she thinks me an older man. Now she doubts my prowess with sword and pistol. Dear God, what will it be next?"

Ariadne laughed and drew back, still keeping her arms wrapped around his waist. "Oh, Colin. You always know just what to say to make me feel better. You have made me laugh in one of the darkest hours of my life."

"Well then, before that hour grows any *darker*," he said lightly, as the green faded from the hills and crickets began to herald the onset of night, "shall we use what time we have left to try to find that confounded stallion of yours?"

"If only you'll let us find a brook first, so I can wash that horrid ink out of your hair."

"It is not important. And I rather like being tall, dark, and handsome."

"It *is* important. And handsome you are, but I prefer you as tall and fair instead."

"My lady—"

"No arguments, Colin. *I'm* the boss, remember?"

He grinned at her, and she took his hand. It was warm, strong, comforting, and hers fit within it as though the two had been made for each other.

The thought hit her with sudden alacrity.

Made for each other.

Shareb-er-rehh was out there somewhere, perhaps in danger, perhaps gone forever. But there was something she had to say to the veterinarian before they did anything. Something she had withheld from him, something she could keep to herself no longer. She squeezed his hand, looked up into his handsome face, and knew it was time to tell him the truth.

As he grasped Thunder's bridle and tried to move out from beneath the tree, she held her ground and said, "Colin."

He paused, raising one brow in question.

She gazed up and into those clear, intelligent eyes that had so entranced her from the very first, and wondered how she had ever been able to keep anything from him. Then, taking both of his hands, she drew a deep breath and looked him straight in the eye. "There is something about Shareb-er-rehh that I have not told you."

"I know," he said, gently, with a little smile. "He's no gait horse, is he?"

She shook her head, still holding his gaze.

"I didn't think so. In fact, if I were to make one guess, based on his build, his carriage, and what I saw today, I'd say he's a racehorse."

"He's more than a racehorse, Colin. *Much* more than a racehorse."

He looked at her, waiting.

And Ariadne stared into those arresting eyes of his and told him the truth.

"He's the Fastest Horse in the World."

Chapter 14

"**T**he Fastest Horse in the World."

He was gazing at her with a patient smile, the sort a parent might bestow upon a child who'd just said she'd seen a fairy queen sitting on her pillow.

"That is what I said."

"Granted, my lady, the horse is obviously a Thoroughbred, but that is an extraordinary claim."

They trudged through the pasture, the wet grass brushing their knees, Thunder between them and Bow leading them back toward the road.

"No, Colin, you're wrong. Shareb-er-rehh is *not* a Thoroughbred. At least, not a Thoroughbred as you might know them."

Overhead, the clouds began to break up, and patches of bright, cobalt sky peeked through.

Ariadne gazed off over hills dotted with sheep and cattle. "My father was a very wealthy man, Colin. He had the money to pursue many interests, most of them eccentric, but his life's passion was horses. In particular, *race*horses. He was an active member of the Jockey Club, and he devoted his life to a project that he had begun long before he and my mother were even married—specifically, a quest to develop a superior racehorse."

Ahead, the road beckoned, a flat, brown ribbon of mud wending through the green pastures. "Do you remember the famous, immortal, and unbeaten Eclipse?" she asked. "Well, Papa bred two swift little mares—one, he'd imported from the Orient and the other was a gift from a Bedouin tribe leader whom he befriended when he went there to study their horses—to Eclipse. Then he bred the finest of *their* fillies back to him. Surely, you know the benefits of selective inbreeding. Well, it took my father decades of meticulous planning to see the embodiment of his dream, but see it he did. Fifteen years ago, he produced the very first Norfolk Thoroughbred, an animal *similar* to our English Thoroughbreds, but one with more intelligence, more heart, more fire—and more speed. They are the fastest horses in the world—and Shareb-er-rehh is the last surviving stallion to represent them."

Colin gazed down at her, and saw the truth—at least, as she believed it—in her eyes. Fastest horses in the world or not, only a timepiece could tell. But after seeing Shareb-er-rehh's blistering display of speed, he wasn't altogether inclined to challenge her claim.

"Is he faster, then, than Black Patrick?" he asked, thinking of the mighty and undefeated King of Newmarket.

"Shareb has never been raced. But he *is* the Fastest Horse in the World, Colin. Trust me on that."

"And he is the last stallion?"

"Yes. And Gazella is the last mare. Because Papa gave her to Lord Maxwell as a betrothal agreement, she was not in the barn when that strange illness claimed the rest of the stock. Shareb-er-rehh was the only horse to survive both that and the fire. And if something happens to him . . ."

"The Norfolk Thoroughbred will be no more."

"Yes." She sighed. "Now you know why I must get him to Maxwell's before my brother can catch up to me. Tristan has no regard for our father's dream, and is in debt to the tune of thousands. Shareb-er-rehh is his only means of paying off his creditors—and to that end, he'll sell him off without blinking an eye."

"How much is the horse *worth*?"

She shrugged. "I don't know. Nobody knows. But the duke of Leighton once offered my father thirty thousand pounds for one of our stallions, which wasn't nearly as nice, nor as fast, as Shareb."

They had reached the road. Ariadne climbed over a small fence and stood there in the mud, gazing off at the wide vistas that rolled away on all sides of them. She cupped her hands to her mouth and called the stallion, throwing her head back and letting the wind carry her voice off over the hills.

Nothing.

She let her hands drop to her sides and stood looking up at him in defeat.

"Colin—I know I should trust in you, but I just don't know where to go from here."

"I have an idea," he said, and held out his hand for the stallion's leather lead shank. Wordlessly, she handed it to him, her brow creased in a frown as he squatted down and called little Bow to him.

Even Thunder pricked his ears, curious.

"Really, Colin, what is Bow going to be able to do—"

But the veterinarian was holding out the lead shank to the dog, who approached it and sniffed it furiously.

"Go find," Colin ordered. "Go find Shareb."

Cocking her head, the little dog yapped and regarded her master with bright, button eyes.

Again, Colin held the lead shank out to the dog. "Bow, *find*!"

Bow barked in agreement and, like a white cannonball, streaked off the road and over the adjacent field.

"Let's go!" Colin cried, and leaving Thunder safely ground-tied, grabbed Ariadne's hand, ducked beneath the fence, and ran as fast as he could after the dog.

Running beside him, her hand caught in his and her legs flying through the wet grass, Ariadne felt exhilaration and hope race through her for the first time since the stallion had escaped. Her cap bounced on her head and she swept it off, stuffing it in her pocket as she tried to keep pace with the veterinarian. Wind drove against her flushed cheeks, dried her wet hair, filled her lungs.

"Hurry, Ariadne, or we'll lose her!"

"Rarf! Rarf, rarf, rarf!" came Bow's voice as the dog paused to wait for them at the crest of a hill. Then, barking, she turned and disappeared from sight, only her excited yaps marking her flight as she raced headlong down the other side.

"Colin, *wait*! I cannot keep up!"

But laughing, he only gripped her hand harder and pounded up the hill after the dog. Higher and higher they climbed, the breath roaring through their lungs, the sweat pouring down their faces—and then, as they reached the crest of the hill, Ariadne looked down and saw a flat, fenced-in field, a barn, and a rambling old brick house. In the paddock was a herd of mares. They looked sleepy, sated, and happy—

And in their midst, preening himself like a proud rooster, was Shareb-er-rehh.

"*Shareb*!"

Gripping Colin's hand, she raced down the hill—and lost her footing.

She shrieked as she landed hard on her backside, dragging the veterinarian down with her. Down the hill they went, sliding in mud and grass, laughing with delight until they both ended up at the bottom looking and feeling like two children who'd just been given a sled and a snowy slope to try it out on.

Ariadne came to a stop first and, giggling hysterically, gazed up into the veterinarian's mud splattered face. He looked more than a little shocked, more than a little embarrassed.

"Oh, Colin, you *found* him!" she cried, and tears of happiness raced down her muddy cheeks. "Never, ever, will I doubt you again!"

"Oh, no, it was Bow who found him."

"And *you* who thought of setting her on Shareb's scent!"

She laughed until her sides hurt. The veterinarian smiled hesitantly, then, as he saw the absurdity of their situation, and the amount of mud that covered them both, he too began to chuckle, until they were both giggling and guffawing uncontrollably.

"I feel like a pig that has just spent the day in a pen of muck!" Ariadne cried, reaching out to wipe away a spatter of mud from the doctor's nose. "And look at you! You sure don't look like any University graduate *now*!"

"Forgive me, my lady, but *you* don't strike me as any nobleman's daughter! Perhaps you should maintain that coat of mud and even your brother will never recognize you!"

"Oh, Colin! I haven't had this much fun since I was a little girl and Tristan and I put earthworms in Nanny's bed!"

With the herd of mares watching them, and Shareb-er-rehh shaking his noble head as though disdaining their childish delight, they both erupted in laughter once again. Then, Ariadne looked into the veterinarian's clear, beautiful eyes, and her laughter stopped abruptly.

As did his.

The moment was as fragile and precious as a raindrop poised at the edge of a spring leaf. Neither moved. Ariadne saw only the intense purple of his eyes and the shape of his mouth, heard only her racing heart and the sound of his breathing. She swallowed, hard. Then, his hand came up to clear the damp hair from her brow, his knuckles grazed her cheek, her jaw—and, heeding the gentle pressure, she moved her head toward his.

"Kiss me, my lady," he said softly.

She swallowed hard, and looked deeply into his eyes. "Yes, Colin."

Closing her eyes, she tilted her head back and sighed as he touched his mouth to hers. This time, there was no punishing savagery, no angry lesson in manners. This time he kissed her slowly, deeply, carefully, giving her time to savor the warmth and firmness of his lips, the taste of his mouth, the wondrous beauty of the sensations that began to pulse through her blood. An involuntarily shudder swept through her; a helpless moan escaped her lips. Her hand came up to encircle his nape, her fingers splaying through his wet, still-black hair, pressing against his skull, and pulling him toward her. His tongue moved against her lips, touching, licking, tasting, until her mouth opened under the gentle onslaught. Oh, the sweet taste of him, the feel of him, the heat of his breath against her cheek, the bold touch of his hand upon her knee! His fingers moved up and down her leg, then her arm, and the sensation of her wet shirt sliding over her damp, heated flesh, and his hot hands touching her so intimately, was enough to send shock waves of sensation driving through regions of herself she hadn't known existed.

She pulled back, feeling drugged, feeling helpless, feeling like she wanted to drown in the fathomless depths of those beautiful lavender eyes.

"Colin...." She reached up, and with a shaky hand, smoothed the wet hair off his brow. "God help me, but every bone in my body goes to water when you kiss me. It's wrong, I know it's wrong, but I want more—"

He eased himself down on one elbow, his hand roving over the curve of her hip and down her wet breeches. She shuddered, loving the feel of that bold hand against the outside of her thigh, wishing there was no fabric to separate her flesh from its questing warmth. His eyes were troubled, and as she touched his muddy shirt to feel his heartbeat, he looked up at her.

"My feelings echo yours, Ariadne," he said. "And never have I wanted a woman as I want you. But you are a lady, and even if you were mine to claim, I would not have you out here in the grass for all the world to see." He grinned then, making her want to press her lips against his face and kiss the water droplets from his lashes, his brows, his cheeks. "Especially, with you garbed as a young boy. What would people think?"

She giggled, her face growing hot. He smiled back, and plucking a blade of grass, touched it to the bottom of her chin.

"Oh, Colin, I do not *care* what people think—"

Shouts and hoofbeats interrupted them and they looked up to see a horse and wagon arriving at the house. Colin lunged to his feet, pulling her up with him just as a farmer, waving his arms and yelling furiously, came charging toward the paddock.

"Hey! That your horse? Get him away from my mares!"

It was obvious, however, that Shareb-er-rehh had already had his way with the ladies. Craning his head to give his attacker a smug, amused stare, the horse waited for the man to get close, then he wheeled on his hind legs and in a lazy, ground-eating canter, flowed across the field toward Ariadne, neighing happily.

She ran toward him, her arms open.

Ears pricked, the stallion bore down on her, tail flying behind him like a banner of black silk. Colin caught his breath, for it didn't look as though Shareb was going to stop. But at the last moment he planted his feet, skidded in grass and mud, and nearly plowed into his mistress. She threw her arms around his neck and the horse rubbed his head up and down against her chest.

"Oh, Shareb, I missed you so!"

"Ariadne, I think it best to leave before—"

"Hey, that your horse? If he bred any of my mares, I'm holding you two personally responsible!" the farmer raged, puffing and panting as he reached them. "This is private property and . . ."

Suddenly the farmer's brows snapped together, his head darted out like a chicken's, and he stared at the horse, his eyes bugging out as he realized that the water dripping down the stallion's brown face was washing away mud and grease and revealing a bright white blaze. . . .

And that the high voice, the fine-boned face, and the obvious breasts beneath the loose coat belonged to a woman.

"Hey! You're—*you're the fugitive the whole countryside's looking for!*"

Everything happened at once. The farmer ran forward; Ariadne made a desperate lunge for Shareb-er-rehh's back, and the man's fingers caught her coat and tried to drag her down. She kicked out savagely, her boot connecting with his elbow—and then Colin was throwing himself at the farmer, trying to give her time to escape. As Shareb reared up and wheeled away, she saw him slip on the wet grass and lose his balance, the farmer's fist crashing high up on the side of his cheek.

"Colin!"

"Get on the horse!" he yelled, even as the farmer swung again, that huge, ham-fisted hand arcing toward his head. She screamed—but again, she had underestimated her protector. He ducked, deflected the blow with a quick, upward thrust of his arm, and, hunching his fist, slammed it into the farmer's belly hard enough to send the man retching, to the grass.

And now a crowd of people came charging up the hill after them, waving their arms and yelling at the top of their lungs.

"Run!" the veterinarian shouted, swatting Shareb across the rump. "Here come the reinforcements!"

Shareb reared beneath her, nearly spilling her from his bare back. "No, Colin, I'll not leave without you!"

"Go!"

"*No!*"

Shareb hit the earth, rose again—and as he came down, Colin vaulted up behind Ariadne and was thrown violently against her back as the enraged steed shot away from the oncoming crowd. Beneath him he felt the powerful churn of mighty, hardened muscles gathering speed, the raw power that the stallion had not even begun to tap. He leaned forward, his arms embracing Ariadne on either side, and managed to grab a hunk of the stallion's sparse mane in both fists.

"Where in God's name is he taking us?!"

Beneath them, Shareb found more speed, his hooves thundering over the ground, the wind beginning to scream in their ears, Bow yapping futilely behind them as she tried in vain to keep up.

"Back to get Thunder!"

"No!"

"Yes! Shareb won't want to pull the chaise!"

There was nothing to do but hang on for their lives. Ariadne dug in with her knees and leaned forward, feeling the veterinarian's hard chest against her back, his thighs embracing hers, and Shareb's mane whipping her face as his legs pounded beneath them. The stallion was flying across the pastures at a full gallop, fast enough to leave anything or anyone who might be chasing them floundering in his hoofprints.

But she alone knew that the stallion was not at full speed.

Far from it.

"Easy, Shareb!" she cried, terrified that he'd hit a hole and snap a leg. "Slow it down!"

But he only stretched his neck, flattened his body, and went faster.

They tore down one hill and up another, racing through the gathering gloom, decidedly back in the direction from which they had come. The sensation of the stallion's flowing muscles beneath her, coupled with the memory of Colin's burning kiss and the hot press of his body against every tingling inch of her back, arms, and thighs was enough to make Ariadne breathless and faint.

And there was Thunder, ahead in the distance.

"Pull him up!" Colin shouted, just behind her. "Pull him up or he's going to go right through that fence!"

"Shareb, whoa!"

The stallion shook his head and, blowing hard, kept running.

"Whoa!"

The roar of the wind in Colin's ears lessened in pitch, and he felt the horse beginning to slow. The great muscles beneath him stiffened, and Shareb-er-rehh broke to a canter, then a plunging, hopping series of jumps until at last he came to a halting

stop ten feet from where Thunder stood. Then, as
though wishing to discharge an unwanted passen-
ger, he reared high, and Colin slid off and over the
stallion's rump, his legs promptly giving out beneath him.

Her Ladyship's high laughter bubbled around
him. Even the stallion swung around to regard him
with amusement, lifting his head, stretching out his
neck, and peeling his lips back from his teeth in an
equine grin. Far off over the hills, Colin heard little
Bow's frantic yapping as she hurried to catch up
to them.

Ariadne slid from the stallion and reached down
to help him up.

Her eyes were sparkling with triumph.

"*Now* do you believe he's the Fastest Horse in
the World?"

Chapter 15

Whether Colin believed it or not was of no consequence, because at that moment Bow came racing over the farthest hill, two horsemen a half mile behind her.

"Time to test that claim!" he said, and seizing Ariadne around the waist, tossed her up on Shareb's back in one easy, fluid movement. Her eyes were bright with excitement, her skin glowing. "There's a pond five miles up the Norfolk Road— I'll meet you there as soon as it's fully dark. Now, prove to me that this confounded nag of yours can indeed run a hole through the wind!"

Laughing, she sent the fiery steed galloping off over the darkening pastures. Colin stared after her, a little smile playing about his mouth, a dreamy look in his eye—then, his heart leapt to his throat as he saw Shareb-er-rehh heading for the tall hedgerow that separated the fields. The mighty racehorse paused only long enough to gather himself, then flowed over it like a dolphin arcing over the waves.

And then he was off, pounding over the hills with his tail streaming behind him, and it wasn't until he was well out of sight that Colin realized that Her Ladyship didn't even have a bridle on him.

The moon was high, fading in and out behind tendrils of cloud and mist by the time Ariadne finally dared to creep out of the copse of trees where she had hidden and venture back onto the road. The night was spicy with the scent of grass and flowers, the air a gentle whisper of a breeze, but the relative quiet did nothing to calm her nerves. Now, as she guided Shareb with her knees and voice, she found herself jumping at every shadow, freezing at every sound of a distant, barking dog.

For the first time since undertaking this adventure, she was alone.

Colin is out here. Just another mile or so and you'll come to the pond. He'll be there, waiting. You know he will. . . .

But what if he hadn't been able to divert the pursuers? What if he *wasn't* waiting at the pond? She didn't know what she'd do, then.

Just as she didn't know what she was going to do about the situation with Maxwell.

Maybe it didn't bear thinking about . . . at least, not yet.

But like a persistent toothache the problem was there, and Ariadne knew that no matter how much she tried to ignore it, it was not going to go away. . . .

Beneath her, Shareb-er-rehh moved quietly, his ears up and his long neck stretched before her, his shoes grinding against little stones in the road. But Ariadne was not thinking about Shareb-er-rehh, nor her pursuers, nor her brother. She reached up and touched her mouth, tracing the shape of her lips as *he* had done with his tongue in the farmer's pasture. Oh, how warm and wonderful that kiss—the memory alone was enough to make her blood burn and little tingles race up and down her spine.

Oddly enough, she felt no regrets. Only, confusion. . . .

Papa—dear, wise, Papa—had arranged the union between herself and Maxwell. Surely, he had known what was best; not only for his daughter, but for the future of his Norfolk Thoroughbreds, whose legacy would be kept alive by Maxwell's own passion for racehorses. The match was a brilliant one, and the earl was everything she should want in a husband. He was well respected in all the right circles, fabulously handsome, darkly sensual, and she had known that he was the man for her ever since the night they'd been introduced. How taken she had been with him! And how taken she would *still* be with him . . .

If not for Colin Lord.

Now, she could barely even recall the details of Maxwell's swarthy face, could not remember quite how tall he was, or what his mouth had tasted like when he'd kissed her. She could only recall his eyes, penetrating black orbs that seemed to look right through her.

Dangerous eyes, and a man who would make a dangerous enemy if ever she crossed him.

The wind blew softly through the branches overhead, and she shuddered.

Best to put Colin Lord and any romantic notions where he was concerned right out of her mind. No matter how attractive she found him, no matter how much she was beginning to fancy him, he was not her social equal and never would be. That fact alone effectively cut off any thoughts of marriage. And even if Ariadne was willing to suffer complete ostracism from the society in which she had been born and raised for giving up an earl in favor of a lowly commoner, there was still Maxwell. *A dangerous enemy indeed*, she thought, remembering those black, unforgiving eyes. She shuddered to think how he might retaliate if she were to break off their engagement. At the very least, he would probably refuse to give the beautiful Gazella back to her. And if that happened, Shareb-er-rehh and Gazella would never be paired, the heir that was so desperately needed to carry on the Norfolk Thoroughbred would never be gotten, and Papa's legacy would die.

It was as simple as that. She *had* to marry Maxwell, or the Norfolk Thoroughbred would be no more.

Tears of frustration, hopelessness, and despair welled up in her eyes, and so absorbed was she in her thoughts that Ariadne never saw the pond where she was supposed to meet the veterinarian. Now, lifting her chin and swiping away her foolish tears—*be realistic, you cannot have Colin Lord!*—she remembered passing a tiny depression in the ground that was barely more than a mudhole some distance back, but the only movement there had been caused by several mallard ducks, some moorhens, and a pair of swans whose plumage had glowed white in the gathering gloom.

Had they traveled farther than five miles?

The road made a gentle bend, and from out of the night came the sounds of racing water. Surely, if there was a brook, it would lead into a pond? Guiding Shareb off the road with gentle pressure of her knees, Ariadne urged him down the hill to its banks, following the stream and allowing him to pick his way through the high grass.

Sure enough, there was a pond, glazed silver with the reflection of clouds and moon. Shareb dropped his head to drink while Ariadne gazed off into the night. Moonlight glinted against grass that was bent and waving in the wind, and she could just see a grove of trees hugging the eastern horizon, dark against the gently rolling hills. Only the rush of the brook, the summer chorus of crickets, and the distant sound of lowing cows broke the stillness of the night.

Shareb's head jerked up and he gave a soft, inquisitive whinny.

"Colin?" Ariadne called, her voice a half whisper.

Silence.

Maybe this was the wrong pond. Maybe she ought to retrace their steps, or continue up the road and see if there was another one. But no. What if Colin had been detained by the reward hunters? What if he had stopped somewhere to wash the ink out of his hair and return it to its rightful color? And what if that decrepit old nag he called a horse had broken down? Surely, its stride wasn't even comparable to Shareb's, and neither was its energy level.

Yes, that would certainly explain the veterinarian's tardiness. In fact, she thought wryly, she could probably count on seeing her companions sometime tomorrow afternoon with the rate of speed Thunder was capable of attaining.

She slid off Shareb-er-rehh, her bottom sore and her legs stiff and wobbly after being astride him for so long. Oh, what she wouldn't give for a hot cup of tea right now—and a bath! Mud caked her clothes, and her hair felt lank and unclean. And that pond, still beneath the night sky, looked dreadfully inviting. . . .

Biting her lip, she glanced back in the direction of the road, but the slope of the hill blocked her view of it. Then she gazed at the pond and, unbuttoning her shirt, pushed through the tall weeds and grasses until she reached the water's edge.

She pried off her boots. Around her the darkness pressed, big and deep and silent. She paused, listening to the crickets, the grunting chorus of a frog, and the lonely sound the breeze made as it whispered through the reeds and sent tiny ripples skating across the pond. She put her foot in the water. Then, the other. Again, it struck her how helplessly alone she was, and her heart began to beat fast and hard.

"Shareb!"

The horse lifted his head, a tuft of grass hanging from the side of his mouth. In the darkness, she could just see the telltale white ringing his right eye.

"Keep a watch for danger," she murmured, and he looked at her blankly before dropping his head once more.

A big help *he* was. Heaven help her, *where* was Colin?

I will not be afraid, she thought, as the night seemed to grow blacker, deeper. *He'll be along shortly, and he'll make certain nothing happens to me. There is nothing to be afraid of. Nothing. . . .*

Leaving Shareb to his grassy meal and trying not to think about how empty her own stomach was, Ariadne waded farther into the pond. The water was warm, still, and unhappy about being disturbed. Deep mud sucked at the soles of her feet, slimy weeds swished against her ankles, and she shuddered in revulsion of what insects and other . . . *creatures* . . . must lurk in the water she was about to bathe in. Again, she paused, listening to the night. If only Colin would appear to smile at her in that shy, private way of his, teasing her and watching her with unspoken admiration in his eyes . . .

Slowly, she turned and looked behind her, her eyes straining to pierce the darkness. But the little slope behind the pond was empty, and the breeze sounded lonelier than ever.

Shivering, Ariadne bit her lip once more, growing worried.

She washed herself as best and as quickly as she could and, wading out of the water, squeezed her arms against her drenched clothing in a futile attempt to dry herself. Miserable and chilly in her wet, scratchy clothes, she lay down on the bare grass and folded her arms beneath her head. Above, the stars looked down, and the utter vastness of the night sky only reminded her how alone she was. She turned her head. Beneath her forearm something was crawling, and, shuddering in revulsion, she got up and moved a few feet away. Tufts of grass were lumpy beneath her arms, and the earth was hard and silent. She moved to press her ear against it, yearning for the quiet vibrations that might signal Thunder's approach.

Nothing but the crickets, the frogs, and the quiet burble of the brook.

And the darkness.

She thought of Tristan out there in the night, hunting her down like an animal. She thought of Maxwell, and wondered why she felt a ripple of foreboding at the very vision of his face. She thought of Colin Lord, and how much she yearned for that gentle healer she could never have. And then she thought of her beloved Papa, and the wonderful horses that had once cavorted around the pastures of Burnham Thorpe. A Papa that she would never see again in this lifetime, and horses that now—like his dream would be if she didn't get the last two of them bred—were all dead.

Tears of silent grief began to roll down her cheeks and into her damp hair, and her chest convulsed on quiet, choking sobs.

Oh, Papa . . . dear God, how I miss you. I am so frightened, so confused. How I wish you were here to counsel me, to comfort me, to keep me company . . . and oh, Papa—how I wish I had the chance to say . . . to say—

She put her hands over her eyes, the tears bursting hotly through her fingers.

Good-bye.

Her soft sobs filled the night, wracking her chest and squeezing it until there were no more tears left to cry. And when at last she opened her eyes, she saw Shareb-er-rehh standing protectively over her, his body huge against the starry sky.

Her Papa's horse.

Comforting her, in her Papa's stead.

He lowered his head and she put her arms around his neck, her face against his jaw until her sobs finally quieted and the wind blew softly against her damp cheeks. She stayed that way for a long, long time.

The Fastest Horse in the World and a soaked, sobbing noblewoman. What a pair they made now.

Her cheek still pressed to the stallion's, she stared off into the night, wishing with all her heart for her veterinarian and the safety and comfort of his arms.

The baying of a hound . . . Shareb's piercing, angry scream, and the earth shaking beneath his hooves as he galloped in a circle around her. At first, Ariadne thought she was dreaming; then, her eyes shot open and she sat up with a gasp, only to see three men standing over her with their muskets pointed at her heart.

She froze, the blood icing in her veins.

"So, what 'ave we here, eh?" one of them said coldly, with a triumphant look at his cohorts. In the moonlight his eyes were small and mean, tiny chips of flint in a fat, bejowled face that was all but dominated by the breadth of his bullish shoulders and great, barrellike body. "A young lad or a *fugitive noblewoman*?"

"A ticket for a fifteen-hundred-pound reward, if you ask *me*," his companion snarled, cocking his musket. "Get up."

Shareb-er-rehh shot past again, the earth shaking beneath his mighty body, his tail flying behind him as he tried to divert the men.

"Somebody grab that damned stallion before 'e falls an' breaks a bloody leg!" the huge bullock of a man shouted. "He ain't going to be worth nothin' to us then!"

One of them, a tall, reedy sack of bones with a broken nose, rushed off after Shareb, trying in vain to catch him.

Ariadne sat up, her heart pounding in her ears. "Really, sir, I don't know what you're talking about," she snapped, trying to sound appropriately indignant. "Do I look like a noblewoman to you?"

Again, Shareb galloped past, his eyes wild, his nostrils huge and wide.

The man thrust the musket against her ribs. "Get up."

Slowly, she got to her feet, her chin high, her stomach sick with fear, her legs like custard. She was shaking so badly she was afraid she would fall, and if she fell, they would probably shoot her and she would die right here, right now, never to be found. But somehow, her legs managed to support her, and she glared defiantly at them, her eyes on their ugly faces, their long muskets, and the growling hound they must have used to track Shareb-er-rehh.

"Somethin' wrong with your legs, *my lady*?" the huge man said with a sneer. "I ain't got time to waste chattin' when I could be collectin' that fifteen hundred pounds for yer return. Now, *move*."

"My brother hasn't the money to pay you," she

retorted. "He is in debt up to his ears, so you might as well just let me go and save yourself a lot of trouble!"

"Oh, he'll pay," the man growled. "I'm goin' to march you an' that horse right back to London an' make *sure* he'll pay. Now shut up an' move, or I'll make you sorry you ever met me."

"I'm already sorry that I met you, you disgusting heap of—"

Her remark was abruptly silenced by a sharp cuff across the mouth that split her lip and nearly knocked her down, and in that moment, Ariadne had no doubt whatsoever that if she tried to fight them, they would kill her.

Dear God. Had they found and hurt Colin?

"Move!" the leader shouted, and shoved her forward with a meaty hand between her shoulders.

Her head high, her legs trembling, she turned and walked stiffly ahead of them, the musket pressing cruelly into the small of her back. Sweat prickled her scalp, ran like ice water down her spine. She had to do something.

In the end, she didn't have to. Shareb-er-rehh did it for her.

The stallion had been circling the field, leading his frustrated pursuer a merry chase; now, he saw the men forcing his mistress away and his savage, angry whistle rent the night. And though Ariadne could not see him, she could hear his hoofbeats, and knew the exact moment he moved out of his lazy canter to come charging across the grassy field in thunderous fury. This time, he did not feint away at the last moment. Head down, ears back, he let out an enraged, stallion scream—and came straight for the little group.

Howling in fear, the men dived for cover as the horse, teeth bared and neck outstretched, bore down on them like a demon straight from hell. The huge one dropped his musket and leapt headfirst into the pond; the other flung himself into the weeds, his musket going off in the process with a thunderous explosion of smoke and fire. Only the dog stood his ground, crouching low, racing alongside Shareb as the stallion swept past, then making a leap for the mighty shoulder. The hound glanced off the flying horse, connected with his hooves, and fell back, shrieking and yelping in pain. A shot rang out and then Shareb was turning, his tail flying, his scream piercing the night as he came galloping back toward Ariadne.

She was already running toward him, and he slowed only long enough for her to make a wild, desperate lunge for his back. Her balance failed her, and she clung to his mane with one leg curled over his back and the ground rushing past beneath her.

Angry voices rang out behind them.

"Stop her! Damn it, *stop her*, that horse is worth fifteen hundred bloody *pounds*!"

Her fists wrapped in the stallion's mane, her leg hooked around his back, his flying hooves inches from her shoulders and head, Ariadne managed to pull herself up onto him as shots rang out behind her. Something whined past her ear, and she bent low over the outstretched neck, burying her face in the sparse, flying mane and feeling the wind ripping through her clothes, her hair, her—

"Go, Shareb, *go*!" she cried, driving her heels into his flanks. "Run, like you've never run before!"

Back went the stallion's ears, and he nearly exploded out from under her in a burst of speed and sound that drowned out everything else. Mighty muscles churned beneath her and Ariadne wrapped her arms around his neck, urging him on with knees and hands and voice.

"Run, Shareb! For God's sake, *run*!"

Behind them the hound set up a frenzied baying, but it could never catch them. Another shot rang out, and instantaneously, pain exploded in her arm. She cried out and sank her teeth into her bottom lip, trying to hold back the sudden dizziness of terror, for blood was running hot and wet down her arm and she knew she'd been hit. Locking her hands beneath the stallion's neck she hung on for dear life, knowing that if she passed out and fell, it would be all over.

"Go, Shareb," she whispered, her lips against the straining neck and whipping mane. "Go . . . find Colin."

The stallion lunged over a hill and hit the road at a blistering gallop, the rapid beating of his hooves beginning to fade to a dull roar in her ears until Ariadne could no longer separate it from the thunder of his mighty strides.

Darkness began to invade her vision and she buried her cheek in his mane, praying she could hold on, that she wouldn't fall when she lost consciousness. Her face bumped against the hard neck and her eyes began to slip shut, and the last thing she felt was the stallion, leveling out into that tremendous, ground-eating stride that was more a flight than a gallop, that fabulous, soaring gait that carried him over the earth faster than any domesticated creature alive. She never saw his ears prick forward, never heard his long, urgent whinny as he thundered down the Norfolk Road with his precious burden perilously balanced on his back, his tail streaming behind him and his dark eyes searching the night.

Shareb-er-rehh screamed again, the sound flowing out over the hills and to the stars above.

Looking for the veterinarian.

Chapter 16

G^{*unfire.*}
G He heard it as a sharp crack in the distant night, and the blood ran cold in his veins. Moments later the baying of a hound echoed over the hills, and then—faintly at first, then growing louder and louder—the sound of a horse bearing down on them.

Fast.

In the darkness, Colin could just see the road ahead, ribboning away behind a low rise. The maddened hoofbeats grew louder and he cautiously steered Thunder over to the side, waiting for the animal to come charging around the hill and hoping it wouldn't run them down.

Louder and louder came that furious crescendo, the baying of the hound—

And then the steed burst around the bend.

It was Shareb-er-rehh, the moonlight glowing in his eyes, fire flying from his hooves.

Fastest Horse in the World.

Colin leapt from the chaise and ran out into the road, waving his arms to intercept the stallion.

"Whoa! *Whoa!*"

Shareb planted his front feet and, nearly sitting

back on his haunches, came to a skidding, sliding halt, the dirt spraying up beneath his hind legs and belly.

And then Colin saw the tiny burden he carried on his back.

"Ariadne!"

She tumbled off and into his arms. The hound's baying was furious, growing louder, and at any moment the dog was going to burst around the bend and God only knew who else would follow.

Colin wasted no time. The unconscious noblewoman in his arms, he slapped Shareb-er-rehh hard on the rump. The horse understood perfectly, and with a shrill whinny charged off down the road. He'd no sooner vanished around the bend when the dog burst into view, baying furiously, a trio of mounted horsemen in hot pursuit.

Colin leapt into the chaise, put Ariadne beneath a blanket on the floorboards and, leaning over her with his elbows on his knees, urged Thunder into a slow, plodding trot.

The hound streaked past, followed by two of the riders. The third paused, breathless, his jowly face dark and angry. "You see a horse go by with a rider on its back?"

Colin raised a brow and kept Thunder walking. He scratched his head. "Horse? What kind?"

"Bay one, a stallion, white blaze down its face!" the man shouted, fighting to keep his own winded mount under control.

"Oh, aye," Colin said slowly. "Saw one go past about ten minutes ago, though I don't think it was the one you're looking for. Little white mare, she was. Definitely no stallion—"

"The hell with ye!" the man yelled, and drove his heels savagely into his frightened mount, sending the protesting animal charging off down the road to join his companions.

Colin waited for the pounding rumble of their hoofbeats to recede; then, with Bow huddling fearfully on his lap and Her Ladyship's body pressed warmly against his toes, he steered Thunder off the road and deep into the dark pastures.

"Faster, boy," he called, urging the old gelding on. The horse tucked his head and pulled a quick trot out of his long-forgotten repertoire of gaits, and the chaise creaked, bounced, and rolled over the dips and rises.

They followed the perimeter of a broken fence. Colin heard water rushing ahead, and saw a flat, bubbling brook cutting through the starlit field. At his feet lay the limp, warm mass of Ariadne's body, and its very stillness caused his heart to pound and cold sweat to break out along the length of his spine. Urgently, he steered the gelding down the bank and into the water, then back up the other side and into a grove of trees. There, he pulled Thunder to a stop, leapt from the chaise, and, sliding his arms beneath the blanketed body, gingerly lifted her.

"Ariadne," he whispered, cradling her to his chest. "Oh, sweetheart. . . ."

He peeled back the blanket, and his heart breaking, pressed his lips to her brow. It was pale and cold in the darkness.

"Colin?" Her voice was the faintest of whispers; then her head fell back against his arm, her hair tumbled over his wrist, and she was still and silent once more.

His face grim, his eyes bleak and worried, he carried her swiftly toward the grove of trees, little Bow whining worriedly at his heels, Thunder following along behind him with his nose at Colin's arm.

Please, God, let her be all right, he breathed, his heart racing. He found a flat spot in the grass, set her and the blanket down, and lowered himself to his knees beside her.

With Bow watching from beside him, he laid his fingers against her cheek. Her face was white in the gloom, her lips parted, her little hand lying at her side with the palm turned upward. Colin swallowed hard. Then, he gently peeled the blanket back—and there, black and ugly in the moonlight, was a huge stain spreading over her left sleeve.

Wordlessly he got up, went to his sea chest, and got his surgical instruments and spectacles. With precise orderliness, he lit the lantern, laid out forceps, tweezers and scalpel, a roll of bandages and a small bottle of rum.

He had never performed surgery on a person before, but he shoved aside the thought and concentrated on the task at hand. Lifting her tiny wrist, he pressed his index finger to her pulse and found it to be steady and strong. Then he pulled the lantern close, rolled her gently onto her side to expose the injured arm, and with two quick, steady slices, slit the sleeve from wrist to elbow, then elbow to shoulder.

His patient moaned and gave a little sob, and he gently laid his hand against her cheek, smoothing the fragile, dewy skin and feeling something thick and burning rising up in his chest.

Please God, help me to help her. Don't take her from this earth. Not yet. Not now. I love her, God. I love her. Let me save her. . . .

He leaned down and tenderly kissed her damp, tangled hair.

"Colin," she whispered, opening her eyes and looking dazedly up at his knee. "I'm so scared. . . ."

"You're going to be all right," he murmured, close to her ear. "Just lie still and think of happy things. Clouds floating over the sky. Birds singing on a sunny morning. Kittens sleeping in the sun-shine."

He pulled back, peeled the wet, bloody fabric from her arm, and with gentle fingers, examined the injury.

Given his former profession, Colin had seen enough gunshot wounds in his life to recognize what he saw now, and hot rage pounded against his temples with such force that he had to sit back and press his fingertips against them to quell it. He shut his eyes, briefly, until his emotions were once again under control. Then, he peered down at Ariadne for a moment before pulling her up and into his lap, and with businesslike efficiency, went to work.

The wound was an open, gaping hole, still trail-ing a bloody thread of crimson. He put his fingers against its perimeter and pushed, hard. Blood bub-bled out and trickled down the white flesh of her arm, and the girl made a sobbing, wrenching noise deep in her throat.

Instantly, Bow was there, licking her face.

"Be brave, my little Ariadne," he murmured, wishing desperately that he wouldn't have to cause her further pain, wishing he could take it on him-self and thus spare her the agony of what he had to do. "It's going to hurt."

"A lot?"

"Maybe, sweetheart. Just . . . hold on to me, all right?"

She whimpered, terrified and dazed, one hand reaching out to grasp a handful of his shirt like a child with a toy. "Am I going to die, Colin?"

His skilled fingers pushed against the wound, forcing more blood out of it to cleanse it, and dimly, it occurred to him that what he was doing was probably the closest he would ever come to phlebotomy. He moved his fingers a fraction of an inch, and sure enough, he felt it—something hard and sharp just beneath the skin and buried in the superficial tissues of her bicep.

"No, my love, you're not going to die," he said, trying to sound cheerful and chiding in the hope of calming her. "Besides, who would pay me the two thousand pounds if I were to lose you?"

"Oh, Colin—" Bravely, she tried to laugh, but the sound came out as a hitching sob of fear, and he enfolded her tiny hand within his own large one, his fingers reaching halfway up her forearm until she stopped trembling. Then he pressed her hand to his lips, not noticing the way her eyes fastened on his in wonder, trust, and . . . something else.

My love, he had said. Maybe he had not caught his words, but Ariadne had. He rambled on about sunshine and kittens, detaching that part of his mind from the part belonging to the professional, competent surgeon she had first seen on his knees in the street. But Ariadne wasn't thinking about kittens. She was looking at his face; the ink black hair tumbling over his brow, the planes of his cheeks, the glint of moonlight off his spectacles, the intensity of his gaze. She thought that maybe if she gazed at him, she wouldn't feel the pain as much. But feel it she did, and when she cried out at the first touch of the scalpel, she saw the muscle twitch in his jaw, the flash of anguish in his beautiful eyes.

My love, he had said.

She closed her eyes and drifted off, feeling herself floating . . . sinking down beneath dark, gentle blankets. . . .

"Colin?" she murmured.

His hand was warm and gentle against her cheek, smoothing the wet hair away and stroking her skin to soothe her. "It's only a flesh wound, with a bit of the musket ball still caught inside. If you can just hold on for a few minutes longer, we'll be all through."

"Shareb-er-rehh—"

"Has led your pursuers a merry chase, and I have complete confidence in his ability to lose them. Now be still, love, and think of all the little foals he shall some day sire. . . ."

"Yes, little foals . . ."

Colin reached for his tweezers and gently palpated the muscle, trying to pin down the exact location of the lead fragment. There. Right . . . *there*.

Balancing her in his lap, he pulled the lantern close to her arm, bent his head, and, knitting his brow in intense concentration, put the tweezers against the wound.

The girl's eyes flew open, her teeth catching her bottom lip hard enough to raise blood.

"Little foals," he repeated softly, in a low, soothing tone. "Little foals, kicking up their heels and running alongside their mamas"—he touched the tweezers to the fragment once more, trying to see what he was doing in the lantern's meager light—"little foals, with little feet and little faces, little foals with fuzzy little whiskers and long, long, legs like their papa's. . . ."

So intent was he on his work that he didn't quite notice the moment she lost consciousness, and it was only the distant thunder of galloping hoofbeats that brought him back to awareness of the present.

His head jerked up in alarm, and he was seized by a flighty impulse to sweep up the girl and make a run for it—but as the pounding rumble grew louder and louder, he realized it was no threat at all, but Shareb-er-rehh.

The stallion burst over the farthest rise and, silhouetted against the night sky, charged along the rim of the hill before plunging down it and toward them. He lurched to a stop, tossed his head, and prancing with triumphant fire, came forward, his nostrils flaring and the breath rushing through his lungs.

"Did you lose them, boy?"

Shareb tossed his head as though to respond, and stepping forward, lowered his nose to his mistress's still body, his nostrils flaring at the pungent scent of blood.

"She's going to be fine," Colin said. Tweezers in hand, he raised his arm and pointed to a spot several feet away. "Now off with you, and let me work. Go chew on some grass or something."

Shareb put his ears back and eyed him flatly.

"Go!" Colin said, waving his hand.

The stallion squealed, trotted a short distance away, and stood staring.

Once more, Colin bent his head, the black hair falling over his brow. He pushed it back with his wrist and hurriedly found the place where the fragment was. Behind him he heard slow, hesitant hoofbeats approaching. They came to a stop, and heavy, hot breathing blasted the back of his neck.

"Go away, Shareb."

The breathing grew hotter.

"Go *away*, Shareb, I will not hurt her!"

But the stallion refused to move, and, trying to ignore him, Colin slid the tweezers beneath the ragged edges of torn skin and skillfully retrieved the leaden fragment.

The girl never stirred. Shareb's head hung protectively over Colin's shoulder, and twice, he had to elbow the stallion away so that he could work. He squeezed more blood from the wound, pinched the edges shut with his fingers, and cleaned the blood away with a piece of linen soaked in rum. Then he wound a bandage around the arm, tied it in a snug knot, and began to get up. His feet and legs had fallen asleep, and he stumbled as he set Ariadne down on the blanket, stood up, and passed a weary hand over his brow. Leaving Shareb-er-rehh to stand watch over her, he retrieved a strong bar of soap, went down to the brook, and washed his hands, face—and, finally, his hair.

It took three washings to get the ink out, but he dared not continue on with that distinctive black hair. Not after being recognized, and not with the countryside looking for a tall, black-haired accomplice to Lady Ariadne's "crime." And so he scrubbed until his scalp ached and the soap was but a mere sliver in his hand, and then, his hair fresh, clean, and fair once more, his body aching with fatigue, stood leaning against a tree.

Thinking.

Moments later, when he returned to the little group, he saw the rum bottle lying empty on the grass, and Shareb eyeing him innocently.

Colin was too weary to scold him. He looked at Thunder, dozing with one hind leg cocked beneath him, and Bow, curled up on the blanket in the hollow of Ariadne's hip and waist. Only Shareb-er-rehh was awake, the dimming lanternlight glowing in his dark eyes, and Colin wondered what was going through that canny, equine mind.

Dismissing the horse from his thoughts, he sat down beside the girl, slid his arms beneath her, and, wrapping her in the blanket against the cool night air, pulled her protectively up against his chest. Shareb eyed him for a long, decisive moment; then, he gave a great sigh, walked a few feet away, folded his long legs beneath him, and lay down. His tail flicked once, his sides heaved, and then he was asleep.

Around them, the night breathed, deep and silent at last. There were no hounds, no reward hunters in hot pursuit, nothing but a clear sky, the crickets, and there, just above the treetops, a bat winging its way through the darkness.

His precious burden sheltered in his arms and held protectively close to his heart, Colin leaned back against the spoked wheel of the chaise and put his lips against her damp hair.

For a long, long, time he remained awake, staring bleakly into the night and aching for the woman he held so tenderly in his arms. Sometime between midnight and the wee hours, his head lolled against the wheel spokes, the spectacles slid from his nose, and the veterinarian joined his companions in exhausted slumber.

Chapter 17

Ariadne became slowly aware of several things at once. A burning ache in her arm that throbbed in time with her pulse. Damp, itchy clothes that clung to her skin. The lingering scent of a spent wick, a soft linen shirt against her cheek, the sound of deep, rhythmic breathing, and a heartbeat thudding beneath her ear.

And warmth. Hard, encompassing warmth, beneath her face and surrounding her back and shoulders.

Enclosing her.

Protecting her.

She opened her eyes, and there, so close she had to adjust her vision to focus on it, was the pale, moonlit wedge of Colin's chest.

Full awareness came quickly back to her, and bits and pieces of things she couldn't fully remember. Those horrible men, she remembered *them*, and the gunshot that had cracked the night the same moment she'd been hit. Shareb-er-rehh, calling on his extraordinary speed to bring her to safety; how she'd remained aboard him she didn't know, but she recalled tumbling from his back and into the doctor's arms, and then, later, his soothing voice and comforting touch as he'd made her arm hurt more and told her to be brave.

And yes, his eyes. . . . She remembered his eyes, those beautiful, gentle eyes, the intense concentration behind his spectacles as he'd stared down at her arm and dug at her flesh with the same fixed purpose he had demonstrated when he had saved that poor, dying dog from bloat.

Colin. . . .

She gazed at all she could see of him; the base of his throat, and the hot, silvery wedge of skin just beneath her lips, where soft, wiry hair lay and a pulse beat rhythmically. She moved her head just enough to nuzzle his shirt aside and put her mouth against it. He smelled clean, of English wind and English pastures, hay, clover, and wild grasses.

Colin. . . .

She kissed that warm, beating pulse.

He did not stir, and, gingerly, Ariadne tried to push herself out of his protective embrace. It was no easy task, with his arms locked loosely around her, but she felt the call of nature and had no choice but to answer it. Holding her breath, she moved back another inch, and the arm that weighed down her shoulders slid off and thumped heavily to the blanket.

She froze. The animal doctor made a soft, unintelligible noise, but did not wake.

She stood and looked down at him. He reposed with his back propped against the hard spokes of the chaise's left wheel, his head at an uncomfortable-looking angle to his body and his lashes long, sweeping crescents atop his cheeks. With a sense of relief and happiness, she saw that he had scrubbed the ink out of his hair, and the fair, beautiful locks that she had so admired were restored to their former glory.

"You are beautiful," she whispered, her heart in her throat. "Perfect. Magnificent."

His spectacles lay upside down on the grass beside his hip, and carefully folding them, she put them on the seat of the chaise. The movement sent pain winging the length of her arm and, gasping, she hesitantly touched the area. A bandage bound the wound, exerting just enough pressure to make it feel snug and secure. Her eyes filled with tears of adoration, and, as she gazed down at her handsome, gentle savior, sleeping like a babe in the starlight, she felt her heart constrict, then overflow with something so powerful it did not even have a name.

In that moment, she knew that she loved him.

Knew that she'd loved him from the moment she'd seen him bending over that dog.

"Dear, dear, Colin..." she whispered, placing her lips against his sleeping brow. Then she drew back and put trembling fingers against her mouth and gave a little, incredulous laugh. "God help me, but I have fallen in love with you."

And then, suddenly, Maxwell, her betrothal, and the plight of the Norfolk Thoroughbred swept upon her like a dark cloud and the smile died on her lips.

She moved stiffly away and down to the brook. Kneeling on the grassy bank, she splashed cool water on her face and tried to make sense of things. The stars reflected on the flat parts of the water and refracted into millions of bright sparkles on those broken areas where the brook tumbled over rocks and rises. She stared down into the depths, her heart aching with longing and despair and something she couldn't quite grasp, couldn't quite understand.

Colin. . . .

Bits and pieces of scenes came back to her. His

hot kisses, promising further, untold delights. His hand on her breast, sweeping up her thigh on a trail of fire. The long gazes, the accidental touches, the silent glances when the other wasn't supposed to be looking, and always, the constant awareness and underlying attraction they each had for the other. She thought of the sound of his voice, the taste of his kiss, that crooked grin and his helpless laughter when she said something outrageous. She was lost. But then, she had been, from the moment she'd first seen him and he'd glanced up and caught her with those striking, oddly beautiful eyes.

Just thinking of his kisses, the gentleness of his strong, warm hands—and the idea of them touching her here, there, and all over—was enough to melt her from the inside out and reduce her to a state of mindless need and want.

Lady Ariadne St. Aubyn got to her feet and stared resolutely across the flat English pastures that stretched away toward the pink rim of the coming dawn.

There was nothing to do but face the truth, vulgar as it might have once appeared.

She loved Colin Lord, veterinarian.

Wanted him more than she had ever wanted anything in her entire life.

Head high, she turned and went back the way she'd come.

He lay sleeping where she had left him, a golden angel lacking only the wings and the halo. In the starlight, his hair was almost silver, and the effect was enough to lend him a sort of ethereal mystique that held her breathless and spellbound.

Ariadne knelt down before him.

She remembered someone saying that if you stare at a sleeper for long enough, he will waken.

Squatting, she propped her elbows on her knees, her chin in her palms, and focused her gaze on his closed eyelids. But after five minutes of this, he still had not moved.

Growing impatient, she reached out and carefully touched his hair.

He flinched but did not wake.

Her hand remained with the soft, still-damp locks caught between thumb and forefinger; then her palm moved lower, tracing the warm, stubbly curve of his jaw and cheekbone. She put her hand against his cheek, and with a soft sigh, he leaned his face into it.

And then his eyes—beautiful, mystical, almost magical in the kiss of the starlight—opened.

He said nothing, only looked at her. There was no fogginess in his gaze, none of the customary adjustment most people must make from sleep to wakefulness. For a moment she thought he was going to kiss her; then, he seemed to remember himself, and reached up to gently encircle her wrist with strong, warm fingers.

The moment was broken.

"Your arm—"

"My arm is fine."

He frowned, seeing her face. "Are you all right, my lady?"

Her eyes pooled with tears. Slowly, she shook her head.

He sat up, leaned against the wheel of the chaise, and patted the ground beside him. She swallowed hard and joined him, feeling very tiny beside him, feeling very foolish for making such a mess of things. Anguish filled her, and the tears slid unchecked down her cheeks. He was too gallant to call attention to them, merely pulling out his handkerchief and dabbing silently at her eyes until she had herself under control. Then he slipped his arm around her shoulders and pulled her close, and only her breeding and manners kept her from huddling against him and burying her face in the warm cup of his shoulder.

"I love you, you know," she said. Then she raised her chin and stared mutely out into the darkness. Her lip trembled, but her voice was firm with resolution. "I love you, Colin, have from the moment I first saw you, I think, and I don't quite know what to do about it."

Sighing, he drew up one knee, lay back against the wheel of the chaise, and gazed wordlessly out at the dawn, a blaze of fire smeared above still-dark hills. His lips were pursed and a vertical frown line creased his brow as he pondered this revelation with all the attention he might've given a particularly difficult scientific problem.

"Colin, did you hear me?" Feeling suddenly foolish, she looked down and began to twirl a clump of grass around her finger.

"Yes, sweetheart, I heard you."

"I . . . don't know what to do about it."

"Yes, it certainly *does* present a problem, doesn't it?"

"Yes, and it is all your fault, Colin, because I wouldn't even *be* in love with you if you'd only stop doing things to make me love you!"

The corner of his mouth lifted in a helpless grin. "Oh, well, yes. I really should have left you to bleed to death."

"And you should not have rescued Thunder from that heinous ogre, and you should not have saved that poor dog from bloat, and you should not show such patience with me, and—"

"My lady."

She sniffled and glanced at him, her dark eyes glassy with tears, her lower lip quivering. "What?"

He smiled, a bit sheepishly. "You are missing a beautiful sunrise."

To his surprise, she began to sob, and buried her face in her hands. "Oh, Colin . . . I am *so confused*."

He tightened his arm around her shoulders. "I know. I—am too."

"I don't know what to do . . . what to say . . . what to feel."

Again, he drew his handkerchief and gently dabbed the tears from her cheeks. "Neither do I."

"What do you think we ought to do about it?"

He looked up again, off into the gathering pink dawn. Anguish burned in his eyes, and his jaw was suddenly hard. "Keep away from each other, I guess. It's . . . safer that way."

"Is that what you *want*, Colin?"

"What I want, and what I shall have, are two different things."

"That is not what I asked you."

"Very well then." He turned to face her, dark pupils framed by the beauty of irises that looked silver in the faint light. "What I want is a lovely little noblewoman who is promised to another. What I shall have, is the heartbreak of having to deliver her into the arms of somebody else."

She pulled her knees up to her chest, locked her hands around them, and propped her chin on her kneecaps. She could feel the heat of him burning through her clothes, could smell his warm scent of man, and grass, and wind. She looked down at the ground, seeing it through a haze of tears. "Colin . . . I'm not so sure I still want to marry Maxwell."

"Have you ever been, Ariadne?" he asked, gently.

She swallowed hard, feeling something thick and harsh catching in her throat.

"No," she whispered. "Not . . . after meeting you."

"You've only known me for a few days. Not so long as you've known Maxwell, and not long enough to consider giving up your future."

"You're too noble."

"No, merely realistic. And older than you."

"You mean, wiser?"

He shrugged and gave a little grin. "Maybe."

Her eyes sad, she gazed at him, her cheek still lying atop her kneecaps. Then she reached out and touched the corner of his mouth. "You will make some lucky woman the perfect husband," she said wistfully, staring into his beautiful eyes. "You are the gentlest, yet strongest, man I have ever met, and you make all those London blades to whom I am accustomed look like a bunch of whining sissies. You stand up for what you believe in, you defend what you think is right and just, you are . . . a *man*."

His mouth curved in that slow, crooked grin she loved so much. "Yes, I was, the last time I checked—"

"Colin?"

"What?"

"Do you love *me*?"

He plucked a blade of grass, began knotting it around his finger, and slanted her a chiding look. "Do birds fly?"

"*Do* you?"

"Fly?"

"No, silly . . . *love* me."

He tossed the grass aside and looked into her eyes, his gaze so full of feeling she thought she would drown beneath the force of its very intensity. Then he gave a great sigh, took her hand, and turned his face to the dawn. "Yes, Ariadne. For all the good it does me, I do."

The words hung in the still air, and there was not even any breeze to sweep them away. They glanced at each other, he looking boyishly sheepish by what he had just said, she gazing at him with a slow grin spreading across her face that lit up her entire countenance. Then, shyly, they both looked away from each other.

She plucked at the grass again. "So now what do we do?"

"*You* need to think about whether you will go through with this marriage to Maxwell, and if not, how to end it."

"And you?"

"I think"—he squeezed his eyes shut and pushed the heel of his hand against his forehead—"I think I need to go take a walk."

He got to his feet and left her sitting there in the grass by herself.

"Why?"

"I need to think."

"Why?"

He stood staring down at her. "Because if I *don't* think, I'll take action, and then both of us might—correction, both of us *will*—regret it."

He turned and began walking away.

"But *would* we regret it?" Feeling rejected, Ariadne stared after him. "And would the 'action'—I presume that means lovemaking—be so very bad, Colin? If we both want to do it, I can't see why—"

He spun around, shoving his hair off his brow. "For God's sake, Ariadne, *think* about it! At the moment you're engaged to another man, and you need to make some major decisions before you can even think about marrying *me*—"

"I never said anything about marrying you."

"What?"

"I mean, I cannot marry you. That should be obvious."

He stared at her, shocked. "You would make

love with me, then go off and marry somebody else?"

"Colin, I *have* to, the future of the Norfolk Thoroughbred depends upon my marrying Maxwell! Don't you understand?"

"No, I guess I bloody well don't!"

He whirled and began walking angrily away.

"Colin!"

He kept walking, his shoulders stiff with fury.

Ariadne leapt to her feet and ran after him. She caught his arm, her fingers sinking through the soft cotton of his sleeve and meeting hard muscle before he spun around, his eyes flashing, his mouth hard. "Damn it, don't you know enough to leave me alone?"

And then, before she could shrink back from his anger, he shoved a hand through her hair, yanked her up against him, and slammed his mouth down atop hers. The kiss was hard, hot and punishing, his lips almost brutal, his tongue plunging deep within her mouth. He caught her behind the waist with his other hand and ground his hips against hers, and she felt his hardness against her belly, the heat of his body burning her through their clothing. Her head fell back beneath the onslaught even as she wrapped her arms around his neck and drove herself upward to meet his kiss, and she would have lost her balance if not for the hand beneath her head, the arm behind her waist. And then, like a storm blowing itself out, he became gentle, loving, the pressure of his mouth growing sweet instead of savage, the hand that crushed her head against his now gently cupping her skull, the thumb caressing her cheek.

He broke the kiss, and breathing hard, let his brow rest against the top of her head. For a moment neither moved, their hearts pounding and their bodies clinging to each other with desire and need. From somewhere off in the distance a crow called . . . then the veterinarian gently cradled Ariadne's jaw in his hands and lifted her head.

They gazed into each other's eyes—

And time stopped.

Her hands caught in his shirtfront as they stared at each other across more inches of space. She blushed and giggled nervously. He gave a slow, defeated grin. And then they sobered, their anger, hurt, and pride forgotten as their bodies began to respond to each other.

He gazed down at her, his body catching fire where it touched hers.

"Will you kiss me?" she asked, in the softest of whispers.

He swallowed hard, and Ariadne knew in that final, triumphant moment that he was hers. She watched his long lashes sweep down over those beautiful eyes; his head bent, his mouth neared hers, and his warm breath feathered against her cheek . . . she felt his fingers thread through her hair and cup the back of her head; then there was only the gentle pressure of his lips, the sweet thrust of his tongue. . . .

And nothing more.

She slid her palms up his chest and sank against him. The kiss went on, drawing her up and into its heat until her head was swimming and her flesh was a writhing mass of liquid fire. She heard herself moan somewhere deep in her throat, and then all thought, all reason fled her, and the only occupant of her universe was . . . *him.*

Colin . . . how I love you, adore you, want you, want—

Dimly, she felt his hand caressing her back, pulling her shirt out from her breeches and then sliding beneath the fabric to move down her spine with hot, feverish eagerness. . . .

Lady Ariadne St. Aubyn sobbed deep in her throat, and began to melt.

Chapter 18

ome hundred feet away, Shareb-er-rehh came awake and raised his noble head. His ears went back and, sulkily, he heaved himself to his feet. He heard the man's gentle voice, Lady A's answering giggle, and jealousy—ripe, hot, and searing—tore through him.

Nostrils flaring, he skulked past the unhitched Thunder and Bow, the former regarding him with a warning look in his old eye and the latter with a curious cock of her head.

Not bothering to honor the pair with even a glance, Shareb-er-rehh stood sulking, pouting.

And then he spotted the doctor's sea chest.

One ear went forward, and he glanced stealthily off toward that slight rise, beyond which *his* human was giving her attentions to the hated veterinarian. He lowered his nose to the chest, lifted out the last remaining rum bottle, and, managing to uncork it with his teeth, consumed every drop of the fiery spirits with a single, triumphant gulp. Then he raised his shod foot and began pawing through the chest, spitefully intending to destroy the contents.

Sharp pain burst in his shoulder and savagely, he whirled around to see what had caused it.

The old gelding stood there, his ears flattened in warning.

They glared at each other for a moment; then, defiantly, Shareb raised his front foot once more. The gelding bit him again, this time, hard, his yellowed old teeth tearing into Shareb's flesh and raising a trickle of blood.

Incensed, Shareb lunged for the other horse, but Bow, barking furiously, leapt between them at the last moment. Her small body hit Shareb squarely between the eyes. The impact was painless, but it knocked some sense into the stallion and, with an angry squeal, he galloped a short distance away, where he stood sulkily eyeing the other animals. They ignored him and, frustrated, he reached for an overhanging tree branch and began to take out his wrath on it, instead.

Savagely, he ripped a spray of leaves and twigs from the branch and ground it savagely between his teeth. *Let them all band together. What in Pegasus' name had any of* them *done to save Lady A?* he thought.

Some *friends*. He'd known horseflies that showed more loyalty.

Snorting, he tore off another branch, began to chew—and suddenly found himself with a stick wedged across the roof of his mouth and braced hard against his teeth.

He shook his head, trying to dislodge it. The stick remained. He stamped his foot and angled his jaw and tried to twist his tongue around it, but the branch was stuck fast. Worried now, he broke out in a hard sweat and, snorting, shook his head once more, furiously this time—but the ends of the branch only dug themselves in deeper, and suddenly the proud young horse knew he was in trouble.

* * *

Colin lay back in the grass, Ariadne atop his ribs and the dawn sky a crown of fire and fading stars around her face. She felt tiny within the cradle of his arms, her shoulders and bones fragile beneath hands that suddenly seemed big and clumsy. Fiercely protective instincts rose within him and he pressed her body close to his, the need to take her, to possess her, so fierce that he was trembling with need and desire.

God help him, he hadn't wanted, hadn't *meant*, that is, to find himself in this position, wasn't he stronger than this?

No.

But it was too late now. Her slight weight inflamed him, her sweetness filled his senses, and now she was passing her tongue over her lusciously red and bruised-from-kissing lips in an unconscious plea for more.

No. He could not do this. She was no dockside tart, no practiced whore, but a fine, well-bred gentlewoman who was still promised, and engaged, to another. He reached up to push her off of him— and found his hands pressing into her shoulders instead, his mouth seeking her lips.

There was no help for him.

None at all.

Cursing himself, and his weakness, he gently rolled her over until they lay side by side in the sweet grass, staring into each other's faces as if seeing each other for the first time.

"I'm glad your hair is no longer black. And I think you have the most beautiful eyes I have ever seen on a man," Ariadne murmured, tracing the curve of one silky brow with her finger. "I could get lost in them and never find my way out. Never *want* to find my way out. Why, if you were to take my pulse right now, I'm sure you would not be able to count it, so rapidly is my heart beating!"

"Perhaps you should take mine instead," he said suggestively, his eyes glinting as he drew his finger down the slope of her nose and traced her lips.

"Why, I wouldn't know what to do," she said, blushing.

"I can show you. . . ." Propping his head on one hand, he offered his wrist and smiled lazily at her. "Put your finger right there, against the underside of my wrist," he instructed, watching her with high amusement. "No, no . . . higher."

"Right there?" she said, shyly, placing her finger where he had directed and feeling no pulse, but hot, hard, male strength.

"Up another half inch—aaah, you have found it. My pulse."

"Yes. . . ."

"Can you count the beats, my lady? Can you tell me if I shall survive this encounter?"

She felt herself going hot with anticipation at what was to come. Beneath her finger, his pulse was racing.

"My lady is blushing," he said teasingly, his eyes darkening with desire. "Perhaps her temperature is rising. . . ."

"Perhaps," she agreed, her own heartbeat matching his.

"Perhaps the good doctor should do something about it, quick."

"Yes . . . perhaps he . . . should."

"Perhaps"—he slowly pulled his wrist from her numb hand, his fingers drifting up to her throat, where her own rapid pulse beat like a butterfly's wings against the fragile skin—"what my lady needs is some cool air to . . . revive her."

"Cool air," she agreed, feeling his fingers, hot and achingly wonderful, moving against the buttons that closed her shirt at the throat. She felt one button slide through the hole; another, and a cooling wash of air against her hot skin. His fingers lingered against the sensitive flesh, beginning to move downward toward her breast. A last, maidenly instinct swept in to save her, and she lightly slapped at his hand, bringing a rich chuckle of laughter from him. He did not make another attempt to undo her buttons, but simply lay there, lazily watching her with his head still propped on his hand, his eyes intense, clear as frost, and beautifully violet.

And then his gaze shifted, looking down, and she saw one brow raise.

"A wonder, what that cool air does to ... *revive* things," he said, suggestively.

She followed his gaze—and saw that her nipples were high, hard, and clearly visible in high relief beneath her shirt.

"Oh!"

Again, his hand came out, making a slow, lazy circle around her shoulder before drifting down toward her breast. But he did not touch that protruding nipple, merely let his fingers softly caress her tingling, hungry flesh through the fabric until the ache of pleasure withheld made her shut her eyes in bliss and yearn to shove herself against his hand. "Perhaps some more cool air is in order, to effectively revive this patient?"

She caught his wrist, guided it back toward her throat in unspoken invitation. "Yes, cool air ... I feel faint."

"Feverish?"

"Dizzy."

"Afraid?"

She opened her eyes, stared into his soft, gentle, understanding ones.

"Yes."

He smiled and gently rolled her over onto her back, his mouth coming down to claim hers as his fingers found the last button at her throat and moved within the gap to caress her hot skin. She was partially aware of her body shifting so that he could drag the shirt up and over her head; cool air tingled over her hot flesh and her leg came up as if of its own accord to encircle his thigh. His kiss grew hot and demanding, his palm—hard with callus, strength, and warmth—dragged fire over her breast. His fingers found her taut nipple. She moaned deep in her throat and arced upward, into him, her insides melting beneath the building heat.

He lifted his mouth, kissed the side of her jaw, her cheek, her throat.

"Still afraid?" he murmured, his breath hot against her skin.

"No, feverish," she said, burning up. "So hot. . . ."

"That is good, my lady . . . because I am *much* better at treating fever than I am fear. . . ."

His lips were touching her throat now, kissing, grazing, tasting the delicate, moist skin, his hand kneading the erect nipple and making her gasp with longing. Her hand came up, her fingers splaying through his hair as he moved lower . . . lower . . .

His lips feathered over one swelling breast, then closed over the aching bud, his tongue tracing wet circles as he drew the tingling peak up and into his hot mouth.

"Oh-h-h-h-h-h . . . Oh, Colin—"

He raised his head, cupped the side of her jaw, kissed her on the lips until she was mindless with desire. Then he gazed admiringly down at her breasts, slowly tracing a finger over one creamy mound, then the other. They were pink with the kiss of dawn, the nipples bright salmon and thrusting eagerly toward him. "I have always thought

you were more than pretty, Ariadne ... but dear
God, you are beautiful."

She blushed and took his hand. "And just think,
now you can take *my* pulse, Colin ... right from its
source."

Closing her eyes, she pressed his palm against
her thundering heart, feeling the fire spreading out
and into her breasts at the close proximity of his
hand to them.

"Aaah, but I crave touching you," he said huskily, leaning down to kiss her once more as his hand
moved away from her heart, only to cup, knead,
and caress her breast once more. Fresh waves of
heat burned through Ariadne's blood as his finger
traced little circles around her softly puckered ar-
eole. The bud felt ready to explode beneath the
sweet torment ... she wanted his mouth, his lips,
his tongue, on her—

"Go ahead, Colin. Please. I *want* you to touch
me."

He looked up, his eyes so dark with desire that
they were almost indigo. "Ariadne, have you ...
done this before?"

"Once. But only for a few minutes."

"Do you know what comes next?"

"I have my suspicions." She smiled tremulously,
trying to show bravery, flippancy even, so that he
wouldn't stop. *Please God, don't let him stop.* "I
should hope you're as good a teacher as you are a
doctor, Colin. You'll show me what comes next,
won't you?"

"Oh, I'll show you, love. 'Twill be a lesson you
won't ever forget."

His mouth moved to her nipple once more, suckling, licking, tasting. Dampness began to blossom
between her thighs, and the heat centered there
stretched tendrils of fire up through her belly.

"Oh ... that feels so, very, nice."

Her body was burning up. She put her hands around the back of his skull, holding him down against her breast and arcing shamelessly up and into his hot mouth.

"... I like that.... Don't stop."

Colin didn't. Couldn't. He felt her hands against the back of his head, tasted the sweetness of her breast and drove himself down into the very source of it, suckling the delicious pink nipple until she began to sob with pleasure. God help him, he was drowning in the feel, the scent, the taste of her; he couldn't take much more of this, his heart was beating fast now, too fast, she was incinerating him into ashes, too much, not enough, and now his hand was skimming down her belly—and such a tiny, flat belly it was—sliding under her trousers, then impatiently undoing the buttons there, finding the silken nest of damp curls and stroking the moist petals of flesh until she was bucking and writhing beneath him—

Calm down.... Take it slow. Make it beautiful for her.

His finger found her entrance, sank within it, and pushed upward, her hot sheath engulfing the digit with delicious wet heat all the way to its base.

She went momentarily stiff in his arms and made a little cry, and for the briefest moment he feared he'd hurt her—but no, she was pressing herself against him, making little gasps and urging him on with tiny, guttural whimpers.

He licked and nuzzled her breast, inflamed her with mouth and tongue and finger; wanting her, needing her, feeling the heat rising up and out of her until her skin was dewy and hot, until she was moaning and gasping beneath him, until she finally caught his head in her hands and gasped breathlessly beneath him.

"Oh, Colin, I ... am so full of feeling, I don't

know where to put it all. It grows ... unbearable. I
love you, Colin ... please, please don't stop ... I
love you. ..."

He had found her wet, inner wall with his finger,
stroking it ceaselessly until he had her sobbing
with the start of climax; he withdrew just before
sending her over the edge, then concentrated on
the hidden nub of her femininity. Dallied in slick
wetness, it grew hard as a cherry pit as he kneaded
it between thumb and forefinger. She cried out,
digging her nails into the back of his head and neck
as he took one of her breasts deeply into his mouth,
all the while pressing and rubbing that secret part
of her, inflaming her to a state of pleading, sobbing
need until she was begging for something she
didn't understand. He felt her beginning to spasm,
and withdrew his hand to let her hang suspended
on the shelf of ecstacy, wanting only to make the
pleasure so fierce that she would never forget it for
as long as she lived.

Gasping, whimpering, she groped frenziedly for
his hand.

"Wait, love ... it will be better if you take it
slowly."

He sat up and began to unbutton his breeches,
but Ariadne, delirious with need, thrust his hand
away and did the task for him. She had never seen
the male organ, didn't know quite what to expect—
but the hard, swelling blade of manly flesh that
popped free, jutting and swelling stiffly against her
hand, had the effect of a bucket of cold water
thrown in her face. She gasped with shock. Desire
fled her like water thrown on a fire, and she buried
her face in the curve of his shoulder, not daring to
look.

He was breathing hard, his heart racing beneath
her ear, and she realized that he was as swept up
in passion as she. Nevertheless, he gently cupped

the back of her head and stroked her hair, under-standing.

"It's all right, dearest. It is part of me. Nothing more."

He lifted her head and kissed her, until her curiosity triumphed over her fear. With a trembling hand, she pushed the flap of the breeches aside, and then—and only then—did she look at him.

Her hand flew to her mouth and the blood drained from her face. "Oh dear heaven, I've never seen anything so horrid-looking in my life!"

To her amazement, he laughed. But Ariadne was still staring at it, that frightening, alien protuberance of flesh that rose straight up and out of the soft brown hair between his legs, and the twin sacs just beneath it. Shock, horror, and withdrawal made her mute, and her gaze shot upward, past the tapered waist and widening ribs, past the broad, lightly furred chest and up into the doctor's eyes.

His *gentle* eyes, regarding her with love and ad-oration.

"I'm still here," he said softly, in understanding, and reached up to touch the bottom of her chin. "Still the same person, Ariadne. It's all right to be afraid of . . . well, the unknown."

"But it's . . . *huge*!"

"Yes, it rather gets that way, when it's aroused."

"How on earth do you keep it safely hidden in your breeches? Do you have to tie it down?

He had the good grace to actually blush. "I don't spend my every waking moment walking around in this state, my lady. Indeed, you have done this to me."

"So *now* what do I do with it?"

"Anything you like," he said, softly. Invitingly.

She clamped her legs against the still-throbbing ache at their junction. Horrified, yet a little eagerly, she gazed up at him. Again, those beautiful eyes were regarding her, with patience, love, and understanding.

He is Colin, she reminded herself. *And he will never hurt me.*

She went bright red, and carefully kept her hand away from that alien tower of flesh. "I'm sorry, Colin. I've seen st-stallions before, but never a man."

He began to look embarrassed, and for a brief, terrifying moment she thought he was going to button his breeches back up and leave her there, hot, desperate, and burning like a candle running out of wick in the deepest part of the night. She saw the hesitation in his eyes, the quick look of regret crossing his face.

Then he gave a guilty little grin and said softly, "I fear that in comparison to a horse ... I am sadly lacking."

He looked up at her and pursed his mouth, and he looked so dreadfully serious and comical all at the same time that she could not help but laugh.

He laughed too, banishing the awkwardness, and when she looked back down at him, that manly appendage was no longer frightening and strange, because it was a part of *him.*

"Touch me, Ariadne."

"You want me to *touch* it?" she squealed, horrified.

"Yes. It does not bite."

She was shaking as she lay back down in the grass and helped him to remove his breeches, stockings and shoes. His manhood was fully bared to her view, along with long, beautifully muscled legs sheathed in sparse, light brown hair. One of them was marked by a gruesome tangle of raised, angry scar tissue, and sucking her lips between her teeth in imagination of what agony the injury must have caused him, Ariadne reached out and put her hand over the puckered, scarred flesh. The doctor regarded her steadily. She swallowed hard, caressed the injured area as though she could smooth away the long-ago pain. He smiled. Then, Ariadne's curiosity over the male organ got the better of her, and hesitantly, she reached out and touched . . .

It.

It jumped beneath her finger and she gave a little shriek.

"I hurt you!"

He laughed, and leaned over to kiss her. "No, no, you could never hurt me."

"But—"

"I know. Touch it again, Ariadne. It is only a part of me and nothing more."

She reached out and gingerly laid her fingers against the blunted apex of the appendage. It was warm and surprisingly soft, as velvety as the hide of a newborn colt, the skin of Shareb's muzzle, the most elegant of silk.

He smiled, watching her.

Gently, she stroked the length of the strange, hard, organ, feeling it growing firmer beneath her touch, larger, stiffer, hotter, until it outgrew her hand and thrust harshly against her palm with every tortured stroke of her fingers. She looked down at Colin; he now lay with his eyes half-closed, as though in the deepest of pain. Anguish, even. She pulled the loose skin down over the rigid top of his organ, exposing a head that was damp, veined, and purply red. She shivered with awe and fear, and felt a warm drop of liquid on the inside of her thumb. She drew the loose skin back up to cover it.

Gasping, he caught her hand, began to guide her away.

"Am I hurting you, Colin?"

"No. But you will soon put me over the edge with such handling."

"Edge of what?"

He slowly shook his head and eased himself onto his back, one arm outflung to gather her close and pull her down atop him until their mouths met once more. She felt his warm breath on her cheek, his tongue exploring her mouth, and unable to leave it alone, put her hand around that hard, hot part of him.

"I'm warning you, Ariadne. . . ."

She kept stroking him, feeling a wicked sense of triumph and femininity as he groaned softly beneath her and let his head fall back, away from her. Finally, his eyes opened and he gazed up at her with a faint smile and eyes glazed with passion. "Sweetheart, I want to make love to you."

He looked intently into her eyes, waiting for her answer.

She swallowed hard, her flesh, her skin, her very blood, on fire.

"Yes, Colin . . . I would like that. Love me. Love me with all of your heart."

Gently pushing her hand aside, he moved over and atop her, one arm coming out to pillow her head, his hand caressing her breasts, her belly, and then, the silky junction of curls at her thighs. She went to butter as his fingers moved toward her hot recesses, spreading the inner lips apart and stroking the soft, pink flesh until she felt her own moisture flooding in fresh, hot waves against his fingers.

His eyes had gone deep and soft, his brow creased with concentration, his breathing thick and heavy. Under his intimate caress, she once again— sharper this time, fiercer, even—felt something huge and cresting start to gather in the most inner part of her.

"Oh, Colin, something's *happening*—"

And then he withdrew his hand, grasped that manly part of himself, and guided it into the center of her need. Quivering, she felt it touching her flesh, felt her very insides stretching as he slowly slipped inside her and began to probe, to thrust, upward.

It was not enough. She ached for his weight, ached for his body, ached for his touch and his soul and the feel of him against her. She ached to have him inside her, as far as he could go, ached for . . .

"Ariadne, I dare not go any farther," he said hoarsely. His eyes were clear as glass, intense, penetrating and brilliant; she thought he must be able to see right down into her soul. He cupped her face in his hands, kissed her brow, and breathing harshly, said, "It's going to hurt you, dearest. I cannot hurt you—"

"I trust you, Colin."

"Do you want this, Ariadne?"

"God help me, I do. . . ."

"Then hold onto me—tightly—and know that I love you, and that it will only hurt for a moment."

"Yes. . . ." She thrust upward, seeking him, her breath hot against his skin.

He lowered himself onto his forearms to take his weight, and kissed her fervently, his lips and breath hot against her temple, her cheek, her brow, her lips. Between her thighs she felt him filling her, stretching her, and the sensation pulsed out from her lower body and sent shards of fire shooting out in every direction. He began to move within her, pulling back and then thrusting slowly back in. She felt her body expanding to accept him, felt his hard staff sliding into her, inch by glorious inch, tearing away reason and control until at last he came up against the fragile membrane that proclaimed her innocence.

He paused, head bent, the hair hanging over a brow that was damp with sweat.

"I love you, Colin. Please . . . just make me yours."

He kissed her, held her tightly, and then, just when she thought that she would die for want of him, he drove himself into her, breaking her maidenhead forever.

The pain was brief, brilliant, and blessed. She felt the warmth running between her legs and was thankful for it, and then there was only *him*, picking up and continuing the rhythm, going deeper with each thrust, harder, until something huge and frightening began to build within her, rising higher, higher, higher—

He gave one last, driving thrust at the same time Ariadne felt herself exploding into shards of feeling. She cried out, arced up, clung to him and drove her nails into his back with the force of her climax, feeling her body convulsing out of control. Sweat sheened their bodies and she heard nothing but his gasps of pleasure and the sound of her name tumbling from his lips, felt nothing but the blood shrieking through her ears and the sky flying, spinning, whirling, above her. She clung to him, sobbing with wonder and joy, until the waves began to ebb, and at last fade away like the ripples in a pond. And then there was just the two of them, bodies entwined on a bed of grass with the stars fading and the dawn coming up in the eastern sky in a beautiful mantle of fire and gold.

They washed in the pond, then lay together on a blanket in each other's arms, watching the sun coming up.

"Oh, Colin, my dear, beloved, wonderful Doctor,

how I love you... want to be with you, forever...."

For a long moment he said nothing. Then she
heard his voice against the inner curve of her neck,
and his words were flat and tortured.

"Ah, but you wouldn't, Ariadne, if you only
knew what disgrace I have suffered, just what I
am—"

"Nonsense, Colin, I would love you whether you
were a marquess's grandson or a Chelsea veterinarian."

"That's all well and good, Ariadne—" He
paused, and she felt cool air against her neck as he
slowly raised his head. "Because you see—"

"What?"

"I *am* a marquess's grandson."

Chapter 19

"And I was born in a coal mine and carted out of it on the back of a mule. Very funny, Colin. You know, you really shouldn't say things like that, because it is very impertinent and disrespectful to those of us who *are* quality—"

"I'm serious, Ariadne."

She giggled and kissed him, loving the way the pinks and golds of the rising dawn gilded his brow, cheek and jaw. Behind him, clouds were dark mauve against the fiery sky. "Oh Colin, you are *never* serious, and besides, if you were the grandson of a marquess, you'd have told me long before now."

"Ariadne, I will say it to you again." Supporting his weight on his elbows, he framed her cheeks with his hands and held her face still as he looked deeply into her eyes. His gaze was intent, almost pleading, and something like fear rippled through her; not quite fear, but a quick flutter of the heart, a heightening of the senses, for she had the sudden feeling he really *wasn't* jesting with her.

Not this time.

Quietly, he continued, "When my grandfather died, the title was passed to my uncle Elliott, who became the marquess of Hampden. Elliott never married, never had children, and when he quit this earth, the title went to my father. Subsequently, I became Lord Morden."

"*Really*, Colin!" She laughed and reached up to kiss his brow.

"Ariadne, you must believe me," he said, his warm breath grazing her face. "*Please*."

Her mirth died a quick death, and she caught her lip between her teeth. She looked at him for a long, searching moment, her eyes pained, a frown creasing her lovely brow. "But . . . you would have *told* me, Colin. You would have told me about something that important."

"That's just it, Ariadne. *You* think it's important. I do not. And that is precisely the reason why I *didn't* tell you." He reached down, thumbed a damp strand of cinnamon-colored hair out of her eyes, and reverently ran his fingers over her brow, her cheek, her jaw, as though trying to wipe the shock and growing expression of betrayal from her face. "I guess I suspected you were becoming . . . er, fond, of me, but if that fondness grew to love, I wanted you to love me because of who I am as a *person*, not because my grandfather happened to be a marquess."

She stared at him in disbelief, cheeks going pink with anger. "What makes you think I'd base my feelings on anything so ridiculous?"

"Your attitude about and toward Thunder. Bow." He looked her in the eye. "Commoners."

"Yes, well that does make me wonder, if you are indeed *Lord Morden*"—she almost spit the name, so vexed was she—"what on earth are you doing practicing veterinary medicine, of all things?"

"Making a living."

"Any nobleman worth his pride would never stoop to dirtying his hands with a *trade*, especially one that is regarded with such contempt!" She heaved upward, displacing his weight and squirming out from beneath him in the dewy grass. Humiliated that he had hit upon the truth, she grabbed her shirt and yanked it down over her head so that he wouldn't see how flushed and hot her face was.

"I wasn't aware that you saw the veterinary art in such a light," she heard him say, softly.

"I don't. *I* happen to love animals and personally think that animal doctors should be given more respect than they glean!" She got the shirt down and yanked her hair free of the collar. "But polite society itself, Colin, does not attach much honor to your trade, and you know it as well as I do!"

"How kind of you to enlighten me, my lady."

"Well, that still doesn't answer the question, does it?"

"What question?"

She glared at him as though he was an idiot. "The question of how you went from Lord Morden to London veterinarian!"

Images flashed through his mind. The shipwreck. The court-martial. The newspapers—

He shrugged and grinned, trying to disarm the moment's tension. "I haven't gone from one to the other. I still *am* Lord Morden."

"For heaven's sake, Colin, don't you care what people *think*?"

"Not particularly," he said quietly. "And besides, I had to find a way to support myself after . . ."

"After what?"

The shipwreck.

"After *what*, Colin?" she persisted.

The disgrace.

"Nothing," he said, keeping his eyes unreadable as he watched her tug on her breeches.

"There you go, doing it again," she said, sullenly. "You and your secrets. I shall never figure you out, Colin! Never! One moment you're laughing and teasing me, the next you're retreating behind a wall of privacy and refusing to let me in! And you know something? I really don't care if you're a London veterinarian or Lord Morden, because I love you, I have always loved you, and nothing you can tell me is going to change that!"

"Oh, there is a lot I could tell you that might change that—"

"Oh, yes, your Deep, Dark, Secret! Well then, here is your chance to confess all, Dr. Lord, go ahead, tell me, tell me this horrible thing that hangs in your past and brings shadows into your eyes whenever I ask you to speak about it, go ahead, *tell me*!"

He looked at her with something like shock at her outburst, opened his mouth to speak—and turned away.

"I can't."

He bent to pick up his shirt. Pulled it on and quietly did up the buttons, his face troubled, the pain emanating from him in waves that she could almost *feel*. She watched him pull on his stockings and step into his breeches, putting first one leg, then the horribly scarred one—*oh, God, that must've hurt*—into the cylinders of fabric.

"Colin?"

He sighed. Stopped. Turned to regard her with hurt, defiance, and pride burning in his eyes.

"What?"

"Colin, I'm—"

"Ariadne, I'm—"

They both stared at each other, and then, in unison:

"Sorry."

She flew into his embrace and buried herself

against his chest, her hands coming up to grasp his shirt, her brow resting against his sternum. He held her tightly, silently, not saying a word but only wrapping her in his arms, and his very silence made her pain and confusion somehow worse, her desperation to know his terrible secret a crusade of obsession.

"Colin—"

At that moment hoofbeats shook the ground and Ariadne barely had time to jerk her head up in alarm before Shareb-er-rehh came bursting out of the nearby stand of trees, his tail streaming behind him, the dawn's light gleaming in eyes that were wild, panicky, and ringed with white.

He screamed, charging toward them at a dead run.

Ice tingled up Ariadne's spine, for she didn't need more than a second glance to know that there was something wrong with her horse.

Something dreadfully, seriously, wrong.

"Shareb!"

She ran forward and grabbed the stallion's neck as he plowed to a stop before her. The force of the action nearly tore her arms from their sockets, and she felt pain explode along her injured limb, felt her teeth smash together as her chin bumped the horse's sweaty throat. She lost her grip and stumbled backward, saw the sky above her as a brilliant splash of pink, orange and mauve—and then Colin's strong arms as he caught her and made a wild grab for Shareb's head—

Screaming, the stallion bared his teeth and struck savagely out, just missing him.

"Colin, do something!" Ariadne cried, trying to corner the horse on the other side. "He's sick!"

"Get back, Ariadne!"

"I will not, he's my horse and—"

But Shareb was clearly out of his mind with

panic. Mighty hooves slashing the air, he reared, wheeled, and thundered off, shaking his head and making a pitiful, horrible noise that raised the hair on Ariadne's neck. He made a tortured circle around them, his hide flecked with sweat, saliva flying from his mouth; then, the grass plowing up before his hooves, he came to a stop, blowing hard and staring at them as though recognizing them for the first time.

Ariadne stood frozen and unable to move.

Slowly, she turned to look at the veterinarian.

He stood as still as a stone, one hand stretched entreatingly toward the trembling horse that stood fifteen feet away from him.

Shareb made a pitiful, crying noise, shook his head, and began to back up.

"Here, boy," Colin murmured, never moving. He stared deeply into the stallion's dark eye, willing the animal to come to him. "Let's have a look at you."

"Oh, Colin, what's *wrong* with him—"

"Get his halter," the veterinarian commanded.

"But Colin, I—"

"Ari, get his halter," he said, again.

Blind with terror she ran to obey, feeling that same horrible, paralyzing nausea she'd experienced upon being told about the stable fire and Papa's death. Frantically, she tore through their belongings in the chaise, trying to remember the symptoms that Papa's other horses had shown just before they died, trying to think of anything that might help Colin save her beloved stallion—

There, the halter. Clenching it in her fist, she ran back.

Colin never turned, merely reaching out to accept the halter while keeping his gaze on Shareb. The stallion took a hesitant step forward, shaking his head. Thick, foamy blobs of blood-flecked spittle arced from his mouth, spattered on the grass.

"Come here, boy," the veterinarian murmured, so softly that Ariadne wasn't even sure he'd even spoken. She watched the stallion take another step forward; saw the barely perceptible movement of Colin's fingers, beckoning the animal closer.

And closer. . . .

Shareb dropped his head in defeat and walked forward, ears drooping, body shaking, the drool running in little rivulets from his mouth. He stopped miserably before Colin, then lifted his head to look at the animal doctor with great, pleading eyes.

Colin hooked an arm around Shareb's poll and buckled the halter into place. Once more, the stallion dropped his head and gazed dejectedly at the ground, his breath coming out in great, labored breaths.

"Ariadne, please bring me my lantern."

She scurried off and found it, lying half on its side in the grass beside the wheel of the chaise. With Bow trotting worriedly at her heels, she carried it back to the veterinarian, her eyes misty with tears that, even now, were running warmly down her cheeks.

Have faith in him, Ariadne. Remember the first day you saw him, and how he saved that dog. He is a healer. He can save animals. Faith, Ariadne, faith. . . .

But out here in a lonely pasture, with daylight approaching and her beloved horse looking sicker than she'd ever seen him, it was not easy to have faith. She picked up little Bow and buried her face in her soft fur. The dog was trembling, and sensing Ariadne's grief and worry, twisted around to lick her cheek. The little animal's compassion was enough to bring on the sobs in earnest, and Ariadne pressed Bow's fuzzy ear against her eyes so that Colin would not notice her distress and be affected by it.

She peered through Bow's fur and risked a glance at his face, fully expecting to see grave concern there. But his handsome features were expressionless, his eyes intent as he murmured to the trembling horse, dragged his drooping head up, and ran a gentle, soothing hand down the stallion's long jaw. Thick ropes of spittle leaked from Shareb's mouth, slid to the ground, and lay glinting upon the grass in the early morning sunlight.

The tears were running freely now, soaking Bow's ear.

Colin. Please, please save my horse. . . .

Her body frozen with fear and grief, she rocked from side to side, watching as he bent sideways and forced the stallion's head high. Shareb squealed and fought him, shaking his head and sending more drool flying from his mouth. Ariadne bit her lip so hard that the coppery taste of blood burned her tongue. The tears came harder, streaming silently down her cheeks and filling up her throat so that she couldn't swallow.

She saw Colin's honeyed hair falling over his brow and picking up the first rays of sun, the intense concentration in his eyes, and the skill in his strong, gentle hands as he pried open the stallion's mouth. He would make everything all right. He *had* to, because if he couldn't *no one* could—

"Is he going to . . . to d-die, Colin?"

"Oh . . . I don't think so," he murmured absently, trying to peer into the dark depths of Shareb's mouth. "Really, Ari, you make a terrible assistant. Bring the lantern over so I can see what I'm doing, would you?"

She didn't like his calm insouciance, the jocular note in his tone, nor the fact that he did not seem as concerned as he should be. Didn't he realize how priceless Shareb-er-rehh *was*? Didn't he sense the gravity of the situation? Pursing her lip, she put Bow down and did as she was told; she held the lantern up and hoped to keep its bright glare out of the veterinarian's eyes as well.

"What do you see?" she managed, swallowing back the sobs and feeling the prickles of fear clawing up her spine.

Be brave, Ariadne. If only for Colin's sake. And, Shareb's.

"Teeth."

Teeth.

The veterinarian turned his back, thrust his thumb between Shareb's lips right where a bit would have gone, and then she saw only the back of his golden brown head, the play of muscles in his shoulders and at his nape as he forced the stallion's jaws wide.

"Eaaaayyuuuk," he murmured.

Raw terror lanced her. "What?"

"Slimy tongue," he said, flashing her a grin and pulling that thick, wet muscle from Shareb's mouth. The stallion protested, and tried to fling his head up and back.

"Hold still, you confounded idiot," Colin commanded.

Shareb tensed, but did as he was told.

"Closer with the lantern, Ariadne. It's dark in there."

Her sore arm aching, she propped her elbow in her palm and held the lantern up.

Colin all but thrust his face between the stallion's jaws.

"Aha!"

"What?"

"Just what I thought. . . ."

"Colin, *what*?!"

Somehow managing to restrain the stallion and

hold his head up at the same time, the veterinarian held Shareb's tongue aside, thrust his hand between his jaws, and craning his neck, peered up into the stallion's mouth. "Our friend here has a foreign object—a stick, by the looks of it—wedged firmly across the dental arcade. Really, Ariadne . . . I do wish you'd be more cautious about what you feed him!"

"But I thought . . . you mean—A *stick*!?" She stumbled backward, feeling such an intense wave of foolishness and relief that her knees went weak and she nearly collapsed. "You mean there's a *stick* caught up there?"

"Right across the roof of his mouth. Tie a string on each end and it would make a lovely bit."

A stick. . . .

He wiggled his hand within the stallion's mouth and triumphantly brought out a wet, chewed up branch for her inspection. Grinning, he gave the sheepish stallion a fond slap on the neck before taking the lantern from Ariadne's suddenly limp fingers, knowing, intuitively, that she would otherwise have dropped it. "Really, Shareb . . . I'm beginning to think you'd be better off with pastry, after all."

Colin might have already won the undying love of the earl of Weybourne's daughter, but with the removal of the stick from the roof of Shareb's mouth, he won the undying—and perhaps unwelcome—devotion of the earl's horse, as well.

It was a devotion that proved to be a mixed blessing.

Shareb-er-rehh followed him back to their little campsite. He followed him down to the brook and stood waiting patiently as the veterinarian washed the spittle and flecks of blood from his hands. He followed him back to where Thunder waited with a horsey smirk on his face, followed him as he carried his sea chest back to the chaise, followed him when he went to Ariadne and put his arms around her tiny shoulders.

When Colin felt the stallion's hot breath blasting against the back of his neck his patience finally reached an end.

"Enough, Shareb. You've made your point."

"You've made a friend for life, now, Colin," Ariadne said.

"I think I'd prefer him as an enemy," he returned, wryly, but he was pleased with himself and happy that his initial diagnosis had proved correct.

Yes, sometimes he *still* felt like a hero. . . .

She laughed and buried herself against him. Her hair smelled like grass and wind, and she was so tiny that he was almost afraid to embrace her too tightly. But she wrapped her arms around his waist and gripped him with a ferocity of strength that belied any image of delicacy her small body conveyed.

He sighed and rested his cheek atop her hair.

"You're wonderful, you know," she whispered, as though he was a god and not just a mere human. "Every day, you do something to make me love you more and more. You don't know how grateful I am that I chose *you*, Colin, to be my horse's veterinarian."

"Dislodging a stick is not terribly difficult, my dear. Certainly not the most challenging problem of my career."

Her hand was sliding down his thigh, heading for his groin. "Then perhaps you need something *more* challenging."

"Such as?"

"Helping me think up a way to break off my engagement to Maxwell . . . without losing Gazella."

"Obviously you think me capable of great miracles."

"Oh, Colin, you are far too modest! What *am* I going to do with you?"

He grinned, and said invitingly, "I can think of a few things. . . ."

"Can you, now?" She cocked her head and looked playfully up at him. "And what are they, my good Doctor?"

He looked down at her, his eyes glinting.

"Hmmm . . . ?"

She never gave him the chance to answer. Laughing, she slid her hand down his hard, muscular back . . . and made him incapable of thinking of *anything*.

Anything at all.

Chapter 20

❦

They reached the Burnhams several nights later.

It should have been a triumph—making it all the way to Burnham from London without capture—but it was not. Ariadne had felt only dread and foreboding as she began to recognize landmarks along the route she'd known and traveled on since childhood. Soon, she knew, she would have to confront Maxwell, and the thought, for some unexplainable reason, filled her with apprehension. She had begun this mad journey wanting only to get to Norfolk, beloved, familiar Norfolk. Now, with every step that Shareb-er-rehh carried her to her destination, she felt the fear breeding in her heart until that organ felt as if it would crack like ice with every labored beat. Even the landscape—which should have provided comfort and reassurance with its beloved familiarity—could not ease her restlessness, and she had felt tears of mixed emotion in her eyes at the sight of it. Sugar beets growing in endless, sweeping fields that were coffee-colored against the green Norfolk grasses; hard wedges of flint and stone peppering the dark earth, wind, windmills, the smell of the marsh, and always, the nearness of the sea.

The sea.

The veterinarian sensed it too. She'd seen the change in him as they'd neared Burnham and the wind swept its salty scent across bent grasses and long, rolling pastures. A faint shadow darkened his beautiful eyes, and she wondered at the cause of it.

He had his secrets.

She would find them out.

And she was beginning to suspect that whatever he was hiding was also keeping him from asking her to marry him. Not that she hadn't pressed him, and tried every clever method she knew, to get some answers out of him. But continually, he had thwarted her efforts, growing angry, even, at her persistence, until she'd finally retreated in sullen hurt and he'd gone off to be by himself, his eyes preoccupied, despairing, and troubled. His reluctance to talk about his past had even begun to affect their lovemaking, making what should have been an intimate, shared act into something distant and tense.

What was wrong with him? Whatever his shameful secret was, Ariadne had no doubt that Colin Lord was the man she wanted to marry. Oh, she had *thought* she loved Maxwell. Thought that all she needed to make a splendid match was a man who was titled, rich, and influential. Now she realized that she had deceived herself, only inventing the idea that she loved Maxwell in an attempt to reassure herself about her future, for that was what her Papa had arranged for her. But the truth was, what she had felt for Maxwell was nothing in comparison to what she felt for Colin Lord. It didn't even come close.

Lord Morden.

Imagine.

But she still preferred to think of him as *Doctor*

Lord, for that was what he had always been to her,
and what he would always be. He was Colin.
Strong, handsome, intuitive, and gentle, steady
where she was erratic and volatile, wise where
she was impulsive. He was everything she wanted
in a man. In a husband. And if there'd been
any doubts in her mind about him—which there
weren't—they would have been eased by the way
animals acted around him, for animals, she knew,
were far better judges of people than humans were.
And the way that Shareb-er-rehh had forgotten his
earlier animosity toward the doctor and now slath-
ered all of his attention on him was almost nauseating. He was no different than any other beast
who'd fallen under the veterinarian's spell.

And neither was Ariadne.

Yet the miles had passed, and he had not proposed to her. With her future so uncertain, Ariadne's anxiety had mounted. With the anxiety came
annoyance, and with annoyance, anger.

Now, ten minutes from Maxwell's estate, she
twisted around in the saddle to gaze through the
starlit darkness at the veterinarian, who followed
with Thunder and the chaise. Elbows resting on his
knees, the reins held loosely in his fists, he looked
preoccupied while gazing out toward the fields beyond which lay the sea—and heartbreakingly
handsome as the wind ruffled his hair and sent his
shirtsleeves rippling against his arms. She gazed
longingly at those hands; he could reduce her to a
puddle of honey just by stroking her flesh with
those long, beautiful fingers, could set her blood
afire with the lightest of kisses, a mere sideways
glance from beneath those beautiful long lashes.
Oh, how she loved him. And she knew in her heart
that she wanted nothing more than to be with
him—forever.

But now, "forever" was a frightening uncertainty, for here, bordering the road, were the eight-foot-high, ivy-choked stone walls that ringed Maxwell's estate, and the gates themselves lay just around the next bend. Soon now, Colin—if he wanted her as much as she hoped, prayed, he did—would have to make a decision.

Please, Colin, ask me—

Thunder stumbled on a rock, and the massive, cast iron gates loomed up before them, dark, skeletal sketches against the night.

"Is this it?" Colin asked, his voice oddly strained, flat.

"Yes."

He pulled Thunder up short. "Ariadne, I . . ."

"Yes?" she said breathlessly.

They stared at each other, their thoughts and longings lying unspoken between them. Colin saw the hopeful expectancy in her eyes, saw that she was holding her breath, her hands tightly clenching the reins. He was no fool, and knew very well what she wanted, what her eyes begged him to do. . . .

Please ask me to marry you, Colin.

But he couldn't. What would her future be like if she consented to be his wife? How would she feel about his continuing to practice veterinary medicine, and the subsequent societal ostracism his actions—and trade—would cost her?

She deserved better than that.

How would she feel when the *ton* turned a collective cold shoulder on the pair of them? Would she resent him for that? Would she miss her lofty, aristocratic friends? Or would they accept him back into their fold simply because he had married one of the wealthiest women in England?

She deserved better.

She deserved better than a disgraced naval officer who didn't even have the courage to tell her the truth about that awful night, nearly five years ago, that had ended his career with tragic finality. Oh, God help him, he *wanted* to tell her, because it was all that kept him from asking her to marry him—but he couldn't bear what her certain reaction would be when she opened the Pandora's box of his past and saw what lurked inside. The love and adoration would fade from her eyes to be replaced by shock, pity, and disgust, her cheeks would drain of blood, and then . . .

And then she would turn away and no longer love him because, in her eyes, he would no longer be a hero.

"Colin?"

He felt Thunder fidgeting, turning his head to regard him in concern. Veils of cloud drifted across the night sky, and a light wind sprang up, ripe with the scent of the salt marshes, grass, the sea.

The sea.

He took a deep, shuddery breath, his nostrils flaring, the old ache starting up in his heart. His eyes fell shut and he took another breath, sucking the sea air deeply into his lungs and feeling every cell in his body imbibing it until he wanted to put his head in his hands and weep with longing.

Five long years, and still . . . oh, did it have to hurt so damned much?

And Ariadne. Looking at him. Waiting.

"Colin, are you well?"

Crickets sang in the night around them. Far, far off in the distance, he could hear the sea running against the land, and knew the tide was coming in.

"I'm fine," he said, his voice sounding hoarse and raw.

He could feel her gaze upon him and knew she was no longer perturbed, but worried. He heard the stallion's shoes clicking against dirt and stone as she turned him and sent him back to the chaise, heard the squeak of leather as she lightly dismounted, then the rustle of her clothes, the soft sounds her feet made as she came up to him. She leaned over the wheel of the chaise, and put her face close to his. Her scent invaded his senses, mingling with the heartrending tang of a sea he had not dared approach since—

"Colin, you're ill." Her hand was against his brow, soft, sweet, light as air.

He opened his eyes, raked a hand over his face, and shook his head. "No, Ariadne. I'm . . . missing something. Someone. We—we need to talk, I think, yes, need to talk, now, while there's still time and my courage is up to it."

The breeze rustled in the trees above them, in the thousands of leaves of star-shaped ivy that fought for space on Maxwell's old wall, through the long, bent grasses of the surrounding fields. A few coarse strands of Thunder's tail skated over Colin's fist. Several feet away, Shareb-er-rehh lifted his head, his wide nostrils flaring as he, too, caught the scents borne on the wind.

Far, far off beyond the fields, beyond Ariadne's worried face, beyond the road that ribboned away into the night, Colin saw the distant, moonlit silver line that was the sea.

"I have not always been a veterinarian, Ariadne," he began hoarsely. The wind blew harder, and he saw sails in the clouds above his head, sixteen years of sails, day in, day out, from the time he'd turned twelve 'til the day the navy threw him out in the twenty-eighth year of his life; sails, stiff with salt and hard with wind, swelling above his head and reaching toward the skies, sails in rain, snow, sunlight, fog, battle, dawn, and darkness. In the breeze whispering against his cheeks, his brow, he could hear distant voices, becoming clearer, distinct, moving across time and space and out of the vault of memory on the gentle kiss of the night wind, the voices of junior officers passing his orders on down the line, the voices of seamen calling to each other from high, high in the tops. He shut his eyes, not wanting to remember. Wanting to escape the memories, the tragedy he must have sensed even as he once again felt the spray on his face, the deck moving uneasily beneath his feet, and yes, even the coldness of brass and leather as he'd pulled out his night glass and trained it aft on HMS *Cricket*, where his admiral had gone to join that ship's captain for a late dinner. . . .

He would have laid down his life for his admiral, newly wed and the brightest star in the Royal Navy.

Something welled up in his throat, and suddenly he couldn't speak.

A hand touched his arm. A voice stirred the hair near his ear, seemed to come from far away. "Colin, are you well?"

He heard the wind rising, growing stronger and heading toward a gale, until his mighty *Triton* was heeled hard over on her beam—

"Colin?"

Rain began to pelt the decks, sporadically at first and then with the tattoo of a thousand drums, hard, brutal, so deafening he couldn't hear himself think. He took shelter beneath the poop deck, eyes growing desperate as he had waited for his admiral to return but no, the admiral was still aboard the frigate Cricket, *still sharing a glass with Captain Young, laughing, probably, and totally unconcerned about the sudden fear and foreboding welling up in the heart of his flag-captain:* Hurry up, Sir Graham. It's running a high sea and I don't like this at all—

He wasn't sure what came first; the spray, bursting suddenly out of the night in huge waterspouts against submerged rocks, or the horrible thunder that had accompanied it. He raced to the shrouds, the rain pum-

meling his face and the wind shrieking like a legion of demons around him. He lifted his telescope to see Sir Graham coming up on Cricket's decks . . . Sir Graham, who would surely die if Colin didn't do something, Sir Graham, who immediately saw their predicament and was ordering him to save Triton, her people, himself, and leave Cricket to her fate. . . .

Colin disobeyed that order.

Beneath him the mighty flagship HMS Triton labored and strained, beginning to slide across mountainous seas toward those terrible, murderous rocks . . . he saw Cricket's foremast toppling, getting carried away, and the little frigate floundering helplessly, driven toward certain death by violent wind and current; he heard her crew screaming, saw his admiral bravely clinging to shrouds that lay nearly vertical beneath the onslaught of wind and storm — and made the decision that cost him his career.

"Prepare to rig a tow line!" he bellowed, his voice cracking as he rammed his speaking trumpet against his lips.

Closer and closer they came to the stricken Cricket . . . men were screaming in terror from her canting decks, the horrible thunder of the breakers boomed ever closer, and still the admiral clung to the shrouds, determined to meet his death with courage and dignity —

Someone was shaking his shoulder. Blinking, Colin opened his eyes and stared at the woman for a long, uncomprehending moment.

Ariadne.

Her face was pure white in the darkness, and her hand was shaking and cold when she put it against his brow.

"I was calling you for the past minute . . . Colin?"

A sudden, violent chill seized him, and he brought his hand up to rake it over his eyes. His face was slick with sweat, cold, clammy, as though coated in sea spray.

Dear God.

"Ariadne, there is something you must know before I can ask you to marry—"

At that moment Maxwell's giant black boarhounds, roaring and howling with fury, came charging out of the darkness and hit the massive iron gates with such force that they clanged with the force of the great beasts' impact. Yelping with fear, Bow dived beneath Colin's legs as the shouts of a guard pierced the night.

"Who goes there?"

The boarhounds' snarling was drowning out all sound. Defeatedly, Colin made a dismissive motion with his hand. "Go ahead, answer him, Ariadne."

"But you were going to tell me something—"

"Later."

"But Colin—"

"I repeat, who's there?" shouted the guard, and the hounds renewed their crazed snarling until little Bow was howling in terror.

The veterinarian turned away, his jaw hard in the moonlight, his eyes large pools of pain. It was obvious he would not speak further to her of love, marriage, or whatever his Deep, Dark Secret was, tonight.

If ever.

"Damn you," Ariadne swore beneath her breath, and, leaving him sitting in the chaise, stormed back to Shareb-er-rehh. She grabbed the reins, swung herself up into the saddle, and drove her heels forcefully into the stallion's sides. He snorted and balked, shying at a shadow that slanted across the road, then prancing skittishly forward as though he had no wish to go near those tall, ominous gates.

Behind her, came the slow plodding of Thunder's footsteps as Colin sent him following after Shareb.

And there was the guard, holding a musket in one hand and straining to hold two snarling, leashed boarhounds in the other as he peered through the thick iron bars.

"I repeat, who goes there?" he bellowed, reaching down as though to unloose the dogs.

Bravely, Ariadne urged the stallion forward.

"Lady Ariadne St. Aubyn," she announced haughtily. And then, aware of the veterinarian behind her, she spat, "Lord Maxwell's betrothed. Now do open the gate. His Lordship is expecting me."

In the darkened stable, the noble Shareb-er-rehh stood in a roomy box stall, Thunder hooked in a nearby one and little Bow whining nervously at the door as the three of them waited for the veterinarian and Lady A to return.

Shareb could not forget his mistress's face, and her wretched despair as she'd led him into this fancy stable. She'd stayed just long enough to put her arms around his neck, and only he had known of the tears that had run warmly against his hide. And then she and the doctor had been led away by a man, leaving him to stew in the scent of his beloved Gazella, to stare malevolently at the stallion in the roomy box just across the aisle from him. *So that was Black Patrick, reigning King of the English Turf?* He snorted in contempt and tried to quell the nervousness that was even now causing his heart to pound.

He yanked back against the lead shank and twisted around, making silent eye contact with Thunder. The old gelding's head was raised, his ears pricked for any sound, his eyes huge and soft and yes, worried.

Worried.

As they all were.

Shareb could still feel the rawness around his gums where the stick had been wedged, could still recall the terrible fear and then the intense, overwhelming wave of love and relief for the doctor as he had reached inside and gently pulled it out.

With his equine sixth sense, Shareb knew the doctor was in danger, and there wasn't a thing a horse could do about it.

"Pay to the order of . . . Colin Lord . . . the sum of two . . . thousand . . . pounds."

"Really, my lord, *I* was the one who offered the sum to Dr. Lord," Ariadne snapped, as the earl waited for the ink to dry on the check while regarding her with a tolerant, sardonic lift of one brow. "I can pay my own debts, thank you."

"Ah, dearest," came the silky reply, "you are to be my wife. What is mine is yours, and what is yours, mine. If I want to pay your escort here for safely bringing you home to me, then that is my business, is it not?"

"You don't understand," she said, her face flushed and hot. "We—"

"Nonsense, my dear." Maxwell, garbed entirely in black, sat back in his chair. It angered him to part with such a large sum of money, but once he was married to the beautiful heiress he would never have financial problems again. No more debts, no more threats on his life, no more fear of debtor's prison. Now, he stirred the fire in the hearth with a poker and, out of the corner of his eye, quietly studied the pair. A bedraggled lot, the both of them, he eyeing the girl with watchful possessiveness, she looking like she'd washed her clothes in a mudhole and had her hair cropped by a drunk. It was bad enough that her tresses were the flaming red of rusted iron; to think that she had been so stupid as to chop off part of that fall of liquid fire was only adding insult to injury.

Insult to injury . . .

Five feet away from her, the lout that had brought her here sat stiffly on the edge of his chair and regarded him from beneath the longest lashes Clive Maxwell had ever seen on a man. A veterinarian, he had called himself. He was quiet and unassuming, but there was nothing benign about his lean, powerful frame, and the eyes that coolly took Maxwell's measure through the wire spectacles shone with intelligence and perception. Those eyes made the earl uncomfortable. Not just their unusual color. But the steady, intense way they looked at him. Through him. As though the man knew those things that no one—except Maxwell himself—knew.

Ariadne, he could deal with. Colin Lord might pose a bigger problem.

The name struck him then. *Colin Lord.* He'd heard it before . . . sometime, someplace. It would be only a matter of time before he placed it.

Unobtrusively, he studied his guest. *Rival*, he corrected himself, for he had not failed to notice the way Ariadne had unconsciously angled her body to lean toward the veterinarian's, nor how he had pulled his chair possessively close to hers.

So, the two were lovers, were they?

Another small problem, but one that was easily remedied.

The earl rose to his feet, consciously aware of his own height, and the image of power and sinister strength he conveyed.

The veterinarian rose to his feet, too. He reached out to take the check that Maxwell thrust toward him, and it was then that the earl saw the ring encircling one long finger.

Not just any ring, but a naval ring.

In that moment, he knew precisely who Colin Lord was.

When Colin accepted the check, Ariadne felt as though someone had slammed a fist into her stomach and then left her to die. The blood drained from her face and her fingers went to ice. She started to get up but every limb in her body had frozen, and she fell back into the chair, gripping the arms with both hands and staring at Colin in shock and betrayal while the flames crackled and popped in the hearth.

"I am in your debt, Mr. Lord, for safely conveying my lovely Ariadne to me," she heard Maxwell saying, and the casual, cultured tone of his voice finally invaded her shock. Feeling flooded back into her, and she managed to rise to her feet.

"H-he's a . . . doctor," she heard herself say.

"Yes, of course," Maxwell murmured dismissively, and his black, depthless eyes flickered over the veterinarian, giving away nothing. "Would you care to see the fabulous Black Patrick before you take your leave, *Mr.* Lord? The syndicate that owns him has stabled him here, in the hopes of breeding some of my fine mares to him. Surely you have heard of this wonderful horse? He is unbeaten, the fastest steed to hit an English turf since Eclipse." The earl reached out and cupped Ariadne's elbow, drawing her away from Colin. "Come, my dear—"

Colin had had enough.

He cleared his throat and rose to his feet.

Maxwell stared at him, flatly. Colin returned the look unflinchingly, then stepped toward Ariadne. The check lay like a diseased thing between his thumb and forefinger, the paper burning his skin and making him want to shudder with disgust.

Still holding Maxwell's gaze, he tore the check neatly in half, balled the two halves in his fist, and tossed them into the fire.

Maxwell raised both brows.

Her Ladyship swallowed hard, her eyes huge in her suddenly white face.

And Colin moved toward her, trying not to limp, and took her cold hand firmly in his own. It was not the way he had intended to propose, it was not even appropriate in manner, circumstance, or style—but desperate situations call for desperate measures, and he had no choice in the matter.

"Lady Ariadne—what I tried to say earlier—will you marry me?"

Her mouth opened and for one terrible moment he thought she was going to refuse him. Her gaze flashed to Maxwell, standing calmly beside the fire, his eyes as black as Hades. She gave the tiniest of nods—and then threw herself into Colin's arms, her body shaking with relief. She had never felt so sweet, so perfect, so right, and, reaching down, Colin cupped her face in his hands, lifted her mouth to his, and kissed her with fierce, total abandon.

She clung to him, and then, at the clearing of a throat, he looked over her head to see Maxwell staring at him with malevolent, barely controlled fury.

The earl's face was perfectly controlled, emotionless, flat. Only the whiteness around the suddenly tense mouth, and the incense glowing in the soulless black eyes revealed the hatred that burned within.

"I should call you out for this, Mr. Lord."

The fire crackled in the hearth. *Snap. Fizz.* A thunk of a falling log, and then a shower of falling sparks.

Colin gently drew Ariadne beside him. "Pistols or swords?" he asked, mildly.

"Oh, I shouldn't think it would matter to you, *Captain*. I daresay you're quite skilled with both, are you not?"

Captain? Confused, Ariadne stared at the two men. What on earth was Maxwell talking about? Then she realized just what was happening, and rage swept through her.

"I will *not* have the two of you fighting like little boys over me!" she cried, stepping between them and glaring at them both in turn. "Colin, I give you my answer: *yes*. Maxwell, I give you my explanation: Colin Lord and I became friends, then lovers, on the journey here, and I have been in love with him from the moment I first met him."

She saw fury darkening the earl's face, a faint quivering about his aristocratic nostrils. He stared at her, shocked and hurt—then turned his back and walked toward the fire, there to stand silently.

Ariadne's heart was too soft to tolerate the fact that she had just injured another so severely. She stared up at the back of Maxwell's dark, handsome head, the fringe of perfectly styled hair just touching his collar, the broad span of his shoulders beneath the black coat. Maxwell was a proud man. She had cut him deeply with her declaration of love for Colin and her acceptance of his proposal. The least she could do was offer a gentle explanation to the man she was supposed to have married.

Embarrassed, and feeling small and mean, she turned to Colin and took his hands in her own.

"Will you allow me a few moments to explain our situation to Maxwell . . . in private?" she asked, pleading with her eyes for him to understand.

She saw the uncertainty and distrust in his perceptive lavender gaze, the hesitation etched in his features.

"Please, Colin?" She squeezed his fingers. "Just a moment?"

The earl remained standing by the fire, his back turned toward them and the burned, blackened bits that had been the check curling at his feet.

Colin pursed his lips and she could see the inner battle he was waging. He gave Ariadne a long, searching glance, and reached up to touch her cheek—then, without another word, he nodded and walked toward the door.

Her hands clammy with sweat and sudden fear, she anxiously watched him close the door behind him. And then she turned and found herself staring into the black eyes of Lord Clive Maxwell.

Chapter 21

A mere hour and a half after Maxwell's boar-hounds had flung themselves at the big iron gates, another traveler appeared there—tired, hungry, and desperate.

Tristan, the new Lord Weybourne.

Splattered with mud, his fine clothes rumpled and dusty, the young earl sat coolly astride his mare while the gatekeeper, holding the two growling dogs, opened the gate. Thank God for the darkness that hid his shaking hands, the sure pallor of his face. Carefully, he schooled his features into an expression of impatience and boredom, though his heart was thundering in his chest and his hands were sweating in their gloves.

"My sister, the Lady Ariadne," he began, glancing down at the fresh hoofprints that cut the road up beneath him. "I have reason to believe that she is here."

"Ah yes, Her Ladyship arrived tonight," the gatekeeper said, straining to hold the boarhounds' collars and letting his gaze rake flatly over Tristan. "In fact, she is probably with my lord right now, as we speak."

Tristan shuddered. "I must see her. Immediately."

"Of course. Right this way, my lord," the gatekeeper murmured, managing to raise his flat, hard voice over the vicious snapping and growling of the boarhounds. He eyed Tristan coolly. "His Lordship is . . . *expecting* you."

Cold sweat broke out on Tristan's brow. He felt the customary prickle of fear threading its way up his spine at the thought of confronting Maxwell, and his arms and hands went suddenly numb. *Think of Ariadne.* He urged the mare forward, and she shot nervously past the open gate.

He kneed her into a gallop once the great iron doors were shut behind him and, without a backward glance, sent her flying down the long drive. Far ahead in the distance he saw the great stone manor house, black and foreboding against the night sky, its windows blazing with light.

Terror swept through him and he leaned low over the mare's neck, urging her faster and faster.

Ariadne was in there.

Dear God, don't let me be too late.

"Really, my dear . . . you never fail to shock and surprise me."

Ariadne swallowed hard, suddenly, inexplicably, afraid. She gazed up into Maxwell's saturnine face, but she could read nothing there; the pain she had seen earlier was gone, replaced with a look of bored indifference, and only the tightness of his words and the way his hand clenched and unclenched around the poker betrayed the sense of betrayal and rage he must surely feel.

Still holding the poker, he began a slow, studied walk, back and forth before the great stone hearth. The fire's light glowed eerily against his hair, the harsh planes of his handsome face, the midnight depths of eyes that suddenly seemed bottomless and empty.

The butler came in, and was ushered back toward the door by the earl, who muttered something to him under his breath, then Maxwell turned and regarded Ariadne.

"You are throwing away your father's dream, you know, with your insistence upon marrying this rabble," he said, noncommittally. "You are one of the wealthiest women in England, Ariadne. Do you think that a lowly animal doctor would really want you for your *looks*?"

That stung. "I should hope my *looks* are at least equal to my financial status, my lord," she replied with cool anger. "And as for my inheritance, I'll have you know that *Doctor* Lord has no interest whatsoever in my money."

"Oh, yes, I'm sure he does not. Perhaps it is your horse that he wants then, eh?"

"Really, Maxwell, I am trying to explain my feelings as a rational, sane adult. Please do not make this any more difficult."

He glanced at her, his eyes raking disapprovingly over her mud-splattered clothes, her ungloved hands, her loose and tangled hair. She felt suddenly unclean and barbaric.

"Difficult," he murmured, softly. "Here I have been worried sick about you while the whole countryside has been up in arms trying to hunt you down. You show up here looking like you just crawled out of a pasture, proclaim your love for another man, and do not expect me to be upset?"

"I had no intention of falling in love with Colin Lord. I sought him out because I needed an escort and also wanted someone to look after Shareb-er-rehh's welfare...."

"And?"

"Well ... things just rather—happened, I guess."

She felt her face flaming red, and the way Maxwell was looking at her made her feel suddenly foolish and ridiculous. "One moment I thought of him as a commoner, beneath my notice and station; the next I did not care. And then, to find that he is really Lord Morden, son of the marquess of Hampden—"

An urgent knock sounded on the door. Trailing off, Ariadne watched as the earl, carrying the poker behind his back like a whip, strode across the room to open it. The butler stood there, his face expressionless. He glanced at Ariadne, and then lowered his voice, murmuring something that she could not catch. Maxwell answered him, his words equally unintelligible.

"Thank you, Mr. Critchley," the earl murmured, and, closing the door after the butler, turned to Ariadne. His eyes glinted, and a slow, triumphant smile began to curve his full mouth.

"It would seem, my dear, that your affections for Mr. Lord are rather one-sided," he drawled, running his fingers almost lovingly over the poker.

"What are you talking about?"

"I left a check for five thousand pounds with Mr. Critchley in the hope of buying your beloved veterinarian off with it," he said smoothly.

Her fists clenched behind her back. "And?"

"It seems, my lady, that he has taken the money and run."

In the darkened stable, Colin sat in the straw at Thunder's foot, leaning his back against the gelding's stout foreleg and cradling Bow in his lap. Although his hand ran rhythmically, soothingly, over the little dog's fur, she was trembling madly, her sclera white and framing huge, frightened irises.

Five more minutes, Ariadne, he thought, pulling

out his watch. He gazed impatiently out the open door and toward the manor house. *Five more minutes, and I'm coming in after you.*

Bow trembled harder, almost nearing convulsions.

"Poor little dog," he murmured, his gentle hand stroking her back. "Still not quite recovered from the terrible scare those boarhounds gave you, are you?"

Bow whined and tried to bury her whiskery face in the crook of his elbow. Something touched his hair and Colin looked up to see Thunder's muzzle there, velvety and smooth. The gelding blew softly through his nose, then lifted his head to regard Shareb-er-rehh.

Colin followed his gaze.

The mighty stallion stood tensely in his private box, ears pricked forward, black forelock falling rakishly over one eye, nostrils flaring wide and red. He was staring out the window and toward the great manor house. Every muscle in his body was rigid, and his sleek coat was dark with nervous sweat.

A tickle of foreboding swept through Colin. Something was not right. . . .

Suddenly, Shareb flattened his ears and bared his teeth, his eyes glowing savagely in the moonlight.

"What is it, boy?"

Gently putting Bow on the straw beside him, Colin got painfully to his feet. He brushed pieces of hay from his breeches, pocketed his spectacles, and, approaching the stallion, ran his hand calmingly over the powerful hindquarters, the sleek ribs, the sharply angled shoulder and crested neck as he peered out the window to follow Shareb's intent gaze.

There, walking stiffly across the drive and toward the stable, was Maxwell's butler, a thin, crook-nosed man with a ring of pale hair encircling his skull. He stopped halfway across the little courtyard and waited while two stable hands materialized out of the darkness and joined him.

Shareb began to blow and snort. One sharp hoof struck angrily out at the wall and his whistle pierced the night.

Frowning, Colin watched as the butler punctuated words he could not hear with urgent gestures toward the stable, the manor house, the flat, Norfolk pastures that rolled away behind the stables. But Shareb must have heard them, maybe even understood them, for his whistle became a high-pitched squeal of rage and he suddenly reared up, jerking angrily at his lead shank and slamming his hooves against the side of his box, hard.

The butler cast a quick glance toward the stable; then he turned abruptly and walked back toward the house, the moonlight glowing against his pate.

Colin watched the man until the darkness swallowed him up. Danger darkened his heart, and he laid a hand on Shareb's neck, finding it hot and lathered. Something was going on, and he didn't like the feel of it. Ariadne had had long enough to explain their situation to Maxwell, and the sooner they collected the animals—including the lovely mare, Gazella—and got the hell out of there, the better.

With Bow trotting at his heels, he strode determinedly out of the box stall and the stable, never hearing Shareb-er-rehh's and Thunder's desperate whinnying behind him.

He reached the big door of the manor house and slammed his fist hard against it. It opened, and the cadaverous butler stood there, smiling.

"Ah, Mr. Lord," the old man said archly, his eyes gleaming through years of cataracts. "We were wondering where you'd gone—"

"I want to see the Lady Ariadne."

"But oh, she does not wish to see *you*."

"I *beg* your pardon?"

The butler smiled malevolently. "I'm sorry, sir, but the lady has changed her mind about her temporary *foolishness*. She has decided to honor her betrothal to my lord, after all."

"What in God's name are you saying, man?" Colin demanded, angrily trying to shoulder his way into the house.

"That you are no longer welcome at Maxwell Hall. Good-day, sir."

And then the big door was shut in his face, and Colin was left alone on the darkened steps.

Ariadne stood in the library, the fire at her back and the darkness pushing against the tall, elegantly draped windows. She stared incredulously at Maxwell, her face white with shock while his last words echoed through her stunned brain.

It seems, my lady, that he has taken the money and run ... and run ... and run. ...

"He *wouldn't!*" she cried, stalking to the heavy, olive green drapes and yanking them aside. But there was nothing to see out there in the night, and letting the heavy fabric fall back in place, she strode to the door, determined to find and confront Colin for herself.

A hand fell upon her shoulder, the fingers digging into her bones and halting her progress. She spun angrily around and found herself face-to-face with Maxwell's fathomless black eyes.

"Unhand me!"

"Ariadne." The single word was spoken with a quiet, almost sinister finality, and the hand on her shoulder never wavered. She tried to wiggle free of it, but the fingers only sank further into her flesh, trapping her. "Can you not face the truth? Your veterinarian has more need of five thousand pounds than he does a wife. Do not make a fool of yourself by running after him." The hand strayed, gently grazing the side of her neck, her cheek.

Ariadne stood frozen. She stared up at the earl's sympathetic face, feeling horror, then hysteria rising up in her throat until she couldn't breathe and her world began to go dark.

"But . . . we *love* each other!"

The dark gaze grew warm, penetrating . . . almost frightening, making her feel like a moth being drawn toward a hot fire out of which there was no escape. "And you are Lady Ariadne St. Aubyn— far too good for a disgraced hero the likes of *Captain* Colin Lord."

Captain. That was the second time she'd heard that word in the past several hours.

"Disgraced hero? Captain? What are you talking about?"

One black brow rose. "You mean you don't *know*?"

"Know what?"

A slow, chilling smile lifted the earl's mouth, and he put an arm around her back. "Why, my dear, it is no wonder he didn't tell you, such a shameful scandal it all was. . . . You see, your veterinarian was formerly a naval officer who was court-martialed out of the navy. Five years ago it was, if I remember right. 'Colin Lord.' Ah, I knew that name sounded familiar—"

She stared at him, disbelieving.

"Don't look so shocked, my dear. The whole of England heard about it, it was in all the newspapers. But then, you were too young then to take notice, were you not?"

Ariadne found her voice. "A *captain*? Court-martialed out of the navy? For *what*?"

Again, that dark, satisfied smile. "A storm, it

was. Against orders, your dear lover made a foolishly heroic attempt to save his admiral's foundering ship—and failed."

And failed.

Relief and incredulity made her legs weak. She put a hand on the back of a stuffed chair to steady herself, while the world reeled around her.

"The navy does not like to lose its ships, you know," Maxwell said, smiling. "Damned expensive things to replace."

Ariadne pushed her fingers against her brow. At last, it was all clear to her. The sea chest. The strange little mannerisms, nautical references, even the name of the little dog that was his companion. At last, she knew the reasons for the militaristic bearing, the air of authority, the visible pain she'd seen on his face, when they'd heard that fiddler in the tavern.

Oh, Colin....

No wonder he hadn't asked her to marry him. He had no wish to disgrace her name as well, and was too ashamed of what had happened to him to think that she'd ever want him. Anger swept through her, and a desperate urge to go running after him. If he had left her, it had nothing to do with money, but with his own pride! And to think he'd been disgraced for trying to save his admiral!

"I'm going after him," she announced, and, turning her back on Maxwell, strode, then ran, toward the door.

And found it locked.

Colin might have been off the sea for five years, but his mariner's instincts were still intact.

It didn't take him long to find a good, stout length of rope in the stable. An hour later, he was standing in the darkness outside the manor house, the rope in one hand, Thunder waiting patiently beside him, and the two windows that proclaimed the wakefulness of its occupant glowing golden between the drapes, three stories above his head.

He had no doubt that that occupant was Ariadne, and didn't believe for a moment that she had changed her mind about him. There was too much tension in the air, too much suspicious behavior on the part of the earl's servants, and his every instinct warned him that Ariadne was in grave danger.

Well, if they wouldn't *let* him into the house, then he'd just have to enter by his own means.

He gazed up at the imposing wall of ivy-choked stone that towered above his head. Wind, ripe with the promise of rain, tickled the leaves of several nearby oak trees, making them shake ominously in the darkness. Bow whined softly and pressed against his ankle. He reached down to reassure her, then looked up once again. The nearest handhold was a good ten feet up.

Too far to reach.

He gauged his task silently for a moment, then brought the gelding up close to the side of the house. As though in collaborative understanding, Thunder braced himself as Colin kicked off his shoes and pulled himself up onto the horse's back. His balance precarious, he crouched, then stood up, one foot on the gelding's withers to try to make his weight more bearable, the other resting just before the animal's kidneys. Thunder groaned beneath his weight, but remained faithfully still.

"Good boy," Colin murmured, and without being told, the gelding took a step closer to the house. The movement was enough to upset Colin's already shaky balance, and, wildly, he managed to grab the stony ledge of the windowsill, there to swing desperately by his fingertips while his feet dangled in space.

He cursed and gritted his teeth. Then, with all

his strength, he pulled himself up onto the ledge, tossed the rope over a grinning gargoyle just above his head, and began to climb. . . .

Never seeing Maxwell's servant watching him, nor the shadow he made as he darted from beneath those trees and ran for the house.

Chapter 22

Tristan had just worked up the courage to knock on Maxwell's door, a half-baked plan to rescue Ariadne in his mind, when he heard Shareb-er-rehh's high, piercing whinny coming from the stable.

Ari *was* here, then. *Oh, God. . . .*

Leading his mare, he crept around the back of the building and slipped inside. Horses moved in the darkness. He smelled their warm hides and heard his own nervous breathing shattering the still quiet.

There, in a roomy box at the end, was the stallion.

He glanced apprehensively behind him, but his entry had gone unnoticed. By the meager starlight beaming down through the window, he could just see Shareb-er-rehh's proud, beautifully chiseled head, his small, pricked ears, the arched crest of his long neck. The stallion was staring fixedly out the window, the moonlight gleaming in his dark eye; then he turned his head and saw Tristan.

Both man and beast froze.

Shareb's huge, shell-shaped nostrils quivered, taking the air. Tristan saw, recognized, the horse's distinctive white blaze. The two stared at each other, neither one moving—and then the stallion's soft, welcoming whinny came soughing through the darkness.

Tristan had never heard a sweeter, more comforting sound in his life. He ran forward and put his arms around the horse's neck, his eyes stinging with emotion as he laid his cheek against the sparse black mane and hugged the horse nearly hard enough to strangle him. Relief and courage coursed through him. Shareb was just a horse, but he had been his *father's* horse, and there in the darkness, the young Lord Weybourne felt his father's presence and knew it was time to confront the devil.

For he hadn't posted the rewards, worried himself sick, and chased Ariadne all the way to Norfolk to lay claim on a horse that was already his.

He'd chased her to stop her before she could marry that fiend to whom Papa had unwittingly pledged her.

A fiend who belonged in the very pit of Hell itself.

Steeling himself, Tristan turned and made his way toward the big manor house.

Ariadne paced the confines of the bedchamber, wearing a rich, grass green gown trimmed in peach and ivory that had been hastily procured from the nearby Weybourne estate.

Fresh from a bath and a maid's attention, her fiery locks entwined with artfully arranged strands of pearl and her hands wrapped in butter-soft gloves, she was once again the Lady Ariadne who had so captivated London society—and, the dashing and very eligible Lord Maxwell. But the bath had failed to leave her feeling clean, the gown (even though it had come directly from her own armoire) was restrictive and uncomfortable after the clothing she'd spent the last week in, and this room that Maxwell had provided for her—*until you can safely return to your family's home, my dear*—seemed more like a prison than a haven.

Especially after she had tried the door and found it locked.

The discovery enraged her. Did Maxwell think her an impulsive child who didn't know her own mind? No doubt he knew she'd go racing off after Colin, and thought a few hours of confinement would restore her to sanity—and, a wish to rethink her decision and honor her betrothal. Well, she objected to such high-handed treatment, knew her own mind very well, thank you, and had no intention of marrying His High-and-Mighty Lordship, not today, not tomorrow, not *ever*.

And Colin—she clenched her fists in rising anger, the gloves stretching tightly across her knuckles. She had a word or two to say to *him*, as well! Oh, she didn't believe for one minute that he'd been bought off by Maxwell's five-thousand-pound check, especially after he'd contemptuously ripped up the first one. She remembered how he'd refused to speak about his past, how he was so ashamed to tell her about his Deep, Dark Secret for fear that she would no longer love him. Maxwell was lying. Colin had not deserted her because of a large sum of money, he'd left because of his shame about the court-martial.

Oh, when she caught up to that foolish man of hers—

There was a noise outside. Something moving against the side of the house. The sill. Her window. Frowning, she tiptoed to the drapes, drew them aside—and nearly screamed.

There, his face reflecting the glow of the room's light, was Colin, crouched precariously on the ledge and motioning desperately to her.

With a little cry, she threw the window open. "Colin!"

It took him but a second to haul himself over the sill and into her arms. She sobbed with relief as he crushed her to his chest and held her fiercely, protectively, against his body. Never had she been so glad to see anyone in her life.

"Oh, Colin, I thought you'd run off and left me here—"

"Shh, Ariadne," he whispered, against her hair. "We don't have much time. I want you to put your arms around my neck and hold on tight. We're going back down—then, we'll have to seize the horses and make a run for it."

"But why—"

She never finished. The door crashed open and a horde of men, pistols in hand, charged inside. Ariadne had no time to even utter a scream before Colin thrust her aside and out of the way. She tripped and fell, grabbing the edge of a chair as she went down and hearing the sickening thuds of fists against flesh. Shouts and curses echoed in her ears; a gun went off, someone screamed, and she gained her feet only to see Colin slam his fist into the jaw of a big, powerful brute with greasy black hair and a mouthful of broken teeth.

"Run, Ariadne! For God's sake, get out of here!"

He whirled, ducked a chair that came swinging around at his head, and managed to fell the assailant before a lucky, well-placed blow to his stomach doubled him over in agony. The attackers rushed forward, and Ariadne cried out as one of them fisted his hands and brought them crashing down on the back of Colin's skull.

With a sigh, he pitched forward and fell sprawling to the floor. One finger twitched, and then he lay still.

For a horrified moment, Ariadne could not

move. Then she fell to her knees on the carpet beside him, gathering him protectively up in her arms even as the door opened and Maxwell stepped inside.

Instantly, everyone fell silent.

Brows raised, the earl surveyed the room with a cool, appraising eye. Outside, a dog—*Bow*, Ariadne thought dazedly—was barking frantically. Maxwell jerked his chin, and one of his minions ran to the window and slammed it shut.

Then he turned and regarded his men, the little heiress, and, with a smile of contempt, the prostrate body of the veterinarian.

"Well, well, is *this* what my meeting with the new Lord Weybourne was interrupted for?" Sighing, he put his hands behind his back and peered down at the man cradled in Ariadne's arms. "I daresay, a thieving intruder." He gazed at one of his servants, just picking himself up from the floor and groaning in pain from Colin's well-placed blow, then the butler who stood faithfully behind him. "Critchley? Please arrange to have this refuse carted out and *shot.*"

"You can't do that!" Ariadne cried, holding Colin's lolling head to her shoulder. "That's *murder!*"

"That's *justice,*" Maxwell corrected her coolly. "The blackguard broke into my house. He shall get the punishment he deserves."

For a moment Ariadne could only stare at Maxwell in horror and disbelief, the blood draining from her face. She suddenly remembered the feeling of danger, fear even, as Maxwell had strode calmly back and forth in front of the fire, the poker clenched behind his back, his eyes black and bottomless.

Oh, my God . . . .

"Please stand up, my dear," Maxwell said softly.

"No!" she cried, locking a trembling arm behind

Colin's shoulders and holding his heavy weight against her. "You'll have to shoot me first, Maxwell, I swear it!"

The earl sighed. His cold, black gaze flickered over his rival's still body, and Ariadne's green skirts pinned beneath it. "I wouldn't dream of harming a hair on your pretty head, my dear," he said smoothly. "Get up."

"I *said*, no!"

"My lady." Maxwell's smile widened, and he reached to take the cheroot offered by his butler. "If you do *not* get up, I will have you forcibly hauled away from your lover by your hair, and *still* have him shot as a thief before the sun is up."

Ariadne glared at him, splaying her fingers through Colin's hair and pressing him against her even more tightly.

"Or," Maxwell continued, gesturing with his cheroot, "you can obey your father's wishes and honor your betrothal to me." He flicked an imaginary bit of dust from his sleeve. "The choice, my dear, is yours. Honor your betrothal to me, or I shall have the good doctor shot."

"That's *blackmail!*"

"That's my offer. Make a decision, or I will make it *for* you."

Swallowing hard, Ariadne was acutely aware of Colin's weight in her arms, his lifeblood flowing through his veins, the slow beating of his heart, so close to hers. She felt his hair against her palm and between her fingers, the weight of his brow against her shoulders—

"What will it be, my dear?"

She directed a cold glare at the earl. "And if I agree to marry you?"

"Why, your lover shall be allowed to go free, of course."

She looked down at the man she loved, lying on

the floor and in her arms as if already dead, and an icy chill came up from the very marrow of her bones and sent shivers through every cell in her body. She had no choice in the matter, really, and Maxwell knew it. *Oh, Papa ... why did you ever pledge me to this man, didn't you know what a monster he is?*

Gently, she pressed a kiss to Colin's brow, whispered a plea for forgiveness that she knew he never heard, and then, carefully, eased him down atop the thick carpet. Her hands were trembling as she pulled her skirts out from beneath his heavy weight, and it was all she could do to maintain her courage, her dignity, as she coldly refused Maxwell's offered hand and got to her feet. She watched in horror as his men shoved her roughly aside to pick up Colin's body as though it were nothing but rubbish for the compost pile. As they lifted him, she reached out to touch his hand a final time, and found it deathly cold. Then, at a nod from Maxwell, the men shouldered her aside and carried him out of the room.

Maxwell followed, closing the door behind him. And so it was that Ariadne didn't hear the earl's last, cold order to his faithful servant, Daley.

"Take him out to the far pasture and put a bullet in his head. And I don't want to see your face again until the deed is done. Is that understood?"

"Yes, my lord."

Ariadne, alone in her room and crying into her pillow, never heard the single shot that cracked the night. By the time the sun came up three hours later, Daley was back, his face sober, his trousers smeared with grass stains, his hands filthy with the dirt of the grave. He gave his hasty report to the earl, who nodded with satisfaction and then, calmly sipping his tea, called for his morning paper.

For Maxwell, life had never looked better. His rival was out of the way. The Fastest Horse in the World was in his stable.

And now, nothing—not the chit's father, her stupid, spineless brother, nor even her lover himself—could stand between him and the great St. Aubyn fortunes.

Tristan, Lord Weybourne, was quite proud of himself. Not only had he cleverly disguised his plan—and a desperate plan it was, too—as a gamble that Maxwell could not resist, but he had carried it through with a cool directness of purpose that would have done his father proud. Surely, it was only the thought of his endangered sister that had infused him with such courage, but nevertheless, Tristan was almost grateful for the abrupt appearance of Maxwell's butler, and the subsequent conclusion of the meeting. Now, as he stalked out of the house, a servant running to open the door before he reached it, his heart was pounding as much with relief as it was with fear, because there were a million and one things that could go wrong with his plan to rescue Ariadne.

A plan that depended solely upon the very one who had gotten her into this mess:

Shareb-er-rehh.

The meeting was still fresh in Tristan's mind. . . .

"What do you mean, she's agreed to marry you?" Tristan had said, jumping to his feet and staring angrily at Maxwell. "I forbid it! You know what my father's wishes were, you know what my *sister*'s wishes were! I demand to see her immediately!"

"Sit down, Tristan."

"I said, I want to see her, *now*!"

"Your sister is indisposed. She retired early, pleading a headache and expressing her wish to take tea in her room. Surely, this reunion between siblings can wait until morning."

He stared into Maxwell's eyes. They gave nothing away and, as usual, were as black and cold as the soul of the monster that looked out of them. Shaking with anger, Tristan sat heavily down in a chair and drained his port with one quick, fluid flick of the wrist. He slammed the glass down, and the elegant crystal shattered into a thousand pieces.

"My, my . . . what *has* the aristocracy come to, if its fine young men can no longer show proper poise and manners in other people's homes," Maxwell drawled.

"Don't goad me," Tristan said heatedly. "I'm not afraid of you. Not this time. Not anymore. My father told me, not two hours before he died, that he'd sent you a letter effectively terminating the engagement between my sister and you! He didn't want Ariadne married to you, not after he found out what you are *really* like!"

"Now Tristan—" the earl began, condescendingly.

"And isn't it strange, that somebody *mysteriously* set fire to his stables the very night he sent that letter?"

"Quite strange indeed," Maxwell said, fixedly staring at Tristan and smiling a thin, evil little smile.

"One would think it was almost in *revenge*," Tristan said, knowing he was walking at the edge of an active volcano.

Maxwell lit a cheroot, appeared to study it thoughtfully. "Pity, that some things can be surmised . . . but never proved."

"You will *not* marry my sister."

Maxwell, still gazing at his cheroot, smiled without looking at Tristan. "Oh, but I will. Because you see, young Tristan, I never received such a note from your dear, departed daddy, and as far as *I'm* concerned, the betrothal is still on."

"I say it's not. And I would like to see my sister, *now*."

"Of course, there *is* the matter of . . . the veterinarian," the earl said, offhandedly. "Tell me, does your sister fall in love with every pretty-faced man who happens to come her way? She arrived here looking like a grubworm that just crawled out of the garden. 'Twould be a pity indeed, if society were to find out that she traipsed across half the English countryside—unescorted, save for the company of a man who managed to get himself thrown out of the Royal Navy for losing not one, but two of its finest ships. . . ."

Tristan was not prepared for this. He had always known that his sister was impulsive and flighty, but to think she could fall in love with the *veterinarian*, someone she'd only known for what, a week?

"My time is valuable. What do you want, Tristan?"

His brain whirling, Tristan had no choice but to seize opportunity from despair. He sat back in his chair, plucked a book on fox hunting from the table beside him, and, to still his shaking fingers, casually flipped through the pages, all the while feeling Maxwell's black, malevolent stare boring into him behind a cloud of blue smoke.

"You are a gambling man," he said, turning another page and pretending to be absorbed in a drawing of a hunting scene. He let a moment go by, just enough for drama and effect. "Therefore, I have a proposal for you, Maxwell. A proposal that, as a sporting man, should prove unbearably tempting to you."

Out of the corner of his eye, Tristan saw one sinister black brow rise, ever so slightly, on Maxwell's forehead. He gestured with his cheroot. "This ought to be interesting. But go ahead. I'm listening."

"Black Patrick is the unbeaten King of the English Turf," Tristan continued, casually reciting a well-known fact but feeling his own hands beginning to sweat at what he was about to propose. "In thirty-five races, he has never been defeated."

Maxwell's unnerving stare was leveled on Tristan's face.

"Shareb-er-rehh is the last of my father's Norfolk Thoroughbreds, excepting, of course, Gazella. He is the Fastest Horse in the World—"

"Purportedly, Tristan, but never proven." Maxwell took a long draw on his cheroot, blew out a perfect ring of smoke, and stamped the cigar out. "After all, the beast has never been raced."

"Precisely. Which is why my proposal should interest you greatly."

"And just what is it you propose?" he asked, condescendingly.

"A match race between Black Patrick and Shareb-er-rehh."

Maxwell laughed softly, a soft, thready sound that froze the blood in Tristan's veins. He shook his head.

"With the horse himself as the stakes," Tristan finished, quietly.

Maxwell stopped laughing. He turned the full effect of his eyes on Tristan, and on a note of scared triumph, Tristan saw the sudden, keen interest that flickered in those black-as-death depths. "Really, Tristan . . . haven't you learned your lesson? You are hopelessly in debt to me already, with no means of paying me off until you reach the age to inherit." He smiled, threateningly. "That is, *if* you reach the age to inherit. All you have left is that horse . . . and you would risk even *that*?"

"I love that horse . . . but I love my *sister* more," Tristan said, his voice beginning to tremble, for the thought of losing Shareb-er-rehh filled him with as much grief as the last memory of his father.

"Well. . . ."

"Despite what my sister thinks, Shareb-er-rehh belongs to *me*," Tristan said firmly. "Therefore, what becomes of the horse is my decision, and what I propose is this: If Shareb-er-rehh wins the race, you must free me from all debts owed to you—and, my sister from a betrothal that neither she, my father, nor I, wish. *Publicly*."

Maxwell leaned back in his chair and calmly folded his arms behind his head, his gaze boring into Tristan like nails. "And if Black Patrick wins the race?"

Sick dread pulsed through Tristan's stomach, making jelly out of his nerves, for such a thing did not even bear thinking about. He raised his chin and resolutely met the earl's black stare. "Then ownership of both Gazella and Shareb-er-rehh goes to you."

Maxwell looked at him for a long, thoughtful moment, his eyes glinting with greed like sparks off a smithy's anvil. He kept that calculated stare on Tristan until the young lord felt his heart beginning to pound, the sweat popping out on his brow. *Please, God, let him accept the proposal, it is the only way I know to save both my sister and my horse—*

"Has it ever occurred to you, Tristan, that the stallion is already *mine*? As part of your *assets*—assets that will be sold off to pay me, I'll remind you, if you don't come up with the money—I can rightfully claim him anyhow as payment of your debt." He smiled, threateningly. "One way or another, the horse is mine."

Tristan met that black gaze, sudden rage bubbling up in his throat like acid. "He is *not* yours, *milord*, and if you resort to such lowly means to gain him, I will find my sister's veterinarian friend and sell Shareb-er-rehh to him for the sum of a mere *pound*, if only to keep him out of your clutches."

Maxwell laughed softly then, and Tristan's very bones felt cold.

"If you love this horse so much, then why would you risk losing him in a match race?" he said, patronizingly.

"Because I know that you won't be able to resist the opportunity to make money—lots of money—that such a race would offer, for not only will it draw crowds from Norfolk, but from all over Britain as well. It will be the sensation of the century."

Maxwell's eyes glinted. "And . . . ?"

"Because I will do anything to save my sister from marrying you."

"And . . . ?"

Tristan leaned forward in his chair, gripping its arms and locking his gaze with Maxwell's. "Because I have every faith in the world that Shareb-er-rehh will win."

He sat back, his heart hammering painfully against his ribs. Maxwell looked at him for a long, assessing moment. Then he gave a slight nod and reached for his calendar.

"You are a fool, Tristan. But then, I have made a fortune off of fools, idiots—and people who don't know when their luck has run out. But what do I have to lose? We shall run the race." He pulled the calendar toward him. "Shall we make it, say . . . one week from tomorrow?"

"One week from tomorrow."

"I shall send a courier to Newmarket, then, to alert my racing friends so they can spread the word," Maxwell said, and Tristan could see that the fire had caught hold of the earl, just as he'd known, hoped, gambled, that it would. "Some advertisements there, in the newspapers, in London—"

The door opened suddenly, and the butler stood there, his body looking like a skeletal corpse that had just crawled out of the coffin—save for the eyes, which were bright with desperation.

"Excuse me, my lord. There is a small ... disturbance, that demands your immediate attention. ..."

Maxwell had risen to his feet, bid Tristan good-evening, and that had been the end of a confrontation that Tristan had been dreading with every waking breath of the last week. Now, he wanted only to escape this Hades incarnate, find this veterinarian of Ariadne's—*bloody hell, why didn't she just run off with the damned groom?*—and demand some answers. And as for the race ... He'd see Maxwell in hell before he gave up either Shareb-er-rehh or his sister to the soulless fiend!

The night was dark, lit only by the silver wash of starlight and the eerie bars of gold slanting across the lawn from Maxwell's windows. Tristan was almost to the stable when he heard shouts and pistol shots coming from behind him.

Within the house.

He froze.

His first instinct was to rush back inside, his only thought for the safety of his sister. But reason took hold of him and he dived for cover behind a block of shrubbery, peeking out just in time to see a door open and several men, carrying a dead body between them, hurrying across the dark lawn. Icy dread prickled the length of Tristan's spine, numbing his limbs and settling in his stomach. In horror, he watched as they slung the corpse over the back of an old, swaybacked gelding, exchanged quick words between themselves, and, leaving only one of their number behind, returned to the house.

The man that remained, a wiry, skittish-looking bugger, was just pocketing a gun and carrying a shovel. As Tristan watched, he took the gelding's halter and tried to lead him away. A little dog came racing out of the darkness, barking frantically; the servant shouted at the animal to no avail, finally raising the shovel until it ran, yelping, into the shadows. The gelding's eyes rolled with fear and he began to stamp and snort, nearly spilling the corpse from his back. The servant jerked down hard on the animal's halter, then, dragging the shovel behind him, led the frightened beast off into the darkness.

Tristan didn't need anyone to tell him where the servant was heading.

Toward the lonely Norfolk pastures.

He scrambled out from behind the shrubbery, half-expecting gunfire to ring out behind him, but the night remained still and quiet save for the scraping, increasingly distant sound of the shovel moving over and through the grass. Tristan waited until he was sure the servant couldn't look back and see him, and then, driven by morbid curiosity and fear, sprinted across the lawn after him, keeping to the shadows and behind trees. For a minute, he thought he'd lost the odd trio; then he saw the old gelding just ahead, and thirty feet away, the little dog following at a safe distance. He heard the panicky drumming of his heart and felt the bile of fear in his stomach at the sight of the corpse, the fingers dangling just above the horse's knees and the lifeless head and arms swinging above the grass with every plodding step the old beast took.

Who was the dead man? Another debtor who had fallen afoul of Maxwell and couldn't pay up?

Tristan shuddered, seeing a sudden vision of his own dark fate. Unless he came up with the money—or Shareb won the race—*he* would be the next one to be murdered and buried in a dark, Norfolk field.

He wiped icy sweat from his brow and continued on.

The house was well behind them now, the night growing darker, deeper, blacker. Out over the lonely pastures he followed the servant and the broken-down old horse. Here the grasses were thick and damp, the brambles clawing, and he felt the moisture seeping through his shoes until his feet were wet and clammy. Somewhere off in the distance a nightbird called; closer, an owl hooted. Finally, two miles away from the manor house, the servant stopped the horse, pulled the corpse from its back, and let the body drop bonelessly to the earth. It landed with a heavy thud on its back, arms outflung and face turned toward the night sky.

Tristan stole closer, unnoticed.

The servant began to dig. Cold starlight flashed against the shovel, and the sound of metal striking rock and flint, the servant's labored breathing as he worked, and loose dirt thumping against the steadily growing pile of earth, filled the night. On and on it went. The digging sound was horrible, and the sweat turned to ice the length of Tristan's spine as he wondered how many other unmarked graves were out here on this lonely, windswept hill.

He crept closer.

And saw the body move its hand.

He froze, the scream hanging in his throat. Then reason and reality swept in, and with it, horror. The bugger was going to bury the man alive!

The shovel flashed, the servant grunting and cursing as he struck rock. Holding his breath, Tris-

tan crept forward. He was thirty feet away now ...
twenty ... fifteen—

The old gelding stepped quietly toward the
fallen man and nosed his shoulder, as though trying to rouse him. The hand moved again, then the
arm, and Tristan heard the poor fellow moan, saw
him drag open his eyes and reach up to touch the
horse's lowered muzzle.

At that moment, the servant turned and saw the
whole thing.

Swearing, he tore a pistol from his pocket and
trained it on the defenseless man.

But he was too late. Tristan had already leapt
forward, his elbow deflecting the servant's aim,
and the shot went wild into the Norfolk night.

Chapter 23

The crack of a pistol, the ground vibrating beneath him as bodies wrestled in the grass, grunts, curses, fists against flesh, and the dark mass of Thunder moving to stand protectively over him—Colin was dazedly aware of the struggle, but he was unable to sit up when he tried. He fell back in the grass and must have blacked out, for when he opened his eyes there was only a hand against his brow and someone hovering over him, breathing hard.

"Ariadne—" he murmured, desperately trying to get to his feet. "Got to get her out...."

The stars wheeled above his head and began to fade out. From a great distance away he felt his rescuer shaking him, slapping his wrists and cheek, forcing him back toward consciousness. An arm slid behind his nape and pulled him up. Dragging open weighted eyelids, Colin saw a youthful, handsome face, intent gray eyes staring worriedly down at him, and a tense, determined mouth that broke suddenly into a relieved smile.

"Another one of Maxwell's debtors, are you?" the youth drawled, in a voice that was educated and highbred.

"Colin Lord . . . veterinarian, London."

The wry smile vanished and the youth leapt to his feet. "You're the bloody bastard who helped Ariadne get to Norfolk! Damn you, I ought to just finish what that idiot started and kill you right here and now!"

Colin, too ill to stand, drew his legs to his chest, and rested his brow against his knees.

"Please, after I get my bearings. Make it a fair fight, at least."

"If it weren't for you, I'd have caught up to her and stopped her before she ended up in the clutches of that—that *monster*, Maxwell!"

"And pray, who are you?"

"Tristan St. Aubyn, her *brother*," the lad declared, with highborn indignance.

"Ah, yes, of course." Colin bent his head and, wincing, massaged the back of his skull. "Young Lord Weybourne. If you're after the stallion, I fear you're too late, lad."

"I'm not too late. Shareb-er-rehh belongs to *me*, not my sister. Besides, I didn't chase her all the way from London because I wanted to get my hands on that horse! That isn't what she thinks, is it?"

"I'm afraid so."

"Bloody hell." The young lord, no less high-strung than his sister, began to pace, cheeks bright with color, fists clenched at his sides. "I chased her all the way to Burnham because she *cannot marry Maxwell*, she doesn't know the danger she's in, doesn't know what Papa tried to do, damn it, she doesn't know *anything*—"

"She thinks you want the horse to pay off your debts," Colin said carefully.

"Debts! I'll tell you about debts!" Then, lowering his voice as though he feared anyone hearing him out here in this desolate pasture, the young lord spit, "I'm in debt to the tune of *thousands*, and it's all owed to Maxwell. Gambling debts, horse-racing debts, cockfighting, dog-fighting, and boxing debts. I made wagers, lost, borrowed from Maxwell because he was the only person I could find who'd lend me the money to support my *obsession*. I gambled more, lost more . . . before I knew it I was in over my bloody head."

He paused, raked both hands over his eyes, dropped them on a sigh of self-disgust before turning his face away.

"Maxwell threatened me with bodily harm if I could not come up with the money. So I went to my father, and when he realized what a fiend Maxwell is—I mean, what kind of a man would lend money to someone *my* age?—he tried to break off Ariadne's engagement to him. He sent a cold note to Maxwell but before anything could be made public, before he could even tell Ariadne, even, that he had broken it off, there was a f-fire—"

"Easy, lad," Colin said gently, in a voice he might have once used to steady a frightened midshipman.

"There was a . . . f-fire, and my father ran into the barn to try and save Shareb-er-rehh. He was the last of the Norfolk Thoroughbreds, but Papa, he—he had an attack, and I was the one who . . . who . . . f-found him. Damn it, damn it all to hell—" The youth bent his brow to his fingers, unable to mask his grief from Colin's sympathetic eyes. "And to think that my sister believes I came here to steal Shareb-er-rehh back. . . ."

Colin pulled himself to his feet. Swaying, he leaned heavily against Thunder's stout old shoulder until the fog cleared from his head and the waves of nausea and dizziness passed. It was then that he saw the shovel lying in the grass, the partially dug grave, the unconscious servant nearby.

He had no doubts as to what his fate was supposed to have been.

"By the way," he said, when the hitching sobs finally stopped, "thanks for saving my life."

"Yes. Well, I couldn't just let the bastard bury you alive."

The youth walked a little distance away, misery emanating from his proud, narrow shoulders as he gazed off into the night.

"So how do you propose to settle your accounts, then?" Colin asked, gently. "If you are not yet of age to claim your inheritance, it would seem that you *have* to give up Shareb-er-rehh in order to pay your debts, and will still lose him after all that your sister went through to keep him."

"Mr. Lord—" Tristan faced him, his composure intact once more, his tone far older, wearier, than his face was. "Shareb is all I have. I had no choice."

"No choice?" Colin stepped forward, the fingers of dread already inching up his spine. "What did you *do*, lad?"

Tristan kicked at a tuft of grass, and looked away, his mouth hard.

"You signed the stallion over to Maxwell," Colin said.

"No."

"You plan to sell him and give the money to Maxwell, then."

"No."

"Then what on earth have you *done*, lad?"

Tristan looked up, his eyes defiant. "I proposed a match race between Shareb-er-rehh and Black Patrick, and made a bet with Maxwell on its outcome. If Shareb wins, then Maxwell must not only publicly declare that the wedding between him and my sister is off, he must release me from my debts. All of them."

"And if Shareb loses?"

Tristan's throat moved, and he turned away. "He can't."

Colin stepped forward, and grasped the youth's shoulder. "I repeat, Tristan, if he loses?"

The wind suddenly whispered through the trees, making the leaves shake ominously above their heads.

"If he loses, ownership of both Shareb-er-rehh and Gazella goes to Maxwell, and I'm as good as dead."

If anyone noticed that young Lord Weybourne's personal groom bore a strong facial resemblance to the intruder that had been shot and buried in one of the far pastures, no one commented on it. If anyone noticed that Daley was unreasonably skittish and unable to meet anyone's eyes, they never guessed the reason for it. And if anyone heard the Lady Ariadne's pitiful sobs far into the middle of the night, no one, not even the maid that Maxwell had assigned to her, made any move to comfort her.

For their master was not a man to be crossed, and those who were in his employ knew that more than just their positions were at stake if they were to rouse his ire in any way. And so the household went about its business, Lord Weybourne—who refused to be away from his sister—was moved into a guest wing, and the servant Daley kept his silence, desperately praying that Maxwell would never find out that the man he was supposed to have killed had escaped and disappeared.

It was Daley's most fervent wish that that man would not turn up in an unexpected—and close—place. Luckily, his tasks did not include anything remotely connected to the earl's stable of prized Thoroughbreds, and so it was that he did not recognize Lord Weybourne's bespectacled, crippled groom for the man he actually was.

The disguise—and getting Tristan placed within the manor house in order to keep a watch over his sister—had been Colin's idea. It was no difficult task to exaggerate the limp that would always pain him, and spectacles, a change of clothes, and another shampoo of black ink to cover the striking shade of his hair was enough to fool anyone who might have gotten too close a look at him during his failed attempt to rescue Ariadne. He waited just long enough to make himself comfortable in his new role—and then he sent the young Lord Weybourne to bring his sister to him.

When a haggard-looking Ariadne was escorted to the parlor, she found a slim figure leaning against the mantel, hat and gloves in one hand, brow resting tiredly in the other.

With a shock, she realized it was her brother.

Her first impulse was to flee the room. Her second was to curse him for making her life hell these past few weeks, and forcing her to become a fugitive in order to save Shareb-er-rehh. She stared contemptuously at his drawn, pale face, his elegant hands, and shot him her most withering look of disgust.

"I have nothing to say to you, Tristan. Good-day."

She turned to leave.

"No, Ariadne!" Abandoning his place by the hearth, he rushed across the room, seized her elbow, and forced her into a chair. She fought him, struggling angrily, until his intent gray gaze was inches from her own.

"Unhand me this instant, Tristan, or so help me God I'll scr—"

"Colin Lord is hiding in the stable, waiting for you," he hissed, desperately, in her ear.

Instantly, she froze and fell silent. Her body all but sank into the depths of the chair, where she sat with bent head and hands folded demurely in her lap. She squeezed them to stop their sudden shaking. She could not speak.

"Maxwell tried to have him murdered," Tristan whispered, just above her ear. "Luckily for your animal doctor, I happened to come along at the right time."

"Oh my God, I must go to him—"

"He's *fine*," Tristan said tightly, restraining her. "A bit sore, but he'll make it. Ariadne, I . . . I did something you must know about."

He told her about the match race.

"For God's sake, Tristan, how *could* you?" she cried, anger staining her cheeks and lending the only color to her face. And then she saw his stricken eyes and knew that despite everything, and all that had happened, he was still too young to know any different, still too young to weigh the risks, and still . . .

Her brother.

"Oh, *Tristan*—"

The two siblings rushed into each other's arms, sobbing with relief, despair, and grief for all that they had so recently lost.

And all that they still had left to lose.

Tristan discreetly left her at the entrance to the stable, and, picking up her skirts, Ariadne ran past the box containing Black Patrick, past the demure and elegant Gazella, past the stall where Thunder—never looking more ugly and deplorable than he did in contrast to a stable containing some of the finest horses in England—quietly munched his hay, and straight toward the big box where her stallion resided.

Shareb-er-rehh—staring lustfully at Gazella—

saw her coming. He pricked his ears, turned his head to look knowingly at the stall's other occupants, and then, walking forward, thrust his muzzle over the partition, his forelock falling over his eyes.

He whickered in welcome—but Lady A brushed rudely past him and Bow with nary a word of greeting and threw herself into the animal doctor's arms.

Shareb tossed his tail against his flanks, sighed, and met Bow's laughing gaze while the two humans hugged each other with shameless abandon.

"Oh, Colin . . . Tristan told me what Maxwell tried to do to you—"

But he was pushing her away, ignoring her outburst, looking like someone had just dealt him a stunning blow. "My God, Ariadne . . ."

Confused, she came up short. "What?"

And then she saw the direction of his gaze. He was staring at her, speechless and awestruck. His throat worked, and almost reverently he reached out and touched her coiffed, upswept hair, the bodice of her gown, and then trailed his fingers down the fragile length of her sleeve.

Then his eyes lifted to hers.

"I have never seen such exquisite beauty in all my life," he murmured hoarsely.

Heat swept into her cheeks and she gave him a coy, playful smile before tapping him lightly on the shoulder to jar him back to reality. "Why, Colin, you act as though you've never seen a lady in a gown before!"

"No, dearest, I have never seen *this* lady in a gown before. He remembered his failed rescue attempt. "Or at least, I've never had the chance to *study* her in it. All the rest of your gender do not count upon my memory or my thoughts. I am totally undone. Overcome."

"Oh, Colin . . ."

And then she remembered what had nearly happened to him, and, with a little cry, she threw herself against his chest. His arms closed tightly around her with fierce protectiveness.

"As much as I relish the sight of you, you cannot stay here, Ariadne. It is far too dangerous."

"No, I'm *not* leaving, Colin," Ariadne declared. "Besides, Tristan is standing guard just outside and will cough if anyone comes. Look at you! You've made your hair black again, and what is this blanket you've spread here on the straw? Is it for you or for Bow? Don't tell me you are actually sleeping out here—"

"I don't trust Maxwell, Ariadne. Not with the race coming up. God only knows what he'll do."

"Do you think he might . . . sabotage the race? Even harm Shareb?"

"I wouldn't put it past him, my dear. You and your brother have too much riding on the outcome of this race, and I'd hate like hell to see that stallion end up in Maxwell's hands. *Or*, anything happen to either of you." He took her tiny hand, enfolding it within his own. Then, poking his head out of the stall to be sure the way was clear, he hurried her out of the box and toward the stairs that led up to the loft.

Ariadne followed eagerly, mindful of her skirts. A beam of sunlight, adrift with dust swirls, slanted through a window. Colin gained the loft first and, kneeling in the hay, reached down to pull her up. Hushing a giggle, she went into his arms, clinging to his solid, comforting warmth before he picked her up and carried her through the whispery hay to a far corner. There he set her on her feet, pulled her close, and kissed her long and hard.

She melted against him, never so relieved and happy to see anyone in her life. Just being near him made all the fear and anguish of the past two days go away, and she wearily gave herself up to him and his strength. His hands came up to cradle her cheeks, then one drifted down to graze her neck, her bodice, her stomach, as though to reassure himself that she was truly well and unharmed. She felt the fire starting within her, as it always did at his touch, and she broke the kiss to gaze at his beloved face.

To think that Maxwell had tried to have him killed. . . .

Dear, gentle Colin, who had dedicated his life to saving God's creatures from pain and illness—

Her eyes filled with hot tears, and his face suddenly went blurry behind them.

"Ah, sweetheart. . . ."

His arms went around her, holding her close and cupping her head against the inside of his shoulder. Choking sobs bubbling out of her throat were muffled against his heartbeat. Her tears soaked his shirt, dampening the warm, hay-scented skin just beneath, and she fisted her hands in the fabric beneath her cheek. How close she had come to losing him, and how much peril they were all still in.

And then she remembered Maxwell's revelation.

Managing to get her tears under control, she pulled back, even as Colin pulled the tail of his shirt free and gently dried her eyes. She stared up at his strong nose, his handsome face, the beautiful, soul-deep eyes that were filled with love and tenderness as he went about this humble task.

"Why didn't you tell me?" she asked.

He stared at her, uncomprehending. "Tell you what?"

"About your former career . . . *Captain* Lord."

His flinched, and his hand, just beneath her eye with the shirttail bunched in it, froze. He stared at her as though she had struck him, then began to lower his hand.

She caught it, unwilling to let it go.

He looked away.

"So . . . you know."

"Yes," she replied, steadily. "Maxwell told me."

"Everything?"

"Everything."

He gave a great sigh, and sat down in the hay, looking defeated and broken. "I told you you wouldn't want me if you only knew what I'd done."

She sat down beside him, arranging her skirts in such a manner that her bare ankles showed temptingly. "Colin Lord, you are one of the most intelligent men I have ever met, but sometimes you really *are* a thickheaded dolt."

His gaze had been on her ankles. He looked at her, confused. "What do you mean?"

"How can you believe that I would think any less of you for what you did?"

"I disobeyed my admiral." He looked down, picked up a piece of straw, began to tie it up in a series of little knots. "Because of me, we lost two ships that night, Ariadne. Not just one."

"You disobeyed him because you were trying to save his life, and that of every man aboard that frigate."

She sidled closer to him, put her hand beneath his chin, and forced him to look at her. Dark, purple eyes met hers, full of pain and anguish. "Maxwell told me about it," she murmured. "And fiend that he is, did so with all the triumphant malice in his black heart. But it did not have the intended effect on me, Colin. I love you all the more for what you tried to do—"

"The wind was too strong," he murmured, looking down at the piece of straw he still held. "Sir Graham ordered me to save my ship, to just get out of there and let the frigate dash itself against the rocks. He *knew* the wind was too strong, that in trying to save him and the frigate, I'd imperil my own vessel, my own people, as well. But I had too much respect for him, Ariadne." The lavender eyes, anguished and pleading, looked up at her. "I *loved* him. Aside from Nelson, he was the finest commander I ever served under. . . ."

She put her arms around him, laid her cheek against his shoulder.

"The frigate was doomed, try as I did to save it. And God help me I tried, though Sir Graham was bellowing at the top of his lungs for me to leave off—I can still see his face, the rage there, but I ignored him and ordered my crew to rig a towrope between the two ships—" He put his hands over his eyes, trying to shut out the horrible memory. "The wind was too strong, Ariadne . . . just too damned strong. . . ."

"Oh, Colin. . . ."

"The towline broke. It bloody *broke*. After that—after that it was too late to save either ship. Some of our crews were able to claw their way through the surf and make it to shore, but many men drowned that night. Had I obeyed Sir Graham's order, perhaps not so many would have been lost." He raised his head and looked at her then, and although sorrow was etched in every line of his face, his eyes were almost fierce. "But I swear to you, Ariadne, that if I could go back and face that same decision all over again, I would not have done any different. *I would not have abandoned my admiral.*"

He stared at her for a long, challenging moment.

She said nothing, only reaching out to squeeze his hand.

He looked away.

"But he abandoned *you*, Colin," she said softly, feeling a sudden, unreasonable hatred for this un-

known officer who had done nothing to save the
career of the man who had tried to save *him*.

"No. He didn't, Ariadne. He was Nelson's own
protégé, the brightest star in the Royal Navy, and
angry as he was with me for what I'd done, he
was right by my side throughout the entire court-
martial. If anyone could have saved me from ruin,
or my family from the shame and disgrace they
suffered because of the whole affair, *he* could
have. And God help him, he tried." He tossed the
piece of straw aside and looked bleakly at the
beam of sunlight slanting over the hay. "But nothing Sir Graham could say in my defense made a
damned bit of difference. The fact of the matter
was, I disobeyed my admiral and in so doing, cost
the navy one of its finest, costliest, warships. A
flagship."

She held him tightly. "I love you, Colin."

"Afterward, I had little money to support myself. I was too proud to ask my father for help,
and though he didn't say as much, I knew his
shame ... he was an admiral himself, from a
proud family with a long naval tradition that I
had been expected to uphold; I couldn't disgrace
him further. And so I found myself in London,
and one day, when I came across a horse being
beaten by a cab driver, I intervened." He gave a
sad smile. "It was sort of like what happened with
Thunder, I guess ... only this horse's name was
Ned. Something happened, then—I have always
shared a rather unusual, uncanny bond with animals, but when that horse looked up at me, I
knew, I just *knew* what my calling was, and what I
had to do to atone for all the lives I had helped
destroy in the name of *war*."

"Save animals, instead."

"Yes." He looked at her, unashamed of the path
his life had taken. "I couldn't ask you to marry

me, Ariadne, until I'd told you about my past. And I was so afraid that if I did, you'd no longer want me. No longer respect me. That you'd pity me—"

"I love you, Colin," she repeated, touching his lips.

"And what about your future? You do know that marrying a veterinarian—a man of *trade*—will get you ostracized from polite society, that you will be an outcast just like me. And I don't even make enough money in my profession to keep you in gowns half as beautiful as this one—"

"Colin."

He came up short. "What?"

"I don't *care* about gowns. I don't care about those stuffy people who will turn their backs on me, as those who are my true friends will not. I don't care about social ostracism and I don't care about money, though God knows I have enough of it to put the whole of Norfolk in beautiful gowns. For heaven's sake, can't you see what you've taught me? I know I used to think that money and class were everything, but they can't equal the happiness I've found in your arms. *You* are all that matters in the world, do you understand me? *You*. I love you, Colin. I wouldn't care if you were a destitute veterinarian or the richest lord in the land." And then, looking into his defiant, beautiful eyes, she pulled off his hat, removed his spectacles, put them on the hay, and began to kiss him.

He shut his eyes, the long lashes draping his cheeks, his hands clenched into fists as her lips feathered against his face. She pressed her lips to his, tasting him, loving him. His breathing grew deeper, and finally, his hands came up to caress her back, at first tentatively, then with increasing surety and confidence as he realized that he *hadn't* lost her, that she loved him more than ever. She felt her heart beginning to beat, hard, and her hand drifted down to slip beneath his shirt and touch the warm skin just beneath.

His belly was flat and hard and warm, the hairs there silky against her fingers. She leaned against him, until he finally sighed and drew her close to lie back in the hay together. It rustled and cracked beneath them, its fragrance coming up to envelop them in its sweetness.

"Colin . . . will you make love to me?"

"You still want me, then?"

"You *are* a dolt," she said, with all the fondness in her heart. She leaned down and buried her lips in hair that was as black as midnight.

His lips curved in a boyish grin. Somewhere beneath them, one of the horses stamped; from beyond the window a pheasant set up a harsh, squawking noise before the whoosh of its wings heralded its departure.

And from just outside came Tristan's loud cough, and the sound of approaching footsteps.

"Someone's coming!" she whispered. "I have to go—"

He hushed her with kisses, and she felt only the strength of his arms, the heat of his mouth against hers, the feel of his hands . . . caressing her back, moving down her leg to catch the hem of her gown and drag the fabric up her leg, until she felt the prickliness of the hay against her flesh.

She sank down atop him, even as the footsteps grew louder.

"Fine day, m'lord, eh?"

They clung together, breath and bodies hot and close, as the conversation wafted up to them.

"I daresay," came Tristan's drawled reply.

" 'Is Lordship wanted me to take Black Patrick out f'r some exercise, seein's how the race is in just a few days. Not that the beast ain't in good condition, but ye can't be too sure, eh?"

"Of course."

Ariadne began to giggle. She felt Colin's fingers dragging the heavy skirts up over her bottom, and his warm touch upon her skin. She sighed and pressed closer, touching her mouth to his.

"I wish Tristan would *leave*," she whispered, against the curve of Colin's neck. "I have no wish for him to hear us!"

"He won't," murmured her lover. "Not if we're quiet."

"Can you be quiet?"

"Aye. *I* can." His fingers roved around the silken skin of her thighs and back over her bottom, until the searing ache was blossoming between her legs and her blood was beginning to beat against her ears. "But, can *you*?"

She settled onto her side so that she could reach his trousers. From below, she could hear the servant going into Black Patrick's stall, the slap of his hand against that powerful black hide, the steed's squeal and the challenging whistle of Shareb-er-rehh.

"You're hard, Colin."

"Mmmm . . . Painfully so, I think."

"Do you need some *medicine*, my good Doctor?"

He gave a short burst of laughter even as she thrust buttons through holes, slid her hand beneath the flap of fabric, and began to stroke his manhood. Softly. Agonizingly. He groaned, and she pressed her mouth against his, her hand against his arousal, her thumb running up and down the rigid side of it with torturous slowness.

"My God, Ariadne—"

"Shhhhh, Colin!"

He grimaced as the pad of her thumb circled and teased the engorged tip of him, and buried his face against her neck, his breathing hot and hard.

Downstairs, the sound of Black Patrick's shod hooves rang against stone as he was led outside.

"This is your punishment for not telling me about your past," she murmured, on a quickly smothered giggle.

"Then . . . I shall never tell you anything again." He sucked in his breath as she stroked and teased him, a sheen of moisture breaking out on his forehead.

She leaned over, kissed his brows, the long, sweeping lashes, his mouth—and then his hand grazed her hip and swept over her inner thighs.

"Colin!"

"Fair is fair, my lady," he gasped. "Bloody hell, you keep doing that and I'm not going to be able to last—"

She persisted, lightly dragging her fingers up, over and around his hard length, until a warm pearl of moisture came oozing out to dampen her thumb. She gasped as he wreaked havoc on her senses as well, his fingers slipping beneath the heavy folds of her skirts and into the silken, cinnamon-colored hair at the junction of her thighs; beneath her the hay pricked and stabbed, and a burr was sticking against her ankle, but none of that mattered.

"Oh, *Colin!*" she gasped, nearly crying out as his fingers parted her damp warmth and slid gently inside her.

"Tell me to stop, then," he murmured, suddenly clenching his teeth as she ringed his arousal with thumb and forefinger and slid her hand slowly up and down his length. "I'll bet you can't."

"You know very well that I—oh!—that I can't. . . ."

"So hush, dearest, and let me make love to you." He kissed her, his finger finding parts of her that she didn't know existed, let alone had feeling, until sobs of pleasure were clogging the back of her throat. His mouth was there, against hers, and she felt him straining against her hand, heard his hot, heavy breathing and the frantic slam of her heart in her ears—

"Make love to me, Colin. *Now.*"

With the very likely chance of someone discovering them, time was not a luxury that they could afford. Colin gently rolled her onto her back, withdrawing his hand only to coax her thighs apart. Her skirts lay bunched between their bodies and he impatiently pulled them aside, even as he looked down at her fair, flushed face with the damp strands of fiery hair caught across her cheeks, even as her hand continued its slow and wicked massage, even as her eyes, jewellike with passion, gazed up at him through the dark fringe of her lashes.

He could not wait any longer. The hay pricking his arms, he eased himself down to her tiny body and drove himself deeply into her, feeling himself sliding in on a tide of liquid heat all the way to the hilt. He groaned with the feel of it. She arched up to meet him, sighing, and then her hands were cupping the back of his head, his neck, his shoulders, her nails driving into his sweat-sheened back as he began the slow, agonizing rhythm, trying to hold out, trying desperately, frantically, futilely to make it last, even as he felt the first waves of climax beginning to seize him and knew that he was lost.

She bucked beneath him, her soft cries quickly muffled by his mouth as it slammed down to capture hers. And when it was over and they lay panting and gasping in the hay, Colin raised his head and put his lips against the damp hair at her ear.

"My lady . . . ?"

"Yes, my lord?"

"There is something I have been meaning to ask you for some time now."

"Yes?"

He pulled back, smiling down into her eyes.

"Do you still want to marry me?"

Chapter 24

Midnight.
Hours before the great match race was to start, hours before the sun was to claw its way out of the sea, hours before the crowds were to line the racecourse, pressing and shoving and making last frenzied bets, Clive Maxwell was awake.

He was sitting in the library, calmly thumbing through a book by the light of a lantern, when the knock came.

"Enter."

The massive doors opened and the sleepy-eyed cook stood there, a burlap bag sheened with flour clenched in one doughy hand.

"Here ye go, m'lord. Early breakfast, just like ye wanted." She opened the bag, bending her grizzled old head over it and inhaling deeply. "Peach pie, apple pie, and some of those blackberry tarts yer lordship fancies . . . fresh from the oven and enough t' feed a horse, if ye don't mind me sayin' so meself!"

Clive Maxwell took the bag with an icy smile that never reached his eyes. *If you only knew . . .*

"Thank you, Cook. You may bring it here, please."

"Though don't know why ye be wantin' me to pack it up like ye did, less'n ye be plannin' t' take it wit' ye t' the racecourse to share wit' those friends o' yers—"

"Yes, Cook, that is exactly what I intend to do. The bag, please?"

She handed it to him, stifled a yawn, and left.

Maxwell waited until her footsteps faded and the great manor house was silent once more. The lantern hissed and sputtered, striking tiny diamonds of light off the sugar that still clung to the outside of the bag. He picked the lantern up—and on second thought, extinguished it. The task he was about to perform was one that demanded total stealth and secrecy.

It was a dark night, and blackness pressed against the windows with a sinister feel all its own. That suited Maxwell just fine. He moved, silent as a shadow, out of the library, down the great hall, and outside, the bag still in his hand.

The stable was warm, silent, and black as his jacket, the air thick with the mingled scents of hay, grain, horse sweat, and leather. He stopped, briefly, at Black Patrick's stall. The night was so dark that he could only see the tiny star in the middle of the great racer's forehead, the bandages that protected his fine, long legs. But Maxwell had no time to dally. If anyone ever found out what he was about to do, all was lost.

He moved swiftly past Black Patrick. Past Gazella, her mane like a unicorn's and her coat so bright it almost glowed in the darkness. He paused, his eyes searching the pitchy darkness, trying to locate Shareb-er-rehh by the distinctive white blaze. Somewhere, a horse sighed, and got to its feet. His face swinging toward the sound, Maxwell turned and saw the stallion.

Wide-awake and staring at him.

The devil's own luck, he thought, on a vicious note of triumph. He moved stealthily toward that telltale blaze, the only thing he could see in the entire stable, and slipped into the stallion's stall with as much sound as a cloud passing over the moon.

The horse snorted softly as it caught scent of the pastry. The big head swung toward him, only the blaze visible in the stygian gloom and the animal's breath coming in short, inquisitive blasts against Maxwell's hand. He shoved the warm muzzle aside and, chuckling softly, pulled a piece of still-warm pie from the bag.

The stallion sniffed it, warm breath blowing against his fingers; then, ever so gently, it lifted the treat from his hand with velvety lips, and began to chew, slowly at first, then, as the taste apparently agreed with it, faster.

No mere legend then, Shareb-er-rehh's fascination for pastry.

Maxwell smiled in the darkness.

The big head pushed against the bag, eager for more, and not daring to risk any more time in the stable, Maxwell quickly dumped the rest of the pastry into the food trough.

Then, with a sarcastically whispered wish of good luck on the morrow, he crept out of the box, the horse's happy munching fading behind him.

Gray light streamed through the windows of the sleeping stable, touching first upon partitions and walls, then hayracks, buckets, and troughs. Both Colin Lord and Shareb-er-rehh were in the deepest stages of sleep, the veterinarian's head pillowed against the stallion's glossy croup, the animal's wiry black tail laced with straw and lying haphazardly over Colin's legs. One dreaming of a red-haired noblewoman, the other of a white-maned mare, neither was aware of the agonized moans coming from the bay horse in a nearby stall.

But Ariadne, sneaking out to the stable for a pre-dawn tryst with her fiancé did and, upon investigation, found Thunder down in his stall and rolling about in anguish.

She took one look at the old gelding and knew he had colic.

Bad.

Colin had been more pleasantly awakened by ship's servants in times of impending battle. One moment he was making love to Ariadne in a dream-hazed field; the next, hands were rudely shaking his shoulders making his teeth snap together, the equally startled Shareb-er-rehh was lunging mightily to his feet, and Colin's back and head thumped painfully to the hard-packed earth beneath the straw.

"For God's sake, Ariadne—"

"Oh, Colin, you must come, *quickly*!"

"Come where?" he muttered, thickly, as he pushed the rumpled hair out of his eyes.

"Thunder! He has colic!"

Together, they ran to the gelding's stall, little Bow crawling out of the hay to come flying after them. Sure enough, Colin found the old horse down, his flailing hooves cutting the air as he rolled about in an attempt to relieve the agony.

"You have to save him!" Ariadne cried, her eyes desperate. "Please, Colin, *do* something, he's suffering, please, please do something, now—"

He reached out, caught her arms, held her until she calmed down. "Stop it, Ariadne!" he ordered, holding her tightly. "I need your help, do you understand?"

Numbly, she jerked her head and stared at him. Then he turned, ran past the curious horses that were now watching him from their stalls, hauled his sea chest out of the chaise and rushed back to the stall.

Ariadne was down on her knees beside the old horse, stroking the sweating hide. Thunder's eyes rolled in his head upon seeing Colin and desperately the horse tried to lunge to his feet, back straining, lips peeled back in pain. He managed to stand, and began pawing his bedding before his legs buckled and he went down once again.

Outside, the day grew a shade brighter.

"Stand back, Ariadne," Colin ordered, and quickly entered the stall, seized Thunder's halter and, with all his strength, began hauling on his head, trying to get him onto his feet.

"Come on boy, get up—"

Thunder groaned, tried to get a leg beneath him, and began to roll onto his side.

"Damn it, Ari, help me!"

She dived forward, instinctively swatting at the gelding's heaving flanks, the sunken rump, while the veterinarian heaved and hauled on the halter. Thunder got a leg under himself once more; another; a good, sharp swat on the rump and he was standing, lurching, walking—

"Why, Colin?" Ariadne was asking, as she stared miserably at the suffering horse. "He seemed fine last night—"

Colin, however, had seen the remains of what Thunder had been eating—several fly-covered chunks of fruity, sugary pie and pastry still sitting in his feed bin. He pulled out his watch and, laying his fingers against the ramus of the mandible, took the gelding's pulse.

Should be forty beats per minute, he thought, his mind racing, his eyes closed as he counted. *I'm counting sixty-five . . .*

"Look in his feed bin," he said darkly.

Thunder groaned, tried to lie down. Roughly, Colin jerked his head back up, knowing if the animal went down again, he might never get up.

Now, servants and stable hands were beginning to filter into the stable to start their morning work, their faces shocked as they saw Lord Weybourne's personal groom attending to the worthless old nag.

One by one they came running, eager to offer their help.

Colin, putting his ear to Thunder's flank, looked at the small gathering. "Where's Maxwell?" he ground out, angrily.

"Gone. Went to the track," one of them offered, lamely.

Colin swore beneath his breath.

"What are you listening for?" Ariadne breathed, holding Thunder's head so the old horse couldn't collapse.

"Abdominal sounds. But I'm hearing nothing. No stomach noises, nothing."

"He's going to die, isn't he?"

"Not if I can bloody well help it."

But he noted that Thunder's mucus membranes were a dark red instead of the normal, healthy pink, and that the sweat was pouring off of him. His patient's prognosis didn't look good at all, but at least he knew the etiology of the colic—not constipation, but an overload of pastry.

Ariadne was there beside him, brave, frightened, wanting to help. "What's happening inside of him, Colin?"

"Too much pastry," he muttered, flipping open the lid of his sea chest with one booted toe. "It's fermenting in the stomach, probably the large colon as well. Expect diarrhea. Then, laminitis."

"Laminitis?"

"Founder," he said, darkly.

Some of the stable hands had come forward,

their faces angry as word was quickly passed what had brought on the gelding's colic.

"Who would do such a bloody awful thing?"

"Don't know; ain't like this here hoss is anythin' *valuable* or anything—"

Ariadne, stroking Thunder's drooping face, jerked her chin up. "He's valuable to *us*," she retorted, and hearing it, Colin suddenly knew the reason for her tears. Not only because she had a gentle heart and couldn't stand to see anything suffer; not only because she felt helpless and scared.

But because she felt guilty for the way she had felt about Thunder.

"Aye, but who would do such a thing?" one of the stable hands insisted, coming forward to help should the gelding's legs buckle once again. "Why would anyone put all that pastry in the feed bin?"

"Because they were trying to sabotage the race," Colin muttered, his voice hard and angry.

"But this here horse ain't racin'!"

"No. But he bears a marked resemblance, in color and markings, to the one that *is*. Somebody obviously poisoned the wrong horse."

Kneeling, he rummaged through his sea chest until he found the stomach tube. Shadows blocked out the light as the small group drew close, exchanging hushed comments and speculations about the strange instrument he was uncoiling. He looked up and saw curious faces, all staring down at the snakelike thing he held in his hands.

"What in God's name is that?"

"A stomach tube. I need help here, and quickly, to rehydrate this animal. Can someone please get me a bucket?"

A pail was set before him, and while Ariadne walked Thunder up and down the aisle to keep him on his feet, the day grew brighter and the birds began to sing, and the grooms were sent running to and fro until he had most of the ingredients he needed for the laxative.

He knew the formula by heart.

Two ounces of venice turpentine, dissolved with two egg yolks . . . an ounce of diascordium and a pint of red wine, to help tranquilize the poor fellow . . . a quart of water to restore fluid and correct the dehydration. . . .

Ariadne was there, watching him stir the evil-looking mixture. She reached out and put her hand on his shoulder, her gentle encouragement bolstering his own fading spirits. "A physick?" she asked, peering down at the mixture.

"Aye. We've got to get that pastry through and out of him as soon as possible. This will help speed it from the stomach and into the intestine so he doesn't absorb so much of it." He stood up, the bucket in his hand.

And saw the stable hands all staring at him—no longer with curiosity, but narrow-eyed speculation.

"You ain't no mere groom, are you?"

Without skipping a beat, Colin lifted the stomach tube from the hands of the nearest one. "No."

"He's a veterinarian," Ariadne offered, proudly.

"A what?"

"An animal doct—"

Just then, Tristan entered the stable, his face flushed. He caught sight of the sick horse, the group of people gathered around it, and his "groom" armed with a bucket in one hand and a long, snakelike, leather-wrapped tube in the other.

Instantly, he ran forward to help, his face darkening with rage as he heard bits and pieces of the tale, all coming at him from every direction from stable hands, grooms, and his sister alike. "Maxwell," he spit, for Colin's ears alone. "That bastard's behind this, I'll bet my bloody balls—"

"We'll deal with *him* later. Right now all that matters is saving this horse."

The veterinarian stepped toward the gelding, laying his hand on the sweating, trembling old neck. Sick as he was, Thunder turned his face against Colin's ribs in a quiet, trusting plea to make the pain go away, to make him better.

It was a tall order, but Colin was determined. Some patients—like old Ned, whose life he'd had to mercifully end with a bullet between the ears, the tears rolling down his face as he'd pulled the trigger—he could not save no matter what he did. But by God, he couldn't, *wouldn't*, let Thunder die.

Face set, mouth determined, he retrieved the mouth gag from his sea chest. Resembling a metal halter, it was a cruel-looking assembly of bars, screws, and a strap of leather, with a metal plate to keep the jaws forced open. Stroking Thunder's face, he pulled the animal's head up, removed the horse's halter, and put the mouth gag on.

One by one, the stable hands, the grooms, and even the horses in the stable all fell silent.

"I'll need an assistant," Colin said as he fastened the leather strap, and even before he straightened up, he knew it was Ariadne who had been the first to get to his side.

He eyed her dubiously, wondering if her fair sensibilities would withstand what he had to do. But she recognized his hesitation, and put her hand on his arm.

"I'm strong, Colin. Please—allow me."

"You won't faint?"

"I shall promise not to," she vowed, her concerned gaze going to Thunder once more and the tears welling up in her eyes.

"Very well. Hold him, then."

The stable went hush-quiet in anticipation. Grasping the stomach tube and feeling like an actor on a stage with so many people watching him, Colin moved to Thunder's left side and gently inserted the tube into the braced-open mouth. The gelding was too sick to protest. Glancing up, Colin saw the color fading from Ariadne's face, but she remained steadfast and still, determined to do her part.

Slowly, he pushed the tube into the horse's mouth; he felt Thunder swallow it, and watched intently for the telltale gulp as it passed into the esophagus.

"God almighty, how do ye know ye got it in the right place, and not the windpipe?" one of the grooms whispered, his voice filled with shocked awe as he peered over the shoulder of one of his colleagues.

"He's not coughing." Colin pushed the tube slowly into the esophagus, watching the customary ripple slide down the left side of the neck; he put his hand there to ensure its progress, envisioning it going through the thorax and past the diaphragm, where he met with mild resistance at the cardia of the stomach. He jiggled the tube a bit to get it into the stomach, held his breath as a sudden wave of foul-smelling gas came welling up through it, and heard Ariadne's voice from Thunder's head.

"I think I'm going to be ill."

"Don't," he warned, and shot her a sharp glance. She was pure white, nearly green, one hand on the gelding's head, the other pinching her nose shut to block out the smell. Something in his look must have sustained her, for she gave a tremulous smile, swallowed hard, and glanced away.

Outside, a rooster began to crow.

"All right, someone please get me the bucket," Colin said, and three of the grooms scrambled to do his bidding. Still holding the tube in place, he affixed a funnel to its end, lifted the pail, and poured the physick down the stomach tube.

"You're going to be just fine, old boy," he murmured, gazing into Thunder's suffering eyes as the physick went down. "Just fine. . . ."

But the words suddenly felt like a horrible lie, for he'd made the same promise to poor old Ned before having to destroy him. A lump rose in his throat and unable to look into the gelding's trusting eye a moment longer, he finally removed the tube, his face grave and expressionless. Then he made his way through the small crowd, got the blanket that had been his bed for the past several nights, and returned to find the stable hands exclaiming over the stomach tube they passed amongst themselves while Ariadne looked quietly down at them.

She raised her head and her gaze—shining with pride, adoration, and hero-worship—fastened on his.

Her lips moved to form the silent words. *I love you.*

He gave a little smile that offered no promises and, unable to face her reverent eyes, turned away to put the blanket on Thunder's back. The old horse was not out of the woods yet.

"Will he founder?" Tristan asked, watching him remove the metal gag and replace it with the leather halter. Colin made some noncommittal reply then, squatting down, he placed two fingers at the pastern and checked the pulse at the posterior digital artery. The hoof itself was too warm, but thankfully, there was no increase in pulse. Nevertheless, he called for several buckets of cold water, and, shortly afterward, the blanketed horse was standing in them, head cradled to Ariadne's chest, little Bow standing on her hind legs to reach up and lick the ugly old nose.

At last, Colin stood back and surveyed his patient, his eyes worried behind his spectacles. In several hours he could give another laxative, but for now there was nothing more he could do. Sunlight was already streaming in through the windows, and soon servants would arrive to tack up Black Patrick; the race would go on, and the late earl of Weybourne's legacy, his children's future and happiness, hinged upon its outcome.

An outcome that was dependent upon one thing, and one thing only.

The stallion met his gaze from across the aisle, and something unspoken passed between them.

Shareb-er-rehh.

Chapter 25

⌒◯⌒

In a special, roped-off area beside the dunes, Lord Maxwell and his Jockey Club friends sat drinking wine and plucking morsels of food from trays carried by servants whose faces were expressionless. The long beach that lay between the sea and Burnham Overy Staithe's marshes and sandy dunes was not the best racecourse he might have imagined, nor was it one that he would've selected had circumstances given him more time to choose otherwise. Nevertheless, his racing friends had come up from Newmarket, Epsom, and London to see the much-heralded contest between the undisputed "King of Newmarket" and Weybourne's purported "Fastest Horse in the World," and the race had drawn villagers, farmers, fishermen, and people of every class and description for miles around.

Maxwell was just far enough away from the crowd milling against his private, roped-off area that he couldn't hear their broad Norfolk accents, couldn't smell their sweaty bodies, didn't have to listen to their gossip and news about births, deaths, and sicknesses. But he could see the money being passed at the betting booth, could feel the excitement in the air, could sense the eagerness the crowd had for its first glimpse of the late Lord Weybourne's mystery horse.

An eagerness that was equally shared by Maxwell's cohorts. After all, old Weybourne had never made a secret of the fact that his lifelong goal was to breed the fastest horse in the world.

And now, it was time to see if he had succeeded.

"I say, Maxwell, this is a most unusual site for a match race!" drawled Sir Randall Tapworth, quirking his thick gray brows. He gestured toward the sea with his wineglass. "A beach! Whoever *heard* of such a thing?"

"Most unusual, indeed," muttered Lord Chittick sourly; he had journeyed all the way from London for the event.

The marquess of Sunningwell, looking polished and elegant despite the day's warmth, stared disdainfully at the long beach. "I daresay you take the Sport of Kings to new lengths, Maxwell." A friend of the late Lord Weybourne, he had bet an enormous sum of money on Shareb-er-rehh.

Too bad he would lose it all, Maxwell thought, as he watched several men pounding a marker into the sand a mile down the beach. *Most unusual indeed*. Well, a good, flat-out, run was what he wanted—a race that would leave Shareb-er-rehh in the dust and the fortunes—and legacy—of the late Lord Weybourne in his hands.

But what was taking so long?

He hoped he hadn't given *too* much pastry to the stallion. He'd merely wanted to throw the animal off, not make him deathly ill.

He was just opening his mouth to reply to Sunningwell's taunt when a roar from the crowd heralded the arrival of the contestants.

He stood up, the platform that had been erected for the benefit of him and his guests affording them a superior view. He smiled with satisfaction. Ah, there was Black Patrick, undisputed King of the English Turf, being led through the parting crowds. Maxwell's eye was unusually sharp; he needed no assistance to see that the Irish import was in fine form indeed, lather flecking his glossy jet hide, nostrils flaring red, noble head snaking out to lash viciously at a child who tried to reach out and touch him. Maxwell saw his jockey slash at the brat with his whip before the mother grabbed it up and shielded it to her breast.

He smiled and reached out to pluck a bit of fruit from a tray that appeared beside his shoulder, never sparing the servant a second glance.

"There's Black Patrick," noted Sir Randall, stretching his neck until its withered old cords stood out in high relief. "A fine animal, a fine animal indeed. Who's that on his back, Maxwell?"

"Spit Jordan."

"Ah, *wonderful!*" Randall exclaimed, rubbing his bony old hands together and making it obvious who he had laid *his* money on.

Maxwell smiled down into his drink, the sea wind ruffling his hair. Spit Jordan was a cunning blackguard who would stop at nothing to win a race, and had been well paid to make sure that his mount didn't lose. He chuckled darkly to himself.

Soon my financial problems will be over. . . .

"Where the hell is Weybourne's nag?"

Forever.

"You sure there's supposed to be two of 'em racing, Maxwell old chap?"

"Maybe he lost his nerve," Randall said, laughing. "There isn't a horse in England that can beat our Black Patrick!"

Maxwell pulled out his watch, arching one brow as he idly studied the time. "I suppose they'll be along shortly."

"Who's riding him?"

"Weybourne's groom," he drawled, thinking that it wouldn't really matter *who* was on Shareb-er-rehh, for no jockey in the world would be able to coax speed from a horse that was too ill to run—

Suddenly the crowd sent up another roar, one that grew so loud and deafening that Black Patrick, just emerging from the throng and stepping onto the beach, shied into several people who were unlucky enough to be near him. The cheering went on, until one by one, Maxwell and his companions were forced to stand up to see what the commotion was all about.

"Bloody rabble," Maxwell muttered—

And went slack-jawed with shock.

It was Shareb-er-rehh. Head high, huge nostrils cupped and flaring, forelock sweeping back from his brow and his tail floating on the wind behind him, he made a magnificent sight. His coat glinted in the sun. His muscles rippled with power. He was fire and beauty and speed incarnate and now, as he caught sight of Black Patrick, he gave a half rear, his shrill stallion call ringing through the wind.

"Is *that* Weybourne's horse?"

"Great God above! I think I've put my money on the wrong one."

"Have you ever seen such bloody long legs?"

"Damn his legs, look at that depth of chest!"

Maxwell, blinking, could only shut his eyes and clench his fists in disbelief. Then, the fury began to build and swell deep within him, rising from the very pit of his soul like smoke from glowing embers, with nowhere to go but up. His head ached, and the rage popped out on his brow as burning droplets of sweat. *Something must've happened. The damned horse must have neglected to eat the rest of the pastry. Either that, or it's built up a re-*

sistance to it, because that bloody stallion had never looked healthier.

He opened his eyes, plucked a glass of wine from a passing tray, and pretended to toast the stallion. "Don't forget, gentlemen, Weybourne's horse has never been raced."

"He's speed. Pure, unholy *speed*."

"Going to be a close race, I tell you!"

"Yes, and look how well that groom is handling him!"

Following their gazes, Maxwell promptly dropped his drink.

It was Ariadne. Her fiery hair was stuffed under a cap, trousers covered her legs, and a light jacket concealed her figure—but there was no mistaking that exquisite, pixie face.

Nor was there any mistaking the identity of the tall, fair-haired man who walked beside the stallion's shoulder, leading it through the crowds.

Colin Lord.

Fury drove against his temples and he felt the very arteries pulsing in his brow. He managed to raise his hand, and instantly his servant was at his elbow. Lowering his voice, Maxwell drew the man hastily aside.

"See that bay horse coming through the crowd?" he snarled, his black gaze boring into servant's. "I want you to make *sure* he doesn't win this race, do you understand?" He drew the servant close. "*Do you understand?*"

The man nodded jerkily, staring into Maxwell's face.

Then Maxwell shoved him roughly away, and the servant melted off into the crowd.

"So gentlemen . . ." Maxwell murmured, the picture of aplomb and poise once more. "You were saying?"

* * *

Shareb-er-rehh tossed his head, sending his black forelock spilling rakishly over his eyes. Fretting and prancing, he danced his way lightly through the crowd, neck arched, head tucked, mouth worrying the bit and his tail riding the wind behind him. His nerves were on fire and he could feel the blood rushing through every cell in his body. But he could think of nothing but the white mare that he'd left behind, the possessive looks that his black-coated rival had bestowed upon her, and the fury, the fire, that was sweeping through his body—

Run ... run ... RUN!

And oh, how he wanted to! He felt the sand beneath his hooves, smelled the strong, wild scent of the sea, felt Lady A's gentle hands on the reins, on the bit, trying to calm him in a futile attempt to bank a fire that wanted to rage out of control. He felt alive, free, and if she'd only give him his head, he'd take her soaring out over the sand, out over the very ocean itself. . . .

Ahead, the black's glossy rump flashed in the sunlight as he was led past the crowd to the starting line, and Shareb-er-rehh raised his head and screamed out a challenge. Seconds later, the other horse answered him, his call piercing the wind.

"Easy, boy," Ariadne murmured, laying a soothing hand against Shareb's hot neck. She felt the taut, raw power coiled beneath her, and had no doubt that her father's stallion would leave Black Patrick floundering in the dust. But her mind was awhirl . . . with the memory of poor Thunder, rolling about in agony . . . with horror that Maxwell had tried to have the gentle man walking beside her murdered . . . and with raw, sickened rage at what Tristan had told her about the man she had almost married.

She looked up. Sunlight was just breaking through the high clouds in a magnificent, reverse-

crown of glory, as though God had opened up the
heavens and was shining His light down upon
them.

Oh, Papa . . . this race is for you.

She looked down at Colin's freshly scrubbed
head, strikingly, beautifully, gold in the sunlight
once again. He was tight-lipped and silent, and his
eyes—normally soft, gentle, and expressive—were
hard with fury as he scanned the crowds for Maxwell. If she didn't hate him so, she could almost
pity the earl.

Then she remembered Thunder and his agony.

Almost.

Hands reached out to touch Shareb's burnished,
gleaming coat as the veterinarian led him through
the packed masses; the stallion's one white-ringed
eye turned to regard the crowds, and he stepped
up his fine prancing, showing off for his many ad-
mirers.

They were almost at the racecourse now. The last
of the crowd parted to let them through, and then
there was only the sea before them, wide open and
stretching into forever, sunlight glittering on
thousands of waves, the tide swirling in great arcs
of foam before eddying back into the azure expanse
with a timeless, gentle roar.

Black Patrick was just ahead, his long strides carrying him along the beach.

"Can this nag of yours run in sand?" Colin
joked, looking up into Ariadne's face and trying to
bolster her courage and confidence.

She grinned in response and in her most haughty
voice, declared, "Shareb-er-rehh's ancestors *came*
from the desert. Of *course* he can run in sand."

Exchanging private smiles, they neared the starting line, where Black Patrick was rearing up on his
hind legs and striking out at his groom. A vicious
animal, that one, Colin thought. He turned and

looked up at Ariadne. "I want you to be careful up there," he warned. "Don't get too close to that demon."

"Really, Colin!" she said airily, tickling his shoulder with her foot. "We don't intend to be anywhere *near* him, do we, Shareb?"

The stallion tossed his head and slammed it so hard against Colin's shoulder that he nearly knocked him over.

"Go to blazes, you arrogant beast!"

Shareb made a soft whickering noise that sounded suspiciously like laughter, and then settled down to business. He resumed his prancing, all elegance and grace as he moved past the crowds. He ignored the children that scooted out from beneath the ropes, trying to touch him before being hastily grabbed by their mothers. He ignored the gulls that wheeled and screamed just overhead. He ignored the waves pulsing at his hooves, ignored the thrumming roar of the crowds, ignored all but that huge, black rival that awaited him at the starting line.

The two stallions exchanged challenges, their high, shrill whistles piercing the wind, and it took all of Colin and Ariadne's combined strength to keep Shareb-er-rehh from attacking the other horse. The starter was there, gesturing to the red marker placed far down the beach.

"Easy course," he said, taking off his hat to wipe his thinning hair back from his brow. "Down to the post and back, two miles, and the first one back wins. Got it?"

Spit Jordan cast a malicious glare at Ariadne and raked his gaze over Shareb's glossy hide, as though dismissing him already.

"When you're ready," the starter said.

But Ariadne's heart was hammering, and she suddenly felt a tickle in the arch of her foot. She tried to press it against the stirrup iron, to no avail. Tried to rub it with her hand, but couldn't reach the itch through the leather sole. Finally, with a quick apology to the starter, she leapt down from Shareb's back and yanked off her boot, hastily rubbing the offending area while Colin raised a brow and bent down to help her.

"Problem?"

"My foot itches," she said, sheepishly.

No one saw the shadowy figure that darted up on Shareb's opposite side and was gone in the blink of an eye. But the stallion did, and let out a sudden scream, one hind foot lashing viciously out.

"Easy, Shareb!" Ariadne soothed, the sudden motion startling her. Then, stepping into Colin's cupped hand, she vaulted back into the saddle.

"*Now* I'm ready," she called to the starter, who nodded and motioned them forward.

Colin reached up and squeezed her hand for good luck. The course stretched ahead of them, open, free, and flat, the ocean on one side, the crowds pressing fifty feet away on the other. It would be a good race. A fast race. He let go of her hand and slapped Shareb's glossy rump as a final farewell.

But as the fiery stallion moved up to take his place at the starting line, sudden dread seized Colin's heart.

"Ready—"

Desperately, he tried to run forward.

"Set—"

And saw it. *The girth.* Cut.

"*Ariadne!*"

The pistol shot cracked the air, and the horses were off.

Colin's desperate cry was lost even as Shareb-er-rehh's mighty lunge broke the threads that held the girth and sent the saddle tilting crazily from his back. He heard his shout of panic over the crowd's sudden roar, felt his legs pounding beneath him as he ran to the tiny figure crumpled on the sand; then there was only Ariadne, clinging dazedly to him as he fell to his knees beside her and gathered her up into his arms.

Shareb-er-rehh came racing back, reins flying, head turned to regard his speeding rival.

The crowd was screaming.

And Black Patrick was already gone, running like fire through a trail of gunpowder.

Ariadne raised her head, her cap falling off to reveal her fiery hair. "Got to ride Shareb . . . got to ride him, Colin."

"You aren't riding him, damn it, *you aren't riding him!*"

"No, Colin . . . *you* have to. . . . "

And then her eyes closed, and her head fell back against his arm. The crowd was in an uproar. The stallion circled his fallen mistress, mane and tail streaming in the wind. He made one pass by Colin. Another.

Ariadne opened her eyes. "Do it, Colin . . . for me."

He looked up, seeing the black horse a quarter mile away now. And then, before he could deliberate any further, the crowd had surged in and it seemed that a hundred hands were there, hauling him to his feet and tossing him up aboard the rearing, plunging Shareb-er-rehh.

"Bloody *hell*," was all Colin had time for—and then the stallion exploded out from under him.

He'd been in battles with shot and lead flying inches from his ear. He'd faced storms, stood up to his admiral's temper, survived a hideous fracture that should have cost him his leg if not his life. But never had Colin felt the desperate, exhilarating fear he felt now, as the mighty steed beneath him thun-

dered down the beach like a man-of-war's un-
leashed broadside. He heard the crowd screaming
off to his right, where nothing but colors passed in
a speeding, dizzying blur.

God help me. The wind tore at his eyes, slashed
at his shirt, whipped the flying black mane into his
face until tears ran down his cheeks. He bent low
over the stallion's surging neck, no longer caring if
he won the race or not, desperate only to stay
aboard the animal as it took him on a ride straight
into Hell.

And Shareb, running like a thing possessed,
showed no signs of slowing, stopping, or tiring. He
poured on more speed, his angry scream echoing
through Colin's head, great muscles pounding beneath him.

The crowd was roaring. Through Shareb's mane
and past the backswept ears, Colin could just see
Black Patrick circling the far marker in a wide arc,
beginning his homestretch run back up the beach.

They'd never catch him now.

Not in a million years.

"Go, Shareb," Colin cried, into the small, savage,
backswept ears. "For God's sake, *go!*

Black Patrick galloped past them, now into his
second and final mile, and Shareb slowed, teeth
bared as he tried to go after his rival without com-
pleting the far turn. With all his strength, Colin
hauled on the far rein, the leather cutting into his
hand as he tried to turn the stallion and keep him
on course. The mighty body rose beneath him in
protest, plunged to the ground, and then Shareb
was on course and galloping toward the marker.
He swept around it, body angled toward the
ground like a ship coming about, and as he finished the turn and plunged down the beach at a
speed that defied belief, the crowd rose to its feet,

hundreds upon hundreds of people screaming, roaring, cheering—

A quarter mile ahead was the churning black rump, the streaming tail. Far beyond, at the finish line, Colin could just see Ariadne, leaning heavily against the starter, Bow at her feet.

"Go, Shareb, damn your lazy, bloody hide!" Colin cried, and touched his heels to the pounding flanks. "Win this damned thing and you can have all the pastry and ale your lazy heart desires! You hear me? *Pastry and ale!*"

It was enough. The great body beneath him seemed to flatten itself to the sand, the reins were torn through Colin's hands, and he buried himself in the whipping mane, the wind screaming past his face leaving him faint for lack of air—

Please, Lord, don't let me fall off now, please, not now—

Knees buried in the stallion's sides, arms wrapped around his neck, he hung on for dear life, knowing that if he fell off now he was a dead man. Through flying mane and watering eyes he saw the black horse's hindquarters coming closer, closer. . . .

By God, they just might make it!

He heard the thunder of the black's hooves, saw Spit Jordan glance under his shoulder to look behind him, and felt clods of sand from the animal's hooves pelting his face. But there was no stopping Shareb-er-rehh. Not now. The black hindquarters were a length away now . . . half a length . . . and then Shareb's head was darting out, snakelike, lunging for his rival's neck as the two pounded furiously down the beach toward the finish line—

The other jockey's whip came savagely down on Shareb's nose; still, Shareb went for the other horse, more intent on killing him than winning the race, even as the two hurtled toward the finish line at a blistering speed, the crowd screaming in a wild frenzy around them.

Shareb was falling back, teeth going for Black Patrick's jugular.

And then Colin looked up and saw Tristan, running out beyond the finish line with a lure.

The lovely white mare, Gazella.

Up went Shareb's ears—and in a blazing burst of speed, he shot past Black Patrick and won the race.

Epilogue

～⌒ↄↄ⌒～

A warm stable in Norfolk, England
One year later

In a roomy box stall piled thick with straw, a tiny colt stood with his mother, his belly full with milk, his body warm and ready for bed. His legs were wobbly, his eyes droopy with fatigue. Beyond the windows darkness had fallen, and it was long past time for the little fellow to go to sleep—but he seemed restless and Colin and Ariadne, their arms wrapped around each other's waists as they gazed fondly down at the new arrival, were reluctant to leave.

"Looks like his papa, doesn't he, Colin?"

The colt's tiny face, one eye ringed with white just like his sire, turned toward them. The fuzzy forelock seemed to stand straight up, and the tiny body swayed on the absurdly long, stiltlike legs as he took a hesitant step forward.

"Oh, I think he rather looks like Thunder, myself," Colin joked, enduring a playful swat from his wife as the old gelding whickered from a nearby stall. He yawned, tiredly. "Damn, is this little fellow ever going to call it a night?"

"He's not going to go to sleep until you tell him a tale, Colin." Smiling, Ariadne put her hands on her hips, her own belly beginning to show beneath her gown. "Don't you know that all babies need a bedtime story?"

"You tell it, love."

"Oh no, you're much better at telling stories."

"And which one would you have me tell him?"

"The one about . . ." She thought for a moment, then her face lit up, her eyes sparkling. "About us. And how I took you by storm!"

He laughed. "Dear God, that will take all night!"

The little colt looked at them, eyes huge and imploring, tiny muzzle frosted with droplets of milk. He stumbled forward, tottering precariously, and put his miniature nose into the palm of the man who had brought him safely into the world.

"See, Colin? He's *asking* you."

Colin gave a heavy sigh, affecting great weariness, but he was grinning. Gazella had had a rough time of it, and for a while there, as he'd struggled to help her through the hard delivery, he'd wondered if the legacy of the Norfolk Thoroughbred was going to die right along with her.

But she hadn't died, and neither had the colt, and now they had a tall, healthy baby to show for all their shared pain and effort. Still smiling, Colin opened the door to the box. He sat cross-legged in the straw to get down to the little one's level and gazed into the huge, dark eyes.

"So you want to hear a story, eh, young fellow?"

The colt stared at him, waiting, tiny ears twitching back and forth. His dam stepped forward and touched her muzzle to Colin's shoulder, and in the adjacent stall, Shareb-er-rehh put his head over the divider, his rapt gaze, like his son's, on the veterinarian.

Even Bow sidled into the stall and put her paw

on Colin's knee, her scraggly tail wagging with anticipation as he patted her fondly.

Audience in place, Colin ran his hand over the colt's sloping shoulder, his fine, long legs. He had a feeling this wouldn't be the last time he'd have to relate the tale—not only to Shareb-er-rehh's children, but, someday, to his own.

And so he settled himself in the straw, smiled up at his wife, and began, starting with the beginning ... about how the Lady Ariadne had abducted him, how they had fallen in love on the journey to Norfolk, how Shareb-er-rehh had defeated Black Patrick in the match race of the decade. His kept his voice low and mild, gentle and soothing, and at the door he saw Ariadne, her chin resting atop her crossed wrists, an adoring smile on her face as she gazed down at him.

The good doctor sighed and gazed affectionately at each equine face. "And then," he said, cradling the head of Shareb-er-rehh's tiny heir in his hands and gazing intently into the wide, attentive eyes, "just as we accepted the prize money for winning the race, Lord Maxwell's servant came running out of the crowd, babbling hysterically about how his employer had set him up to kill me. Later, at the trial, he and several other chaps came forward and testified that Maxwell had set the fire that burned down Ariadne's papa's barn, all because he was angry that her papa was breaking off their betrothal. The authorities came and took the earl off to jail, Lady Ariadne married me so that we could live happily ever after, we bought this fine home in Burnham, and then ... well then, your mama and papa had *you*."

The little colt wobbled with fatigue, but his eyes were wide with wonder. He turned his head and stared up at his proud father, as though seeing him for the very first time. Colin smiled, and touched the fuzzy little neck. "And someday," he said, "you, too, will grow up and be a famous race-horse—just like your papa."

Colin got to his feet, running his hand over the downy back, aware of Ariadne watching him with her heart in her eyes. He moved across the stall, plumped the straw piled thickly in the corner, and beckoned the colt with his hand.

"Time for bed, little fellow."

But the colt's eye was challenging, his stance defiant.

"I think he wants a bedtime snack," Ariadne said, her voice bright with laughter. "Pastry and ale."

"Well, he can want it all he likes, he's not getting any!"

As though in understanding, the colt threw a tantrum, squealing and kicking his tiny heels against the door. He turned a defiant stare on Colin, the breath whooshing in short, angry bursts through his flared nostrils.

Colin and Ariadne looked at each other and burst out laughing. And in the end, it was Shareb-er-rehh who sighed heavily, leaned over the divider, and flattening his ears with fatherly authority, scowled fiercely at the young scalawag.

The colt returned his stare; then, his tiny head drooped and, with a heavy sigh, he turned and flung himself down at his dam's feet.

Grinning, Colin crept out of the stall and joined his wife just outside. For a long moment, the two of them stood gazing down at the little one.

"What do you think Shareb just said?" Ariadne whispered, as Colin put his arm around her shoulders and the two stood watching the little baby drift off into slumber.

He looked up at Shareb-er-rehh. The stallion's

dark eye gleamed, and he seemed to smile as he looked steadily at Colin.

"I think," the veterinarian murmured, returning that equine smile, "that he just agreed with me."

And then he put his arm around his wife's widening waist and, with little Bow following at their heels, led her from the stable.

Avon Romances—
the best in exceptional authors and unforgettable novels!

MONTANA ANGEL   **Kathleen Harrington**
77059-8/ $4.50 US/ $5.50 Can

EMBRACE THE WILD DAWN   **Selina MacPherson**
77251-5/ $4.50 US/ $5.50 Can

MIDNIGHT RAIN   **Elizabeth Turner**
77371-6/ $4.50 US/ $5.50 Can

SWEET SPANISH BRIDE   **Donna Whitfield**
77626-X/ $4.50 US/ $5.50 Can

THE SAVAGE   **Nicole Jordan**
77280-9/ $4.50 US/ $5.50 Can

NIGHT SONG   **Beverly Jenkins**
77658-8/ $4.50 US/ $5.50 Can

MY LADY PIRATE   **Danelle Harmon**
77228-0/ $4.50 US/ $5.50 Can

THE HEART AND THE HEATHER   **Nancy Richards-Akers**
77519-0/ $4.50 US/ $5.50 Can

DEVIL'S ANGEL   **Marlene Suson**
77613-8/ $4.50 US/ $5.50 Can

WILD FLOWER   **Donna Stephens**
77577-8/ $4.50 US/ $5.50 Can

Avon Romantic Treasures

*Unforgettable, enthralling love stories,
sparkling with passion and adventure
from Romance's bestselling authors*

CAPTIVES OF THE NIGHT *by Loretta Chase*
76648-5/$4.99 US/$5.99 Can

CHEYENNE'S SHADOW *by Deborah Camp*
76739-2/$4.99 US/$5.99 Can

FORTUNE'S BRIDE *by Judith E. French*
76866-6/$4.99 US/$5.99 Can

GABRIEL'S BRIDE *by Samantha James*
77547-6/$4.99 US/$5.99 Can

COMANCHE FLAME *by Genell Dellin*
77524-7/ $4.99 US/ $5.99 Can

WITH ONE LOOK *by Jennifer Horsman*
77596-4/ $4.99 US/ $5.99 Can

LORD OF THUNDER *by Emma Merritt*
77290-6/ $4.99 US/ $5.99 Can

RUNAWAY BRIDE *by Deborah Gordon*
77758-4/$4.99 US/$5.99 Can

America Loves Lindsey!

The Timeless Romances
of #1 Bestselling Author

KEEPER OF THE HEART   77493-3/$5.99 US/$6.99 Can

THE MAGIC OF YOU   75629-3/$5.99 US/$6.99 Can

ANGEL   75628-5/$5.99 US/$6.99 Can

PRISONER OF MY DESIRE   75627-7/$5.99 US/$6.99 Can

ONCE A PRINCESS   75625-0/$5.99 US/$6.99 Can

WARRIOR'S WOMAN   75301-4/$5.99 US/$6.99 Can

MAN OF MY DREAMS   75626-9/$5.99 US/$6.99 Can

SURRENDER MY LOVE   76256-0/$6.50 US/$7.50 Can

YOU BELONG TO ME   76258-7/$6.50 US/$7.50 Can

Coming Soon
UNTIL FOREVER
76259-5/$6.50 US/$8.50 Can